The Penguin Poets
The Penguin Book of New Zealand Verse

Ian Wedde was born in Blenheim in 1946. As a child he lived in East Pakistan, Europe and England, and he has travelled extensively as an adult. Ian Wedde was educated at the University of Auckland, where he gained an MA in English. He now lives in Wellington with his wife and two children.

Ian Wedde has published a number of volumes of poetry, including *Spells for Coming Out* (1977), joint winner of the National Book Award for poetry, *Tales of Gotham City* and *Georgicon* (both 1984). He has also published *Dick Seddon's Great Dive* (1976), winner of the National Book Award for fiction, and *The Shirt Factory and Other Stories* (1981).

Harvey McQueen was born in Little River, Banks Peninsula, in 1934. After gaining an MA in history from Canterbury University he taught in secondary schools in the Waikato. He joined the Department of Education in 1971 where he is now Assistant Director, Curriculum Development, Wellington. Harvey McQueen has edited two anthologies of New Zealand poetry for schools, *Ten Modern New Zealand Poets* (with Lois Cox, 1974) and *A Cage of Words* (1980), and has published two volumes of his own poetry, *Against the Maelstrom* (1981) and *Stoat Spring* (1983).

Margaret Orbell was born in Auckland in 1934. From 1962 to 1966 she was the editor of *Te Ao Hou* magazine. She taught for two years in the Anthropology Department at the University of Auckland, and in 1978 gained her PhD with a thesis on 'Themes and images in Maori love poetry'. She is currently a Senior Lecturer in Maori at the University of Canterbury. Margaret Orbell's publications include *Maori Folktales* (1968), *Contemporary Maori Writing* (1970), *Traditional Songs of the Maori* (with Mervyn McLean, 1975) and *Maori Poetry: an Introductory Anthology* (1978).

The Penguin Book of
New Zealand Verse

Edited by Ian Wedde and Harvey McQueen

Introductions and Notes by Ian Wedde and
Margaret Orbell, consultant to the editors

Penguin Books

Penguin Books (NZ) Ltd, Cnr Rosedale and Airborne Roads,
Albany, Auckland 1310, New Zealand
Penguin Books Ltd, 27 Wrights Lane,
London W8 5TZ, England
Penguin USA, 375 Hudson Street,
New York, NY 10014, United States
Penguin Books Australia Ltd, 487 Maroondah Highway,
Ringwood, Australia 3134
Penguin Books Canada Ltd, 10 Alcorn Avenue, Toronto,
Ontario, Canada M4V 3B2

Penguin Books Ltd, Registered Offices: Harmondsworth,
Middlesex, England

First published 1985
10 9 8
Copyright © Ian Wedde and Harvey McQueen 1985
Introduction copyright © Ian Wedde 1985
The Maori Tradition copyright © Margaret Orbell 1985
Notes copyright © Margaret Orbell and Ian Wedde 1985
All rights reserved

Designed by Deborah Brash
Printed in China

Contents

Acknowledgements

For those poems with notes (p. 527), the acknowledgements are included therein.

For permission to reprint the poems in this anthology, acknowledgement is made to the publishers and copyright holders of the following:

Fleur Adock: *The Eye of the Hurricane* (A.H. & A.W. Reed, 1964, and the Author); and *Tigers* (Oxford University Press, London, 1967, © Oxford University Press 1967); *The Scenic Route* (Oxford University Press, London, 1974, © Oxford University Press 1974); *The Inner Harbour* (Oxford University Press, 1979, © Fleur Adcock 1979); *Selected Poems* (Oxford University Press, London, 1983, © Fleur Adcock 1983); reprinted by permission of Oxford University Press.

K.O. Arvidson: *Riding the Pendulum* (Oxford University Press, 1973).

James K. Baxter: *Collected Poems* (Oxford University Press, 1979).

Christina Beer: *This Fig Tree Has Thorns* (Alister Taylor, 1974); the Author for 'waiheke 1972—rocky bay' and '1974—the sounds'; all poems copyright Christina Conrad.

Mary Ursula Bethell: *Collected Poems* (Caxton Press, 1950).

Tony Beyer: *Dancing Bear* (Melaleuca Press, Canberra, 1981).

Charles Brasch: *Disputed Ground, Poems 1939–1945* (Caxton Press, 1948); *The Estate and Other Poems* (Caxton Press, 1957); *Ambulando* (Caxton Press, 1964); *Not Far Off* (Caxton Press, 1969); *Home Ground* (Caxton Press, 1974); Alan Roddick for the poems by Charles Brasch.

Alan Brunton: *Black and White Anthology* (Hawk Press, 1976); *O Ravachol* (Red Mole Publications, 1979); poems © Red Mole Enterprises 1974 and 1978.

Meg Campbell: *A Durable Fire* (Te Kotare Press, 1982).

Gordon Challis: *Building* (Caxton Press, 1963).

Allen Curnow: *An Incorrigible Music* (AUP/OUP, 1979, and the Author); *You Will Know When You Get There, Poems 1979–1981* (AUP/OUP, 1982, and the Author); *Selected Poems* (Penguin Books, 1982, and the Author).

Ruth Dallas: *Country Road and Other Poems, 1947–1952* (Caxton Press, 1953); *The Turning Wheel* (Caxton Press, 1961); *Shadow Show* (Caxton Press, 1968); *Walking on the Snow* (Caxton Press, 1976); *Steps of the Sun, Poems* (Caxton Press, 1979).

Eileen Duggan: *Poems* (The New Zealand Tablet, 1922); *New Zealand Bird Songs* (H.H. Tombs, 1929); *New Zealand Poems* (Allen and Unwin, London, 1940); *More Poems* (Allen and Unwin, London, 1951).

Lauris Edmond: *In Middle Air* (Pegasus Press, 1975); *The Pear Tree* (Pegasus Press, 1977); *Seven: Poems* (Wayzgoose Press, 1980); *Salt from the North* (Oxford University Press, 1980).

Murray Edmond: *Entering the Eye* (Caveman Press, 1973); *Patchwork* (Hawk Press, 1978); *End Wall* (Oxford University Press, 1981).

A.R.D. Fairburn: *Collected Poems* (Pegasus Press, 1966).

Janet Frame: *The Pocket Mirror* (Braziller, New York, and W.H. Allen, London, 1967; Pegasus Press, 1968); permission granted by Janet Frame c/o Curtis Brown (Aust.) Pty. Ltd., Sydney, Australia.

Ruth France: *Unwilling Pilgrim* (Caxton Press, 1955); *The Halting Place* (Caxton Press, 1961).   .

Ruth Gilbert: *Lazarus and Other Poems* (A.H. & A.W. Reed, 1949, and the Author); 'Green Hammock, White Magnolia Tree' was first published in the *NZ Listener*.

Denis Glover: *Selected Poems* (Penguin Books, 1981); published with the Executor's permission.

Peter Hooper: *Selected Poems* (John McIndoe, 1977).

Sam Hunt: *Collected Poems 1963–1980* (Penguin Books, 1980); published with the Poet's permission.

Robin Hyde: *Houses by the Sea and the Later Poems of Robin Hyde* (Caxton Press, 1952); poems copyright D.A. Challis.

Kevin Ireland: *Educating the Body* (Caxton Press, 1967); *A Grammar of Dreams* (Wai-te-ata Press, 1975).

Michael Jackson: *Latitudes of Exile* (John McIndoe, 1976); *Wall* (John McIndoe, 1980).

Louis Johnson: *Poems Unpleasant* (with James K. Baxter and Anton Vogt, Pegasus Press, 1952); *New Worlds for Old* (Capricorn Press, 1957); *Bread and a Pension* (Pegasus Press, 1964); *Land Like a Lizard* (Jacaranda Press, Brisbane, 1970); *Fires and Patterns* (Jacaranda Press, Brisbane, 1975); 'The Seventies' is from *Coming and Going* (Mallinson Rendel, 1982).

M.K. Joseph: *Inscription on a Paper Dart, Selected Poems 1945–1972* (AUP/OUP, 1974).

Jan Kemp: *Against the Softness of Woman* (Caveman Press, 1976); *Diamonds and Gravel* (Hampson Hunt, 1979); all poems © Jan Kemp.

Fiona Kidman: *Honey and Bitters* (Pegasus Press, 1975).

Hilaire Kirkland: *Blood Clear and Apple Red* (Wai-te-ata Press, 1981).

Rachel McAlpine: *Fancy Dress* (Cicada Press, 1979, and the Author); *House Poems* (Nutshell Books, 1980, and the Author).

Heather McPherson: *A Figurehead: A Face* (Spiral Publications, 1982).

Cilla McQueen: *Homing In* (John McIndoe, 1982).

Bill Manhire: *The Elaboration* (Square & Circle, 1972, and the Author); *How to Take Off Your Clothes at the Picnic* (Wai-te-ata Press, 1977, and the Author); *Zoetropes* (The Murihiku Press, London, 1981, and the Author); *Good Looks* (AUP/OUP, 1982, and the Author).

R.A.K. Mason: *Collected Poems* (Pegasus Press, 1962).

Barry Mitcalfe: *Beach* (Coromandel Press, 1982, and Barry Mitcalfe, Waiomu, Thames).

David Mitchell: *Pipe Dreams in Ponsonby* (Stephen Chan, 1972, and the Author); the Author for 'Van Gogh', first published in *Fifteen Contemporary New Zealand Poets* (edited by Alistair Paterson, Pilgrims South Press, 1980); poems © D.J. Mitchell 1971, 1979, and 1980.

Peter Olds: *Lady Moss Revived* (Caveman Press, 1972); *Doctor's Rock* (Caveman Press, 1976); *Beethoven's Guitar* (Caveman Press, 1980).

W.H. Oliver: *Out of Season* (Oxford University Press, 1980).

Bob Orr: *Poems for Moira* (Hawk Press, 1979); the Author for 'Parable'.

Vincent O'Sullivan: *Our Burning Time* (Prometheus Books, 1965); *Bearings* (Oxford University Press, 1973); *From the Indian Funeral* (John McIndoe, 1976); *Brother Jonathan, Brother Kafka* (Oxford University Press, 1980); *The Rose Ballroom and Other Poems* (John McIndoe, 1982); *The Butcher Papers* (Oxford University Press, 1982).

Alistair Paterson: *Birds Flying* (Pegasus Press, 1973); *The Toledo Room* (Pilgrims South Press, 1978); *Incantations for Warriors* (Earle of Seacliff Press, 1984).

Gloria Rawlinson: *The Islands Where I Was Born* (Handcraft Press, 1955, and the Author); 'A Simple Matter' was first published in *Private Gardens: An Anthology of New Zealand Women Poets* (edited by Riemke Ensing, Caveman Press, 1977).

Keith Sinclair: *Songs for a Summer* (Pegasus Press, 1952); *A Time to Embrace* (Paul's Book Arcade, 1963, and the Author); *The Firewheel Tree* (AUP/OUP, 1974, and the Author).

Kendrick Smithyman: *Flying to Palmerston* (Oxford University Press for Auckland University Press, 1968, and the Author); *Earthquake Weather* (AUP/OUP, 1972, and the Author); *The Seal in the Dolphin Pool* (AUP/OUP, 1974, and the Author); *Dwarf with a Billiard Cue* (AUP/OUP, 1979, and the Author).

Charles Spear: *Twopence Coloured* (Caxton Press, 1951).

Mary Stanley: *Starveling Year* (Pegasus Press, 1953).

C.K. Stead: *Crossing the Bar* (AUP/OUP, 1972, and the Author); *Quesada* (The Shed, 1975, and the Author); *Walking Westward* (The Shed, 1979, and the Author); *Geographies* (AUP/OUP, 1982, and the Author).

Apirana Taylor: *Eyes of the Ruru* (Voice Press, 1979); *Three Shades* (with Lindsay Rabbitt and Lewis Scott, Voice Press, 1981).

Brian Turner: *Ladders of Rain* (John McIndoe, 1978); *Ancestors* (John McIndoe, 1981); *Listening to the River* (John McIndoe, 1983).

Hone Tuwhare: *No Ordinary Sun* (Blackwood and Janet Paul, 1964); *Something Nothing* (Caveman Press, 1974); *Year of the Dog* (John McIndoe, 1982); published with the Poet's permission.

Ian Wedde: *Made Over* (Stephen Chan, 1974); *Earthly: Sonnets for Carlos* (Amphedesma Press, 1975); *Spells for Coming Out* (AUP/OUP, 1977); *Castaly, Poems 1973–1977* (AUP/OUP, 1980); *Tales of Gotham City* (AUP/OUP, 1984); 'hardon ("get one today"' from *Georgicon* was first published in *Islands*.

Hubert Witheford: *The Falcon Mask* (Pegasus Press, 1951); *The Lightning Makes a Difference* (Brookside Press, London, 1962); *A Native, Perhaps Beautiful* (Caxton Press, 1967); *A Possible Order* (Ravine Press, Harrow, 1980).

Acknowledgements are also due as follows:

Arapera Hineira Blank: the Author for the text and translation of 'He kōingo', first published in *Into the World of Light* (edited by Witi Ihimaera and Don S. Long, Heinemann, 1982).

Alistair Campbell: the poems by Alistair Campbell are reprinted from *Collected Poems*, published 1982 by Alister Taylor Publishers, Russell.

David Eggleton: the Author for 'Painting Mount Taranaki' and 'These Rumours of Hexagonal Rooms in Gone Bee City'.

Herman Gladwin: 'Dear Miss' is reprinted from *In Praise of Stalin*, published 1977 by Alister Taylor Publishers, Russell.

Rowley Habib: the Author for 'Moment of Truth', first published in *Into the World of Light* (edited by Witi Ihimaera and Don S. Long, Heinemann, 1982); the Author for 'Ancestors', first published in *Landfall*.

Michael Harlow: the Author for 'Vlaminck's tie, the persistant imaginal'; the Author for 'Poem then, for love', first published in *Landfall*; poems © Michael Harlow.

Keri Hulme: the Author for 'He Hōhā', first published in *Into the World of Light* (edited by Witi Ihimaera and Don S. Long, Heinemann, 1982); © Keri Hulme, Okarito.

Kingi M. Ihaka: the Author for the text and translation of 'Te Atairangikaahu'.

'L.S': the Wai-te-ata Press for 'Pan in Battle', from *The Iron Hand*, edited by Les Cleveland (1979).

Katerina Te Hei Koko Mataira: the Author for the text and English interpretation of 'Waiata mo te whare tipuna'.

Hirini Melbourne: the Author for the texts and translations of 'He aha te hau mai nei' and 'Tāmaki-makau-rau'.

Elizabeth Nannestad: 'Portrait of a Lady' was first published in *Islands;* 'Queen of the River' was first published in *Landfall*.

Margaret Orbell: the Author and Mervyn McLean for translations first published in *Traditional Songs of the Maori* (A.H. & A.W. Reed, 1975); *Maori Poetry: an Introductory Anthology* (Heinemann Educational Publishers, 1978); some translations were first published in the *Journal of New Zealand Literature*, the *NZ Listener*, *Pacific Quarterly Moana* and *Tu Tangata*; previously unpublished translations by Margaret Orbell are published with the permission of Richards Literary Agency.

Kohine Whakarua Ponika: the Author for the text and translation of 'He waiata murimuri-aroha'; Sam Karetu and the Advisory Committee for the Teaching of the Maori Language for the text and translation of 'Karanga! karanga!'; published with the Author's permission.

Elizabeth Smither: 'The best cowboy movie' is reprinted from *Here Come the Clouds*, published 1975 by Alister Taylor Publishers, Russell; *You're Very Seductive William Carlos Williams* (John McIndoe, 1978); *The Legend of Marcello Mastroianni's Wife* (AUP/OUP, 1981, and the Author); *Casanova's Ankle* (Oxford University Press, 1981).

The text of 'David Lowston' is from the *Maorilander*, Journal of the New Zealand Folklore Society, Spring 1970 (researched by Frank Fyfe); the text of 'Come All You Tonguers' is from the *Maorilander*, Spring 1970/Autumn 1971 (researched by Frank Fyfe); the texts were collected in the USA by John Leebrick and published, with music also collected by John Leebrick, in *Shanties by the Way* (Rona Bailey and Bert Roth, Whitcombe and Tombs, 1967). 'Waitekauri Every Time!' was also published in *Shanties by the Way* and is published here with acknowledgement to the *Thames Valley Gazette*.

Every effort has been made to trace copyright holders, but in a few cases this has proved impossible. The publishers would be interested to hear from any copyright holders not here acknowledged.

Introduction

1

The history of a literature with colonial origins is involuntarily written *by* the language, not just in it: the development of poetry in English in New Zealand is coeval with the developing growth of the language into its location, to the point where English as an international language can be felt to be original *where it is*.

The 'here-anywhere' controversy that followed upon Allen Curnow's essay in *The Penguin Book of New Zealand Verse* (1960) had a lengthy senescence. The problems it raised are dynamic rather than solvable. As late as 1971 Mike (Charles) Doyle could satirically advance some themes of the argument in a section of his long poem *Earth Meditations*:

> Material
> as the purlieus they scarpered from
> those vestrymen took scales
> to weigh profit rather than justice
> (or imagination). Thin milk,
> alas, do they sigh, will trickle
> from the fattest cow. Now, spent
> a hundred years, half a globe
> (fearing their history's
> chimerical clamourings?)
> craven towards phenomena:
> we are offered—geraniums.[1]

—where the 'geraniums' refer us to Allen Curnow's poem 'A Small Room with Large Windows' (*see* p. 201).

On both sides of what became a confusingly opaque argument (not always the fault of the immediate protagonists) there was an exercise of will in relation to language. It was going to have to be *taught* to do the job of making us feel 'at home' (or not) within whatever

[1] *Earth Meditations* II (xvi), The Coach House Press, Toronto, 1971.

conception of that relationship we felt adopted by—the
'drizzle' of kowhai flowers in spring; gin in the suburbs;
the Korean War seguing into our involvement in
Vietnam; the re-emergence of racial issues from the
smug obscurity to which liberal assimilationist optimism
had consigned them; the linguistic republic of
postmodernist words; and so forth—many intersections
of identity and language could be added.

Within such a grid of intersections the important
consideration must be relation, rather than mere
location. As Murray Edmond (he would have been
eleven in 1960) put it in 'Von Tempsky's Dance'
(*see* p. 504), a poem collected in 1973:

> & on that island, in South Chile too,
> the gold sophora grows.[1]

—where, by substituting 'sophora' for 'kowhai', he
wryly defused the derisive function that flower had
come to have in our literary indexing, recalling in the
same lines a relationship with the American west coast
that had survived since the commonplace traffics of
early colonial times. His is an attitude that takes the
indigenous pretty much for granted, though he likes to
think about it (he does not simply 'assume . . .
environment', as Robert Chapman put it in 1956[2]),
seeing its meaning as deriving from a sense of
relationship.

The much vaunted renaissance in poetry during the
1960s and 1970s had as much to do here with an
atrophy of the sense of will-to-language, as with wider
literary-historical developments. The language seemed
to have flowed more naturally from the hieratic towards
the demotic: two terms shifted from the Canadian critic

---

[1] *Entering the Eye*, Caveman Press, 1973.
[2] Robert Chapman, Introduction to *An Anthology of New Zealand Verse*,
   selected by Robert Chapman and Jonathan Bennett, Oxford
   University Press, 1956, p. xxxii.

Northrop Frye's use of them in a literary-critical context[1]
to a more immediately linguistic one—where 'hieratic'
describes language that is received, self-referential,
encoded *elect*, with a 'high' social threshold emphasising
cultural and historical continuity; and where 'demotic'
describes language with a spoken base, adaptable and
exploratory codes, and a 'lower' and more inclusive
social threshold emphasising cultural mobility and
immediacy. Although we need to distinguish between
industry and poetry, this flow must have been freed by
the progressive erosion of various cultural dams. And
certain 'derivative' developments out of Modernism,
increasingly American from the late 1960s, appear since to
have taken their guide-book elements of poetic language
with them into an interior where language is original:
there has come to be little residual missionary sense of
poets operating at a frontier where you have to carry a
life-supporting canteen from some distantly-located
spring.

It is time to demonstrate that language can, happily,
be subtly resistant to the standardising influences of
international communications systems and the received
orthodoxies of languages of administration and
education. The best way to demonstrate this is by
means of the issue of translation. This book contains a
greater quantity of Maori composition than did *The
Penguin Book of New Zealand Verse* (1960). The problems
of translation will be dealt with elsewhere in the
Introductions; they should remind us here that
translation occurs through varying degrees, one of
which is the transposition of language from one *context*
to another; for example, the transposition of a largely
oral literature, with a vitally public and usually
performed and musical context, to the written, private,
passive, and literary context of an anthology.

---

[1] Northrop Frye, *The Well-Tempered Critic*, Indiana University Press,
1963.

Wingatui

Sit in the car with the headlights off.
Look out there now
where the yellow moon floats silks across the birdcage.
You might have touched that sky you lost.
You might have split that azure violin in two.[1]

In this sense of a transposition of context, we can get
away with saying that translation occurs when a poem
in English by a New Zealand poet is published in an
English magazine. Bill Manhire would seem to be one of
the least conspicuously 'craven towards phenomena'
poets now writing here. His poem 'Wingatui' was
published in *The Times Literary Supplement*, and was
quickly hijacked to the derisive 'Pseud's Corner' section
of a satirical magazine where, by implication, it had
earned a place as an example of a preciously fatuous
surrealism. However, knowing that 'Wingatui' is the
name of a racecourse on the Taieri Plains (obscure), but
more importantly knowing what 'the birdcage' is at the
races, and what 'silks' would be (not so obscure), it is
natural to read the poem as one of those miniatures at
which Manhire excels, where the language enacts a
cipher game with what turn out to be particular
referents. What Manhire's small poem *does*, without by
any means slipping us a decodeable paraphrase, results
from a natural gearing-together of poem, language, and
context, including the ironically absent context in which
many 'poetry lovers' do *not*, in fact, know what 'the
birdcage' really is. We might guess that there was
considerable humour for Manhire in publishing
'Wingatui' where he did, with the results that followed.
   Location, then, not just in terms of place, but in the
fullest cultural sense, is the consummation of a sense of
relation.
   A major 'imported' poetic influence must inevitably
bring its larger context with it. Earlier this century, the
transposition to a somewhat garrison situation of

[1] From 'Two Landscapes', *Good Looks*, AUP/OUP, 1982.

Tennyson's Italianate English salon sonorities, for
example, resulted in some startlingly inappropriate
collisions of language, time and place in the poetry of
Hubert Church[1], whose good intentions were no
protection against his inability to read his influences in
the full context in which he now found them.

It is equally possible that some poets importing such
influences desire the milieu rather than the poetics:
prising language and context apart, they go for a poetics
that will best decode its desired milieu, as a kind of
template, in their own situation. The success of
influence seems to depend largely on the confidence of
the receiving culture, its ability to find consummation in
location.

Kendrick Smithyman has been one of the most
consistently confident tuners of such relationships here.
'An Ordinary Day Beyond Kaitaia'[2] is a good example.
Into a 'setting' examined with his usual shrewd
patience, Smithyman introduces a meditation on Rilke's
Apollonian dictum that we must change our lives,
concluding that

> If we live, we stand in language.
> You must change your words.

Far from being a banal assertion that words are stuck to
(and with) things ('craven towards phenomena'), this
emerges as a subtle declension of epistemological
relationship, through which flows the suggestion that
you cannot 'stand in' an unchanging language.

Another fine long Smithyman poem, 'Tomarata'
(*see* p. 287), sleuths observantly ('why the dog did not
bark') through the changing geology of a landscape. The
musing voice that we hear is free of the anxieties of a
language unsure about the tuning of its relationships: it
gives us Sherlock Holmes at Tomarata, and Rilke and

---

[1] (1857–1932)—the author, between 1902 and 1912, of four books of
  verse, including several lengthy poems such as 'New Zealand' and
  'A Fugue'.
[2] *Earthquake Weather*, AUP/OUP, 1972.

Heraclitus at Kaitaia, without needing to explain away any incongruity—we accept these presences because the language has. The voice is 'indigenous', as Murray Edmond puts it in 'Von Tempsky's Dance', 'as it walks about/where it is'.

And 'Tomarata' incidentally reminds us of the importance of, for example, the geographer Carl Saur in the 1950s development of postmodern American poetry, particularly in the work of Charles Olson and Edward Dorn. Olson's instinct told him that a 'New World' literature, if it was to advance its sense of relationship beyond nationalism or cultural alienation, would have to do so by studying geography and anthropology as much as literary culture.

It is a theme that recurs frequently in this anthology. It is there in Janet Frame's wry line from 'Letter' (see p. 301): 'I came your way walking from paddock to field'. And it is more implicitly there in David Eggleton's 'Painting Mount Taranaki' (see p. 515)— the poem's sense of natural relation is instinctively satisfying evidence of language centred in a culture whose dimensions are internally familiar. It is possible to read influences there without doubting the originality of the poetry. The poem *is* the subject, not just about it—where 'about' implies will, a philosophic determination.

The claims to be made for such refreshed language should not be overstated. It is a question of relation, again. We need the hieratic depths, which need the demotic inputs of newer cultures. The relationship is ecological—a reticulation of nourishment. As Northrop Frye, one of the most disenchanted champions of his own culture, has put it, we expect a vision of beauty to be the end of the hieratic view of literature, and the possession of some form of imaginative truth to be the proper end of the demotic, 'but if either is separated from the other and made an end in itself, something goes wrong'.[1] Something often does.

---

[1] *The Well-Tempered Critic*, p. 137.

Poets early this century, Hubert Church again, for example, had inherited a hieratic 'vision of beauty' language that had begun to be an end in itself. The process of undamming that leads to the sense of 'rightness' (or uprightness, as Allen Curnow might say) in David Eggleton's poem has been a lengthy and progressive one of readjusting the relation in favour of the demotic. Only in this way could a locally original culture establish its relation 'in the world' to the point where it became internally familiar rather than willed.

The uneven history of this process, as well as participating in the wider literary-historical developments of Modernist and postmodern change, has been the short history of our developing English-language literature in New Zealand. And that history has been coeval with the growth of language into its centring ganglia of relationships, to the point where we can feel ourselves to be its original poets, its consummators.

What is called 'New Zealand poetry' is thus a process, not a national condition. Anthologising it has involved us in a selecting process which we, as editors, came to organise along lines of thought like those outlined above. It should be obvious that these lines have derived from reading the poetry, all of it that we could find.

2

A *Times Literary Supplement* reviewer, writing about Charles Brasch's 1948 volume *Disputed Ground*[1], had this to say:

> . . . shows an acute historical sense, a great awareness of ancestry, of the formation of New Zealand as a country and a nation. It is, in fact, about what one would expect good Dominion poetry to be, but about which it so rarely is.

[1] *Disputed Ground*, Caxton Press, 1948.

These sentences, which sound as though they were
being muttered by someone probing for a tomato seed
under their dental plate, manage to convey also a sense
of chagrined surprise. And while the last sentence of
the quotation probes for its seed between 'about' and 'to
be', most readers with half an ear for plain language
will have assumed that 'about' is a qualifying word
attached to 'what', not a preposition attached to 'to
be'—so that the final part of the sentence comes as a
confusing surprise; what you *thought* you were
reading was a construction along the lines of 'about
right' or 'about what you'd expect'; what you get is
correct enough, perhaps, but it sounds . . . foreign. This
quotation appears on the dust jacket of Brasch's 1957
volume, *The Estate and Other Poems*. The total effect is of
being stranded at some pivotal mid-point in the process
outlined earlier.

To get a fix on the essential question that demands to
be asked at this mid-point you need to leapfrog back to
something like Tennyson's use of language in *Maud*:

> Walk'd in a wintry wind by a ghastly glimmer, and found
> The shining daffodil dead, and Orion low in his grave.[1]

Isn't this symptomatic of over-fertilised and
consequently exhausted language, like a tillage that
expends six bushels of topsoil in the production of one
bushel of wheat? And again, doesn't such language,
which is almost literally nowhere except in a salon like a
time-capsule, decorated with Italian souvenirs, demand
the refreshment of language that is alert to its situation,
to relation, to *location*? It seems fair to suggest that, in
measuring the distance 'good Dominion poetry' had
travelled in time and space to get from *Maud* to *The
Estate*, the essential question to ask would be, not *who*
are you, but *where* are you?—another of Northrop Frye's
acutely applied levers.[2]

---

[1] *Maud* III, i, 13–14.
[2] '[Canadian sensibility] is less perplexed by the question "Who am I?"
than by some such riddle as "Where is here?"' '— from 'Conclusion to *A*

After 1957, say, or the 1951 publication of Eileen Duggan's last book *More Poems*, the question becomes less appropriate. The emergence into the 1950s of a generation of poets including James K. Baxter moved the process into another phase. The judgement-inviting sense of will-to-language begins to fade over the next decade. Prior to this, Frye's lever comes in handy.

3

My name is David Lowston . . . .
. . .
We were set down in Open Bay . . . .

It is unlikely that 'David Lowston' (*see* p. 71) had much interest in where he was beyond hoping that someone else knew too, and would come and get him. Nonetheless, since Frye's question 'not *who* . . . but *where* are you?' contains the ghost of his hieratic-demotic relation, the superbly plain lines of this folk lyric contain the structure of the whole relation too.

The *who* and the *where* are interdependent, yet at times one will be a more appropriate question than the other. The concern with *who* you are implies a sense of tenure: returned beyond migration, an immature whakapapa can become legendary and nostalgic. Satirists of colonial insecurity have ridiculed the colonial desire to seek identity through legendary ancestry—to find a European aristocrat to ground that rootless *who*. The reciprocal hungers for each other of impoverished European nobility and New World heiresses is a kind of comic imprint of the same traffic. A sentimental attachment to the British Royal Family might be considered a related phenomenon. This *who* is hieratic: if you ask for it too early in the history of your tenure you are going to get lost in the illusory comforts of legend (which also come in proletarian guises), or in racially xenophobic culture, much as Hubert Church got lost in Tennysonian visions of beauty. By the time you

Literary History of Canada', in *The Stubborn Structure, essays on criticism and society*, Methuen, London, 1970, p. 284.

have got it straight about *where* you are (where *here* is), the *who* may follow more naturally: the tenure of your whakapapa will be extensive enough to stand between you and delusion; the legendary can properly have become the mythic, an integral part of your sense of history.

Quite apart from its quality as poetry, therefore, 'David Lowston' seemed an apt place to mark the English beach-head of an historical anthology. It is outflanked by a classic and, in formal terms, hieratic, oriori of Ngati Kahungunu (*see* p. 67), and by the Ngati Porou waiata 'E kui mā, e koro mā' (*see* p. 73); both compositions would have been largely concerned with instructing the young in matters of *who*, allowing their *where* correlatives to be treated in formulaic ways. Thus, between two classic poems recording and commemorating whakapapa, is the marooned English sailor, on a desolate beach . . . historic archetype of Pacific translation.

Where was the melancholy Edward Tregear as he contemplated Te Whetu Plains (*see* p. 97)? Not quite there—his description drops wearily into negatives:

> All still, all silent, 'tis a songless land,
>   That hears no music of the nightingale,
> No sound of waters falling lone and grand
>   Through sighing forests to the lower vale,
>   No whisper in the grass, so wan, and grey, and pale.

It is a language that subtracts rather than names, that reveals Tregear's alienation. And in our own times the misuse of the word 'culture', or 'cultured' (as in fake pearls), in a negative sense similar to Tregear's subtractions, is still not uncommon—where 'culture' is what is *not* there, or what you think should be, rather than what is: used this way, the word signals alienation, not just ordinary dissatisfaction.

In the 1870s Australian poets such as Adam Lindsay Gordon, in 'The Sick Stockrider', for instance, had begun to name; the mythic topography is thin and

sentimental, but New Zealand had no real
equivalent.

It is with Blanche Baughan that we first sense the
beginnings of an internal relation of *where* to the
language of the poems. 'A Bush Section' (*see* p. 110),
written soon after her arrival in New Zealand in 1900,
deals ostensibly with the same subject as William Pember
Reeves's elegy 'The Passing of the Forest' (*see* p. 100). It
has as its central character 'Thorold von Reden, the last of
a long line of nobles', whose connection with European
nobility Blanche Baughan is clearly terminating; and this
childish, isolated *who* is set down in the midst of a
desolation whose negatives the poet co-opts for their
wider symbolic significance, suggesting at the same time
that for Thor this landscape is original, full of magic, full
of names.

Optimist with a social conscience that she was,
Blanche Baughan was not above using 'Thor Rayden' as
the sentimental emblem of her hopes and fears. This
optimism re-emerges in 'Maui's Fish' (*see* p. 114).
Amidst a great deal of mawkish and boring retailing of
indigenous myth by numerous colonial poets, Blanche
Baughan's poem stands alone. This is not least because
the language can scarcely keep up with its theme's
opportunities to deal ecstatically with the question
where? A half-century or so further on, Allen Curnow's
assumption of the same myth into his austere
meditation on violence in 'Canst Thou Draw Out
Leviathan with an Hook?' (*see* p. 206) might make
Blanche Baughan seem naive and innocent ('Live! Dare!
Be alive!' as against, 'and you're caught, mate'). Yet the
distance her poem has come from the alienated,
negative gloom of Tregear's 'Te Whetu Plains' is not
only astonishing in itself, it was also necessary as a
stage on the way to Curnow's own disenchanted
occupancy of that *where*.

In her own time, critical commonplace admired Ursula
Bethell's more literary manner. Now we are likely, as
did a few contemporaries, to recognise the qualities of
her intimate miniatures. These personal poems,

collected in her 1929 volume *From a Garden in the Antipodes*[1], were intended for a friend in England (that 'from' implies a 'to'). And yet it is obvious that these are not nostalgic cables 'Home'. What is striking about these poems, released by an absence of literary expectations into the clearest of subtly highlighted speech, is that their informative purpose leads them not to large brochure vistas, nor into mythopoetic visions, but to finely observed domestic exteriors, in which the 'subjective correlative' is carefully pruned: a more unexpected achievement than her literary manner in 'The Long Harbour' (*see* p. 125). And, her perception of relation edited to essentials by personal grief, she was able to write, in '9th July, 1932' (*see* p. 129):

> There shall be no insistence upon symbolism;
> let each eye take the tokens, heart interpret,
> individual tongue make fit respond.

'By the River Ashley' (*see* p. 129), the unfinished major sequence she was working on at the time of her final illness and death, which we now have in the version edited rather too scrupulously perhaps by Lawrence Baigent and Charles Brasch for publication in the 1950 *Collected Poems*, reveals her as having begun to expand within this concept much as Robin Hyde did in her own autobiographical trilogy of sequences, 'The Beaches', 'The Houses', and 'The People'[2].

The individual response of Eileen Duggan's best poems subverts their Georgian decorum. As both Robin Hyde and Gloria Rawlinson had to over the next decade, Eileen Duggan struggled for independence within, and occasionally from, those muffling conventions. James Kelly, editor of the Catholic *New*

---

[1] Published under the pseudonym 'Evelyn Hayes', Sidgwick and Jackson, London, 1929.
[2] *Houses by the Sea and the Later Poems of Robin Hyde*, edited by Gloria Rawlinson, Caxton Press, 1952.

Zealand Tablet, and her first keen promoter, can't have seen the early evidence of this intellectual and emotional toughness in such youthful poems as 'Rosa Luxembourg' (*see* p. 136), first published in *The Democrat* in Dunedin in 1919; in his blithely irrelevant view, her *Poems* (1922) 'are the products of a heart and mind inspired by two forces—Catholicism and a love for Ireland—rare in a girl who never saw the land from which her parents came many years ago'. *Rare,* certainly. Clearly, Eileen Duggan had to combat the anachronistic expectations of 'cultural' conventions in addition to those of a saccharine variety of literary Georgianism, among them assumptions about the kind of verse 'properly' composed by women, particularly women with sincere religious convictions.

'Rosa Luxembourg' pretends to pass disguised as a conventional expression of regret for childless womanhood. 'The Shag' (*see* p. 136) falls with unexpected emphasis on ears delicately attuned to animistic flora and fauna set-pieces. 'Ballad of the Bushman' (*see* p. 138) packs a somewhat dour punch in the folksy context of such genre writing. Most striking of all, perhaps, is the way the ironically reactive rhetoric of a late poem, 'Prophecy' (*see* p. 141), published in *More Poems* in 1951, is unsettled by the incongruous disturbance of the Tennysonian line, 'And of men wanning away from a weird roaring of waters'. The only other place I have ever come across a verb cooked-up out of 'wan' is in poor *Maud*: 'And ever he mutter'd and madden'd, and ever wann'd with despair'[1]. The surprise caused by the appearance of this word in 'Prophecy' is a measure of the otherwise 'fit respond' of that poem, and others, which had succeeded in unsettling numerous conventions, not least those underlying James Kelly's broguish pat-on-the-head Introduction of 1922.

When Robin Hyde left New Zealand in 1938 she took Eileen Duggan's poems with her, comparing their 'china' to her 'clay'. She didn't take poems by Hubert

---

[1] *Maud* I, iii, 1–2.

Church. But then, neither are we surprised at Church's Tennysonian verbs—they are about what we come to expect of his *where*.

This structural line from the ecstatic mythopoetics of Blanche Baughan through the economic focus of Ursula Bethell to the intellectual confidence of Eileen Duggan, thence to Robin Hyde's late poetry, thence to Gloria Rawlinson's, is one of the great strengths of the process we call 'New Zealand poetry'. And as the struggles involved begin to be better known, we are able to turn that knowledge back into the ground of the poetry, the culture of what is there. Such an attitude is not just chauvinistic or self-serving; it derives from a recognition of the development of language towards the naming qualities of, for example, Eileen Duggan's 'Invasion' (*see* p. 138):

> War shows what each man's country is to him.
> Ah look with me on this great windy sod,
> Richer by lines of leaves than Adam's loam,
> Its kowhais' fiery drizzle in the Spring,
> Its paddocks' green oblivion of grass[1]

—where, now, we might find it irrelevant to wince at the kowhai, or at the 'windy sod'; we might be less inclined, as did Walter de la Mare in his Introduction to her *Poems* of 1937, to suggest that 'Macaulay's New Zealander' may have the 'duty and privilege, in those lovely and remote islands of his, to say the final word on the literature of England'; and more inclined to notice *within* the poetry the upwelling vigour of original language.

And to notice a code of alert irony which has seldom been recognised, but which is characteristic of much poetry by women from Ursula Bethell down: having heard it in Eileen Duggan, in Robin Hyde, Janet Frame, Fleur Adcock, Elizabeth Smither, we may feel the celebrated humour of A.R.D. Fairburn and Denis Glover, for example, to be more confident than witty.

[1] *New Zealand Poems*, Allen and Unwin, London, 1940.

4

> The tall pine in the bracken. 'Tis the place
> Still as a catacomb; the waving mound,
> Manuka-braided, where they buried deep
> Wakefield's beleaguered men. A massacre
> May roll from memory like a drinking song
> Chorused in murky taverns, dead the throats
> That hurtled it; or stab us through the years—
> 'This was a field unholy for our race.'
> You will not walk tonight, old pioneers,
> Te Rauparaha's stroke was curt and shrewd,
> And Charon paddled you . . . .[1]

Here, as also in his very long poems like 'A Fugue' ('. . . a bowshot from my casement Wakefield died . . .')[2], Hubert Church laboured to find in his foreground suitable subjects for poems. Not only is it ludicrously impossible to bend the so-called 'Wairau massacre' to this suitable end (and even harder to time-warp Colonel Wakefield into a kind of 'Lady of Shalott' medievalism), but Church's programme for local subject matter is also constantly sabotaged by the language he was stuck with: Tennysonian struggling, without a trace of irony, to advance through a Miltonic sieve into late-Victorian Browningesque dramatic monologue. It is not just that he was a second-rate poet, nor that we now enjoy the gloating benefits of retrospection. What we notice, in page after page of Church's earnest castings at the indigenous, is the total failure of the language he used to hook into any 'subject'; and we notice, too, that the direction of this diligent flinging-out of grapples is always away from the poet, out towards 'a subject'. In diagrammatic form, we can represent Church's position as: poet and indigenous-programme 'subject' on opposite sides of a chasm, with language failing to make any connection across.

[1] 'Tua Marina' 1–11, from *Egmont*, T.C. Lothian, Melbourne, 1908, p. 16.
[2] 'A Fugue' IX, 1, from *Poems*, T.C. Lothian, Melbourne, 1912, p. 168.

A half-century later, in Charles Brasch's long poem
The Estate, the diagram has contracted: the poet is now
on the ground of his poem, using a more demotic
Wordsworthian thought-language to examine his
situation. At the human centre of this examination are
repeatedly solipsistic images: closed rooms, cosy fires,
books, companionable silence, billowing white curtains.
Outside in the world are, for example, those

> Who are planting
> Deep in desert Otago Athenian olive,
> Virgilian vine, pledges perhaps of a future
> Milder and sweeter to mellow blunt hard natures
> Of farmer and rabbiter, driver, storekeeper, orchardman,
> With usage of wine and oil from grove and vineyard
> Shading stony terraces, naked gorges
> Scoured now by frost and fire, no human country.[1]

Brasch's alienation is Eurocentric; and it is marked by
legendary delusion: you cannot import the immense
cultural depth of history implicit in 'Virgilian vine' any
more than 'Thor Rayden' could maintain an unbroken
connection with his European forbears. Nor was there
anything very 'mild' or 'sweet' for Virgil in the
dispossession of small farmers for the resettlement of
demobbed legionaries: unlike Smithyman's language in
'Tomarata', Brasch's does anything but put us at ease
with the presences it invokes.

Charles Brasch's return to New Zealand from Europe
committed him to a willed relationship of his art to its
situation. This missionary sense he extended into a
programme of constant struggle to find the tones and
alignments in poetry that would bring harmony to the
relationships between himself, his art, and 'the world'.
Because he thought aloud a lot in what he wrote, and
studied landscape for its significance ('Nature' for its
structure), and because of the powerful element of will
in his commitment, Brasch produced the kinds of
sibylline lines by which we can trace, in stages, this

---

[1] *The Estate* iii, 29–36.

lifelong struggle. His careful attention to the echoes and developments within his work removes much chance of misinterpretation: in the space between the often-quoted lines from 'The Silent Land':

The plains are nameless and the cities cry for meaning,
The unproved heart still seeks a vein of speech[1]

and the much later line from his last major poem 'Home Ground' (*see* p. 185), 'I tramp my streets into recognition', we can read the record of a deliberate measuring of his own persistent progress towards some fitting occupancy, in his art and his life, of that 'home ground' he desired too much to ever quite live on without will. And certainly, in the single line quoted above, we can read his belief in the programmatic function of poetry in advancing the possibility of a natural relation, an internally familiar culture. In diagrammatic form, however, and certainly in 1957, Charles Brasch can be represented as a square peg in a round hole: Church's chasm has gone, but there still isn't a fit.

We must not attach too much *value* to these dialectical developments. Nonetheless, the historical process towards the sense of consummation in location that comes a quarter-century after *The Estate* with a poem like David Eggleton's 'Painting Mount Taranaki' is also a development towards a sense of culture that is internally familiar: a development that, to some extent, cuts across literary styles or genres which cannot themselves be assayed together—though our literary history is almost wholly post-Romantic: unlike Australia, we had no eighteenth-century mode.

There is no programme left in 'Painting Mount Taranaki', except in the vestigial sense of a satirical tone that undercuts the idea of an indigenous programme-piece—a tone that may also be targeting some of the ambitiously well-done poetry of the 1970s, for example Murray Edmond's 'Von Tempsky's Dance'. In spite of

[1] *The Penguin Book of New Zealand Verse*, edited by Allen Curnow, 1960, p. 183.

its ironies, the poem immerses us in its process. Its
literary influences can be guessed at (John Ashbery,
perhaps), but it remains completely familiar at a local
level. It is inside its history. Its language is a confident
if erratic blend of vernacular, lyric, and 'high demotic';
this confidence allows for mobile and ironic cross-
currents animating the texture and depth of the
language throughout. And, in the central shape of the
mountain, there is a cipher for the latest contraction of
the diagram of development from Church's colonial
abyss, through Brasch's existential struggle to fit, to the
natural sense of relation of Eggleton's poem.

'Painting Mount Taranaki' is not a 'better' poem than
The Estate, that goes without saying; but it was written
at a more integrated stage of our literary history, and it
enacts that integration. Allen Curnow's also much-
quoted lines

> Not I, some child, born in a marvellous year,
> Will learn the trick of standing upright here.[1]

are often flourished at such moments over the poet
considered fortunate enough to have coincided with this
moment in evolution. In fact, the lines conceal a couple
of delayed-action warnings: at the moment of
presentation we realise that we may be congratulating
the nominee for nothing better than a currish party-
piece; a less malign signal informs us that you can't
'learn' without being taught, which may not imply
teachers, but certainly does imply process or
development. And so you put the award away; it will
never be presented, except perhaps to 'history', which
is continuous anyway, though not by that token
linear—in my own mind, I can't help sliding the figure
of Thor Rayden into the persona whose literal vision drew
him to the modern wastes surrounding 'the cone
shape,/like a pile of drenched wheat, of Mount
Taranaki'.

[1] 'The Skeleton of the Great Moa in the Canterbury Museum,
Christchurch', *see* p. 199.

5

In these historical and dialectical terms, our
'mainstream' poets show variously related profiles.
A.R.D. Fairburn's sentimental lyricism, in such Georgian
poems as 'Winter Night' seldom reveals the subversive
quality with which Eileen Duggan can alert us. It is
more often in poems that combine a kind of visionary
bitterness with a laconic music, a characteristic falling
rhythm, that the extremes at which Fairburn worked are
welded into a tough, inimitable eloquence, for example
in 'Tapu' (see p. 144): a precarious amalgam which can
disappointingly curdle out again, as it does at the end of
'The Cave' (see p. 143): '. . . lovers' breaths who by
salt-water coasts/in the sea's beauty dwell'.

R.A.K. Mason's 'drab blade', his monosyllablism and
the quantitative Latinate flatness of his rhythms, seems to
come out of nowhere in the late 1920s stage of the
process we call 'New Zealand poetry'; yet this austere
demotic atmosphere sustains syntactical inversions and
'poetic' effects in a relationship of condensed irony; this
intensity, which was Mason's genius, reveals how alert
he was to the location of the language he was using.
Forty years later, the poems of David Mitchell often
achieve a similar intensity: demotic austerity containing
intense lyrical pressure.

It is a relation which is reversed in a poem such as
'Young Knowledge' (see p. 164) by Robin Hyde, into
which the poet seems to have brought much of the verbal
excess of her 'child prodigy' poetry, but where the 'poetic'
settings are constantly jarred and eroded by blunt
phrases:

> What your hard soles have taught you, and rough hands,
> What your wet eyes have dealt with, and tight mouths,
> What your bewilderment gave you, and hot heart,
> That only is your knowledge. Take and bear it.

—an effect that accumulates through the poem towards
the final dramatically bathetic image of a man 'of good
sense', the scientist Charles Heaphy, climbing back up

out of a real incursion of the mythic into the everyday, and acknowledging to himself that this cannot be presented to the world-at-large—the rational world, 'the cities', will not have it. In this context, Hyde's precariously poetic language, fissured with disenchantment and the ironies of its curt interruptions, is superbly appropriate.

This alertness to the situation of language, an unwillingness to allow the tensions of relationship to escape unused from the poems, has been a consistent quality of Allen Curnow's poetry. Always more integrated in its effects than Fairburn's, never as suffused with pressure as Mason's, never as risky as Robin Hyde's, and rarely enacting the existential struggles of Brasch's, Allen Curnow's poems, sometimes to the exasperation of commentators, have held pretty steadily to their urbane alignments for close on fifty years. If this rigour has not often produced poems that are endearing or 'accessible', it has abundantly paid off in the translucent qualities of his late work, in, for example, *You Will Know When You Get There*[1]. The title poem, concluding a book that can be read as a disquisition on death, confronts that reality with the lone figure of the poet, who includes himself in the human community through the unemphatic use of the pronoun 'you':

A door

> slams, a heavy wave, a door, the sea-floor shudders.
> Down you go alone, so late, into the surge-black fissure.[2]

The familiarity of a location, and of a 'human history', have been assumed into language that has itself achieved a lucid poise of relation. The distance from 'willed' qualities of commentary in 'House and Land' (*see* p. 197) to the translucent assumption of context (and of myth: Hine nui te po) into language in 'You Will Know When You Get There' is not just a matter of literary

[1] AUP/OUP, 1982.
[2] *See* p. 209.

history or personal achievement—between historical and personal there exists an exactly derived cartography of the reclamation of the language we now 'stand in'. Not all 'New Zealand poets' will care to acknowledge that language as theirs, in any personal sense; but few will be able to deny the precision of the tide-charts.

In the earlier poems of James K. Baxter, it is the demotic which is always reclaiming poetry from an insecure hieratic tone committed to abstractions:

> How many roads we take that lead to Nowhere,
> The alley overgrown, no meaning now but loss:
> Not that veritable garden where everything comes easy.

In these lines from the first verse of 'The Bay' (*see* p. 333), a poem of the late 1940s, it is only the last two words ('comes easy') that stall our urge to deflate (for example by substituting 'vegetable' for 'veritable'). The tension of this relation is much less finely tuned than in Allen Curnow's poems; yet it is obvious that Baxter was shrewdly aware of it, despite the banality of his critical comments, for example in the Introduction to his plays *The Devil and Mr Mulcahy* and *The Band Rotunda*, where he distinguished between 'street language' and 'bureaucratic language': 'A modern playwright has the choice. . . .'[1]

In his finest poems, this awareness produces a characteristic tone of covert humour. It is a tension, too, that enacts the persistent dualisms of those earlier poems. 'On the Death of her Body' (*see* p. 336) releases a sweetness of understanding only after its anxieties have produced the literal image of an abyss—less a pit to fall into than an image of the violent prising-apart of love and disgust. And this fundamental diagram, by implication, returns us to the 'beauty' and 'truth' of Northrop Frye's interdependent terms: to hieratic and demotic, and to *who* and *where*.

One reason Baxter's poetry achieved an unparalleled readership in this country is that its language structures

---

[1] Heinemann Educational Books, 1971.

consistently enacted, and developed upon, the relations
involved in achieving consummation in location—a
phrase whose camouflaged sexual and recreative
metaphor he also understood. With the exception of the
great Ngati Porou composer Tuini Ngawai (her work is
virtually unknown among non-Maori speakers anyway),
James K. Baxter is probably the nearest we have come
this century to a 'folk poet' whose circumference our
reading does not seem able to reach. His poetry, and
the ways he balanced relations of language and context,
produced, I believe, deep-seated and even subliminal
sympathetic reactions in his readers. The qualities of his
late, great sequences *Jerusalem Sonnets* and *Autumn
Testament* result from integrations of language as much
as from the related integrations of conflict:

> In the corner I can hear now

> The high whining of a mason fly
> Who carries the spiders home to his house

> As refrigerated meat. 'You bugger off,' he tells me,
> 'Your Christianity won't put an end to death.'[1]

—where we hear, simultaneously, a 'truth'; the
characteristic humorous tone of a self-parodying, living
voice; the easy movement of prosody that has mastered
an inimitable use of elision and caesura; all located in a
context that has everything to do with relation, but little
to do with the will-to-location, or the will-to-language.

Using signs that were always big and clear enough to
generously risk parody, Baxter has gifted us with an
immense and uneven body of work that has done more
than anything else in our literature to bring into
balance, for us and in us, that precariously alert yet
instinctive sense of internal relation between *who* and
where, between language and location: the culture of
what *is*. This anthology is as much 'post-Baxter' as it is
'post-1960'.

[1] *Autumn Testament* 42, see p. 346.

6

Expatriatism, which as editors we had thought might be
a problem, proved to be less so once our reading had
produced the lines of thought discussed so far. I was
reminded of Antony Alpers' description of Katherine
Mansfield as 'an epiphyte of the language'[1], and her
implicit denial of this in sentence after sentence that
draws sustenance from location. It is with regret that we
abandon, for example, William Hart-Smith to the
Australians, and younger writers such as Nigel Roberts,
Mark Young, and Eric Beach also. The contributions
made by Peter Bland (U.K.) and Mike ('Charles')
Doyle (Canada) to poetry in New Zealand are
gratefully acknowledged: in particular we miss Doyle's
Earth Meditations, with which he began to signal his
readiness to move on. An edition twenty years hence
may leave Alan Brunton in New York, and Fleur
Adcock and Kevin Ireland in England; in the meantime
we recognise their continued connection. Our decisions
in this area were influenced by the clear need for Maori
content in this anthology, as well as by the general
principles outlined in this Introduction—the two, of
course, are closely related.

7

The need for Maori content was obvious and
problematical. The difficulty of translation of context has
been mentioned. Insistence on the primacy of texts in
Maori goes some way towards solving this; however
translations themselves can seldom do justice to the
condensed simplicity of waiata such as Hera Katene-
Horvath's 'I ngā ra' (*see* p. 223, and note p. 539),
which in Maori has a resonance tapping into tradition
which English cannot reproduce: even the very best
translations must serve rather than equal their originals.
We hope that Margaret Orbell's Introduction and the

[1] *The Life of Katherine Mansfield*, The Viking Press, New York, 1980,
  p. 177.

notes provided will establish a context for the
non-specialist reader. The Maori poetry offered here can
only sample the amount that exists already in variously
recorded forms.

For help with this work we are indebted to the Centre
for Maori Studies and Research at the University of
Waikato, particularly to Hirini Melbourne and Katerina
Mataira; to Sam Karetu and to the Advisory Committee
for the Teaching of the Maori Language, Education
Department, and to Hone Apanui of the Maori section
of the Education Department's School Publications; and
to the Maori and South Pacific Arts Council. We are
deeply indebted to Ngoi Pewhairangi of Tokomaru Bay
and to Maaka Delamere-Jones (Te Aomuhurangi Te
Maaka) of Omaio in the Bay of Plenty, for long talks
and for their advice; to Mervyn McLean for his patient
and enthusiastic explanations in the early planning
stages; and to the many others who raised objections or
gave advice.

And in particular we are indebted to Margaret Orbell,
who agreed to take on the difficult task of assembling a
selection of traditional and 'transitional' compositions.
Her job was not easy: she was to ensure representation
in tribal and in genre terms; to choose examples which
were accessible to the general reader without losing a
sense of the complexity and diversity of the tradition;
and as far as possible to use sources which could ensure
tribal assignation. In addition, her lucid translations,
with their refusals to import interpretation or
explanation *into* the texts, are ideal for the purposes of
an anthology such as this.

Margaret Orbell's position in the middle of this
process has not been an easy one: we are grateful for
her commitment and for her fine attention to detail.

The contemporary material was assembled largely
through personal contacts. The difference between this
process and that of selecting English texts from library
reading is an obvious indicator of the difficulties of
translating context. Inevitably there were compositions,
for example by Wi Te Tau Huata of Hastings, which

were too deeply imbedded in their location and in their oral or dramatic context to survive the damage of translation. Other contemporary compositions, for example Pita Sharples' waiata-a-ringa 'Te mihini ātea', (*see* p. 438), make the transition at the expense of the loss of the drama, humour and subtlety of their performance.

Translations and notes for material after 1900 have been variously provided. In general, composers' translations have been preferred.

We have decided to do without a short glossary of Maori terms. Since most of the words that might appear there would be familiar in New Zealand, the inclusion of such a glossary seems at best irrelevant. There are now several good dictionaries: if you don't know a word, look it up—you may find out more about context that way than by flipping through a kind of tourist phrase-book at the end of this anthology.

8

That there are contemporary Maori compositions whose 'publication' normally consists of their being known literally 'by heart' reminds us of how little poetry we have in English that achieves an equivalent 'folk' quality. Certainly there are no poets whose work has the immensely familiar range of Tuini Ngawai's; while most schoolchildren in New Zealand learn some version or other of 'Pōkarekare ana' (*see* p. 105), few will ever know that Paraire Tomoana composed it; if you wish to indicate your location within Ngati Kahungunu, you have only to stand up and sing Tomoana's 'E pari rā' (*see* p. 106); Kohine Ponika's 'Karanga! karanga!' (*see* p. 259) is as permanently published in song-memory as any stock anthology poem; Pita Sharples' 'Te mihini ātea' was being sung around the Tomoana showgrounds soon after its performance by Te Roopu Manutaki at the 1983 Polynesian Festival in Hastings.

The anthologist who goes hunting for English equivalents to these will mostly be disappointed. Although we tried to avoid a too exclusively literary selection, we have therefore been sparing in representing so-called 'popular' poetry. We disagreed with Allen Curnow's judgement of William Pember Reeves's 'The Passing of the Forest' as 'beneath him'[1]. David McKee Wright we find well worth preserving. 'Historic' folk material such as 'Covered Wagons', commemorating the use of scab labour in the 1951 Waterfront Dispute, doesn't survive into print.

Of the poets writing from the working movement, Henry Kirk ('The Mixer')[2] is the most notable; he pushes his poems and songs well past the limits of conventions that braked Harry Holland, for example, short of anything better than pious apostrophizings of the 'Red Dawn', or the good socialist intentions which Peter Fraser diverted to feeble verses. It is worth noting that these politician *poètes-manquées* both display advanced symptoms of what might be called 'telephone voice', whereas the unapologetic language of 'The Mixer', in particular, relishes its frequent literary references and pastiches without unease or condescension—and without what Eileen Duggan, in 'Shades of Maro of Toulouse'[3], skewered with three annihilating lines of which the first contains an ironic miniature of the awkwardness of 'telephone voice':

> There is somewhat which flatters,
> Which sends the thumbs to the armpits
> In this role of dialectical defender.

One of these days someone will resurrect and translate all the Serbo-Croat poems of Ante Kosović[4]; here we offer a reminding sample. James K. Baxter's 'Ballad of the Stonegut Sugar Works' (*see* p. 339) is included less as a sample of *his* work than as a sample of the satirical ballad, which he happened to write brilliantly. The

---

[1] Introduction to *The Penguin Book of New Zealand Verse*, 1960, p. 36.

[2] *See* p. 153.

[3] *More Poems*, Allen and Unwin, London, 1951.

[4] *See* p. 132.

claims made for Denis Glover as a popular poet are probably better matched in the work of a painter such as Russell Clark than in poetry as it approaches folk-lyric. More recently, Sam Hunt, through tireless touring and reading, has achieved a popular folk standing which sometimes obscures the potential subtleties of his verse. David Mitchell publishes largely through reading. Alan Brunton, moving his poetry increasingly into theatre and cabaret scripts, was reaching large live audiences before his departure for New York.

The concept of a discrete 'folk poetry' is, however, misleading. We hope that this anthology gives a sense of the integrated levels at which poetry in New Zealand works. Too bad there isn't room for the unintentional hits scored by the likes of Dr A.S. Thompson, MD, Surgeon-Major 58th Regiment, in the 1850s, in his officers' mess attempt to pastiche Maori oratory:

I am going to Auckland to-morrow,
The abode of the Pakehas,
The place tobacco and blankets are sold;
Where the governor and the soldiers live,
Where the prison stands,
Where the large ships lie,
The fire boats are seen,
Where men are hung;
To-morrow I shall go to Auckland.[1]

—or for samples of the kind of 'popular' rubbish penned by the likes of Martin Farquhar Tupper, DCL (1810–1889), graduate of Christ Church, Oxford:

Like a Queen of swarming bees,
England, hived amid the seas,
Sends you by a favouring breeze,
        Canterbury pilgrims.[2]*

[1] Thompson, *The Story of New Zealand*, 1859, vol. 1, p. 84.
[2] No. 4, Canterbury Papers, 1850.
* Both quotations from Horace Fildes, *Fugitive Verse of Early New Zealand*, manuscript notebook, Rare Books, Victoria University Library.

9

Obviously the greatest pressure on selection came from
the need to accommodate a further highly-productive and
varied twenty years' writing since *The Penguin Book of
New Zealand Verse* of 1960. In doing this it became
obvious that there was a need for a comprehensive
anthology of contemporary poetry in New Zealand.
What we have done here, however, is to condense and
redefine the period dealt with by Allen Curnow, and to
give as generous a selection as possible of the poetry
written since then. In several cases (Curnow,
Smithyman, Baxter and Alistair Campbell, for example)
this has resulted in an emphasis on later work. This
result, which was not planned in advance, seems to us
satisfactory, and consistent with our method as it
emerged from reading.

Not all poets are best represented by matching
quantities of pages and/or poems. Poets such as C.K.
Stead who have often worked with longer, closely-
integrated forms cannot, with the best will in the
world, adequately survive their 'translation' into
anthologies like this. On the other hand, it seemed
essential to us to include complete longer poems by, for
example, Robin Hyde, Kendrick Smithyman, and
Alistair Campbell: there are poets who cannot be 'heard'
without this scope. We have tried to weigh the
proclivities of the poet with the need to represent the
poetry fairly, and with the coherence of the book as a
whole. We have also tried to be generous with space;
future anthologists of New Zealand poetry will find this
increasingly difficult.

The 'structural line' of women poets spoken of earlier,
from Blanche Baughan through Gloria Rawlinson, was
profoundly altered by the early death of Robin Hyde in
1939; the progression into self-sufficient reticence of
Gloria Rawlinson during the 1950s; the silence of Mary
Stanley after the publication of her one book, *Starveling
Year*, in 1953; by the tragically early death of Hilaire
Kirkland in 1975. The larger implications of this

damage, together with the failure of commonplace criticism to see past the Georgian surface of Eileen Duggan's poetry, for example, needs to be examined in the full context of a 'New Zealand poetry' where male hegemony has achieved the dubious status of orthodoxy. We have tried to offer selections that would make such examination possible.

In the parallel context of composition in Maori in the twentieth century, the immense contributions of women composer-teachers are obvious: Te Puea Herangi, Tuini Ngawai, Kohine Ponika, Ngoi Pewhairangi, Merimeri Penfold and Te Aomuhurangi Te Maaka, for example, have nurtured a tradition that embraces Arapera Blank and Katerina Mataira and the emerging bilingualism of Keri Hulme.

These selections allow cross-references and comparisons for which we should be grateful: tradition can be various as well as structured. I like to 'hear' Tuini Ngawai next to Charles Spear's medallions of decadent endgame; to read the certainty of Arapeta Awatere's language next to the doubt of Allen Curnow's 'House and Land'. I never did much warm to the terms of Charles Brasch's approving estimation of Allen Curnow's 1945 Caxton anthology, *A Book of New Zealand Verse 1923–1945* as 'a hard frost'[1]. Mere survival isn't everything, any more than good posture is.

10

Independently of each other, Harvey McQueen and I read everything, and made our own large preliminary selections. Where these coincided, we often had workable short lists; otherwise, collective bargaining took place. Our relationship was cordial, and our co-operation made us think twice, as often as it pushed us to defend our certainties.

[1] *Indirections: A Memoir 1909–1947*, Oxford University Press, 1980, p. 391: 'Like a hard frost, it killed off weeds, and promoted sound growth.'

We wished to include some poems by Alan Loney; unfortunately this could not be arranged.

Our thanks are due to the librarians of the Wellington Public Library, the General Assembly Library, the Alexander Turnbull Library, the Victoria University Library and J.C. Beaglehole rare books collection, and the Auckland Public Library, Rare Books and Sir George Grey collections.

For help and advice with 'folk' material we are indebted in particular to Noel Hilliard, Rona Bailey, and Bert Roth.

We are grateful to the Literary Fund and the Lottery Board, who were able to buy us some reading time.

Finally, we thank our editor at Penguin Books, John Barnett, for his support, industry, and scholarship.

Ian Wedde

The Maori Tradition

In the eighteenth century most of the Maori were living
in the warm, fertile coastal regions in the north of the
North Island, where kumara grew readily, and fern-root
flourished, and there was access to good fishing and
shellfish beds. In this part of the country there were many
heavily fortified pa—refuges in times of war and
ceremonial centres containing the finely carved houses of
chiefly families and other treasures. Elsewhere there was
less horticulture or none at all, and the people were more
scattered and often more nomadic. Everywhere, though,
they were generally similar in appearance, speech and
customs.

All this was described by the first European explorers,
missionaries and traders. They observed as well that the
chiefs and warriors were fiercely proud and
independent, that they were impassioned, skilful
orators, and that they performed furious war dances,
keeping perfect time with their 'horrid' gestures and
shouted choruses. Sometimes they described other
occasions on which there was singing, as when in 1793
two Maori men were kidnapped and taken to Norfolk
Island, and the governor of the island wrote that they
would 'almost every evening at the close of the day . . .
lament their separation by crying and singing a song
expressive of their grief; which is at all times very
affecting'. Later, when these men were being returned
to their homes, they met some strangers and asked for
news of their country: 'this was comply'd with by the
four strangers, who began a song in which each of
them took a part, sometimes using fierce and savage
gestures, and at other times sunk [sic] their voices,
according to the different passages or events they were
relating'. One of the returning exiles, 'who was paying
great attention to the subject of their song, suddenly
burst into tears', having learnt that the son of his chief
had been killed by enemies, with many of his warriors;

'he was to[o] much affected to hear more, but retired
into a corner . . . where he gave vent to his grief, which
was only interrupted by his threats of revenge'.[1]

But at first the Europeans had little knowledge
of the language, and such songs were meaningless to
them. It was only much later, after many of the Maori
had been converted to Christianity and the country had
become a British colony, that their songs were recorded.
When George Grey arrived in New Zealand as governor
in 1845, he began a collection of Maori poems, myths
and legends because, as he tells us, he found to his
surprise that many of the chiefs, especially 'some of the
oldest, least civilized, and most influential', frequently
quoted in their speeches and their letters to him

> fragments of ancient poems or proverbs, or made allusions
> which rested on an ancient system of mythology; and,
> although it was clear that the most important parts of their
> communications were embodied in these figurative forms,
> the interpreters were quite at fault, they could then rarely (if
> ever) translate the poems or explain the allusions, and there
> was no publication in existence which threw any light upon
> these subjects . . . I should add that even the great majority
> of the young Christian Maoris were quite as much at fault
> on these subjects as were the European interpreters.[2]

Grey did not, however, regard this as merely a practical
matter. Like many Victorians he had a scholarly
fascination with folklore and antiquities, and he was a
born collector who amassed as well a considerable
collection of incunabula and other rare works. When in
1853 he published a large volume of Maori poetry, he
described it in a preface as being of interest to students
of the history of the human race and as containing,
along with 'so much that is wild and terrible . . . many

---

[1] 'The Journal of Lieut.-Governor King', in *Historical Records of New
Zealand*, edited by Robert McNab, Wellington, 1914, vol. II, pp. 539,
547.

[2] This is from the preface to *Polynesian Mythology*, a volume of prose
translations first published by Grey in 1855 and several times
reprinted, most recently in Christchurch in 1961.

passages of the most singularly original poetic beauty'.[1]

Maori life and thought were changing rapidly at this time, and the ancient poems were 'fast passing out of use'.[2] On the other hand a great many Maoris were now literate, having been taught by the missionaries, so there were plenty of younger men able to write down poems and traditions from the dictation of their elders. Grey's high standing with the Maori ensured their trust and collaboration, and he was fortunate in having among his assistants several young men of European descent who had grown up in New Zealand and knew the language and the people well. Two of his interpreters were later to become important scholars themselves: C.O.B. Davis produced a fine collection of songs and oratory, and John White an indispensable six-volume compilation of traditions and songs.[3] And there were others who acted independently of Grey, though no doubt encouraged by his example—for it took much tenacity and a most enquiring and literary mind to pursue such studies in a colonial environment. A missionary, Richard Taylor, and a government official, Edward Shortland, published major works.[4] When war came in the 1860s, a military man named John McGregor, becoming friendly with the Maori prisoners whom it was his duty to guard, asked them to write down the love songs they knew, promising to publish them; and he did so, in his retirement thirty years later, in a wonderful, uncensored collection.[5] Many songs were preserved in Maori-language periodicals, and in letters published in official papers.

[1] *Ko Nga Moteatea, me nga Hakirara o Nga Maori*, Wellington, 1853. There are no translations.

[2] Grey, op. cit.

[3] C.O.B. Davis, *Maori Mementos*, Auckland, 1855. John White, *The Ancient History of the Maori*, Wellington, 1887–90.

[4] Richard Taylor, *Te Ika a Maui, or New Zealand and its Inhabitants*, London, 1855; 2nd ed., 1870. Edward Shortland, *Traditions and Superstitions of the New Zealanders*, London, 1854; 2nd ed., 1856.

[5] John McGregor, *Popular Maori Songs*, Auckland, 1893; also four supplements published 1898, 1903, 1905, 1909. There are no translations.

Then in 1892 a new generation of scholars led by
S. Percy Smith and Elsdon Best founded the *Journal of
the Polynesian Society* as a means of preserving the
knowledge of Maori elders whom they considered to be
the last of the true authorities. Though their main
purpose was to write the history of the Maori, they
recorded much poetry in the process.

The manuscripts of nearly all the early collectors of
Maori poetry and tradition are now in public libraries in
New Zealand; they are more voluminous than one
might expect, for they contain a great deal that has
never been published. Though the collectors were
Pakeha, the writers of these manuscripts were nearly
always Maori, and in most cases their names and tribes
are known. In this century, two Maori scholars, Apirana
Ngata and Pei Te Hurinui, have produced a
monumental collection of three hundred poems, giving
the historical explanations and linguistic annotation
that they require; many of their poems are ones
recorded by Ngata, while others are taken from Grey's
untranslated collection.[1] Further insights have come
more recently from the work of Mervyn McLean, an
ethnomusicologist who has transcribed the music of the
songs and recorded more than 1300 performances by
expert singers.[2] And there are now good dictionaries,
and innumerable books and articles that can be
consulted on Maori language, history and religion.
When there is a close concern for historical background,
and when the poetry is approached with the respect
and care accorded to other ancient literatures, and the
usual methods of literary scholarship are employed—

[1] *Nga Moteatea*, part I, by Apirana T. Ngata, Wellington, 1959, and *Nga
Moteatea*, parts II and III, by Apirana T. Ngata and Pei Te Hurinui,
Wellington, 1961 and 1970. Translations are also provided.

[2] In so doing, he has preserved the words of many songs that have
not been recorded elsewhere. McLean's recordings, with other
material, are in the Archive of Maori and Pacific Music in the
Department of Anthropology at the University of Auckland.
Transcriptions, texts and translations of fifty of these songs are in
Traditional Songs of the Maori, by Mervyn McLean and Margaret
Orbell, Wellington, 1975.

such as the comparison of recurring images, and the analysis of thematic structure and formulaic language— these often difficult poems generally yield their meaning.

Each kind of song has its own social purpose and its own poetic and musical conventions. McLean's analysis of the music shows that they may be grouped into two general categories, depending upon whether they are recited or sung. The recited songs are rhythmically chanted. They do not have a repeated melody but are through-composed,[1] and they are performed with rapid tempos. Among them are karakia or spells, haka or dance songs, patere or vaunting songs replying to insults, work songs, and pokeka, or laments for the dead. Most of these recited songs are expressive of group sentiment, and they were almost invariably accompanied by dancing, gestures, or action of some other kind. They were frequently performed when one social group confronted another, so there is often an element of social interaction and challenge, even when this is not at once apparent; the pokeka, for example, is not so much a lament for a person who has died as a contemplation of death itself, and a kind of confrontation of it. In all recited songs the verbal rhythms are relatively close to those of speech, though the language is very different in its imagery and concentrated energy from that of ordinary discourse. Songs accompanied only by gestures, such as pokeka and patere, tend to have long, flowing sentences, while haka, which are accompanied by vigorous posture dancing, have choppy rhythms and especially terse, emphatic language, with much repetition.

Songs that are sung rather than recited are strophic, with a melody repeated in each line. These are more personal and contemplative than the recited ones, and they often take the form of a communication

---

[1] Strictly, then, the texts of recited songs should be set out as prose. In this anthology they are arranged in lines to make for ease of reading. It should also be noted that translations of songs have in some cases been given explanatory titles by the translator.

addressed to one person by the poet. There were
formerly three kinds of sung song. Witty, epigrammatic
couplets known as pao—unrhymed, like all Maori
poems—commented upon local events and scandals, or
taunted enemies, or sometimes were addressed to
sweethearts, or farewelled visitors; unfortunately they
are not very well recorded, having been regarded as
frivolous and unimportant by most collectors of the
poetry. Another kind, known as oriori, were
composed for young, high-born children by relatives,
and were often sung by people who were nursing them;
generally they are concerned with the child's origins,
and the loyalties and feuds he had inherited from his
elders. The lines and stanzas of oriori are flexible in
length, and this, coupled with their fast tempos and
relatively simple melodies, made for a swift, economical
diction well suited to the elliptical conveyance of brief,
complex allusions to persons, places and events. Oriori
have an extraordinary poetic energy and express an
astonishing range of ideas.

The third kind of sung song, the most common and
poetically the most important, is the waiata. Its
language is elaborate, with specialised expressions and
much use of imagery, and it is more or less
declamatory, for these are rhetorical songs that were
usually sung publicly, on a marae or elsewhere, to
relieve the poet's feelings and to sway the emotions of
his or her listeners. All waiata take the form of
complaints. Most of them are waiata aroha, 'songs of
yearning' in which women complain about gossip, or
unrequited love, or the way their husbands are treating
them; and waiata tangi, which may bemoan an illness
or some other trouble but usually lament the death of a
relative. Such laments were, and sometimes still are,
sung at tangihanga or funeral ceremonies, which are
occasions of great social importance. They were also
sung at later meetings of kinsmen. In 1817, for example,
a missionary at the Bay of Islands described a meeting
of parties of Maoris from the surrounding districts:
'there was a general mourning for two days and two

nights successively', and people 'continued to rise up
alternatively during the whole time and sing a mournful
song to the memory of their departed relatives . . .
[they] did not cry nor cut themselves, as they usually
do when a person is recently dead'.[1] In 1860, a
government agent in the Waikato witnessed the
mourning for 'a dashing leader' who had been killed
while fighting European troops: 'Every evening, for
months afterwards, the women of Tamahere met at
sunset to raise the "tangi" for the dead, and moaned
forth the doleful dirge until nightfall. The traveller
riding about the neighbourhood constantly came upon
small parties, who, meeting each other, had alighted
from their horses, and were sitting in the dust',
weeping and singing.[2]

Maori poetry was generally inspired not by success
and happiness but by sorrow and loss; great men, for
example, were praised in song only after they had died.
But these songs were composed as a positive response
to unhappy circumstances, a way of dealing with them.
Words had power for the Maori; they were a kind of
action, so that correctly performed spells were a means
of ensuring success in an undertaking, and curses and
insults, even accidental ones, could not be withdrawn
but always led to trouble. When they were faced with
separation and defeat, and no other form of action was
open to them, poetry provided an outlet and a means of
assertion, and their song became a kind of triumph over
their circumstances. This was especially the case with
the waiata, in which a poet publicly lamented a
situation, stated its consequences, and often envisaged
some further action. A woman who had been unlucky
in love, and who knew that everyone knew it, might
save face by singing a waiata aroha, for the very act of
making a vigorous, ingenious poetic statement would

[1] From Thomas Kendall's journal, excerpted in *Marsden's Lieutenants*,
edited by J.R. Elder, Dunedin, 1934, p. 137.
[2] *The Maori King*, by J.E. Gorst, published 1864 and reprinted in
Auckland in 1959, edited by Keith Sinclair, p. 101 of the 1959
edition.

do much to redeem her social position. And when people were in the presence of death, waiata tangi served to unburden their hearts, to send the soul of their departed relative on its journey to the skies or the underworld, and to threaten enemies with revenge when they were responsible. Above all, the act of singing was a means of assertion in the face of Aitua, or Disaster, an affirmation of the human will, and capacity, to survive adversity.

The great, classic tradition of Maori poetry began to decline in the 1830s and 1840s, when many of the people became Christian, and the old myths and images began to lose much of their significance. New interests were to some extent replacing the old ones, and the virtual cessation of warfare after the country became a British colony meant that there were now no glorious deaths in battle for poets to mourn. The great tradition of wood sculpture, which in its fierce intricacy has much in common with the poetry, was falling into abeyance at the same time. Yet both art forms have continued, changing in subtle ways. In the poetry, Christianity was at first another subject to be celebrated, especially in laments for Christian teachers. The poets began to introduce references to the new possessions that were of so much interest to them, and sometimes they employed transliterations of English words and phrases for conscious effect. Another stimulus came, tragically, from wars fought with the land-hungry settlers, especially in the Waikato in the early 1860s. There were songs of protest against Pakeha greed, and songs by, or about, a series of prophetic leaders, notably Tawhiao, Te Kooti and Te Whiti. In the late nineteenth century some laments for the dead were still being composed, along with pao and other songs. And as in the past, ancient laments were revived when the need arose, often being sung in adapted form.

In the early years of this century, new kinds of songs appeared. The waiata-a-ringa, or action song, often makes use of popular European tunes, is performed with movements illustrative of the sentiments expressed, and often draws ideas and phrases from earlier pao and waiata. Some are songs of welcome or farewell, some are love songs (addressed now to women rather than men), and others are exhortatory in their purpose. Many were composed to farewell men who were leaving to fight in the two world wars, to lament those who lost their lives and to welcome those who returned. Among the famous composers of the first half of this century are Te Puea Herangi, who was one of the leaders of the King Movement and who celebrates it in her poetry, Apirana Ngata and Tuini Ngawai of the East Coast, and Paraire Tomoana of Hawke's Bay. And now, in the last decade or so, there has been a remarkable resurgence of interest and confidence in the Maori language and Maori means of expression. In songs of protest and celebration, contemporary poets are renewing and extending the ancient tradition.

Margaret Orbell

Ko tumi euwha*

(Moriori, Chatham Islands)

Tumi euwha, e eueuwha,
Tumi apō, e apoapoā!
E euwha i te tumu o ta rakau,
Euwha i te take o ta rakau,
Euwha i te aka o ta rakau,
Euwha i te more o ta rakau,
Euwha i te pakiaka o ta rakau!

E euwha ka tipu! E euwha ka ora! Ka ora ko ta rangi e!
Tumi euwha, tumi euwha!
E tchu ta rangi ka ora!

E euwha i ru pua o ta rakau,
Euwha i ta rau o ta rakau,
Euwha i te maewa o ta rakau,
Euwha i te makoha o ta rakau,
Euwha i te tauira o ta rakau,
Euwha i te whakaoti o ta rakau!

E euwha ka tipu! E euwha ka ora! Ka ora ko ta rangi e!
Tumi euwha, tumi euwha!
E tchu ta rangi ka ora!

* Notes for poems begin on p. 527.

Spell for making the first man

Stem heaped up, heaped, heaped up,
Stem gathered together, gathered, gathered together!
Heap the stem of the tree,
Heap the base of the tree,

Heap the fibrous roots of the tree,
Heap the butt of the tree,
Heap the root of the tree!

Heap it, it grows! Heap it, it lives! The sky lives!
Stem heaped up, stem heaped up!
Let the living sky stand!

Heap the flowers of the tree,
Heap the leaves of the tree,
Heap the swaying of the tree,
Heap the waving of the tree,
Heap the pattern of the tree,
Heap the finishing of the tree!

Heap it, it grows! Heap it, it lives! The sky lives!
Stem heaped up, stem heaped up!
Let the living sky stand!

Translation by Margaret Orbell

He hari no mua

(tribe unknown)

E te hihi o te rā e kōkiri kei runga ē,
Tarahaua, ē, pikipiki ake ra, ē,
Ngā moutere tahoratia mai te moana!
Kāore iara, pikipiki ao, pikipiki ao,
Ka puta iara kei tua ē!

An old song of rejoicing

The sun's rays that shoot up, stretched out,
Climb up over the islands spread out on the sea!
Oh climb up over the world, climb up over the world,
Reach the other side!

Translation by Margaret Orbell

Ngā taura, kumea kia ita

(Ngāti Whātua)

te kaea	Ngā taura, kumea kia ita!
te katoa	Kumea, kumea ki uta
te kaea	Ngā tamariki o Tangaroa
te katoa	E pepeke mai, e pepeke atu
te kaea	Ana i ngā hīrautanga o te kupenga o
	Kahukura!
te katoa	Kumea, kumea mai!
te kaea	E tama mā,
te katoa	Kumea mai!

Fishermen's song

leader	The ropes, pull them tight!
chorus	Pull, pull to the shore
leader	Tangaroa's children
chorus	Leaping here, leaping there
leader	In the entangling folds of Kahukura's net!
chorus	Pull, pull them in!
leader	Men,
chorus	Pull them in!

Translation by Margaret Orbell

He oriori mo Te Hauapu

(Noho-mai-te-Rangi of Ngāti Kahungunu)

E tama i whanake i te ata o Pipiri,
Piki, nau ake, e tama,
Ki tōu tini i te rangi!
E puta rānei koe, e tama,
I te wā kaikino nei?
Taku tamaiti, hohoro te korikori
Kia tae atu koe ki te wai ahupuke i ō tīpuna,
Kia wetea mai ko te tōpuni tauwhāinga
Hei kahu mōhou ki te whakarewanga taua!
Ko te toroa uta, nāku i tautara
Ki te akerautangi—
Ko te toroa tai, nāku i kapu mai
I te huka o te tai!
Whakangaro ana ki ngā tai rutu ī!

Song for Te Hauapu

Son who came forth on a winter's morning,
Ascend, mount up, my son,
To your multitude in the sky!
Will you survive, my son,
These evil times?
My child, go quickly
That you may reach the sacred waters of your ancestors,
That they may unfasten the black dogskin cloak of war
For you to wear when the expeditions set forth!
I have bound to my weapon
The albatross plume of the land,
I have caught from the foaming waves
The albatross plume of the sea
As it was going down in stormy waters!

(c. mid eighteenth century)
Translation by Margaret Orbell

Na Murupaenga ra

(Taranaki)

Na Murupaenga ra tana kawenga mai,
I kite ai au i ngā moana nei!
Ko wai ka mātau ki tō tau e awhi ai?
Tērā anō ia ngā mahi i ako ai,
Kei ngā hurihanga ki Ōkehu ra ia!

Slave girl's song

It was Murupaenga who brought me here
So that I saw these seas!
Who knows what lover you embrace?
Oh the things that I learnt over there
In the river-bends at Okehu!

(c. 1810)
Translation by Margaret Orbell

Mātai rore au

(tribe unknown)

Mātai rore au ki te taumata,
Te ngākau whakapuke tonu.
Me aha iho ka mauru ai,
Whiuwhiu kei te muri, kei te tonga?

Love song

On the hill tops I visit the snares
And my heart keeps surging up.
Oh how can I quiet my heart,
That is tossed from north to south?

Translation by Margaret Orbell

He waiata aroha

(? Ngāti Porou)

E haere noa ana, ī, te takutai one, ē, ki Huri-rakau ra ē,
Tērā aku koro te pehapeha noa ra, ē, tē hōhā a Te
    Ngutu!
Ehara i a au, na te ure i hara-mai, ī, he kimi i te hoe ē!
Hokotahi te pounga, waiho nei au ki' mānuka nui ana
    ai!

Go right along the seashore

Go right along the seashore, and you'll come to
    Huri-rakau!
That's where my fathers are talking, their lips are never
    tired!
It wasn't my fault, a penis came seeking to paddle!
Twenty times it plunged, and left me in such trouble
    here!

Translation by Margaret Orbell

David Lowston

(anon.)

My name is David Lowston, I did seal, I did seal,
My name is David Lowston, I did seal.
Though my men and I were lost,
Though our very lives 'twould cost,
We did seal, we did seal, we did seal.

'Twas in eighteen hundred and ten we set sail, we set
   sail,
'Twas in eighteen hundred and ten we set sail.
We were left, we gallant men,
Never more to sail again,
For to seal, for to seal, for to seal.

We were set down in Open Bay, were set down, were
   set down,
We were set down in Open Bay, were set down.
Upon the sixteenth day,
Of Februar–aye–ay,
For to seal, for to seal, for to seal.

Our Captain, John Bedar, he set sail, he set sail,
Yes, for Port Jackson he set sail.
'I'll return, men, without fail,'
But she foundered in a gale,
And went down, and went down, and went down.

We cured ten thousand skins for the fur, for the fur,
Yes we cured ten thousand skins for the fur.
Brackish water, putrid seal,
We did all of us fall ill,
For to die, for to die, for to die.

Come all you lads who sail upon the sea, sail the sea,
Come all you jacks who sail upon the sea.
Though the schooner *Governor Bligh*,
Took on some who did not die,
Never seal, never seal, never seal.

(*c. 1810–1815*)

E kui mā, e koro mā

(Ngāti Porou)

E kui mā, e koro mā, kāore nei aku mahara i piri mai
tau tahi ei!
Kātahi ka tū tonu, he au huri-waka kei waho te moana,
He tai whakatū kei te awa i Hangarua ei!
Ko te whenua anake te āmaia ana e aku mahara ki ngā
pūtea.
Kia ahatia hoki ā te mate hanga?
Ngau atu ana te ahi a Tamatea, he paura kei tawhiti,
kei Tautehere ei!
Ko wai e hua ake nei kai mamao?
Kāore iara, e waiho tata i te pārua o te roto i mate ai a
Te Whakahu.
Na wai ra aronui te ngau rekereke o ngā tamariki?
Huru kurī, ē, te whakawehi o te ope taua!
Pēnei pea me tiro ake ki runga te whare, me whakahoki
roimata ki roto ra ī!
He puna wai e utuhia, he wai kei aku kamo,
He pua kōrau e ruia, e tipu i te waru.
Tēnā ko Tangaroa maheni tirotiro noa ana ki rō
pungarehu ī!

O women, O men

O women, O men, my thoughts will not come to rest in
a year!
They surge up like a canoe-wrecking current out at sea,
A high tide in the river at Hangarua!
That place alone is encircled by my thoughts—I think of
those fine baskets!
What can be done about the works of Death?
Tamatea's fire attacks us, powder from afar, from
Tautehere!

Who thought that it was far off?
Alas, it came close to the edge of the lake where Te
    Whakahu died.
Who could have foreseen the cowardice of those
    children?
How fearsome the war party, in dogskin cloaks!
Perhaps they looked up at the top of the house, then
    weeping, returned inside!
The tears in my eyes are a spring from which water is
    drawn,
Spore of the mamaku spread around in summer.
But smooth-skinned Tangaroa stares about in vain
    in the ashes!

Translation by Margaret Orbell

He tangi mo Te Heuheu Herea

(Te Heuheu Tūkino of Ngāti Tūwharetoa, 1780–1846)

Tītaka kau ana ngā manu o te ata, ka riro ko koe ra ii!
Hare ra, e pā, i te hāhātanga o Piripi.
E kore au e mihi, me i riro ana koe
I te puta tū ata, i whakarakea i te awatea.
Aku ika huirua tēnei ka tū,
Ka pae kei ō tāua aroaro.
Tiria atu ra ki te aroaro no te atua,
I whakakateatia i te ahiahi.
Taku manu noho mātārae, i whāngaia ki te hau,
Kawau aroarotea, ka tū tēnei kei te paenga i ō riri.
Taku kōkōmako whakahau i te ata
No ngā rake manawa i te tahatika ki Pungarehu,
Ka whāngaia koe ki runga te ahurewa,
Ka kai Uenuku, e ra!

Kōmako noa ana i tōku pō ko au anake.
Tē au ko te moe; tokona ake ana ki runga, e ra,
Na te mamae ra ka huri rōnaki.
Ko 'e ika pāwhara na te atua ki runga te tīepa.
Whatiia mai ra tītapu maroro,
Ka tōkia tō kiri e te anu kōpata.
Kāpā ianei he wehenga tau koe.
Te wehe i te matua, no hea e hoki mai ki ahau?
Te matua i te whare, me rauhī mai e te ringa,
Te matua i te waka, me whakatangi ki te waihoe!
Me uta ki te patu, me uta ki te tao—
Ngā mahi ra, ē, i whakarararawetia, ka rewa kei runga
Te apaapatū kei ō tuākana,
I te waka e tau ana
I te nui 'Āti Tū, i te rahi 'Āti Rangi—
Māna e hoatu ki te mata-uraura,
Māku e whakamau ngā tai-toru ātea o te wai!
E pā mā, tirohia mai ko au anake tēnei!
Ka riro te mumu, ka riro te āwhā,
Ka tere te parata,

Ka maunu te ika i tōna rua.
Taku kākā haetara ki te iwi ra ia,
Wātea kau ana ko te tūranga kau o Rehua,
Takoto ana mai te marama i te pae ki a koe.
Ka eke i ō hē, ka tau ki raro, e ra ii!

Lament for Te Heuheu Herea

The birds at dawn fly around in confusion now you are
    gone.
Go, sir, while the mist rises from the frozen earth!
I would not have greeted you if you had been taken
In a dawn attack, to be seen in the light of day.
My warriors who killed two men at a time
Now lie before us.
They are offered to the god,
Scattered in the evening.
My bird of the headlands, fed by the wind,
The white-breasted shag stands on your battlefields.
My bellbird that hastened the dawn
In the thickets on the cliff-shore at Pungarehu,
You are a food-offering on the shrine,
And Uenuku eats!

In the night I am a solitary bellbird, singing on my
    own.
Sleep does not come, for my thoughts spring up
As grief turns me about endlessly.
You are a gutted fish on the shrine of the god.
The drooping heron-plume is broken,
And your skin is wet with the cold dew.
If this were a parting for a season!
But when we part from a father, what can bring him
    back?
If it were the body of a house, hands would be at work,
If it were the body of a canoe, the paddlers' song would
    be chanted!

Place his clubs about him, place his spears about him!
With them he did great deeds—and your fame arose
Among the company of your elder brothers
And the anchored canoes
Of the hosts of 'Ati Tu, the multitudes of 'Ati Rangi—
They will go forth to war,
And I will confine the surging tides of the ocean!
My fathers, see me here alone!
The strong wind is gone, the storm is gone,
The canoe prow has drifted away,
The fish has left its den.
My kaka envied by the tribes,
The place is empty where Rehua used to shine,
And because of you the moon lies on the horizon.
Misdeeds brought you evil, and you lie low!

(c. 1820)
Translation by Margaret Orbell

He tangi mo Te Iwi-ika

(? Kāi Tahu, Kāti Mamoe)

E kimi ana i te mate o Te Iwi-ika,
Waniwani amu a wekuna i whakapiki
Ka reo o tini o te iwi o te ao.
Waiho kia mate ana te tangata—
Tāruatia nei e koe te mamae ki a au,
He tikanga huri kino i a au!
Whatungarongaro, ē, te tahu—
I ngaro tonu atu koe i ahau!
Hare ra i te ara whānui,
He rori ka tika i a Hine-tītama,
I a Tahi-kūmea, i a Tahu-whaera—
Ka tika te ara ki te mate!
Hua parau noa 'e tāne ki te whai atu—
Koia 'nō i tapoko atu ai ki rō te tatau
O te whare o Poutukutia, ko Poutererangi!
He oti tonu atu koe, e te tahu ei!
Hoki kau mai 'e tāne ki te ao nei,
Kōmiro kino ai tōna kākau, pēnei me au ē—
Momotu kino nei taku manawa
Ki a koe, e te tahu ei!
Whakapiki te haere a Tāne
Ki te raki i a Rehua i ruka,
Whakatika te haere a Tāne
Ki te raki i a Tama-i-wa[h]o,
Whakapiki titaha te haere a Tāne
Ki te rangi i a Rangi-whakaūpoko-i-runga—
Ka tūturu anō te kāhui ariki
Kai te mutuka o kā rangi!
Heke iho nei Tāne ki te whenua,
Ka kitea he mahara mo te tōhuatanga,
Ko tōna ika whenua, ka tipu he tāngata
Hei noho i te ao mārama ei!

Lament for Te Iwi-ika

Seeking Te Iwi-ika's death
The voices of the multitudes in the world
Mount up, speaking bitterly.
Let the man be dead—
How you make my pain increase,
So that I turn about in sorrow!
Oh my husband is lost—
You are lost to me always!
Set out on the wide path!
Straight is the road of Hine-titama,
Tahi-kumea, and Tahu-whaera—
The path goes straight to death!
I had thought there would be a man to follow,
But he disappeared through the doorway
Of Poutererangi, Poutukutia's house!
Husband, you are gone from me for ever!
When he visits this world again
His heart is cruelly twisted, as is mine—
My heart is cruelly broken,
Husband, because of you!
Tane made his way upwards
To the sky of Rehua above,
Tane made his way straight
To the sky of Tama-i-waho,
Tane made his way up slantingly
To the sky of Rangi-whakaupoko-above—
The lordly company remains always
In the last of the skies!
Tane came down to this land
And saw how it might be made fertile—
His mainland here—and people grew up,
To live in the world of light!

Translation by Margaret Orbell

He pōkeka

(? Arawa, Mātātua)

Titi, titi kawe kura, poupoua te rangi e tū iho nei, e tū
   iho nei!
Kāore iara, ko te tiki pounamu!
Ko Āniwaniwa i te kauhanga nui, ka takoto kei te āio.
Tīkina, tirohia, pātaia. Tēnā ka riro kei te one i Hawaiki,
Kei te tupuranga mai o te kauheke—kauheke,
   kaumātua!
He atua! Ko atua tonu te hoa e takoto mai nei i tana
   moenga—
Moenga kino, moenga kura, moenga a Tiki-rau-hanga, a
   Tiki!
He pare kawakawa te pare o Ruaumoko—Ruaumoko!
Hīa, ka tārewa te atua Māori whiowhio—
Atua taniwha o te moana nui a Kiwa e takoto mai nei!
He horonga! Nāna i huna iho te tini o Manaia i
   Pōwhitiao!
Ko te tai anake o Maketū e ngunguru nei i te pō, i te
   ao!
Uhi wero! Whano, hara-mai te toki! Haumi e, hui e,
   tāiki e!

Lament

Spell, treasure-bearing spell, prop up the sky standing
   above, standing above!
O alas, it is the greenstone tiki!
Rainbow is in the spaces of the sky, and all is calm.
Go and see, and ask. He is taken away to the soil of
   Hawaiki,
The place of origin of the ancestors—ancestors,
   forebears!

A spirit! Our friend is a spirit indeed, lying here on his
   bed—
An evil bed, a precious bed, the bed of Tiki-rau-hanga,
   of Tiki!
Ruaumoko's chaplet is of kawakawa leaves—Ruaumoko!
The whistling Maori spirit is raised up, floats up—
The taniwha spirit of the great ocean of Kiwa that lies
   before us!
A battle lost! When night became day, thus were
   destroyed the hosts of Manaia!
At Maketu only the tide sounds in the night, in the
   day!
Uhi wero! Come, bring the adze! Join together, come
   together, bind together, *e!*

Translation by Margaret Orbell

E Hōhepa e tangi

(? Te Rarawa)

E Hōhepa e tangi, kāti ra te tangi!
Me aha tāua i te pō inoi, i te pō kauwhau?
Me kōkiri koe ki te wai Hōrana
Kia murua te kino, kia wehea te hara, e tama e!
Me kawe ake koe ki te whare i a Tāna
Kia tohutohungia ki te rata pukapuka—
Te upoko tuatahi, te upoko i a Kēnehi,
Te rongopai o Mātiu, kia whakamātau ai,
Kia kite te kanohi o te tinana, e tama e!

Song for Joseph

Joseph, you are crying, but you have cried enough!
What must we do on the night of prayers, the night of
    preaching?
You must leap into the waters of the Jordan
That evil may be forgiven, and your sins removed, my
    son!
You must make your way to Turner's house
And be taught the letters in the book—
The first chapter, the chapter of Genesis,
And the gospel of Matthew, that you may learn,
That the eyes of your body may see, my son!

(*c. 1823–1827*)
Translation by Margaret Orbell

Come All You Tonguers

(anon.)

Come all you tonguers and land-loving lubbers,
Here's a job cutting in and boiling down blubbers,
A job for the youngster, or old and ailing,
The Agent will take any man for shore whaling.

I am paid in soap, and sugar, and rum,
For cutting in whale and boiling down tongue.
The Agent's fee makes my blood so t'boil,
I'll push him in a hot pot of oil!

Go hang the Agent, the Company too!
They are making a fortune off me and you.
No chance of a passage from out of this place,
And the price of living's a blooming disgrace!

I am paid in soap, and sugar, and rum,
For cutting in whale and boiling down tongue.
The Agent's fee makes my blood so t'boil,
I'll push him in a hot pot of oil!

(*c. 1830*)

Kia nui ō pākiki maunga

(Kie Tapu, tribe unknown)

Kia nui ō pākiki maunga, hei neke ki Tuia, hei rapa mo
    Kaipuke—
Tō waka, e Kawa, hei pīhau tere kai Te Rimurapa ii!
Kai raro Potau, e awhia ana Rakura—he tangata hou
    koe no te rā tō ei!
Ka mea, e Whare, ka utaia au ki te arero ra ia!
Kia huri, ē, Hui, te hoa i a Kuia—nāku rawa i rore atu!
Tukua kia pahu ki Tangi-noa, arā te hoa o Te Hukinga
    ii—
Ko taku tangata hokoi tērā, i ako ai au te ai rape ie!
E tama mā, whakapono tahi ake he taru i onge rawa ii!
Na Maru koi patu, whiua ki tōku, koia tonu anō!
Kia huri, ē, Uta, i Rangipō ra, te hoa i a Riu—
Nāna rawa i mahi nei, pine ana Raro i taku ohinga ii!
No muringa nei koe hei urungi kau, ka tere kai te
    moana ii!

Song by a woman accused of adultery

Since you're asking so many questions I'll be off to Tuia
    and seek Ship—
Your vessel, Kawa, will send me on with the wind to
    Te Rimurapa!
Potau is below there, who's embraced by Rakura—
    you're a determined man from the setting sun!
Whare, I think I am put on board those tongues
    there!
Oh let me turn to Hui, Kuia's companion—it was I who
    snared him!
Let me dart off to Tangi-noa, who's Te Hukinga's
    companion—

He was a man I loved, who taught me sex with tattooed
   buttocks!
O men, truly he was a most rare treasure!
Then Maru struck, flung a blow at mine, and that's how
   it was!
Oh let me turn to Uta there at Rangipo, Riu's
   companion—
Yes it was he who did it, pinned me below when I was
   young!
Now you are only a steering-paddle drifting upon the
   ocean!

(*c. 1820–1850*)
Translation by Margaret Orbell

He tangi na te tūroro

(Harata Tangikuku of Ngāti Porou)

E timu ra koe, e te tai nei, rere omaki ana ia ki waho ra!
Hei runga nei au tiro iho ai ngā roro whare ki
   Mihi-marino—
Nāku iana koe i kakekake i ngā rangi ra ka hori nei!

E tangi ra koe, e te kihikihi! Tēnei koe ka rite mai ki
   ahau!
Me he hūroto au kei rō repo, me he kāka e whakarāoa
   ana!

Tirohia atu koia me ko Tāwera whakakau ana mai ki
   uta—
Hohoro mai koia hei hoa moe ake mōku ra, e tiu nei!
Me he pōrangi au e keha ana, he haurangi kai waipiro;
Me he tāhuna rere i te amo hau, he perehia rere ki
   tawhiti!

Tiro iho ai au ki ahau, rinoi ra, ē, te uaua:
Te koha-kore o te kai ki ahau, heke rāwaho i te kiri ora.
Waiho au kia pōaha ana, he rimu pukā kei te ākau!

Invalid's song

Ebb on, tide, moving swiftly outwards!
Here above, I look down at the house porches at
   Mihi-marino—
You that I climbed in those days that are gone!

Sing on, cicada, for your case is like mine!
I am like a bittern in the swamp, a bittern with its
   choking cry!

I see the morning star rising towards the shore—
Come quickly to keep me company as I reel about!
I am like a madwoman making strange sounds, one
  drunk with alcohol,
Like raupo seed flying in the wind, sand-bent seed
  flying far off!

I look down, and see my twisted sinews.
Food does not sustain me, it passes through my body
Leaving me empty, dry seaweed on the shore!

(*c. 1860–1875*)
Translation by Margaret Orbell

Tangi a taku ihu

(Te Whetū of Te Āti Awa)

Tangi a taku ihu e whakamakuru nei, ko au pea, ē, te
    tūria ki runga!
He maihi whare koe ki' miti mai te arero! Ma ringa tohu
    au e whakapoi ai, e tika
Taku tākiritanga te kahu o te Kuini! Ka piki ngā rongo o
    Te Whiti kei runga,
Hāpainga atu au ki runga o Parihaka! Kia whakarongo
    mai Moeahu i reira,
Hei pānui atu ki te iwi o Tītoko! Ki taku whakaaro he
    makau tupu koe,
Ka mutu pea, ē, ngā rangi hanihani! Tēnei anō ra tō
    raukura ka titia,
Ma te 'au o waho e tiki mai, e whawhati! Te weherua
    pō i wake ai kōrua,
He kai mutunga koe ki taku tinana nei! No hea ngā
    mate e patu ra i aku hoa,
Te karawhiu ai ki te kino i ahau? Kei noho au i te ao
    hei kome au ma te ngutu ii!

The sound of my sneezing nose

The sound of my sneezing nose tells me that I am
    raised up on high!
You are the bargeboard of the house that the tongue
    will assail! My hand with my poi affirms it was right
To cast off the cloak of the Queen! Te Whiti's fame
    mounts on high,
I am carried up over Parihaka! Let Moeahu hear news
    of it then,
And proclaim it to Titoko's people! You are a man
    beloved, I know,

And these days of slanderous talk will end! In our hair
    we wear your plumes,
Though the wind from outside come to break them! You
    two walk in the darkest hour of night,
You are my mainstay and my sustenance! Whence come
    the evils that attack my friends,
The misfortunes crowding upon me? Let me not remain
    in the world as an object of derision!

(c. 1880)
Translation by Margaret Orbell

Ē, i te tekau mā whā

(tribe unknown)

Ē, i te tekau mā whā ka ū te whakapono ei
Ki runga o Ōihi, ki te iwi Māori ei!
Ka tū Te Mātenga, ko te kupu tēnei ei,
'Kei te rangi te Atua, me titiro whakarunga ei!'
Ka huri te Māori, ka titiro whakararo ei
Ki te papa oneone i Aotearoa ei,
Ka taiapatia mai ki te pāraharaha ei,
Ki te pātītī, ki te paraikete whero ei,
Ki te rōria rino nāu, e Kāwana!
Kua riro te whenua, e tere ra i te moana ei!

The land is gone

Oh, in the fourteenth the faith landed
At Oihi, brought to the Maori people!
Marsden stood there, and these were his words:
'God is in the sky, you must look up!'
The Maori turned, and looked down
At the soil of Aotearoa,
Fenced off from us by iron tools,
By hatchets and red blankets
And your iron jew's harps, Governor!
The land is gone, drifting out to sea!

(c. 1880)
Translation by Margaret Orbell

He waiata tohutohu

(Te Kooti Rikirangi of Rongowhakaata, c. 1830–1893)

Kāore te pō nei mōrikarika noa!
Te ohonga ki te ao, rapu kau noa ahau.
Ko te mana tuatahi ko te Tiriti o Waitangi,
Ko te mana tuarua ko te Kōti Whenua,
Ko te mana tuatoru ko te Mana Motuhake!
Ka kīia i reira ko te Rohe Pōtae o Tūhoe,
He rongo ka houhia ki a Ngāti Awa.
He kino anō ra ka āta kitea iho
Ngā mana Māori ka mahue kei muri!
Ka uru nei au ki te ture Kaunihera,
E rua aku mahi e noho nei au:
Ko te hanga i ngā rōri, ko te hanga i ngā tiriti!
Pūkohu tāiri ki Pōneke ra,
Ki te kāinga ra i noho ai te Minita.
Ki taku whakaaro ka tae mai te Poari
Hai noho i te whenua o Kōtitia nei,
Pā rawa te mamae ki te tau o taku ate.
E te iwi nui, tū ake ki runga ra,
Tirohia mai ra te hē o aku mahi!
Māku e kī atu, 'Nōhia, nōhia!'
No mua iho anō, no ngā kaumātua!
Na taku ngākau i kimi ai ki te Ture,
No konei hoki au i kino ai ki te hoko!
Hī! Hai aha te hoko!

A song of instruction

Alas for this unhappy night!
Waking to the world, I search about in vain.
The first mana is the Treaty of Waitangi,
The second mana is the Land Court,
The third mana is the Separate Mana:

Hence the Rohe Potae of Tuhoe,
And peace made with Ngati Awa.
It would indeed be an evil thing
To abandon the mana of the Maori!
If I submitted to the law of the Council,
Two things I would do:
Building roads, and building streets!
Yonder the mist hangs over Wellington,
The home of the Minister.
I fear that the Board will come
To live in this land of Kootitia,
And I am sick at heart.
All my people, be watchful,
See the evil of these things!
I say to you, 'Remain, remain on your land!'
It is from former ages, from your ancestors!
Because my heart has searched out the Law,
For this reason I abhor selling!
Hi! Why sell!

(1883)
Translation by Margaret Orbell

Waitekauri Every Time!

(Edwin Edwards)

There's a good old war-cry sounding, it hangs on every
    lip,
In the city, in the township, in the mine and on the tip,
A phrase that gives the story of the old prospectors'
    pluck,
Their doings with the pick, and gad, their cursèd bally
    luck,
When the battered dish flowed empty, bar a tail of new-
    chum gold,
Or it gave a ring of 'colour' that betokened wealth
    untold.
I can weave it in my ballad, I can swing it in my
    rhyme,
It's Waitekauri, Waitekauri, Waitekauri Every Time!

Oh, the days of Hughey's tribute and the doings that
    they did!
You had to drink your grog those times from out a billy
    lid.
When all the picks were furnished by poor old
    Pick-handle Dan,
And Harry Skene retorted in a broken frying pan.
When the dirt went fifteen ounces, and every now and
    then
They used to weigh the bullion not by troy weight, but
    by men.
I can swing it in my ballad, I can weave it in my
    rhyme,
Waitekauri, Waitekauri, Waitekauri Every Time!

They never growled at road or track, or at the county
    groan,
With a compass and a slasher they would travel on
    their own.
I used to pack the tucker to the 'Perseverance Push',

And the only road I knew of then was blasphemy and
  bush.
There was no Rae nor Ryan, but the bhoys could get
  their fill
At the shanty in the ti-tree, up at Paddy Sheehy's hill.
Ah, the tears come in my ballad, and the sadness in my
  rhyme,
Those times 'twas Waitekauri, Waitekauri Every Time!

But now they've got a boarding house, a lock-up and a
  cop,
And a milkman, and a parson, and Good Gawd, a
  barber's shop!
John Bull he owns the country, and he snaffles every
  find,
And the poor old-timer—well, he gets the dust that
  blows behind.
Perhaps it's for the better, but somehow it seems to me,
That up there at the Beehive they ain't what they used
  to be.,
There isn't just the accent as they howled it in their
  prime,
When the ranges used to echo—Waitekauri Every Time!

I think of those vast aisles of bush and fern where I
  have heard
The whistle of the tui and the screeching of that bird,
The gloomy, lonesome kaka, whose gloomy lonesome
  ring
Breaks the solemn silence where no other songsters
  sing.
He's dead, the bush is fallen, and there's dust and
  cyanide,
And syndicates, and companies, and God knows what
  beside.
Well, it's in the way of all things—you must climb and
  climb and climb.
Anyhow, we'll yell the chorus—Waitekauri Every Time!

(*c. 1890–1900*)

Ko te tangi mo Tāwhiao

(Waikato)

Ka ngau Mōkau, ka ngau Tāmaki,
Ka rū te whenua, ka mate te marama,
Ka taka te whetū o te rangi
I te unuhanga o te taniwha i te rua!
Auē, auē, auē, te mamae ē!

Waikato awa e tuwhera kau nei,
Waikato tāngata e tangi kau atu nei:
Auē, auē, auē, te mamae ē!

E Tupu e, kei whea tōu ariki?
Kua unuhia i runga i te ahurewa,
A, kua pouarutia ngā iwi o te motu nei!
Auē, auē, auē, te mamae ē!

E Whiti e, kei whea tō tamaiti?
Kua unuhia i runga i te takapau hora-nui!
Auē, auē, auē, te mamae ē!

E tama e, ka tohe au, ka tohe au,
Ka tohe au ki te Kauhanganui,
Ki tōu torona i waiho i te ao,
E tū nei, e tū nei, e tū nei
Runga i te mana Maori motuhake, e tū nei!

E ngā Minita, e ngā Matariki, e ngā Manukura,
Kia ū, kia mau ki tō karauna i waiho i te ao,
E tū nei, e tū nei, e tū nei
Runga i te mana Māori motuhake, e tū nei!

Lament for Tawhiao

Mokau roars, Tamaki roars,
The earth shakes, the moon dies,
The stars fall from the sky
As the taniwha is raised up from its den!
Alas, alas, alas, what sorrow!

Waikato river lies empty,
And Waikato men lament:
Alas, alas, alas, what sorrow!

Tupu, where is your lord?
He is raised up at the shrine,
And the tribes of the land are widowed!
Alas, alas, alas, what sorrow!

Whiti, where is your child?
He is raised up on the widespread mat!
Alas, alas, alas, what sorrow!

My son, I strive, I strive,
I strive for the Kauhanganui,
For your throne left in this world,
Standing, standing, standing here
Because of the separate Maori mana, standing here!

Ministers, Matariki, Manukura,
Hold firm, hold fast to your crown left in this world,
Standing, standing, standing here
Because of the separate Maori mana, standing here!

(1894)
Translation by Margaret Orbell

Te Whetu Plains

A lonely rock above a midnight plain,
  A sky across whose moonlit darkness flies
No shadow from the 'Children of the Rain',
  A stream whose double crescent far-off lies,
  And seems to glitter back the silver of the skies.

The table-lands stretch step by step below
  In giant terraces, their deeper ledges
Banded by blackened swamps (that, near, I know
  Convolvulus-entwined) whose whitened edges
  Are ghostly silken flags of seeding water-sedges.

All still, all silent, 'tis a songless land,
  That hears no music of the nightingale,
No sound of waters falling lone and grand
  Through sighing forests to the lower vale,
  No whisper in the grass, so wan, and grey, and pale.

When Earth was tottering in its infancy,
  This rock, a drop of molten stone, was hurled
And tost on waves of flames like those we see
  (Distinctly though afar) evolved and whirled
  A photosphere of fire around the Solar World.

Swift from the central deeps the lightning flew
  Piercing the heart of Darkness like a spear,
Hot blasts of steam and vapour thunder'd through
  The lurid blackness of the atmosphere.
  A million years have passed, and left strange quiet
    here.

Peace, the deep peace of universal death
  Enshrouds the kindly mother-earth of old,

The air is dead, and stirs no living breath
  To break these awful Silences that hold
  The heart within their clutch, and numb the veins
    with cold.

My soul hath wept for Rest with longing tears,
  Called it 'the perfect crown of human life'—
But now I shudder lest the coming years
  Should be with these most gloomy terrors rife;
  When palsied arms drop down outwearied with the
    strife.

May Age conduct me by a gentle hand
  Beneath the shadows ever brooding o'er
The solemn twilight of the Evening Land,
  Where man's discordant voices pierce no more,
  But sleeping waters dream along a sleeping shore.

Where I, when Youth has spent its fiery strength
  And flickers low, may rest in quietness
Till on my waiting brow there falls at length
  The deeper calm of the Death-Angel's kiss—
  But not, oh God, such peace, such ghastly peace as
    this.

He pao

(Ngāti Tūwharetoa)

Āwangawanga, ē, ki aku tau e rua ei!
Ko tēwhea e pine mai ki te uma iara ei?

Kia inu ake au, inu tahi te aroha ei!
Kāore he rangi tāmututia iara ei!

Piki ake ai au, ka eke ki ngā hiwi ei!
Me te hau te aroha te piki ake i raro ei!

E hoki, e Hira, ki tō tau tūturu ei!
Waiho ko Kīngi ki ngā kuru reiri iara ei!

Punaruatia ki te tau a Merania ei!
Ko au ki te taha ki waenganui, e kare ii!

Women's songs

Oh I can't decide between my two loves *ei!*
Which one shall I pin on my bosom *iara ei?*

Let me drink of love, drink deep *ei!*
Not a day without it *iara ei!*

I climb the hills and reach the top *ei!*
Love mounts up like the wind *ei!*

Hira, go back to your own true love *ei!*
Leave Kingi to the good ladies *iara ei!*

Take Merania's love as your second wife *ei!*
I'm the one in the middle, my darling *ii!*

(c. 1900)
Translation by Margaret Orbell

The Passing of the Forest

All glory cannot vanish from the hills.
   Their strength remains, their stature of command
O'er shadowy valleys that cool twilight fills
   For wanderers weary in a faded land;
Refreshed when rain-clouds swell a thousand rills,
   Ancient of days in green old age they stand,
Though lost the beauty that became Man's prey
When from their flanks he stripped the woods away.

But thin their vesture now—the trembling grass
   Shivering and yielding as the breeze goes by,
Catching quick gleams and scudding shades that pass
   As running seas reflect a windy sky.
A kinglier garb their forest raiment was
   From crown to feet that clothed them royally,
Shielding the secrets of their streams from day
Ere the deep, sheltering woods were hewn away.

Well may these brooding, mutilated kings,
   Stripped of the robes that ages weaved, discrowned,
Draw down the clouds with soft-enfolding wings
   And white, aerial fleece to wrap them round,
To hide the scars that every season brings,
   The fire's black smirch, the landslip's gaping wound,
Well may they shroud their heads in mantle grey
Since from their brows the leaves were plucked away!

Gone is the forest's labyrinth of life,
   Its clambering, thrusting, clasping, throttling race,
Creeper with creeper, bush with bush at strife,
   Struggling in silence for a breathing space;
Below, a realm with tangled rankness rife,

Aloft, tree columns in victorious grace.
Gone the dumb hosts in warfare dim; none stay;
Dense brake and stately trunk have passed away.

Gone are those gentle forest-haunting things,
  Eaters of honey, honey-sweet in song.
The tui and the bell-bird—he who rings
  That brief, rich music we would fain prolong,
Gone the woodpigeon's sudden whirr of wings,
  The daring robin all unused to wrong,
Ay, all the friendly friendless creatures. They
Lived with their trees and died and passed away.

Gone are the flowers. The kowhai like ripe corn,
  The frail convolvulus, a day-dream white,
And dim-hued passion-flowers for shadows born,
  Wan orchids strange as ghosts of tropic night;
The blood-red rata strangling trees forlorn
  Or with exultant scarlet fiery bright
Painting the sombre gorges, and that fay
The starry clematis are all away!

Lost is the resinous, sharp scent of pines,
  Of wood fresh cut, clean-smelling for the hearth,
Of smoke from burning logs in wavering lines
  Softening the air with blue, of brown, damp earth
And dead trunks fallen among coiling vines,
  Slow-mouldering, moss-coated. Round the girth
Of the green land the wind brought vale and bay
Fragrance far-borne now faded all away.

Lost is the sense of noiseless sweet escape
  From dust of stony plain, from sun and gale,
When the feet tread where quiet shadows drape
  Dark stems with peace beneath a kindly veil.
No more the pleasant rustling stir each shape,
  Creeping with whisperings that rise and fail
Through glimmering lace-work lit by chequered play
Of light that danced on moss now burned away.

Gone are the forest tracks, where oft we rode
   Under the silver fern-fronds climbing slow,
In cool, green tunnels, though fierce noontide glowed
   And glittered on the tree-tops far below.
There, 'mid the stillness of the mountain road,
   We just could hear the valley river flow,
Whose voice through many a windless summer day
Haunted the silent woods, now passed away.

Drinking fresh odours, spicy wafts that blew,
   We watched the glassy, quivering air asleep,
Midway between tall cliffs that taller grew
   Above the unseen torrent calling deep;
Till, like a sword, cleaving the foliage through,
   The waterfall flashed foaming down the steep:
White, living water, cooling with its spray
Dense plumes of fragile fern, now scorched away.

The axe bites deep. The rushing fire streams bright;
   Swift, beautiful and fierce it speeds for Man,
Nature's rough-handed foeman, keen to smite
   And mar the loveliness of ages. Scan
The blackened forest ruined in a night,
   The sylvan Parthenon that God will plan
But builds not twice. Ah, bitter price to pay
For Man's dominion—beauty swept away!

DAVID McKEE WRIGHT (1867–1928)

While the Billy Boils

The speargrass crackles under the billy and overhead is
    the winter sun;
There's snow on the hills, there's frost in the gully, that
    minds me of things that I've seen and done,
Of blokes that I knew, and mates that I've worked with,
    and the sprees we had in the days gone by;
And a mist comes up from my heart to my eyelids, I
    feel fair sick and I wonder why.

There is coves and coves! Some I liked partic'lar, and
    some I would sooner I never knowed;
But a bloke can't choose the chaps that he's thrown
    with in the harvest paddock or here on the road.
There was chaps from the other side that I shore with
    that I'd like to have taken along for mates,
But we said, 'So long!' and we laughed and parted for
    good and all at the station gates.

I mind the time when the snow was drifting and Billy
    and me was out for the night—
We lay in the lee of a rock, and waited, hungry and
    cold, for the morning light.
Then he went one way and I the other—we'd been like
    brothers for half a year;
He said: 'I'll see you again in town, mate, and we'll
    blow the froth off a pint of beer.'

He went to a job on the plain he knowed of and I went
    poisoning out at the back,
And I missed him somehow—for all my looking I never
    could knock across his track.

The same with Harry, the bloke I worked with the time
    I was over upon the Coast,
He went for a fly-round over to Sydney, to stay for a
    fortnight—a month at most!

He never came back, and he never wrote me—I wonder
    how blokes like him forget;
We had been where no one had been before us, we had
    starved for days in the cold and wet;
We had sunk a hundred holes that was duffers, till at
    last we came on a fairish patch,
And we worked in rags in the dead of winter while the
    ice bars hung from the frozen thatch.

Yes, them was two, and I can't help mind them—good
    mates as ever a joker had;
But there's plenty more as I'd like to be with, for half of
    the blokes on the road is bad.
It sets me a-thinking the world seems wider, for all we
    fancy it's middling small,
When a chap like me makes friends in plenty and they
    slip away and he loses them all.

The speargrass crackles under the billy and overhead is
    the winter sun;
There's snow on the hills, there's frost in the gully,
    and, Oh, the things that I've seen and done,
The blokes that I knowed and the mates I've worked
    with, and the sprees we had in the days gone by;
But I somehow fancy we'll all be pen-mates on the day
    when they call the Roll of the Sky.

PARAIRE HĒNARE TOMOANA
(1868–1946; Ngāti Kahungunu)

Pōkarekare ana

Pōkarekare ana ngā wai o Waiapu.
Whiti atu koe, e hine, marino ana ē!

E hine ē, hoki mai rā!
Ka mate ahau i te aroha ē!

E kore te aroha e maroke i te rā.
Mākūkū tonu i aku roimata ē!

E hine ē, hoki mai rā!
Ka mate ahau i te aroha ē!

Tuhituhi taku reta, tuku atu taku rīngi.
Kia kite tō iwī, raruraru ana ē!

E hine ē, hoki mai rā!
Ka mate ahau i te aroha ē!

Whatiwhati taku pēne, kua pau aku pepa.
Ko taku aroha mau tonu ana ē!

E hine ē, hoki mai rā!
Ka mate ahau i te aroha ē!

The waters of Waiapu

Stormy are the waters of Waiapu.
If you cross them, girl, they will be calm.

Come back to me girl,
I am so much in love!

My love will never dry in the sun.
It will always be wet with my tears.

Come back to me girl,
I am so much in love!

I write my letter and send my ring.
If your people see them, there will be trouble.

Come back to me girl,
I am so much in love!

My pen is broken, my paper used up.
My love for you will always remain.

Come back to me girl,
I am so much in love!

Translation by Margaret Orbell

E pari rā

E pari rā ngā tai ki te ākau,
E hotu rā ko taku manawa!
Auē, me tangi noa ahau i muri nei.
Te iwi e, he ngākau tangi noa!

Tēnā rā, tahuri mai!
E te tau, te aroha!
Tēnei rā ahau te tangi nei
Mōhou kua wehea nei!
Haere rā, mahara mai!
E te tau, kia mau ki a au!
Haere rā, ka tūturu ahau!
Haere rā!

Ngaro noa koe, e tama, i ngā marae nei,
Ko te aroha, e tama, e pēhi kino nei!
Kei Īhipa koe, e tama, kei Karipori rā.
Auē, te mamae, e tama. Haere, haere rā!

Kāore hoki, ē, te pō nei te hari wairua mai,
He aroha ki ngā iwi ka hinga ki pāmamao.
Kei Īhipa koe, e tama, kei Karipori rā,
Kei Paranihi, e tama. Haere, haere rā!

Haria mai te aroha ki ahau,
Auē, me tangi noa ahau i muri nei!
Haere rā, e tama, haere rā!

Full tide

Full tide on the shore,
And my heart is sobbing.
Alas, I must keep weeping here.
You people, my heart is weeping!

Oh, turn back to me!
Beloved, what sorrow!
Here I am weeping
For you who are gone.
Oh farewell, think of me!
Beloved, be true!
Farewell, I am yours always.
Farewell!

You are lost, my son, to these marae
And sorrow weighs me down.
You are in Egypt, my son, and Gallipoli.
Alas, what pain! Farewell, farewell!

Oh alas, how this night brought our souls to me!
I long so much for those fallen in far places.

You are in Egypt, my son, and Gallipoli,
And France, my son. Farewell, farewell!

Send your love to me!
Alas, I must keep weeping here.
Farewell, my son, farewell!

Translation by Margaret Orbell

The Old Place

So the last day's come at last, the close of my fifteen
    year—
The end of the hope, an' the struggles, an' messes I've
    put in here,
All of the shearings over, the final mustering done,—
Eleven hundred an' fifty for the incoming man, near on.
Over five thousand I drove 'em, mob by mob, down the
    coast;
Eleven-fifty in fifteen year . . . it isn't much of a boast.

Oh, it's a bad old place! Blown out o' your bed half the
    nights,
And in summer the grass burnt shiny an' bare as your
    hand, on the heights:
The creek dried up by November, and in May a
    thundering roar
That carries down toll o' your stock to salt 'em whole
    on the shore.
Clear'd I have, and I've clear'd an' clear'd, yet
    everywhere, slap in your face,
Briar, tauhinu, an' ruin!—God! it's a brute of a place.
. . . An' the house got burnt which I built, myself, with
    all that worry and pride;
Where the Missus was always homesick, and where she
    took fever, and died.

Yes, well! I'm leaving the place. Apples look red on that
    bough.
I set the slips with my own hand. Well—they're the
    other man's now.
The breezy bluff: an' the clover that smells so over the
    land,

Drowning the reek o' the rubbish, that plucks the profit
    out o' your hand:
That bit o' Bush paddock I fall'd myself, an' watched,
    each year, come clean
(Don't it look fresh in the tawny? A scrap of Old-
    Country green):
This air, all healthy with sun an' salt, an' bright with
    purity:
An' the glossy karakas there, twinkling to the big blue
    twinkling sea:
Ay, the broad blue sea beyond, an' the gem-clear cove
    below,
Where the boat I'll never handle again, sits rocking to
    and fro:
There's the last look to it all! an' now for the last upon
This room, where Hetty was born, an' my Mary died,
    an' John . . .

Well, I'm leaving the poor old place, and it cuts as keen
    as a knife;
The place that's broken my heart—the place where I've
    lived my life.

from A Bush Section

Logs, at the door, by the fence; logs, broadcast over the
    paddock;
Sprawling in motionless thousands away down the
    green of the gully,
Logs, grey-black. And the opposite rampart of ridges
Bristles against the sky, all the tawny, tumultuous
    landscape
Is stuck, and prickled, and spiked with the standing
    black and grey splinters,
Strewn, all over its hollows and hills, with the long,
    prone, grey-black logs.

For along the paddock, and down the gully,
Over the multitudinous ridges,
Through valley and spur,
Fire has been!
Ay, the Fire went through and the Bush has departed,
The green Bush departed, green Clearing is not yet
    come.
'Tis a silent, skeleton world;
Dead, and not yet re-born,
Made, unmade, and scarcely as yet in the making;
Ruin'd, forlorn, and blank.

At the little raw farm on the edge of the desolate
  hillside,
Perch'd on the brink, overlooking the desolate valley,
To-night, now the milking is finish'd, and all the calves
  fed,
The kindling all split, and the dishes all wash'd after
  supper:
Thorold von Reden, the last of a long line of nobles,
Little 'Thor Rayden', the twice-orphan'd son of a
  drunkard,
Dependent on strangers, the taciturn, grave ten-year-
  old,
Stands and looks from the garden of cabbage and
  larkspur, looks over
The one little stump-spotted rye-patch, so gratefully
  green,
Out, on this desert of logs, on this dead disconsolate
  ocean
Of billows arrested, of currents stay'd, that never awake
  and flow.
Day after day,
The hills stand out on the sky,
The splinters stand on the hills,
In the paddock the logs lie prone.
The prone logs never arise,
The erect ones never grow green,
Leaves never rustle, the birds went away with the
  Bush,—

There is no change, nothing stirs!
And to-night there is no change;
All is mute, monotonous, stark;
In the whole wide sweep round the low little hut of the
  settler
No life to be seen; nothing stirs.

            *   *   *

Darker the grey air grows.
From the black of the gully, the gleam of the River is
  gone.
Scarcely the ridges show to the sky-line,
Now, their disconsolate fringe;
But, bright to the deepening sky,
The Stars creep silently out.
'Oh, where do you hide in the day?'
. . . It is stiller than ever; the wind has fallen.
The moist air brings,
To mix with the spicy breath of the young break-wind
  macrocarpa,
Wafts of the acrid, familiar aroma of slowly-smouldering
  logs.
And, hark, through the empty silence and dimness
Solemnly clear,
Comes the wistful, haunting cry of some lonely,
  faraway morepork,
'Kia toa! Be brave!'
—Night is come.
Now the gully is hidden, the logs and the paddock all
  hidden.
Brightly the Stars shine out! . . .
The sky is a wide black paddock, without any fences,
The Stars are its shining logs;
Here, sparse and single, but yonder, as logg'd-up for
  burning,
Close in a cluster of light.
And the thin clouds, they are the hills,
They are the spurs of the heavens,

On whose steepnesses scatter'd, the Star-logs silently
lie:
Dimm'd as it were by the distance, or maybe in mists of
the mountain
Tangled—yet still they brighten, not darken, the thick-
strewn slopes!
But see! these hills of the sky
They waver and move! their gullies are drifting, and
driving;
Their ridges, uprooted,
Break, wander and flee, they escape! casting careless
behind them
Their burdens of brightness, the Stars, that rooted
remain.
—No! they do not remain. No! even they cannot be
steadfast.
For the curv'd Three (that yonder
So glitter and sparkle
There, over the bails),
This morning, at dawn,
At the start of the milking,
Stood pale on the brink of yon rocky-ledged hill;
And the Cross, o'er the viaduct
Now, then was slanting,
Almost to vanishing, over the snow.
So, the Stars travel, also?
The poor earthly logs, in the wan earthly paddocks,
Never can move, they must stay;
But over the heavenly pastures, the bright, live logs of
the heavens
Wander at will, looking down on our paddocks and
logs, and pass on.
'O friendly and beautiful Live-Ones!
Coming to us for a little,
Then travelling and passing, while here with our logs
we remain,
What are you? Where do you come from?
Who are you? Where do you go?'

*   *   *

Ah, little Thor!
Here in the night, face to face
With the Burnt Bush within and without thee,
Standing, small and alone:
Bright Promise on Poverty's threshold!
What art thou? Where hast thou come from?
How far, how far! wilt thou go?

from Maui's Fish

. . . Toward the Dawn,
Lo, a Sea of thick shining! Behold the thick waves of
    great fishes!
This way and that way darting and shooting in masses,
Anxious, in haste to escape.
What is lifting them? *Pull!*
What is under them? *Pull!* . . .
The first beam strikes on the water . . .
The Brothers rub at their eyes . . . *O pull!*
Pull! What is this that they see?

    Thro' the waves, flashing!
    To the light, flashing!
  Bright, bright up-bursting, startling the light.—
Oh, the sharp spears and spikes! Oh, the sparkle of
    summits of crystal,
        Springing up, up!

Tongariro! O Taranaki,
Your splendour! your shooting of spear-points, keen,
    sea-wet to the sun!
Ruapehu, Kaikoura, Aorangi, Tara-rua, long-arm'd
    Ruahine!—
Midsummer clouds, curling luminous up from the
    skyline:
Far-fallen islands of light, summon'd back to the sun:
Soaring Kahawai-birds—

How ye soar'd, shining pinions! straight into the heaven
   high above you:
How ye shot up, bright Surprises! seizing, possessing
   the sky:
How firm, great white Clouds, ye took seat!

Pull, Maui! Pull!
For what follows, beneath them?
A waving, a waving and weaving of light and of
   darkness—
A waving of hands and of hair in the dance!
Lo, is it a garden of kelp?
Is it Night, coming up from the deep, up through fold
   upon fold of the Sea?
Pull!
Behold, it approaches! it darkens, it pierces the water—
   Lo! Lo!
Tree-tops! Lo, waving of branches! Lo, mosses and fern
   of the forest!
—How sweet on the salt came the breath of the forest,
   that summer sea-morning!
Sweet on the spacious silence the ring of the Tui's rich
   throat!
Kauri and Totara, Rimu, and Matai and Maire,
Red-as-blood Rata, and bright-as-blood Pohutu-kawa,
Manuka dark-ey'd, Convolvulus, Clematis star-ey'd—
The glittering of you that morning! fresh, dripping with
   dews of the Ocean,
New rays to the young, early sun!
The host of your taua, address'd as to fight! of your
   lances and meres of green-stone,
Bristling all suddenly upward, lustrously tossing in
   glory,
A green sea, high in the air!

Pull on! Pull away!
I see shining and shining below here.
Is there a Sun in the Sea? a young Sky in the water?
A Sea, deep in Sea?
Or is a great paua-shell, empty, vividly variegated,

Shadow playing with shine, blue and green in the arms
  of each other,
As they lie on the lap of the Sea?
Lo! it nears! it arrives! on the face of the water it
  floats—
Land—Ho! Land!
Yea, sparkling with freshness, audacious with newness,
  laughing with light,
Land! a young Land from the Sea!
A dark land, of forest; a bright land, of sky and of
  summits,
Of tussock sun-gilded, of headlands proclaiming the
  sun:
Tattoo'd with blue—behold Waikato! lo Wanganui!
Ey'd with quick eyes—Wakatipu, and over there Taupo:
Plumed with sky-feathers, with clouds and with snow:
  begirt with the mat of the Ocean
Border'd with foam, with fine fringes of sand, with
  breast-jewels of clear-coloured pebbles:—
Up it sprang, out it burst from the folds of the foam,
  out it stood,
Bare-bright on the jewel-bright Sea:—
A new Land!

There it stood!
And the Sea, now at rest, laid her down with her arms
  round about it,
Thrusting the tongue and the touches of love 'gainst the
  limbs of the living,
Caressing her newly-born, laughing and singing for joy.
And, up-coiling his line, disentangling his fish-hook,
  now Maui laugh'd also—
'Ha, ha, ha!' laughed Maui the Fisher,
'Behold, I have caught me a Fish!'
Enough—Even so!
With a hook of the Dead, with a bait of the the Living,
With the thought of his head, with the blood of his
  body, the sweat of his heart,
With pangs and with laughter, with labour and loss,

He truly had caught him a fish—the canoe was
   aground—
O *Te Ika a Maui*—The Fish!

               *   *   *

Alive! Yea, Te Ika—
Of the Bone of the Past, of the Blood of the Present,
Here, at the end of the earth, in the first of the Future,
Thou standest, courageous and youthful, a country to
   come!
Lo, thou art not defiled with the dust of the Dead, nor
   beclouded with thick clouds of Custom:
But, springs and quick sources of life all about thee,
   within thee,
Splendid with freshness, radiant with vigour,
   conspicuous with hope,
Like a beacon thou beckonest back o'er the waters,
   away o'er the world:
The while, looking ahead with clear eyes,
Like Maui, thou laugh'st, full of life!

And do not regard overmuch
Those tedious old Brothers, that still must be pribbling
   and prabbling about thee
(Paddlers inshore: when a Maui has fish'd, then they
   claim the canoe!) . . .
Laugh at them, Land!
They are old: are they therefore so wise?
Thou art young, Te Ika: be young!
Thou art new: be thou new!
With keen sight, with fresh forces, appraise those old
   grounds of their vaunting,
Dip in deep dew of thy seas what swims yet of their
   catch, and renew it,—
The rest, fish very long caught,
Toss it to them!
And address thee to catches to come.
Rich hauls to bold fishers, new sights to new sight, a
   new world to new eyes,

To discoverers, discoveries! Yea,
Offspring of Maui! recall the experience of Maui:
A dead fish he did not receive it? No, No!
He endured, he adventured, he went forth, he
  experimented,
He found and he fetch'd it, alive!

Yea, alive! a Fish to give thanks for.
Ah, ah, Tangaroa, well done!
Thou livest, Te Ika a Maui!
Enough! My last word:—
Live! Dare! Be alive!

E rere rā te kirīmi

Tērā te mahi pai rawa
E kīia ana mai,
He mahi rā e puta ai
Ngā moni nuinui noa!
E whanga rā, e tama mā,
Ki ngā pei marama—
Kua riro kē i ngā nama,
Auē ngā wawata!

E rere rā te kirīmi,
Ki roto ki ngā kēna nei!
Kia tika hāwerewere,
Kei rere pārorirori,
Kia rite ai ngā nama!

Tērā ngā tino momo kau
E kīia ana mai,
Kei Taranaki rā anō,
Na Māui Pōmare!
Ko ngā kau rā i rere ai
Te Nāti ki te hao!
He rau māhau, he rau māku,
Ka ea ngā wawata!

E rere rā te kirīmi
Ki roto ki ngā kēna nei!
Kia tika hāwerewere,
Kei rere pārorirori,
Kia rite ai ngā nama!

Tērā te pata rongo nui,
He Nāti te ingoa,
Te wāhi rā i mahia ai,

Ko Ruatōria!
Hara-mai rā Te Pirimia,
Māhau te kawanga
E pono ai te mahi nei,
He mahi kai anō!

E rere rā te kirīmi
Ki roto ki ngā kēna nei!
Kia tika hāwerewere,
Kei rere pārorirori,
Kia rite ai ngā nama!

The cream song

There's some really good work
We've been told about,
Work that will make us
Lots and lots of money!
Just wait, you fellows,
For your monthly pay—
But our debts have taken it,
So much for our dreams!

Flow on, cream,
Into these cans!
Go straight in,
Don't go crooked,
So our debts can be paid!

There are some pedigree cows
We've been told about,
Over in Taranaki.
They belong to Maui Pomare!
They're the cows the Nati
Rushed to get hold of!
A hundred for you, a hundred for me,
And our dreams will be realised!

Flow on, cream,
Into these cans!
Go straight in,
Don't go crooked,
So our debts can be paid!

There's some famous butter,
Nati is its name,
The place where they make it
Is Ruatoria!
Welcome, Prime Minister,
You have come to perform
The opening ceremony
For this food-producing work!

Flow on, cream,
Into these cans!
Go straight in,
Don't go crooked,
So our debts can be paid!

Translation by Margaret Orbell

Response

When you wrote your letter it was April,
And you were glad that it was spring weather,
And that the sun shone out in turn with showers of
   rain.

I write in waning May and it is autumn,
And I am glad that my chrysanthemums
Are tied up fast to strong posts,
So that the south winds cannot beat them down.
I am glad that they are tawny coloured,
And fiery in the low west evening light.
And I am glad that one bush warbler
Still sings in the honey-scented wattle . . .

But oh, we have remembering hearts,
And we say 'How green it was in such and such an
   April,'
And 'Such and such an autumn was very golden,'
And 'Everything is for a very short time.'

Pause

When I am very earnestly digging
I lift my head sometimes, and look at the mountains,
And muse upon them, muscles relaxing.

I think how freely the wild grasses flower there,
How grandly the storm-shaped trees are massed in their
   gorges
And the rain-worn rocks strewn in magnificent heaps.

Pioneer plants on those uplands find their own footing;
No vigorous growth, there, is an evil weed:
All weathers are salutary.

It is only a little while since this hillside
Lay untrammelled likewise,
Unceasingly swept by transmarine winds.

In a very little while, it may be,
When our impulsive limbs and our superior skulls
Have to the soil restored several ounces of fertiliser,

The Mother of all will take charge again,
And soon wipe away with her elements
Our small fond human enclosures.

Detail

My garage is a structure of excessive plainness,
It springs from a dry bank in the back garden.
It is made of corrugated iron,
And painted all over with brick-red.

But beside it I have planted a green Bay-tree,
—A sweet Bay, an Olive, and a Turkey Fig,
—A Fig, an Olive, and a Bay.

Erica

Sit down with me awhile beside the heath-corner.

Here have I laboured hour on hour in winter,
Digging thick clay, breaking up clods, and draining,

Carrying away cold mud, bringing up sandy loam,
Bringing these rocks and setting them all in their places,
To be shelter from winds, shade from too burning sun.

See, now, how sweetly all these plants are springing
Green, ever green, and flowering turn by turn,
Delicate heaths, and their fragrant Australian kinsmen,
Shedding, as once unknown in New Holland, strange
     scents on the air,
And purple and white daboecia—the Irish heather—
Said in the nurseryman's list to be so well suited
For small gardens, for rock gardens, and for graveyards.

Elect

You have been my treasure, Rose Pilgrim,
Because of your beautiful name.
But because of your name I would not pamper you,
And I chose you to be planted in a difficult place,
In the pathway of the east wind;
Where at times, too, your roots might become thirsty,
Although I have a thirty-foot hose.

You have thriven in spite of of these disadvantages.
When your first shoots were battered by the spring
     storms,
Others pushed forth perseveringly.
You have been my treasure, Pilgrim Rose.

And you are up near the frontier, near the gateway,
So that when I come home, tired, in the evening,
Home to my hill-garden, Rose Pilgrim,
You are the first flower I find there,
You are the very first flower, my Rose Pilgrim,
Pilgrim, my sweet rose.

The Long Harbour

There are three valleys where the warm sun lingers,
gathered to a green hill girt-about anchorage,
and gently, gently, at the cobbled margin
of fire-formed, time-smoothed, ocean-moulded
    curvature,
a spent tide fingers the graven boulders,
the black, sea-bevelled stones.

The fugitive hours, in those sun-loved valleys,
implacable hours, their golden-wheeled chariots'
inaudible passage check, and slacken
their restless teams' perpetual galloping;
and browsing, peaceable sheep and cattle
gaze as they pause by the way.

Grass springs sweet where once thick forest
gripped vales by fire and axe freed to pasturage;
but flame and blade have spared the folding gullies,
and there, still, the shade-flitting, honey-sipping
    lutanists
copy the dropping of tree-cool waters
dripping from stone to stone.

White hawthorn hedge from old, remembered England,
and orchard white, and whiter bridal clematis
the bush-bequeathed, conspire to strew the valleys
in tender spring, and blackbird, happy colonist,
and blacker, sweeter-fluted tui echo
either the other's song.

From far, palm-feathery, ocean-spattered islands
there rowed hither dark and daring voyagers;
and Norseman, Gaul, the Briton and the German
sailed hither singing; all these hardy venturers
they desired a home, and have taken their rest there,
and their songs are lost on the wind.

I have walked here with my love in the early
   spring-time,
and under the summer-dark walnut-avenues,
and played with the children, and waited with the aged
by the quayside, and listened alone where manukas
sighing, windswept, and sea-answering pine-groves
garrison the burial-ground.

It should be very easy to lie down and sleep there
in that sequestered hillside ossuary,
underneath a billowy, sun-caressed grass-knoll,
beside those dauntless, tempest-braving ancestresses
who pillowed there so gladly, gnarled hands folded,
their tired, afore-translated bones.

It would not be a hard thing to wake up one morning
to the sound of bird-song in scarce-stirring willow-trees,
waves lapping, oars plashing, chains running slowly,
and faint voices calling across the harbour;
to embark at dawn, following the old forefathers,
to put forth at daybreak for some lovelier,
still undiscovered shore.

Warning of Winter

Give over, now, red roses;
Summer-long you told us,
Urgently unfolding, death-sweet, life-red,
Tidings of love. All's said. Give over.

Summer-long you placarded
Leafy shades with heart-red
Symbols. Who knew not love at first knows now,
Who had forgot has now remembered.

Let be, let be, lance-lilies,
Alert, pard-spotted, tilting

Poised anthers, flaming; have done flaming fierce;
Hard hearts were pierced long since, and stricken.

Give to the blast your thorn-crowns
Roses; and now be torn down
All you ardent lilies, your high-holden crests,
Havocked and cast to rest on the clammy ground.

Alas, alas, to darkness
Descends the flowered pathway,
To solitary places, deserts, utter night;
To issue in what hidden dawn of light hereafter?

But one, in dead of winter,
Divine *Agape*, kindles
Morning suns, new moons, lights starry trophies;
Says to the waste: Rejoice, and bring forth roses;
To the ice-fields: Let here spring thick bright lilies.

Spring Snow and Tui

We said: there will surely be hawthorn out
down in the sun-holding folds of the hills by the sea;
but suddenly snow had forestalled the thorns there,
death-white and cold on their boughs hung the festival
   wreaths.

It is all one. The same hand scatters the blossoms
of winter and spring-time. The black-robed psalmodist,
traversing swiftly the silent landscape like Azrael,
echoed in clear repetition his well-tuned antiphon;
a waking bugle it might be, a passing bell,
of life, death, life, life telling: it is all one.

Decoration

This jar of roses and carnations on the window-sill,
Crimson upon sky-grey and snow-wrapt
   mountain-pallor,
(Sharp storm's asseveration of cold winter's on-coming,)
How strange their look, how lovely, rich and foreign,
The living symbol of a season put away.

A letter-sheaf, bound up by time-frayed filament,
I found: laid by; youth's flowering.
The exotic words blazed up blood-red against death's
   shadow,
Red upon grey. Red upon grey.

Midnight

All day long, prismatic dazzle,
Clashing of musics, challenge, encounter, succession;
Gear-change on the up-and-down hill of hypothesis;
Choice, choice, decision, events rivetting shackles;
Hazardous tests, new wine of escape . . .
       oh, strange noviciate!
Bright stimulus, venture, tension, poised preparedness.

But at midnight, infinite darkness,
Opulent silence, liberty, liberty, solitude;
The acrid, mountainy wind's austere caresses;
Rest, rest, compensation, very suspension of death;
Deep stillness of death, dark negation . . .
      ah, thy heart-beat,
Origin, Signification, dread Daysman, Consummator.

9th July, 1932

Grey sky, grey city-smoke;
garden all gone bare, gaunt mountains;
pitiful pipe of well-nigh homeless birds . . .

But then these stinging sun-roused messages
tossed hither salt-cold from the pacific sea;
those foremost, dawn-dyed, rose-red eminences,
those snow-fast, soon-to-be-incarnadined strongholds
   beyond . . .

There shall be no insistence upon symbolism;
let each eye take the tokens, heart interpret,
individual tongue make fit respond.

from By the River Ashley

IV

Sauntering home from church we lingered
looking away northwards over the white gates.
I see our visitors in go-to-meeting dress.
I do not see my parents. Perhaps that day they chose
to 'stay behind'—mysterious phrase of those times,
meaning reserved from children, I must think.

Above that gate the downs. I see them now,
I see them gentle brown and amethyst.
Our grown-up guests the landscape viewed
and commented—Lovely! perhaps a sketch?
My eager praises added met with prompt rebuff.
Too young, too young to notice lovely views.

Wrong, Madam, wrong—dear Wordsworth was more
   reasonable.
Too late! the great African bishop rhetorician

cried out upon himself, too late have I sought thee,
Beauty!—His vision abides. Let us begin here
upon the downs . . . A few years gone
I passed them by in autumn and their fields
a basket of ripe fruit, of purple plums
and yellow, apricots, ruddy pears—
but to my memory of earlier day, soft pasture.

The guardian Mt Grey still casts a spell
of greatness, majesty that does not go with
    measurement,
a mien of kinship with all renowned heights,
a look of having kept inviolable for a thousand years
a secret of great comfort. Who has not traced,
looking from southward hills, its noble outline?
Who has not watched the pencilled shadows deepen
upon its flanks? I do not see you there,
Mt Grey, looking down at the end of our village streets,
but I was conscious. I have found you, since,
something familiar, and I salute you now, for your
    significance.

V

That bridge from the city, that was Waimakariri.
Greater than our River Ashley, the playground.

The rivers, over and over again the rivers.
They hasten to you, look up them, up the riverbeds.
From the soft dark forest they come down,
Or from the snows, carving their patterns
Of tawny terraces they come hastening down
To where by archipelagos of silver,
Lizard twists of azure, tranced lagoons,
We hear the ripples and the silence sing together
With the small soft sighing of the tussock,
And flax-spears' rattle, and, might be, a seabird's call.
These were the harmonies, splashed often now
By sudden hue of alien weed, still beautiful.

Too late we hear, too late, the undertones
Of lamentations in all the natural songs—
What have you done with my mountains?

What have you done with my forests?
What have you done to your rivers?
Too late.

VI

The hour is dark. The river comes to its end,
Comes to the embrace of the all enveloping sea.
My story comes to its end.

Divine Picnicker by the lakeside,
Familiar friend of the fishermen,
Known and yet not known, lost and yet found,
The hour is dark, come down to the riverside.
The strange river, come find me.
Bring if it might be companions
In the tissue of the Kingdom, but come thou,
Key to all mystery, opening and none shall shut
     again,
Innermost love of all loves, making all one.
Come.

ANTE KOSOVIĆ (1882–1958)

from Dalmatinać iz Tudjine
   (Dalmatian in Exile)

. . . Ah Dalmatia, if only I could send word of your
   dear sons,
How this wild, hard country beats them down,
What plight traps them, what they suffer here. . . .

*   *   *

In the morning before dawn-light
We cook our lonely breakfast—
Enough to keep body and soul together,
And set out for the gumfields
With a slab of bread, a billy of tea
To keep us working till dark.
The gum-digger shoulders his spade, and sets off—
At the gumfield begins to dig, merciless,
Ignoring rivers of sweat, head bent to the ground,
No time to squint up at the sun, hardly time to stretch,
Doggedly grouts himself six feet down into the dirt,
Endures his pain, takes his spade and digs further
Till he's thigh-deep in swamp-muck—
What life could be harder than that?
And when it rains there's water above him also,
Till he could drown just standing there—
A gum-digger's lot: resignation, dreams of rich strikes.
You see our plight: we graft like beasts,
In soul-danger of sudden, unshriven death,
Lost to the sweet ceremony of Mother Church,
No bells, no bell towers. . . .

Translation by Amelia Batistich and Ian Wedde

E noho, e Rata

E noho, e Rata, te hīri o Waikato!
E huri tō kanohi ki te hauāuru,
Ngā tai e ngunguru i waho o Te Ākau,
Auē hai auē!

Tō pikitanga ko te ao o te rangi,
Tō heketanga ko Karioi maunga,
Tō hoenga-ā-waka ko Whāingaroa,
Auē hai auē!

Takahia atu rā te moana i Aotea,
Kia whatiwhati koe i te hua o te miro—
Te tihi o Moerangi, te puke okiokinga,
Auē hai auē!

Piua ō mata ki Kāwhia moana,
Ki Kāwhia-ā-tai, ki Kāwhia-ā-tāngata—
Ko te kupu tēnā a ō tūpuna,
Auē hai auē!

E tū tō wae ki te kei o Tainui!
Tēnei tō hoe, ko te Tekau-mā-rua
Ngā tai e ngunguru i waho o Karewa,
Auē hai auē!

E huri tō kanohi ki Pirongia maunga,
Ki te rohe pōtae ki Arekahanara,
Te haona kaha o te Rungarunga Rawa,
Auē hai auē!

Whākia ō mata ki te Kauhanganui,
Te Paki o Matariki, ngā whakaoati—
Ko Kemureti rā tōna oko horoi,
Auē hai auē!

E hoe tō waka ki Ngāruawāhia,
Tūrangawaewae o te Kīngitanga,
Te tongi whakamutunga a Matutaera,
Auē hai auē!

Remain, Rata

Remain, Rata, the shield of Waikato!
Turn your face westward,
To the waves that sound beyond Te Akau,
Aue hai aue!

You will mount up on the clouds of the sky,
You will go down at Mount Karioi!
Your paddling-place is Whaingaroa,
Aue hai aue!

Tread the shore at Aotea,
That you may pluck the fruit of the miro
On the peak of Moerangi, the mountain lookout,
Aue hai aue!

Gaze upon the ocean at Kawhia,
The 'sea Kawhia' and 'human Kawhia'
Of which your ancestors spoke,
Aue hai aue!

Place your foot by the stern of Tainui!
In the waves that sound beyond Karewa
Your paddle is the Twelve,
Aue hai aue!

Turn your face to Mount Pirongia
And the boundary at Alexandra—
The strong horn of the Most High,
Aue hai aue!

Let your eyes rest upon the Kauhanganui,
And Te Paki o Matariki, who have pledged their word!
Cambridge was his wash bowl,
Aue hai aue!

Paddle your canoe to Ngaruawahia,
The foothold of the Kingitanga,
Matutaera's last, small possession,
Aue hai aue!

Translation by Margaret Orbell

Rosa Luxembourg

For some the shuttle leaping in the sun,
  Laburnum leaves above the quiet door,
  And song that drips like water, cool and slow:
And when the hands are still, and day is done,
  The swaying crib upon the firelit floor.
  Ah! How could you these gentle things forego?

Wild heart that beat beneath its tattered shawl,
  Wild voice that broke upon its ceaseless cry
  For those whose lips are dumb beneath the sky,
Whose feet beneath the stars must stumbling fall,
  Whose hands must twist in toil until they die!
  Which is the nobler task? God knows, not I.

For you, no threaded spool, no singing time,
  No young bees flying through laburnum boughs,
  No little rolling head upon the breast.
But now, beyond the bourn of flower or chime,
  May He, who set the storm between your brow,
  Pity your broken bones, and give them rest.

The Shag

(For E.C.)

Wanaka, mother of Clutha,
Says to the Shag in her shallows:
'Back, you thief of the twilight,
Highwayman of the headland,

After your line flew down,
A nest in Hell was empty.'

Wanaka, little old woman,
Wrinkles and rocks and mutters:
'Out of the land forever,
Out of the sky forever,
Back to the blight of God,
In the land of hungry waters!'

Dreamily answers the bandit:
'My head is sold for silver,
But God, where all is gentle,
May weary of much meekness,
May turn unto the outlaw,
May bless the Shag, the sinner.'

The Tides Run up the Wairau

The tides run up the Wairau
That fights against their flow.
My heart and it together
Are running salt and snow.

For though I cannot love you,
Yet, heavy, deep, and far,
Your tide of love comes swinging,
Too swift for me to bar.

Some thought of you must linger,
A salt of pain in me,
For oh what running river
Can stand against the sea?

Invasion

War shows what each man's country is to him.
Ah look with me on this great windy sod,
Richer by lines of leaves than Adam's loam,
Its kowhais' fiery drizzle in the Spring,
Its paddocks' green oblivion of grass,
Its alps, those proud desires, arrested sighs,
Of earth's old hopeless passion for the blue—
Oh some would weep and some go numb and cold
As an Australian in Antarctic snows
But we would burn until our souls ramped flame.
For if I held the freehold of this land
From Cape Reinga to Oreti Beach
I could not feel that it was more my own.
A zone of earth came to its hour of us
And, wary in the wash of continents,
Poised 'twixt the flowing sea and flowing sky,
As lightly and as nobly as a stag,
New Zealand flings its heavy antlers up
And senses little but the lonely pole.
So leave us anger, leave us like a world
That has not yet the calm despair of sod
But keeps the insurrection of its core.
I grant you grief may be a gracious thing,
But, countrymen, this ire is better dry,
Only the cooling stars give way to seas.

Ballad of the Bushman

Only a fool would eat his heart out so,
    And I am old enough to have more sense,
But lying by the window makes it worse—
    Look out across that fence!

I have to die, they say, so let it come.
   A clean break is the best I have always said.
And better burn than blight for any crop.
   So I am better dead.

My wife says do no fretting over her.
   She will be soon upon my heels up there.
We have been in it ankle-deep at times.
   She always pulled her share.

No son of hers was ever rocked to sleep.
   She bore me three here in the bush alone,
She is as hard as maire in some things,
   But faithful to the bone.

Each day to us was just so many trees.
   Night was a minute then. Short is the world!
Ah who will wake me out of my last sleep?
   Her clock was the first bird.

It is not for my sons I grudge to go.
   Good lads like them will never come to harm,
The neighbours envy us the name they have,
   But God, if one of them could farm!

Cloudy Bay

Where the racing Wairau slows, homesick for its
   snowshed,
Tua Marina murmurs in the south,
Caught in a loop of sighing, saltless waters
Running intently into one great mouth.

I was born inland between the creek and river
In the heart of paddocks shaken by their stir
For in between hills' great river horseshoe
Land and all seemed flowing with lonely, long demur:

And the west sinking with its light so low there
Left the sunset growing in the fences' hold,
Paradisal grasses, knee-deep and molten,
Running in their stillness sap of ember-gold.

Once a great aurora played to the southward—
And, fetlocks burning, foal after foal—
Clodding the icefloes as a colt the paddocks,
Rushed up, uncalkined, from the silver Pole.

Where the horseshoe opened in came the morning,
There to the eastward lay the hidden sea,
The same footloose mountains that taunted Magellan,
Massive and flying and nothing to me.

We were held fast by the glitter of a solstice,
Or by a smoulder of autumns to the land,
But in the winter the booming of its groundswell,
Thundered a shoreline back upon the sand.

Lunged in our ears and forced us to remember
What was too wild, too great for any law,
Holding us in from the tip of Reinga
To where the Bluff folds down a heavy paw.

Here the great air-currents, cloven by the alp-line,
Roll and soar above us with a salty boast–
Almost any seawind, streaming from the Tasman,
In these narrow islands blows from coast to coast.

Love is around me like that hidden ocean
And I, inland, forget I have a shore.
It needs the breakers of your anger to remind me
That I am yours and yours forevermore.

Truth

Some can leave the truth unspoken.
Oh truth is light on such!
They may choose their time and season,
Nor feel it matters much.

I am not their judge, God help me!
Though I am of the crew
For whom is only truth or treason—
No choice between the two.

But pity wrestles with my fury
Till, spent and dumb and dry,
I envy bees which, barbed with reason,
Give the whole sting and die.

Prophecy

No ears could hear then the mutter of the Milky Way,
Nor could the four great points of space cry out
    together
That earth shall lose its place in time and in delight.

Though we use on the world the brand of our own
    being,
Till latitudes flow terror as wet colours run,
Its flash cannot consume the line of man forever.

It is past all power save love to douse that
    conflagration,
The love that suffers cross-wise to make an enemy holy,
The hardest lesson learned that no-one is especial.

The mystic is no refuge if it forsake the human.
Such love is isolated that soars not for its fellows.
The volatile is sealed—a clinic sanctity.

Though languages fear death if Babel's voice grows
   single,
And nouns and verbs clutch only an exile's hasty
   baggage,
By agony stripped to the bare of hate and of love,

Though speed becomes our staple and air-maps
   bewilder,
Bleak, and blank, and vital, all else dissolved in sky,
If chart and tongue elide, both land and sea are
   constant.

Though doom may shoot a burning pip between its
   fingers,
It shall not shake our spin, nor shall it confound our
   orbit,
Since it is not fore-ordained, nor is it the end of earth.

Nor can it strike the dread of words heard each
   December
Of signs in the sun and in the moon and in the stars
And of men wanning away from a weird roaring of
   waters.

When the powers of the heavens shall be moved and
   sentence appear in state
Above an abyss of light, then shall the heart wither
Not for death but for shame, which is the gap between
   fear and awe.

The Cave

From the cliff-top it appeared a place of defeat,
the nest of an extinct bird, or the hole where the sea
   hoards its bones,
a pocket of night in the sun-faced rock,
sole emblem of mystery and death in that enormous
   noon.

We climbed down, and crossed over the sand,
and there were islands floating in the wind-whipped
   blue,
and clouds and islands trembling in your eyes,
and every footstep and every glance
was a fatality felt and unspoken, our way
rigid and glorious as the sun's path,
unbroken as the genealogy of man.

And when we had passed beyond
into the secret place and were clasped
by the titanic shadows of the earth,
all was transfigured, all was redeemed,
so that we escaped from the days
that had hunted us like wolves, and from ourselves,
in the brief eternity of the flesh.

There should be the shapes of leaves and flowers
printed on the rock, and a blackening of the walls
from the flame on your mouth,
to be found by the lovers straying
from the picnic two worlds hence, to be found and
   known,
because the form of the dream is always the same,
and whatever dies or changes this will persist and
   recur,

will compel the means and the end, find
   consummation,
whether it be
silent in swansdown and darkness, or in grass
   moonshadow-mottled,
or in a murmuring cave of the sea.

We left, and returned to our lives:

the act entombed, its essence caught
for ever in the wind, and in the noise of waves,
for ever mixed
with lovers' breaths who by salt-water coasts
in the sea's beauty dwell.

Tapu

To stave off disaster, or bring the devil to heel,
   or to fight against fear, some carry a ring or a locket,
but I, who have nothing to lose by the turn of the
   wheel,
   and nothing to gain, I carry the world in my pocket.

For all I have gained, and have lost, is locked up in this
   thing,
   this cup of cracked bone from the skull of a fellow
     long dead,
with a hank of thin yellowish hair fastened in with a
   ring.
   For a symbol of death and desire these tokens are
     wed.

The one I picked out of a cave in a windy cliff-face
   where the old Maoris slept, with a curse on the
     stranger who moved,

in despite of tapu, but a splinter of bone from that
   place.
  The other I cut from the head of the woman I loved.

from Dominion

from Album Leaves

Back Street

A girl comes out of a doorway in the morning
with hair uncombed, treading with care
on the damp bricks, picks up the milk,
stares skyward with sleepy eyes;
returns to the dewy step; leaves
with the closing of the door
silence under narrow eaves
the tragic scent of violets on the morning air
and jonquils thrust through bare earth here and there.

At ten o'clock a woman comes out
and leans against the wall
beside the fig-tree hung with washing; listens
for the postman's whistle. Soon he passes,
leaves no letter.
She turns a shirt upon the barren tree
and pads back to the house as ghost to tomb.
No children since the first. The room
papered in 'Stars', with Jubilee pictures
pasted over the mantel, spattered with fat.

Up the street
the taxi-drivers lounging in a knot
beside the rank of shining cars
discuss the speed of horses
as mariners the stars in their courses.

The Possessor

On my land grew a green tree
that gave shade to the weary,
peace to my children, rest to the travel-stained;
and the waters ran beneath, the river of life.
My people drank of the waters after their labour,
had comfort of the tree in the heat of noon,
lying in summer grass ringed round with milk-white
    flowers,
gathering strength, giving their bodies
to the motion of the earth.

I cut down the tree, and made posts
and fenced my land,
I banished my people and turned away the traveller;
and now I share my land with sparrows that trespass
upon my rood of air. The earth
is barren, the stream is dry; the sun has blackened
grass that was green and springing, flowers that were
    fair.

Conversation in the Bush

'Observe the young and tender frond
of this punga: shaped and curved
like the scroll of a fiddle: fit instrument
to play archaic tunes.'
                          'I see
the shape of a coiled spring.'

Full Fathom Five

He was such a curious lover of shells
and the hallucinations of water
that he could never return out of the sea
without first having to settle a mermaid's bill.

Groping along the sea-bottom of the age
he discovered many particulars he did not care to speak
   about
even in the company of water-diviners
things sad and unspeakable
moss-covered skulls with bodies fluttering inside
with the unreality of specks moving before the eyes of a
   photograph
trumpets tossed from the decks of ocean-going liners
eccentric starfish fallen from impossible heavens
fretting on uncharted rocks
still continents with trees and houses like a child's
   drawing
and in every cupboard of the ocean
weary dolphins trapped in honey-coloured cobwebs
murmuring to the revolution Will you be long.

He was happy down there under the frothing ship-lanes
because nobody ever bothered him with statistics
or talk of yet another dimension of the mind.

And eventually and tragically finding he could not
   drown
he submitted himself to the judgement of the desert
and was devoured by man-eating ants
with a rainbow of silence branching from his lips.

A Farewell

What is there left to be said?
There is nothing we can say,
nothing at all to be done
to undo the time of day;
no words to make the sun
roll east, or raise the dead.

I loved you as I love life:
the hand I stretched out to you
returning like Noah's dove
brought a new earth to view,
till I was quick with love;
but Time sharpens his knife,

Time smiles and whets his knife,
and something has got to come out
quickly, and be buried deep,
not spoken or thought about
or remembered even in sleep.
You must live, get on with your life.

A Naked Girl Swimming

Air, earth and water meet at the sea's edge:
   see, Dian cold thrusts in with lustless hand
her watery wedge
   where, whirled through skies and walled with rock,
     cling wind and land.

One element was lacking till you came:
   you, lovely wife of Sol, life-giving fire,
you are the flame
   that welds clashing worlds of matter and desire.

I'm Older than You, Please Listen

To the young man I would say:
Get out! Look sharp, my boy,
before the roots are down,
before the equations are struck,
before a face or a landscape

has power to shape or destroy.
This land is a lump without leaven,
a body that has no nerves.
Don't be content to live in
a sort of second-grade heaven
with first-grade butter, fresh air,
and paper in every toilet;
becoming a butt for the malice
of those who have stayed and soured,
staying in turn to sour,
to smile, and savage the young.
If you're enterprising and able,
smuggle your talents away,
hawk them in livelier markets
where people are willing to pay.
If you have no stomach for roughage,
if patience isn't your religion,
if you must have sherry with your bitters,
if money and fame are your pigeon,
if you feel that you need success
and long for a good address,
don't anchor here in the desert—
the fishing isn't so good:
take a ticket for Megalopolis,
don't stay in this neighbourhood!

Terms of Appointment

I speak of walls and chains; of the vials
of wrath; of limitations, denials,
derelictions, fallings from grace,
making them yours to save my face:

Though you live in the desert eating manna, you will
   not be happy until you have raised a house;
Though you build, yet chaos will stoop like a girl by the
   hedgerow to pluck your towers like lilies;

Though you gather flowers, yet the dust of a thousand
    carriage-wheels will settle upon them;
Though you go a journey into the interior you will long
    for the reek of salt and the noise of gulls;
Though you cross the seas your heart will remain
    buried beneath the hearthstone;
Though you stay on one acre you will sweat with rage
    to see your enemies riding upon the hilltops;
Though you conquer your enemies at last, you will wish
    you had spent the time making summer love;
Though you tumble her in every haystack from here to
    Paradise, there will be a question at the end and no
    answer from the night;
Though you grow wise with the sloughing of years,
    time will not forgive you for deserting your youth;
Though you live you will long for death; though you
    die you will lack breath.

Beggar to Burgher

I am a man defeated in his loins:
    custom and law have hit me where I live.
Look me over. Laugh at me. Toss no coins.
    I'm asking nothing, sir, that's yours to give.

You have no news to tell me, bad or good.
    I know it all, what soul or body lacks.
I sweat, and sleep, and starve—or chop your wood
    for tucker. When I go mad I fire your stacks.

Sir, here we are, the two of us, rich and poor,
    I in my winter doss, or summer ditch,
you in your linen, comfortable, secure.
    One of us should be envious—tell me which?

I am a man confounded. Yet my defeat
    is something short of absolute. O bold

hunter, O proud proprietor, I repeat—
 I'm asking nothing, sir, that's yours to withhold.

Exhibit her proudly, the trophy of your chase,
 like a horned head (true symbol of your power!),
but know that your corn-stack was our lying-place,
 learn that the man of straw has had his hour.

Down on my Luck

Wandering above a sea of glass
 in the soft April weather,
wandering through the yellow grass
 where the sheep stand and blether;
roaming the cliffs in the morning light,
 hearing the gulls that cry there,
not knowing where I'll sleep tonight,
 not much caring either.

 I haven't got a stiver
  the tractor's pinched my job,
 I owe the bar a fiver
  and the barman fifteen bob;
 the good times are over,
  the monkey-man has foreclosed,
 the woman has gone with the drover,
  not being what I supposed.

 I used to get things spinning,
  I used to dress like a lord,
 mostly I came out winning,
  but all that's gone by the board;
 my pants have lost their creases,
  I've fallen down on my luck,
 the world has dropped to pieces
  everything's come unstuck.

Roaming the cliffs in the morning light,
   hearing the gulls that cry there,
not knowing where I'll sleep tonight,
   not much caring either,
wandering above a sea of glass
   in the soft April weather,
wandering through the yellow grass
   close to the end of my tether.

Diogenes

I would rid myself of an old way of life
that has clung about me since the day I was born,
covering me with its cloak of smiling hatred,
with its shield of nonchalance and easy scorn.

I have worn this armour, kept my soul inviolate,
mocking the estate of kings with cool bravado;
but I am tired now; I have lain too long
in the gutter of the world, crossed by a King's shadow.

I have done, indeed: as well be a whining moralist,
vile slave to a viler god, picking a sermon
from every cruel stone, as waste my breath
on this abominable world and all its vermin.

I would escape all this, and all things else;
I would creep within my life and lie there curled
like a flower in ice, or a pharoah in his tomb,
lulled in a sleep that should outlast the world.

To the Poets

('The Mixer': Henry Kirk)

Let us have a rest about the sunset,
   The chirping of the birds, the babbling brook;
Write us something up about the wharfie,
   The man who wields the shovel and the hook;
Let us know his work and his surroundings,
   And show the sort of life he battles through—
Never mind 'the summer trees are bowing,
   The water lilies or the honey-dew.'

Leave the fawns that play within the woodland,
   The nymphs that on the greensward dance and skip;
Write about the man who keeps the steam up
   While working in the bowels of the ship,
Through the blinding sweat and heat that brings him
   The nearest he has ever been to hell—
Never mind 'the cuckoo or the redbreast,
   Or Grecian maids within the mossy dell.'

Let us have a spell about the moon-rays,
   That glitter on the calm and placid sea;
Pen your thoughts to something of the sailor,
   And what his home on board the ship should be;
Let us know the kind of den he lives in,
   The risky work he's often called to do—
Never mind the 'buttercups and daisies,
   The castle turret, or the oak and yew.'

Let us have a breathe about the rainbow,
   The jewelled stars that through the heavens flit;
Write us up an ode about the miner,
   Who sells his life when working in the pit;
Write about his family that's grieving
   Across the mangled corpse that's borne away—
Never mind 'the blue Alsatian mountains,
   Or in the cavern-tomb the Roman lay.'

Write us nothing up about the twilight,
    The autumn foliage rustling in the glen;
Lead us to something that's elevating
    And interesting to the working-men;
Try to make their lives a little brighter
    Than what their masters ever tried to do—
Never mind 'the silver halo gleaming
    As princely swords across each other flew.'

Let us have a rest about the cloisters,
    The curfew and the knell of parting day;
Bring to light the reason for improvement
    Between the worker and his under-pay;
Ply your pen to better his conditions,
    And try to raise his status as a whole—
Never mind 'the chiming bells of Shandon
    Or belted knight dare quaff the vassal bowl.'

                                        (1926)

Old Memories of Earth

I think I have no other home than this
 I have forgotten much remember much
 but I have never any memories such
 as these make out they have of lands of bliss.

Perhaps they have done, will again do what
 they say they have, drunk as gods on godly drink,
 but I have not communed with gods I think
 and even though I live past death shall not.

I rather am for ever bondaged fast
 to earth and have been: so much untaught I know.
 Slow like great ships often I have seen go
 ten priests ten each time round a grave long past

And I recall I think I can recall
 back even past the time I started school
 or went a-crusoeing in the corner pool
 that I was present at a city's fall

And I am positive that yesterday
 walking past One Tree Hill and quite alone
 to me there came a fellow I have known
 in some old times, but when I cannot say:

Though we must have been great friends, I and he,
 otherwise I should not remember him
 for everything of the old life seems dim
 as last year's deeds recalled by friends to me.

Body of John

Oh I have grown so shrivelled and sere
>   *But the body of John enlarges*
>   and I can scarcely summon a tear
>   *but the body of John discharges*

It's true my old roof is near ready to drop
>   *But John's boards have burst asunder*
>   and I am perishing cold here atop
>   *but his bones lie stark hereunder.*

Sonnet of Brotherhood

Garrisons pent up in a little fort
    with foes who do but wait on every side
    knowing the time soon comes when they shall ride
    triumphant over those trapped and make sport
    of them: when those within know very short
    is now their hour and no aid can betide:
    such men as these not quarrel and divide
    but friend and foe are friends in their hard sort

And if these things be so oh men then what
    of these beleaguered victims this our race
    betrayed alike by Fate's gigantic plot
    here in this far-pitched perilous hostile place
    this solitary hard-assaulted spot
    fixed at the friendless outer edge of space.

The Spark's Farewell to its Clay (1)

Well clay it's strange at last we've come to it:
    after much merriment we must give up
    our ancient friendship: no more shall we sup
    in pleasant quiet places wanly-lit
    nor wander through the falling rain, sharp-smit
    and buffeted you, while I within snug-shut:
    no longer taste the mingled bitter-sweet cup
    of life the one inscrutable has thought fit

To give us: no longer know the strife
    that we from old have each with each maintained:
    now our companionship has certain end
    end without end: at last of this our life
    you surely have gained blank earth walls my friend
    and I? God only knows what I have gained.

Latter-day Geography Lesson

This, quoth the Eskimo master
    was London in English times:
    step out a little faster
    you two young men at the last there
    the Bridge would be on our right hand
    and the Tower near where those crows stand—
    we struck it you'll recall in Gray's rhymes:
    this, quoth the Eskimo master
    was London in English times.

This, quoth the Eskimo master
    was London in English days:
    beyond that hill they called Clapham
    boys that swear Master Redtooth I slap 'em
    I dis-tinct-ly heard—you—say—Bastard
    don't argue: here boys, ere disaster

overtook her, in splendour there lay
a city held empires in sway
and filled all the earth with her praise:
this quoth the Eskimo master
was London in English days.

She held, quoth the Eskimo master
ten million when her prime was full
from here once Britannia cast her
gaze over an Empire vaster
even than ours: look there Woking
stood, I make out, and the Abbey
lies here under our feet *you great babby
Swift-and-short do—please—kindly—stop—poking
your thumbs through the eyes of that skull.*

On the Swag

His body doubled
    under the pack
    that sprawls untidily
    on his old back
    the cold wet dead-beat
    plods up the track.

The cook peers out:
    'oh curse that old lag—
    here again
    with his clumsy swag
    made of a dirty old
    turnip bag.'

'Bring him in cook
    from the grey level sleet
    put silk on his body
    slippers on his feet,
    give him fire
    and bread and meat.

Let the fruit be plucked
      and the cake be iced,
      the bed be snug
      and the wine be spiced
      in the old cove's night-cap:
      for this is Christ.'

Judas Iscariot

Judas Iscariot
      sat in the upper
      room with the others
      at the last supper

And sitting there smiled
      up at his master
      whom he knew the morrow
      would roll in disaster.

At Christ's look he guffawed—
      for then as thereafter
      Judas was greatly
      given to laughter.

Indeed they always said
      that he was the veriest
      prince of good fellows
      and the whitest and merriest.

All the days of his life
      he lived gay as a cricket
      and would sing like the thrush
      that sings in the thicket

He would sing like the thrush
      that sings on the thorn
      oh he was the most sporting bird
      that ever was born.

Footnote to John ii 4

Don't throw your arms around me in that way:
    I know that what you tell me is the truth—
    yes I suppose I loved you in my youth
    as boys do love their mothers, so they say,
    but all that's gone from me this many a day:
    I am a merciless cactus an uncouth
    wild goat a jagged old spear the grim tooth
    of a lone crag ... Woman I cannot stay.

Each one of us must do his work of doom
    and I shall do it even in despite
    of her who brought me in pain from her womb,
    whose blood made me, who used to bring the light
    and sit on the bed up in my little room
    and tell me stories and tuck me up at night.

Ecce Homunculus

Betrayed by friend dragged from the garden hailed
    as prophet and as lord in mockery
    hauled down where Roman Pilate sat on high
    perplexed and querulous, lustily assailed
    by every righteous Hebrew cried down railed
    against by all true zealots—still no sigh
    escaped him but he boldly went to die
    made scarcely a moan when his soft flesh was
        nailed.

And so he brazened it out right to the last
    still wore the gallant mask still cried 'Divine
    am I, lo for me is heaven overcast'
    though that inscrutable darkness gave no sign
    indifferent or malignant: while he was passed
    by even the worst of men at least sour wine.

The Young Man Thinks of Sons

Did my father curse his father for his lust I wonder
            as I do mine
and my grand-dad curse his sire for his wickedness his
   weakness his blunder
            and so on down the whole line

Well I'll stop the game break the thread end my race: I
   will not continue
            in the old bad trade:
I'll take care that for my nerveless mind weakened brain
   neglected sinew
            I alone shall have paid.

Let the evil book waste in its swathings the ill pen write
   not one iota
            the ship of doom not sail,
let the sword rot unused in its scabbard let the womb
   lack its quota:
            here let my line fail:

Let the plough rust untouched of the furrow, yea let the
   blind semen
            stretch vain arms for the virgin:
I'll hammer no stringed harps for gods to clash
   discords, or women:
            my orchard won't burgeon.

I'll take care that the lust of my loins never bring to
   fruition
            the seed of a son
who in his nettle-grown kingdom should curse both my
   sins of commission
            and what I left undone.

Be Swift O Sun

Be swift o sun
    lest she fall on some evil chance:
    make haste and run
    to light up the dark fields of France.

See already the moon
    lies sea-green on our globe's eastern rim:
    speed to be with her soon:
    even now her stars grow dim.

Here your labour is null
    and water poured upon sand
    to light up the hull
    which at dawn glimmers on to the land

And here you in vain
    clothe many coming sails with gold
    if you bring not again
    those breasts where I found death of old.

Why bring you ships
    from that evil Dis of a shore
    if you bring not the lips
    I kissed once and shall kiss no more:

O sun make speed
    and delay not to send her your rays
    lest she be in need
    of light in those far alien ways.

That you may single
    my love from the rest; her eyes
    her wide eyes commingle
    all innocence with all things wise:

Raindrops at eve fall
    in your last rays no lovelier:
    her voice is the madrigal
    at your dawn when the first birds stir.

Be swift o sun
    lest she fall on some evil chance:
    make haste and run
    to light up the dark fields of France.

Prelude

This short straight sword
    I got in Rome
    when Gaul's new lord
    came tramping home:

It did that grim
    old rake to a T—
    if it did him,
    well, it does me.

Leave the thing of pearls
    with silken tassels
    to priests and girls
    and currish vassals:

Here's no fine cluster
    on the hilt, this drab
    blade lacks lustre—
    but it can stab.

Young Knowledge

Knowledge, I know, is sure, of gradual thought,
A mare in foal, who pastures with dew eyes,
Cropping the grasses of a certitude
By many seasons sweetened for her sake;
Waiting with heart untroubled till it come
That by the straw-beds and the breathing clover
Like frost shall brittle one brief night of pain,
And then her treasure nuzzles at her side.
Knowledge has sunlight sleeked about her limbs,
White-headed reverent trees to partner her
In days of no event but steady growth.
And in the orchard where the crab-tree blooms,
Where surpliced tui chants one orison
Too wild, and shakes his petalled pulpit down,
None plucks unripe, none has a lust for bane
Or thieves across a fence ungiven sweet.
The labours of the world make road for knowledge,
Handling their time-known tools, the scythe for stooks,
Blue wheel in ruts, the brown and running sacks
Wide mouthed forever on the threshing floor.
Proud-nostrilled, chestnut in the sun, shines knowledge,
And singled men will tend her all her days . . .

Or knowledge is the hour that strikes but once,
Strikes, and demands, and never comes again.
Old vine on walls, thick-jointed, stiff with knots,
Knowledge creeps up the mortised centuries;
White grapes from this; but here with darkling pride
Burgundian clusters silk their sides in sun.
A thousand stamping feet across the vats
Press out each grape-year; now the rosy foam
Seethes up in hillocks, and the vintner's rods
Stir the dark coil of potency beneath.

Awhile the new wine in the barrel hisses,
Singing the song of grapes with savage lips
Still sensual for the air, the straight-backed vineyards,
And brown hands thrust among the clustering leaves.
Slowly comes settling, slowly wine forgets,
Sinks into silence, dreams its sunny rage
Away in distillate of centuries.
At last when cobwebs thicken sweating wood
Sure hands draw off the spigot; so much red,
So much bouquet, just so much bite in crystal.
Set the dew to your lips, friend, this is knowledge.

Or knowledge is the thin, contemptuous wine
Of wit from him you met once, in a tavern,
The grudging fellow sprawled across the fire,
Who for no reason (smell of sopping cloth,
Click of the cautious weather fingering latch,)
Poured out his lees of laughter, crude 'I know';
One spoke his soul, but next day in the street
Passed you a stranger, never spoke again.

And knowledge is a thunder in the night,
Huge claps of mirth, a frightened woman flung
Over the bed in oil-lamp's yellow gleam;
One half your soul an awe of burning blue,
One half your life a flower of burning flesh,
Touch her and laugh, whisper the comfort-things;
While still the leaden sky is great with child
And adder flashes dart against the pane.

Knowledge has gardens planted, rooted, so
    companioned
The lichen on the cobhouse sees the way
The flowering damsons in your driveway spill,
And sets its orange cap to catch the smile
Of timid daisies, scared across the lawns
By that old gardener, whipcord like his boughs.
Long since the roots of ash-tree learned the gentle
Contact of fibrous-fed forget-me-not,
The creeper on the walls grown intimate

Swarms just so far, and then for its encroachment
Sees the remonstrance of the garden shears.
The bellbird half-afraid drops down his song
Into the thin and metal campanile
Of glittering pear-trees, white mirage of mosques.
Each bee has learned his choosing. Here you walk
By careful paths, no bruising, nor no stumbling,
And only age and almond be upon you,
Here in the garden; smooth to tread is knowledge.

Or knowledge was the second while you listened
Waiting for raindrops, in the little start
Like claws of birds that patter on the leaves . . .
And dreamed that your two hands had made a
     rainbow.

Knowledge is flint-fire crackling in the road,
The hard impatient message in the breast,
Big words like bloodshot smoke behind old houses,
Loud bells like fishwives clattering their news,
The loneliness of rocks where ships went down,
Black horse that broke his heart to reach the post,
The fool who fell too soon, or lived for failure,
Knowledge is blindness coffined in a world
Where every bloom black-clappered with its bees
Rings out a fragile warning on the wind;
And none to heed; and all to toss aside
The stumbling words, the hand upon their sleeve.

Knowledge is all that grasps and breaks and strives,
The flat tide flowing red between the mangroves,
The little evil roots that suck in mud,
The broken faces; all the broken faces
That put together make the mask of knowledge.

O fretted minds, bear yet your sheaths a little.
Not on the high fields you go, nor in command,
Not greatly owe to captains of wise mien,
For these were ordered; but your march as rough
As the first jagged troops that flung at Alps.

Like vagabonds and thieves you go by night,
Brandishing childish cudgels, circling torches,
And for a sudden burning you shall strive,
And at a sudden evil you shall strike,
But not for long; and God knows well or ill.
What your hard soles have taught you, and rough
   hands,
What your wet eyes have dealt with, and tight mouths,
What your bewilderment gave you, and hot heart,
That only is your knowledge. Take and bear it.

And die at last, like nettle in the ditch,
And burn at last, like gorse across the hills,
Because you stung the cloth and pricked the proud,
And are a bane to what shall come hereafter,
This also, is your knowledge; take and bear it.

Kauri they split with wedges, when too vast
The grey trunks rose for any ripping-saw;
It rounded off in masts that reigned on seas.
Gum-tree from Sydney makes the keels of boats,
But tall puriri, cut in six-foot lengths,
(After the berry-day that snared the pigeons,)
Rides evenly, and never rots in water,
And burns at evening with the hottest flame
For travellers, met ripe with early knowledge.
Soak the lithe toro-toro, and best yarn
Was not so strong for tying up stockades,
Three pickets for defence, a carved head fixed
Red-ochred, on the height of every gate.
The nikau born in shade plait hard together,
(One of the sacred four from lost Hawaiiki,)
Lay over toi-toi, or the raupo, tough
When used for thatching; but if huts take fire
They sheaf in yellow flame seen twenty miles.
The mangrove roots were ground for making powder
At the three secret mills among the Maoris,
When the lost war-dance thudded through the North.
They cut the yellow twisted horoeka
For sticks; the grass springs best when thin-bellied cattle

Trample their path, dung-dropping in the fern;
And the young shoots were burned off once a year,
But food for bellies when the crops were drowned.
And these I know, and ghosts of dead men's
    knowledge,
(And ghosts of young, rebellious, chidden knowledge,
Dunce at its class and stalking out of school,)
By bridges slender as the ake ladder
Where Heaphy, climbing, found the Greenstone People,
Saw the wide nets wash out in thundering surf
Too huge for the canoes, drawn in by moonlight;
Watched the brown women drying out inanga
For fodder in the nights of eaten moons
When wind prowls round the thatch with thievish
    fingers;
Saw the marled greenstone littered on the ground,
And how they fine the edge with whalebone drills—
And turned away at last, and climbed the ladder,
And standing on the clifftops, saw their smokes
Final steam up, blue parting of a dream.
There standing on the clifftops weighed his
    knowledge—
The thin precarious weight of early knowledge—
And staring in a sun, half steeled his heart
To tell the cities there was no such world.

The Last Ones

But the last black horse of all
Stood munching the green-bud wind,
And the last of the raupo huts
Let down its light behind.
Sullen and shadow-clipped
He tugged at the evening star,
New-mown silvers swished like straw
Across the manuka.

As for the hut, it said
No word but its meagre light,
Its people slept as the dead,
Bedded in Maori night.
'And there is the world's last door,
And the last world's horse,' sang the wind,
'With little enough before,
And what you have seen behind.'

from The Beaches

VI

Close under here, I watched two lovers once,
Which should have been a sin, from what you say:
I'd come to look for prawns, small pale-green ghosts,
Sea-coloured bodies tickling round the pool.
But tide was out then; so I strolled away
And climbed the dunes, to lie here warm, face down,
Watching the swimmers by the jetty-posts
And wrinkling like the bright blue wrinkling bay.
It wasn't long before they came; a fool
Could see they had to kiss; but your pet dunce
Didn't quite know men count on more than that;
And so just lay, patterning the sand.
   And they
Were pale thin people, not often clear of town;
Elastic snapped, when he jerked off her hat;
I heard her arguing, 'Dick, my frock!' but he
Thought she was bread.
I wished her legs were brown,
And mostly, then, stared at the dawdling sea,
Hoping Perry would row me some day in his boat.

Not all the time; and when they'd gone, I went
Down to the hollow place where they had been,
Trickling bed through fingers. But I never meant

To tell the rest, or you, what I had seen;
Though that night, when I came in late for tea,
I hoped you'd see the sandgrains on my coat.

VII

Cool and certain, their oars will be lifted in dusk,
    light-feathered
As wings of terns, that dip into dream, coming back
    blue; but the motionless gull
With his bold head, hooked beak, black-slit humped
    harsh back
Freezing in icy air gleams crystal and beautiful.
No longer the dark corks, bobbing bay-wide, are seen:
Dogs bark, mothers hail back their children from
    ripple's danger:
People dipped in the dusk-vats smile back, each
    stranger
Than time; each has a face of crystal and blue.
In the jettisoned boat, the child who peered at her book
Cannot lift her glance from the running silk of the
    creek:
It is time to return to her mother, to call and look . . .
The sea-pulse beats in her wrists: she will not speak.
But the boats, in salt tide and smarting sunrise
    weathered,
Swing by an island's shadow: silver trickles and wets
The widening branch of their wake, the swart Italian
    faces,
Fisherman's silver fingers, fumbling the nets:
And the island lies behind them, lifting its glassy cone
In one strange motionless gesture, light on stone:
Only the gulls, the guards of the water-lapping places,
Scream at the fishermen lifting the water-lifting nets.

Far and away, the shore people hear a singing:
Love-toned Italian voices fondle the night: the hue
Of the quietly waiting people is velvet blue.

from The Houses

III

Adolicus; that's a creeper rug, its small
Pink-and-white piecemeal flowers swarm down a fence:
So little, no scent to be by; show, pretence—
Nothing to do, but hide the rotting wall.
Three slats were broken: but the street-boys' eyes
Can't climb in here like ants and frighten us.
Stare if they like: we've the adolicus.

IV

Hares on their forms at dusk were not so still
Nor those soft stones, their eyes, so warily bright
As yours, held captive by my story's will:
Candle-flame pricked between us: night
Lapped like grey water over the sill.

Why did you listen? Little enough to learn . . .
Scraps from a baked street's platter; folk we knew
Seen slantwise, through vined doorways that discern
The secret child. Did blue
Flame in my eyes so steeply burn?

Why didn't you answer back? Perhaps the wind
Was I; you the deep earth, that wouldn't care
(So dreaming) for the littler left behind:
Flame pieces out your hair,
Your hands; never that quiet coast, your mind.

V

None of it true; for Christ's sake, spill the ink,
Tear out this charnel's darnel-root, that lingers
Sprouting words, words, words! Give me cool bluegum
    leaves
To rub brittle between my fingers.

I had the touch of hillside once: the ever-
So-slender cold of buttercup stems in brink:
Pebbles: great prints in mud: Oh, Lazarus, bring me
Some mountain honesty to drink!

Ku Li

Two words from China: 'Ku li'—bitter strength.
'This coolies' war!' tinkle the sweet-belled idle.
His face and Hundred Names sweep on below,
Child-like, he plays at horse without the bridle:
And carts a world along, and carts a war,
Tugging perhaps to mountain heights at length:
The new vernacular chronicles exhort him,
And waste their breath.
His grinning face can't know
Half the fixed meanings of the flags he saw:
He had a happy childhood: then time caught him,
Broadened his shoulders, but forbore his head.

Eight years his life between the shafts: eight hours
(With luck) between Changsha and Hsuchowfu,
Picks swinging like pendulums in a noon of flowers:
Shining their freedom, bombers spot his blue,
But cease to count. Too poor for marriage-bed
He looks for dreaming in the big dim shed,
Rolled in the quilt where other warmth has dossed.

Turns to Yunnan, hacks the next strategy through,
Cheerful; and often killed; and always bossed.
And not on Tiger Head or Purple Mountain
His grave-mound rises: worlds live on, to slake
Their ashy gullets at his bitter fountain
Of blood and vigour. Enemy armies break
Somehow on this, as somehow cracks the stone
Under his pick: but now he rots alone
(Not claiming to have died for something's sake,)

Only the earth makes ready for his bone,
The green rice sees him with unflattering eyes:
Too cheap a partisan for man to prize,
Men seldom know him for their broadest river,
And burnt in the immortal tiles forever.

The Deserted Village

In the deserted village, sunken down
With a shrug of last weak old age, pulled back to earth,
All people are fled or killed. The cotton crop rots,
Not one mild house leans sideways, a man on crutches,
Not a sparrow earns from the naked floors,
Walls look, but cannot live without the folk they
    loved—
It would be a bad thing to awaken them.
Having broken the rice-bowl, seek not to fill it again.

The village temple, well built, with five smashed gods,
    ten whole ones,
Does not want prayers. Its last vain prayer bled up
When the women ran outside to be slain.
A temple must house its sparrows or fall asleep,
Therefore a long time, under his crown of snails,
The gilded Buddha demands to meditate.
No little flowering fires on the incense-strings
Startle Kwan-Yin, whom they dressed in satin—
Old women sewing beads like pearls in her hair.
This was a temple for the very poor ones:
Their gods were mud and lathe: but artfully
Some village painter coloured them all.
Wooden dragons were carefully carved.
Finding in mangled wood one smiling childish tree,
Roses and bells not one foot high,
I set it back, at the feet of Kwan-Yin.
A woman's prayer-bag,
Having within her paper prayers, paid for in copper,

Seeing it torn, I gathered it up.
I shall often think, 'The woman I did not see
Voiced here her dying wish.
But the gods dreamed on. So low her voice, so loud
The guns, all that death-night, who would stoop to
     hear?'

Dear Miss

How does one get outside
the actual

Within it we do our (whats known
as duty) we
go to work
the rent (our portion of it) has to be
paid
and we bath
to keep our bodies
free of unpleasantness
see
that the curtains are clean
and the tip paid
and all the right things
said
on the right occasions
we gaze
at the offerings male female
wood iron bronze fabrics from
Manchester (unemployed 10,000)
keep the heels from running down
wash our once trendy (last weeks)
clothes
comb our hair
(we are not savages you know)
see that the grass is under control

on the front lawn see
that
the dog has his walk
his
leather collar on

his phone number on his collar
(our shoes are made of plastic)
see
that the insurance on the car
is solvent
(massacres this year 10,000) see
to all
these
avoiding any untoward
events
that would make us feel
we can't cope
and then
we get to the edge
where the uncouth jungle
grows
just as it always did
before
inventions fitted us with corsets
strait jackets
neighbours
books on loan
and busfares
and following this question
the application amid bottles
glasses kegs
and hankies
of liberal embalming
fluid

The mound is lonely
in the moon-lit night—
the birds
(and the bodies in the parking
lot)
are silent

Word by Night

Ask in one life no more
Than that first revelation of earth and sky,
Renewed as now in the place of birth
Where the sea turns and the first roots go down.

By the same light also you may know yourselves:
You are of those risen from the sea
And for ever bound to the sea,
Which is but the land's other and older face.

It is time to replant the seed of life
At this rich boundary where it first sprang,
For you are water and earth,
Creatures of the shore, disputed ground.

For too long now too many have been deceived,
Renouncing the bare nursery of the race,
Trying to shed the limiting names
That link them to their kind;

Have sought sufficiency
In the contingent and derivative,
Wishing to rise from doubtful earth
And move secure among the abstract stars;

But faltering, losing the prime sense of direction,
Fell at last in mindless lassitude
Among the traffic,
Chattering, withered, unrecognizable.

Come again to the shore, the gathering place,
Where cries of sea-birds wring the air,

And by the poverty of rocks remember
Human degrees.

Water rises through the sand, but near
Are the first pastures,
Dyed by the shadow of a leaf,
Promise of the mind's kingdoms.

Seasons that bore you bring renewal,
But do not alter
The nature of your never-finished nature,
Nor the condition of time.

from The Estate

XXIV

What have you seen on the summits, the peaks that
   plunge their
Icy heads into space? What draws you trembling
To blind altars of rock where man cannot linger
Even in death, where body grows light, and vision
Ranging those uninhabitable stations
Dazzled and emulous among the rage of summoning
Shadows and clouds, may lead you in an instant
Out from all footing? What thread of music, what word in
That frozen silence that drowns the noise of our living?

What is life, you answer,
But to extend life, press its limits farther
Into the uncolonized nothing we must prey on
For every hard-won thought, all new creation
Of stone bronze music words; only at life's limit
Can man reach through necessity and custom
And move self by self into the province
Of that unrealized nature that awaits him,
His own to enter. But there are none to guide him

Across the threshold, interpret the saying of perilous
Music or word struck from that quivering climate,
Whose white inquisitors in close attendance
Are pain and madness and annihilation.

Ambulando

I

In middle life when the skin slackens
Its loving clasp of our loose volumes,
When the bone tree stiffens and its well-jointed
   branches
Begin to creak, to droop a little,
May the spirit hold out no longer for
Old impossible terms, demanding
Rent-free futures where all, all is ripeness,
But cry pax to its equivocal nature and stretch
At ease with wry destiny,
Supple as wind bowing in every reed.

II

Now that the young with interest no longer
Look on me as one of themselves
Whom they might wish to know or to touch,
Seeing merely another sapless greyhead,
The passport of that disguise conducts me
Through any company unquestioned,
In cool freedom to come and go
With mode and movement, wave and wind.

III

Communicate with stones, trees, water
If you must vent a heart too full.
Who will hear you now, your words falling
As foreign as bird-tongue

On ears attuned to different vibrations?
Trees, water, stones:
Let these answer a gaze contemplative
Of all things that flow out from them
And back to enter them again.

IV

I do not know the shape of the world.
I cannot set boundaries to experience.
I know it may open out, enlarged suddenly,
In any direction, to unpredictable distance,
Subverting climate and cosmography,
And carrying me far from tried moorings
So that I see myself no more
Under some familiar guise
Resting static as in a photograph,
Nor move as I supposed I was moving
From fixed point to point;
But rock outwards like the last stars that signal
At the frontiers of light,
Fleeing the centre without destination.

Life Mask

Blake shuts his eyes.
He seals himself in the vault of his head
Behind the drawn mouth
Inside the tight-drawn skull

Which is St Paul's dome and the Dome of the Rock, the
    house of the Holy Wisdom, the Colosseum,
The caves of Ajanta and Lascaux
And the Tuscarora Deep,
The underworld silence, the reeling spaces.

Blake goes into his skull
Where the visions start.

A rose shatters the sod there
To sail vermilion energies through heaven.

Quivering nostril that snuffs the scent of being,
He is all inhalation,
The worlds transpire, deliquesce, pour into him
In the rage of their streams.

Yet no breath flutters the marbled countenance
Where Albion breaks from sleep
A winged Mercury and morning Apollo
Scattering fireflags, word-stars.

In factories of bone walls roofed with thatch of hair
Anvils ring in the black haloes of forges,
Swords white-hot from the furnace are plunged to cool
    in vats of tears;
Their thirst for tears will never be quenched.

He will not speak again.
All things are enacting speech in him: wielding the
    eternal compasses
He is cube and circle, he is pyramidal crimson and
    everlasting azure,
Green maenads of the dance, vanishing point of
    diamond white.

Shoriken

1

Feel the edge of the knife
Cautiously—
Ice-keen
It lies against your cheek
Your heart
Will pierce at once if you should stir
Yet offers
A pillow loving to your head
A sword to cross the malevolent sea.

2

The wood of the world harbours
Lamb and lion, hawk and dove.
A world of lions alone
Or a world of doves—would it
Capture our headstrong devotion
Harness the wolf-pack of energies
That unsparing we spendthrift
Earning our lives till death?
Where in its white or black would be work for love?

3

The merciless strike with swords
With words
With silences
They have as many faces as the clouds
As many ruses as the heart
The fountains of their mercy never run dry.

4

In a world of prisoners
Who dare call himself free?

5

Every mark on your body
Is a sign of my love.
Inscribed by the years, you tell
Unwittingly
How we travelled together
Parted and met again
Fell out sometimes, then made peace.
Crowsfoot, scar, tremulous eyelid
Are not matters for shame
But passages of the book
We have been writing together.

6

Giver, you strip me of your gifts
That I may love them better.

7

To remember yesterday and the day before
To look for tomorrow
To walk the invisible bridge of the world
As a tightrope, a sword edge.

8

What wages are due to you
Unprofitable servant?
You come asking for wages?
Fifty years long you have breathed
My air, drunk my sweet waters
And have not been cut down.
Is it not a boon, living?
Do not your easy days mark
The huge forbearance of earth?

9

The bluntest stones on the road will be singing
If you listen closely
Like lilies or larks
Those that may stone you to death after.

10

Rising and setting stars
Burn with the same intensity
But one glows for the world's dark
One whitens into tedious day.

11

All yours that you made mine
Is made yours again.

12

To speak in your own words in your own voice—
How easy it sounds and how hard it is
When nothing that is yours is yours alone

To walk singly yourself who are thousands
Through all that made and makes you day by day
To be and to be nothing, not to own

Not owned, but lightly on the sword edge keep
A dancer's figure—that is the wind's art
With you who are blood and water, wind and stone.

13

One place is not better than another
Only more familiar
Dearer or more hateful
No better, only nearer.

14

He is earth, dying to earth.
The charge of life spends itself
Wears, wears out.
His sole enemy is the self
That cannot do otherwise
Than live itself to death
                    death
The desert sand
That dries all tears
                    death
Our rest and end.

15

Selfless, you sign
Your words mine.

16

To cross the sea is to submit to the sea
Once venture out and you belong to it
All you know is the sea
All you are the sea
And that sword edge itself a wave-crest of the sea.

Note. Shoriken is the Japanese name of one of the
eight Taoist Immortals. A kakemono by Motonobu in
the British Museum shows him crossing the sea,
balanced on the edge of his sword.

from Home Ground

III

I tramp my streets into recognition.
They know me now and make no sign, they keep
Silence for my step
Giving nothing away, but poker-faced
Enact their numbers
Dependable under sun and moon.
I can just run that gauntlet of stone lids,
Making my lips stone.

Do not betray, stiff
My streets, the pulsing inward of your port—
Great King, Filleul, London, Albany Steps—
Paling and crossed curtains, petrol station,
Blossoming plum, hospital, blood-red church:
Tell your frailties over to yourselves
As I retail mine,
Behind the advertised face, between fly
Mocking and despair.
I could not run the gauntlet of your tears.

XIII

Before the light of evening can go out
The mountains have their features to compose,
The sea will commence its orisons,

And I must find a way
Among the indignant directions of the trees
Commanding to every compass point.

I ask the streets to guide me,
Past the shifty eyes of window-panes,
Beyond the forums and advertisements,

To some rough sketch of ground
Out of the traffic's ear
Where I may pitch a tent with plantain and pimpernel

Beneath the Pointers and the east wind,
And listen long to the night prowling
Over roof-skin and raw nerve-ends,

Unravelling the skeins that bind me
Into the world's close cocoon
To cover up my clamouring nakedness.

XXV

In drab derelict marsh near the madhouse
Fenced off and cancelled as dead ground
The spur-winged plover steps and probes.
The swamp-pools and the reeds, brief sky, grant him
    circuit.
He gives no sign to heed the scorching traffic
Eat up the road that swings above his lifeland,
But stray nearby to watch and he will cry alarm
And run, distracting from his callow nest.
He lives, breeds, dies by instinct, nothing willed,
Habit-hovering in a stream of lives
Bent to the arc-flight of the seasons.

And yet, at moments habit cannot point,
Does he divine a consenting sky,
Consent of earth
To his necessity that is hers also?
Necessity, consent, slip through our fingers
That touch and lost the pulse of time.
It is he sustains the world, outside our care.

from Night Cries, Wakari Hospital

Winter Anemones

The ruby and amethyst eyes of anemones
Glow through me, fiercer than stars.
Flambeaux of earth, their dyes
From age-lost generations burn
Black soil, branches and mosses into light
That does not fail, though winter grip the rocks
To adamant. See they come now
To lamp me through inscrutable dusk
And down the catacombs of death.

Arohaina mai

Arohaina mai, e te Kīngi nui,
Manaakitia rā ō tamariki ē!
Horahia mai rā te mārie nui
Ki te Hokowhitu a Tū toa!

Ngā mamaetanga me ngā pōuri nui,
Pēhia rawatia ki raro rā ē!
Me anga atu, ka karanga ki
Te Matua e, auē, aroha mai!

Ngā hapū katoa o Aotearoa ē,
Tauawhitia rā ko tōku rongo!
Kia mau te tihe mauri ora a
Ngā tīpuna, he tohu wehi ē!

Great king

Great king, bless your children,
Take them into your loving care!
Spread wide a great calm
For the warrior band of Tu!

We must strive to overcome
All our grief and sùffering,
We must turn and call upon our Father:
'Bestow your blessings upon us!'

All you tribes of Aotearoa,
Hold fast to our great name!

Proclaim as did our ancestors
Tihe mauri ora, words of power!

Translation by Margaret Orbell

Ngā rongo

Ngā rongo o te pakanga nei
Ka kapakapa te manawa ē
Ka māharahara te tinana ē
Auē auē te aroha ē!
Ka raparapa noa ngā whakaaro
He aha i riri ai te ao katoa?
He nui rawa no te mātauranga!
Purari Hitara, tangata hao!
Ngā rongo o te pakanga ē
Ka kapakapa te manawa ē
Ka māharahara te tinana ē—
Auē auē te aroha ē!

Ka tangi wairua atu ahau
Ki a koutou rā e Te Hokowhitu
I roto i te kino o tēnei wā!
Kia kaha, kia kaha rā!
Ka raparapa noa ngā whakaaro
He aha i whakaheke toto ē?
Hei aha ma purari Hitara,
Ka tohetohe! Nō reira rā
Ka tangi wairua atu ahau
Ki a koutou rā e Te Hokowhitu
I roto i te kino o tēnei wā!
Kia kaha, kia kaha rā!

The news

The news of this war
Makes our hearts beat,
Our minds and bodies are confused.
Alas, alas, what sorrow!
We keep on wondering
Why the world is at war.
There are far too many smart people!
Bloody Hitler, that greedy man!
The news of this war
Makes our hearts beat,
Our minds and bodies are confused.
Alas, alas, what sorrow!

We cry in spirit
For you, the sons of Tu
In these terrible times.
Be strong, be strong!
We keep on wondering
Why there is this bloodshed.
And still bloody Hitler
Fights to the bitter end!
We cry in spirit
For you, the sons of Tu
In these terrible times.
Be strong, be strong!

Translation by
Kumeroa Ngoingoi Pēwhairangi

Memoriter

Ovals of opal on dislustred seas,
Skyshine, and all that indolent afternoon
No clash of arms, no shouting on the breeze;
Only the reeds moaned soft or high their empty rune.

The paladins played chess and did not care,
The crocus pierced the turf with random dart.
Then twanged a cord. Through space, from Oultremer,
That other arrow veered towards your heart.

The Disinherited

They cared for nothing but the days and hours
Of freedom, and in silent scorn
Ignored the worldly watchers and the powers,
Left staples shattered and uptorn,
Filed window-bars and dynamited towers.

What was their wisdom whom no vice could hold?
Remote as any gipsy rover,
They stared along the cliffs, mauve fold on fold,
And watched the bees fly over.

From velvet hills, trees in the river-bed,
From glassy reefs in skeins of foam,
They reared the shell of vision and of words unsaid
To be their haunting and their earthly home.

At a Danse Macabre

The glittering topaz in your glass
Was vintaged forty years ago;
Your emerald has seen eight kings pass,
A thousand thousand candles glow.

Watched in a jewel, the taper curls;
The royal men, the wine that flows
Are tints and crowns; the peerless girls
Are broken shadows of a rose.

Environs of Vanholt I

White and blue, an outspread fan,
The sea slopes to the Holmcliff, and the dawn
Spins vaporous spokes across the Broken Span
To light up Razor Drop and Winesael Yawn.

Beanpod sleeps out beside his malt-filled pot;
Behind him lies the still and silver land;
No atom bomb drops from a shapely hand,
But birds of boding in a greasy knot
Pick at the rusted corpse half-hid in sand.

The Watchers

The bulging rampart streaked with pink and jade
Shelters the quay where heedless drinkers sit,
Discoursing love with gin and orangeade,
Or Marcel Proust to a banana split.

The waiters on their monorail recur
Like an old and boring complex; all aglow
The ironclads out at sea fire through the blur
And sink to the rhythms of *El Chocolo*.

Vineta

Fire in the olive groves throughout the night,
And charred twigs crackling like the living coal;
The flame-splash spread across the wounded height;
Came flash on cannon flash and thunder-roll;
Then through the black smoke roared the bomber flight:
He crouched part-stricken in his shallow hole.

Strangely, at last he put his arms aside
And seemed to drift away. It was the rising tide
That heaped its star-shot depths upon a sunken town
Of brittle amber. There he thought to drown
Against a church haled over on its side,
So with the torpid ghosts he laid him down;
But pain and breath were not so easily denied.

Remark

High-coiffed the muse in green brocade
Hears waltzes that are not for her,
And haunts, by time yet unbetrayed,
A breath-dimmed pane's curved lavender.

Studiously minor, yet attuned to doom,
Like an old gramophone this modish muse—
She may grow spiteful in a little room,
Attack the glass with crystal shoes,
Get airborne on a witches' broom.

He tangi mo Kēpa Anaha Ēhau

I te maruawatea
he wera koroirangi
kōpehupehu ana
taku rau kōtuku.
I te maruahiahi,
he matangi hehengi,
kua parohea ia
taku taonga whakaepa!

Tirohia te rangi
'parewaikohu ana
mōu ra, e te hoa,
'takuatetia nei—
te kākā kura
te manu tohikura
te manu kōrero
kua tāoki na!

Kua wehe nei koe,
e te pūkōrero!
Ma wai e taki
te hono tātai
heketanga-ā-rangi
o Te Arawa iwi?
Ma Muruika pea?
Ma Te Papa-i-ouru?

Takahia, e te hoa,
i te ara a Tāne,
kia tae na koe
ki Tatau-o-te-pō,
ki te whāioio

kua rūpeke atu
hei karanga i a koe
ki Te Pōtangotango!

Lament for Kepa Anaha Ehau

In broad daylight
the shimmering heat
strikes down
my kotuku leaf.
In the evening
the breeze is gentle,
but withered is
my symbol!

See the sky
mistily weeps
for you, friend,
lamented by us—
the tried leader,
the fount of lore,
the orator supreme
now gone to rest!

Now you are gone,
wise man of words,
who will recite
the family tree
rooted in heaven
of Te Arawa people?
Will Muruika speak?
Will Te Papa-i-ouru?

Follow, friend,
the path of Tane
until you reach

Tatau-o-te-po,
and the myriad
now assembled
to greet you
to the Underworld!

Translation by
Arapeta Awatere

House and Land

Wasn't this the site, asked the historian,
Of the original homestead?
Couldn't tell you, said the cowman;
I just live here, he said,
Working for old Miss Wilson
Since the old man's been dead.

Moping under the bluegums
The dog trailed his chain
From the privy as far as the fowlhouse
And back to the privy again,
Feeling the stagnant afternoon
Quicken with the smell of rain.

There sat old Miss Wilson,
With her pictures on the wall,
The baronet uncle, mother's side,
And one she called The Hall;
Taking tea from a silver pot
For fear the house might fall.

People in the *colonies*, she said,
Can't quite understand . . .
Why, from Waiau to the mountains
It was all father's land.

She's all of eighty said the cowman,
Down at the milking-shed.
I'm leaving here next winter.
Too bloody quiet, he said.

The spirit of exile, wrote the historian,
Is strong in the people still.

He reminds me rather, said Miss Wilson,
Of Harriet's youngest, Will.

The cowman, home from the shed, went drinking
With the rabbiter home from the hill.

The sensitive nor'west afternoon
Collapsed, and the rain came;
The dog crept into his barrel
Looking lost and lame.
But you can't attribute to either
Awareness of what great gloom
Stands in a land of settlers
With never a soul at home.

Polynesia

Surf is a partial deafness islanders
All suffer from, committed to the land;
A resonant hades, traversing, the fathers
Left cold or sweltering a world behind;

A drumming, drumming, drumming till there leapt
Fully afforested from the well of ocean
Valley and peak; the glove of blindness clapped
On trusting eyes; perpetual collision

Indistinguishable in those eyes,
Of salt of tears within and spray without;
Currents not warm or cold, of abstract seas
By any sense unfathomed, but where float

Small gods in shawls of bark, blind, numb, and deaf,
But buoyant, eastward, in the blaze of surf.

The Skeleton of the Great Moa in the Canterbury Museum, Christchurch

The skeleton of the moa on iron crutches
Broods over no great waste; a private swamp
Was where this tree grew feathers once, that hatches
Its dusty clutch, and guards them from the damp.

Interesting failure to adapt on islands,
Taller but not more fallen than I, who come
Bone to his bone, peculiarly New Zealand's.
The eyes of children flicker round this tomb

Under the skylights, wonder at the huge egg
Found in a thousand pieces, pieced together
But with less patience than the bones that dug
In time deep shelter against ocean weather:

Not I, some child, born in a marvellous year,
Will learn the trick of standing upright here.

Tomb of an Ancestor

I. In Memoriam, R.L.M.G.

The oldest of us burst into tears and cried
Let me go home, but she stayed, watching
At her staircase window ship after ship ride
Like birds her grieving sunsets; there sat stitching

Grandchildren's things. She died by the same sea.
High over it she led us in the steepening heat
To the yellow grave; her clay
Chose that way home: dismissed, our feet

Were seen to have stopped and turned again down hill;
The street fell like an ink-blue river

In the heat to the bay, the basking ships, this Isle
Of her oblivion, our broad day. Heaped over

So lightly, she stretched like time behind us, or
Graven in cloud, our farthest ancestor.

Spectacular Blossom

Mock up again, summer, the sooty altars
Between the sweltering tides and the tin gardens
All the colours of the stained bow windows.
Quick, she'll be dead on time, the single
Actress shuffling red petals to this music,
Percussive light! So many suns she harbours
And keeps them jigging, her puppet suns,
All over the dead hot calm impure
Blood noon tide of the breathless bay.

Are the victims always so beautiful?

Pearls pluck at her, she has tossed her girls
Breast-flowers for keepsakes now she is going
For ever and astray. I see her feet
Slip into the perfect fit the shallows make her
Purposefully, sure as she is the sea
Levels its lucent ruins underfoot
That were sharp dead white shells, that will be sands.
The shallows kiss like knives.

Always for this
They are chosen for their beauty.

Wristiest slaughterman December smooths
The temple bones and parts the grey-blown brows
With humid fingers. It is an ageless wind
That loves with knives, it knows our need, it flows
Justly, simply as water greets the blood,

And woody tumours burst in scarlet spray.
An old man's blood spills bright as a girl's
On beaches where the knees of light crash down.
These dying ejaculate their bloom.

Can anyone choose
And call it beauty?—The victims
Are always beautiful.

A Small Room with Large Windows

I

What it would look like if really there were only
One point of the compass not known illusory,
All other quarters proving nothing but quaint
Obsolete expressions of true north (would it be?),
And seeds, birds, children, loves and thoughts bore
  down
The unwinding abiding beam from birth
To death! What a plan!
                    Or parabola.
You describe yours, I mine, simple as that,
With a pop and a puff of nonchalant stars up top,
Then down, dutiful dead stick, down
(True north all the way nevertheless).

One way to save space and a world of trouble.

A word on arrival, a word on departure.
A passage of proud verse, rightly construed.
An unerring pen to edit the ensuing silences
(That's more like it).

II

                    Seven ageing pine trees hide
Their heads in air but, planted on bare knees,
Supplicate wind and tide: See if you can

See it (if this is it), half earth, half heaven,
Half land, half water, what you call a view
Strung out between the windows and the tree trunks;
Below sills a world moist with new making where
The mangrove race number their cheated floods.
Now in a field azure rapidly folding
Swells a cloud sable, a bad bitching squall
Thrashes the old pines, has them twitching
Root and branch, rumouring a Götterdämmerung.
Foreknowledge infects them to the heart.

Comfortable

To creak in tune, comfortable to damn
Slime-suckled mangrove for its muddy truckling
With time and tide, knotted to the vein it leeches.

III

In the interim, how the children should be educated,
Pending a decision, a question much debated
In our island realms. It being, as it is,
Out of the question merely to recognise
The whole three hundred and sixty degrees,
Which prudence if not propriety forbids,
It is necessary to avail oneself of aids
Like the Bible, or no Bible, free swimming tuition,
Art, sex, no sex and so on. Not to direct
So much as to normalize personality, protect
From all hazards of climate, parentage, diet,
Whatever it is exists. While, on the quiet,
It is understood there is a judgement preparing
Which finds the compass totally without bearing
And the present course correct beyond a doubt,
There being two points precisely, one in, one out.

IV

A kingfisher's naked arc alight
Upon a dead stick in the mud
A scarlet geranium wild on a wet bank
A man stepping it out in the near distance

With a dog and a bag
                    on a spit of shell
On a wire in a mist
                    a gannet impacting
Explode a dozen diverse dullnesses
Like a burst of accurate fire.

from Trees, Effigies, Moving Objects

I. Lone Kauri Road

The first time I looked seaward, westward,
it was looking back yellowly,
a dulling incandescence of the eye of day.
It was looking back over its raised hand.
Everything was backing away.

Read for a bit. It squinted between the lines.
Pages were backing away.
Print was busy with what print does,
trees with what trees do that time of day,
sun with what sun does, the sea
with one voice only, its own,
spoke no other language than that one.

There wasn't any track from which to hang
the black transparency that was travelling
south-away to the cold pole. It was cloud
browed over the yellow cornea which I called
an eyeball for want of another notion,
cloud above an ocean. It leaked.

Baldachin, black umbrella, bucket with a hole,
drizzled horizon, sleazy drape,
it hardly mattered which, or as much
what cometing bitchcraft, rocketed shitbags,
charred cherubim pocked and pitted the iceface

of space in time, the black traveller.
Everything was backing away.

The next time I looked seaward,
it was looking sooted red, a bloodshot cornea
browed with a shade that could be simulated
if the paint were thick enough, and audible,
to blow the coned noses of the young kauri,
the kettle spout sweating,
the hound snoring at my feet,
the taste of tobacco, the tacky fingers
on the pen, the paper from whose plane
the last time I looked seaward
would it be a mile, as the dust flies,
down the dulling valley, westward?
everything was backing away.

VII. A Family Matter

Adam was no fool. He knew that at his age
a man must plan for his retirement. Or else.
He saw no better way than back to the bush.

An image in disrepair could study itself
in a pool, or such distraction from itself
as a bird flashing a scale upon his ear.

There was Cain to take over the business. There were
    signs.
Light no fires. Discharge no firearms.
Ten acre block for sale. Your private kingdom.

Lianes noosed harmlessly, the water ran
down above and below the road ran down
primevally babbling. Close to the foot

of a young totara, *Podocarpus hallii*,
Adam stumbled, and very nearly fell
over an old survey peg, half rotted.

If it blew like the wrath of God it was all blown over
ages ago, the angel hooked it, having lashed
round with a sword in a flaming bad temper.

Regeneration, conservation, were words
with which he comforted his mind, if angels,
vandals, vermin, got muddled in his mind.

Cain used to come over at the week-ends
and bring the children, who loved it.
Something must be done with it when the old man
  went.

XVII. Lone Kauri Road

Too many splashes, too many gashes,
too big and too many holes in the west wall:
one by one the rectangles blazed and blacked where the
sun fell out of its frame, the time of the day
hung round at a loose end, lopsided.

It was getting desperate, even a fool could see,
it was feverish work, impossible to plug them all.
Even a fool, seeing the first mountain fall
out not into the sea or the smoking west but into
the places where these had been, could see the spider
brushed up, dusted, shovelled into the stove, and
how fast his legs moved, without the least surprise.

A tui clucked, shat, whistled thrice.
My gaze was directed where the branch had been.
An engine fell mute into the shadow of the valley
where the shadow had been.

Canst Thou Draw Out Leviathan
with an Hook?

I

An old Green River knife had to be scraped
of blood rust, scales, the dulled edge scrubbed
with a stone to the decisive whisper of steel
on the lips of the wooden grip.

You now have a cloud in your hand
hung blue dark over the waves and edgewise
luminous, made fast by the two brass rivets
keeping body and blade together, leaving
the other thumb free for feeling
how the belly will be slit and the spine severed.

The big kahawai had to swim close
to the rocks which kicked at the waves
which kept on coming steeply steaming,
wave overhanging wave
in a strong to gale offshore wind.

The rocks kicked angrily, the rocks
hurt only themselves, the seas without a scratch
made out to be storming and shattering,
but it was all an act that they ever broke
into breakers or even secretively
raged like the rocks, the wreckage of the land,
the vertigo, the self-lacerating
hurt of the land.
                              Swimming closer
the kahawai drew down the steely cloud
and the lure, the line you cast
from cathedral rock, the thoughtful death
whispering to the thoughtless,

Will you be caught?

II

Never let them die of the air,
pick up your knife and drive it
through the gills with a twist,
let the blood run fast,
quick bleeding makes best eating.

III

An insult in the form of an apology
is the human answer to the inhuman
which rears up green roars down white,
and to the fish which is fearless:

if anyone knows a better it is a man
willing to abstain from his next breath,
who will not be found fishing from these rocks
but likeliest fished from the rip,

white belly to wetsuit black, swung copular
under the winching chopper's bubble,
too late for vomiting salt but fluent at last
in the languages of the sea.

IV

A rockpool catches the blood,
so that in a red cloud of itself
the kahawai lies white belly uppermost.

Scales will glue themselves to the rusting blade
of a cloud hand-uppermost in the rockpool.

V

Fingers and gobstick fail,
the hook's fast in the gullet,
the barb's behind the root
of the tongue and the tight
fibre is tearing the mouth

and you're caught, mate, you're caught,
the harder you pull it
the worse it hurts, and it makes
no sense whatever in the air
or the seas or the rocks
how you kick or cry, or sleeplessly
dream as you drown.

A big one! a big one!

from Moro Assassinato

II.   An Urban Guerrilla

*The real stress came from life in the group . . . we were
caught up in a game that to the present day I still don't
fully see through.*—Michael Baumann, 'Most sought after' German
terrorist

It was a feather of paint
in a corner of the window,
a thread hanging from the hem
of the curtain, it was
the transistor standing on the corner
of the fridge, the switches
on the transistor, the way they were placed
in a dead design, it was where
the table stood, it was the label
Grappa Julia on the bottle
not quite half empty,

the faces that came and went,
the seven of us comrades
like the days of the week repeating
themselves, themselves,
it was cleaning your gun ten times
a day, taking time
washing your cock, no love

lost, aimlessly fondling
the things that think faster than fingers,
trigger friggers, gunsuckers.
People said, Andreas Baader

'had an almost sexual relationship
with pistols', his favourite fuck
was a Heckler & Koch. Not that sex
wasn't free for all and in all
possible styles, but not all of us
or any of us all of the time—
while agreeing, in principle,
that any combination of abcdefg
encoded orgasm, X being any
given number—got our sums right.

Dust thickened on the mirror,
the once gay playmate,
on the dildo in the drawer,
dust on the file of newspapers;
silence as dusty as death
on the radio, nobody can hear
the police dragging their feet;
sometimes we squabbled, once
could have shot one another
in the dusty time, we had to be
terrible news, or die.

You Will Know When You Get There

Nobody comes up from the sea as late as this
in the day and the season, and nobody else goes down

the last steep kilometre, wet-metalled where
a shower passed shredding the light which keeps

pouring out of its tank in the sky, through summits,
trees, vapours thickening and thinning. Too

credibly by half celestial, the dammed
reservoir up there keeps emptying while the light lasts

over the sea, where it 'gathers the gold against
it'. The light is bits of crushed rock randomly

glinting underfoot, wetted by the short
shower, and down you go and so in its way does

the sun which gets there first. Boys, two of them,
turn campfirelit faces, a hesitancy to speak

is a hesitancy of the earth rolling back and away
behind this man going down to the sea with a bag

to pick mussels, having an arrangement with the tide,
the ocean to be shallowed three point seven metres,

one hour's light to be left and there's the excrescent
moon sponging off the last of it. A door

slams, a heavy wave, a door, the sea-floor shudders.
Down you go alone, so late, into the surge-black fissure.

Home Thoughts

I do not dream of Sussex downs
or quaint old England's
quaint old towns—
I think of what may yet be seen
in Johnsonville or Geraldine.

All of These

Consider, praise, remember all of these—

All, blueprint in hand, who slowly rivet
the intricate structure, handle girders like feathers,
take the inert and formless cement, give it
meaning, rearing new walls against weather;

these, guiding surely the sky-swung cargo bales
yawing over black hold; against all gales
they steady with merchandise the rolling mast,
pack tightly the walls of a ship, storm-fast;

these, building together the parts of an engine,
till revolutions, sweetly tension-strung,
instantly answer as control sends in
message to metal, giving lovely tongue;

these whose laboured cunning plough
carves deeply the sweep of the hill's brow;
now with horses clumsily swinging anew
they've creamed over the black earth, arrow-true;

hands, timber-tried, that round the vessel's bow
to take the wave, know prematurely how
the unsalted hull will lift to breaking seas—
consider, praise, remember all of these.

Their easy partnership of hand and eye
divides them not; life they identify
with effortless use of tools, lovely, articulate,
striking clear purpose into the inanimate.

Holiday Piece

Now let my thoughts be like the Arrow, wherein was
    gold
and purposeful like the Kawarau, but not so cold.

Let them sweep higher than the hawk ill-omened,
higher than peaks perspective-piled beyond Ben
    Lomond;
let them be like at evening an Otago sky
where detonated clouds in calm confusion lie.

Let them be smooth and sweet as all those morning
    lakes,
yet active and leaping, like fish the fisherman takes;
and strong as the dark deep-rooted hills, strong
as twilight hours over Lake Wakatipu are long;

and hardy, like the tenacious mountain tussock,
and spacious, like the Mackenzie plain, not narrow;
and numerous as tourists in Queenstown;
and cheerfully busy, like the gleaning sparrow.

Lastly, that snowfield, visible from Wanaka,
compound their patience—suns only brighten,
and no rains darken, a whiteness nothing could whiten.

The Magpies

When Tom and Elizabeth took the farm
The bracken made their bed,
And *Quardle oodle ardle wardle doodle*
The magpies said.

Tom's hand was strong to the plough
Elizabeth's lips were red,
And *Quardle oodle ardle wardle doodle*
The magpies said.

Year in year out they worked
While the pines grew overhead,
And *Quardle oodle ardle wardle doodle*
The magpies said.

But all the beautiful crops soon went
To the mortgage-man instead,
And *Quardle oodle ardle wardle doodle*
The magpies said.

Elizabeth is dead now (it's years ago);
Old Tom went light in the head;
And *Quardle oodle ardle wardle doodle*
The magpies said.

The farm's still there. Mortgage corporations
Couldn't give it away.
And *Quardle oodle ardle wardle doodle*
The magpies say.

Threnody

In Plimmerton, in Plimmerton,
The little penguins play,

And one dead albatross was found
At Karehana Bay.

In Plimmerton, in Plimmerton,
The seabirds haunt the cave,
And often in the summertime
The penguins ride the wave.

In Plimmerton, in Plimmerton,
The penguins live, they say,
But one dead albatross they found
At Karehana Bay.

from Sings Harry

Songs

I

These songs will not stand—
The wind and the sand will smother.

Not I but another
Will make songs worth the bother:
    The rimu or kauri he,
    I'm but the cabbage tree,
        Sings Harry to an old guitar.

II

If everywhere in the street
Is the indifferent, the accustomed eye
Nothing can elate,
It's nothing to do with me,
        Sings Harry in the wind-break.

To the north are islands like stars
In the blue water

And south, in that crystal air,
The ice-floes grind and mutter,
    Sings Harry in the wind-break.

At one flank old Tasman, the boar,
Slashes and tears,
And the other Pacific's sheer
Mountainous anger devours,
    Sings Harry in the wind-break.

From the cliff-top a boy
Felt that great motion,
And pupil to the horizon's eye
Grew wide with vision,
    Sings Harry in the wind-break.

But grew to own fences barbed
Like the words of a quarrel;
And the sea never disturbed
Him fat as a barrel,
    Sings Harry in the wind-break.

Who once would gather all Pacific
In a net wide as his heart
Soon is content to watch the traffic
Or lake waves breaking short,
    Sings Harry in the wind-break.

III

When I am old
    Sings Harry
  Will my thoughts grow cold?
Will I find
    Sings Harry
For my sunset mind
Girls on bicycles
Turning into the wind?

Or will my old eyes feast
Upon some private movie of the past?
        Sings Harry.

Once the Days

Once the days were clear
Like mountains in water,
The mountains were always there
And the mountain water;

And I was a fool leaving
Good land to moulder,
Leaving the fences sagging
And the old man older
To follow my wild thoughts
Away over the hill,
Where there is only the world
And the world's ill,
        Sings Harry.

Thistledown

Once I followed horses
And once I followed whores
And marched once with a banner
For some great cause,
        Sings Harry.
But that was thistledown planted on the wind.

And once I met a woman
All in her heart's spring,
But I was a headstrong fool
Heedless of everything
        Sings Harry.
—I was thistledown planted on the wind.

Mustering is the life:
Freed of fears and hopes

I watch the sheep like a pestilence
Pouring over the slopes,
    Sings Harry.
And the past is thistledown planted on the wind.

Dream and doubt and the deed
Dissolve like a cloud
On the hills of time.
Be a man never so proud,
    Sings Harry.
He is only thistledown planted on the wind.

from Arawata Bill

Arawata Bill

With his weapon a shovel
To test the river gravel
His heart was as big as his boots
As he headed over the tops
In blue dungarees and a sunset hat.

Wicked country, but there might be
Gold in it for all that.

Under the shoulder of a boulder
Or in the darkened gully,
Fit enough country for
A blanket and a billy
Where nothing stirred
Under the cold eye of the bird.

Some climbers bivvy
Heavy with rope and primus.
But not so
Arawata Bill and the old-timers.

Some people shave in the mountains.
But not so
Arawata Bill who let his whiskers grow.

I met a man from the mountains
Who told me that Bill
Left cairns across the ravines
And through the scrub on the hill
—And they're there still.

And he found,
Together with a kea's feather,
A rusting shovel in the ground
By a derelict hovel.

It had been there long,
But the handle was good and strong.

The River Crossing

The river was announcing
An ominous crossing
With the boulders knocking.

'You can do it and make a fight of it,
Always taking the hard way
For the hell and delight of it.

But there comes the day
When you watch the spate of it,
And camp till the moon's down
—Then find the easy way
Across in the dawn,
Waiting till that swollen vein
Of a river subsides again.'

And Bill set up his camp and watched
His young self, river-cold and scratched,
Struggling across, and up the wrong ridge,
And turning back, temper on edge.

Camp Site

Earth and sky black,
And an old fire's sodden ashes
Were puddled in porridge clay
On that bleak day.
An old coat lay
Like a burst bag, worn
Out in a tussle with thorn.
Water ran
Through a hole in the rusted can.

The pass was wrapped
In a blanket of mist,
And the rain came again,
And the wind whipped.

The climbers had been there camping
Watching the sky
With a weatherwise eye.
And Paradise Pete
Scrabbling a hole in the sleet
When the cloud smote and waters roared
Had scrawled on a piece of board
RIVERS TOO DEEP.

Wata Bill stuck his shovel there
And hung his hat on the handle,
Cutting scrub for a shelter,
Lighting wet wood with a candle.

The Old Jason, the Argonaut

I sit beside my old ship, the timbers rotting,
Some damned old woman with her entrails telling
How Argo's hull will fall upon my head
For expiation of those expeditious deaths.

What's death? Argo in life was more
Than death's one stroke, as stroke on stroke
Beyond the rubbing-strake
Our oars combed out the water.

Was the Fleece worth it, and the Medea offering
Her warm, cold calculating front?

Yes, but it was, though labours brought
Nothing but glory and the name of Argonaut.

I took her with me on the long haul home.
Trouble and danger there, dark-sleeping
On that sheepskin on the thwart. Dark
Was the homeward voyage, my head at rest
On that dark, treacherously loyal breast.

But she gave me no rest.

Hero-tremendous, and I played the fool.
Vengeful she left me, she
Dragoned in air

—And I sit here, neither alive nor dead,
Waiting beside the Argo and the sea,
An old woman's triumph pouring on my head.

Brightness

I am bright with the wonder of you
And the faint perfume of your hair

I am bright with the wonder of you
You being far away or near

I am bright with the wonder of you
Warmed by your eyes' blue fire

I am bright with the wonder of you
And your mind's open store

I am bright with the wonder of you
Despite the dark waiting I endure

I am bright with the wonder of you.

Printers

I speak now of printers and bookmen,
Praise men acknowledged great
Whose business has been display of words
Fragile as bones of birds,
Careful of how hyphens mate,
Considering each comma, establishing
A style as precedent for the mile-
Wide errors of authors laughers
At their own inaccuracy.

John Johnson said 'A title page with red
Is affectation. Printing for reading
Or posterity needs only clarity.'
I said to him, 'This book is hand-set, look!
And there's no mention of the fact!'
'What affectation could we get to—
And yet, of course, it's affectation not to.'

'Do you like that?' said Oliver Simon.
'Myself I could wish it one-point leaded.'
I who could make no room
On the crowded page of my mind
Had no imperfection to find.

Then Stanley Morison squatted me on the floor
To examine big letter designs and pore
Over the refinement of serifs
With a diffident explanation of why

There was a problem in the kern
Of italic *g* plus *y*.

'That initial's too coarse,' I told Bob.
Lowry said, 'You're a perfectionist, a snob.
I'll get away with it before I'm old,
And to hell with you and Doug Robb.'

'What is perfection?' then I said,
'For type and coffin, both are lead.
Those who sought it did their best
And now find honourable rest,
Dead, dead, dead.'

HERA KĀTENE-HORVATH
(1912–1987) Ngāti Toa, Ngāti Tama, Te Āti Awa, Te Rarawa

I ngā rā

I ngā rā o mua noa atu
Waiatatia te waiata o mua
Auē! e hine mā, auē! e tama mā
Kia mau ki tō reo Māori e
Auē! Auē! Auē!

I ngā rā o mua noa atu
I mahi i ngā mahi Māori
E te iwi, e te iwi, hāpai ake ki runga
Tēnei whakatupuranga e
Auē! Auē! Auē!

Akona ai te haka taparahi e
Akona ai te poi pōwhiri
Poi porotiti, tāpara patua!

Kia mau ki tō Māoritanga
Ki ngā taonga a ōu tūpuna
Tēnei hei kahu kiwi mō tōu pakihiwi
Mō ake, ake tonu atu e
Mō ake, ake tonu atu e.

In days gone by

In days gone by
The ancient songs were sung.
Young women, young men,
Keep your Maori tongue!
Aue! Aue! Aue!

In the days gone by
Whatever happened was Maori.
O people, bring up, raise up
This generation.
Aue! Aue! Aue!

Learn the war dance,
Learn the welcoming poi,
Beat the whirling double poi!

Hold on to your Maoritanga
And the treasures of your ancestors
As a kiwi-feather cloak for your shoulders
Forever,
Forever and ever.

Translation by Hera Kātene-Horvath

Pan in Battle

('L.S.')

Remembering dark trees of home that keep
Their rivers flowing and their valleys green—
Tendril-delicate smells, or a trunk of bees:
The leafy god within my heart has found
Another haven in these olive trees . . .
Roofed by the wave of their wind-rippled sheen
From the bare menace of the droning skies,
From curiosity of camera-d eyes,
(Trench shadow-hidden in their olive loam).
A little while these crooked trunks were home;
Some are quick crosses to the quiet now,
But men remember their green breathing space,
The short sleep in the sweet summer night,
(All fate marching with the earliest light)
And the rifle hanging from the bough.

(1942)

RUTH FRANCE ('PAUL HENDERSON')
(1913–1967)

Return Journey

Wellington again slaps the face with wind
So well remembered; and now the mind
Leaps; all sea, all tossed hills, all white-
Edged air poured in tides over the tight
Town. Bleached bones of houses are hard
To distinguish, at some distance, from a graveyard.

But do not consider death; we have tucked
Too snugly into the valleys; we have mucked
With the rake of time over the tamed
Foreshore. Battering trams; Lambton, lamed
With concrete, has only a hint of ghost waters
On the Quay stranded among elevators.

There is no need to remember swamp-grass,
Or how the first women (let the rain pass,
They had prayed) wept when the hills reared up
Through the mist; and they were trapped
Between sea and cliffed forest. No ship could be
More prisoning than the grey beach at Petone.

No need to consider (here where we have shut
The tiger tight behind iron and concrete)
How we might yet drown deep under the wind;
And the wind die too; and an insect find
(Columbus of his day) the little graveyard town
Set in a still landscape like porcelain.

Shag Rock

This time of pause is as though,
Coming beside the rock and the tide full,
Quite suddenly was found a new country
Where familiar over the bright childhood bar
(Always children exploring the grotto, the green pool)
Cast the old nets, but into a stranger, a cold sea.

Then are the bounds broken, and the mind
Knows no remembered place, but falls
Into the ghostly silence of mirrors, of universe
Crowding under the curved bewildered hand
That, lately alone, perfects its own perils
And will explore, willing, the indicated course.

Will explore, later. Here for a moment dwell
On the years' knowledge of rock, surf, sand
Thrusting in tongues to trip the unwary, low
Lying ship; notice the swerve of bird, and marvel
Not for the strange insinuating omen, the wronged
Habitude, but that we are home, and are here now.

This time of pause is as though,
Coming beside the rock and the tide full,
Quite suddenly was found a new vision;
And seaward over the bright blinding bar
(Fishermen wade the shallows, following the channel)
Ebb the silver, the sloughed sea-scales, and are gone.

M.K. JOSEPH (1914–1981)

Mercury Bay Eclogue
(*For Rachel and David*)

I

The child's castle crumbles; hot air shimmers
Like water working over empty sand.
Summer noon is long and the brown swimmers
For fear of outward currents, lie on land.
With tumbleweed and seashells in its hand
The wind walks, a vigorous noonday ghost
Bearing gifts for an expected guest.

Hull down on horizon, island and yacht
Vanish into blue leaving no trace;
Above my head the nebulae retreat
Dizzily sliding round the bend of space
Winking a last red signal of distress.
Each galaxy or archipelago
Plunges away into the sky or sea.

In the dry noon are all things whirling away?
They are whirling away, but look—the gull's flight,
Stonefall towards the rainbows of the spray
Skim swim and glide on wing up to the light
And in this airy gesture of delight
See wind and sky transformed to bless and warn,
The dance, the transfiguration, the return.

The turning wheels swing the star to harbour
And rock the homing yacht in a deep lull,
Bring children to their tea beneath the arbour,
Domesticate the wind's ghost and pull
Islands to anchor, softly drop the gull

Into his nest of burnished stones and lead
The yachtsmen and the swimmers to their bed.

II

A shepherd on a bicycle
Breaks the pose of pastoral
  But will suffice to keep
  The innocence of sheep.

Ringing his bell he drives the flock
From sleepy field and wind-scarred rock
  To where the creaming seas
  Wash shoreward like a fleece.

The farmer and his wife emerge
All golden from the ocean-surge
  Their limbs and children speak
  The legend of the Greek.

The shadowy tents beneath the pines
The surfboards and the fishing-lines
  Tell that our life might be
  One of simplicity.

The wind strums aeolian lyres
Inshore among the telephone wires
  Linking each to each.
  The city and the beach.

For sunburnt sleepers would not come
If inland factories did not hum
  And this Arcadian state
  Is built on butterfat.

So children burn the seastained wood
And tell the present as a good
  Knowing that bonfires are
  Important as a star.

And on his gibbet the swordfish raised
With bloody beak and eye glazed
  Glares down into the tide
  Astonishment and pride.

Machine once muscled with delight
He merges now in primitive night;
  The mild and wondering crowd
  Admire the dying god
  Where Kupe and where Cook have trod.

III

Over the sea lie Europe and Asia
  The dead moulded in snow
The persecution of nuns and intellectuals
  The clever and the gentle
The political trials and punishment camps
  The perversion of children
Men withering away with fear of the end.

Fifteen years of a bad conscience
  Over Spain and Poland
Vienna Berlin Israel Korea
  Orphans and prostitutes
Unburied the dead and homeless living
  We looked on ruined cities
Saying, These are our people.

We sat in the sun enduring good luck
  Like the stain of original sin
Trying to be as God, to shoulder
  The world's great sorrow
Too shaken to see that we hadn't the talent
  That the clenching heart is a fist
And a man's grasp the reach of his arm.

Be still and know: the passionate intellect
  Prepares great labours
Building of bridges, practice of medicine.

Still there are cows to be milked
Students to teach, traffic direction
    Ships unloading at wharves
And the composition of symphonies.

IV

The poets standing on the shelf
Excavate the buried self
Freud's injunction they obey
Where id was, let ego be.

Yeats who from his tower sees
The interlocking vortices
Of the present and the past,
Shall find the centre hold at last.

Eliot whose early taste
Was for the cenobitic waste
Now finds the promise of a pardon
Through children's laughter in the locked garden.

Pound in his barbed-wire cage
Prodded into stuttering rage
Still earns reverence from each
Because he purified our speech.

Cavalier or toreador
Is Campbell expert to explore
The truthful moment when we face
The black bull in the arid place.

And Auden who has seen too much
Of the wound weeping for the healer's touch
A surgeon in his rubber gloves
Now cauterises where he loves.

The summer landscape understood
The morning news, the poet's mood,

By their imperatives are defined
Converging patterns in the mind.

V

Come fleet Mercury, messenger of gods and men
Skim with your winged sandal the resounding surf
Quickly come bearing to all things human
Celestial medicine for their tongueless grief.
Heaven's thief and merchant, here is your port
Lave with your gifts of healing and of speech
All mortals who shall ever print with foot
These silent hills and this forsaken beach.

Come sweet Venus, mother of men and beasts
While meteors fall across the yellow moon
Above the hills herded like sleeping beasts,
Gently come, lady, and with hand serene
Plant fruits of peace where by this mariner's mark
The torrents of your sea-begetting roar
And trouble in their dreams of glowing dark
These sleeping hills and this forbidden shore.

Come swift ship and welcome navigators
Link and line with your instruments this earth
To heaven under the propitious stars,
Show forth the joined and fortune-bearing birth
And set this fallen stone a meteorite
Where Mercury and Venus hand in hand
Walk on the waters this auspicious night
And touch to swift love this forgotten strand.

Whitianga, January 1952

Distilled Water

From Blenheim's clocktower a cheerful bell bangs out
The hour, and time hangs humming in the wind.
Time and the honoured dead. What else? The odd
Remote and shabby peace of a provincial town.
Blenkinsopp's gun? the Wairau massacre?
Squabbles in a remote part of empire.
Some history. Some history, but not much.

Consider now the nature of distilled
Water which has boiled and left behind
In the retort rewarding sediment
Of salts and toxins. Chemically pure of course
(No foreign bodies here) but to the taste
Tasteless and flat. Let it spill on the ground,
Leach out its salts, accumulate its algae,
Be living: the savour's in impurity.
Is that what we are? something that boiled away
In the steaming flask of nineteenth century Europe?
Innocuous until now, or just beginning
To make its own impression on the tongue.

And through the Tory Channel naked hills
Gully and slip pass by, monotonously dramatic
Like bad blank verse, till one cries out for
Enjambement, equivalence, modulation,
The studied accent of the human voice,
Or the passage opening through the windy headlands
Where the snowed Kaikouras hang in the air like mirage
And the nation of gulls assembles on the waters
Of the salt sea that walks about the world.

Girl, Boy, Flower, Bicycle

This girl
Waits at the corner for
This boy
Freewheeling on his bicycle.
She holds
A flower in her hand
A gold flower
In her hands she holds
The sun.
With power between his thighs
The boy
Comes smiling to her
He rides
A bicycle that glitters like
The wind.
This boy this girl
They walk
In step with the wind
Arm in arm
They climb the level street
To where
Laid on the glittering handlebars
The flower
Is round and shining as
The sun.

Epilogue to a Poetry Reading

Ladies and gentlemen, that is the end of the
    programme.
You may think you have been entertained (we hope you
    have)
But don't be deceived, you have also been—'got at'.
For the poet is like a kindly children's physician

Dazzling the young patients' eyes with baubles and
   vanishing coins
And just when you least expect it, *in* goes the
   hypodermic;
For Apollo the god of medicine is also the lord of verse
(Keeping the Muses nine in a kind of platonic harem)
And the poet is also a doctor, a mountebank if you like,
Or bluntly, a quack. Though his nostrums won't always
   cure
He has an infallible knack of diagnosis.

Or since we are met in a picture-gallery, let's change
   the metaphor
Saying with Horace that poems resemble pictures—
An old and fallacious belief, yet true since the poet
Is also Madam Zaza, the figure with the crystal ball
In which can be seen the past, the present, the future,
Three scenes in which you, we, everyone, have a part.
Think then of a kind of triptych, three tall panels
In each of which there is something of each of us,
somewhere.

On the left, the past, small and clear like an old monk's
   missal—

The swarthy ploughman in his green hood pushes his
   plough
Behind two round-eyed oxen, and bent to labour
He ignores the swifts who tumble away in a cold breeze
Towards the white castle from whose gate emerges a
   procession
Of horsemen in blue and crimson, and seigneurs and
   ladies
Canter across the watermeadows into the woods,
Where horns are winding and dogs bell-mouthed give
   tongue
At running boars, and a tall stag bears a gold
Cross between his antlers. Yet for none will he stand
At gaze until the hunter-prince shall turn hermit.

The main panel, the largest and least composed, is the
   present—

In our centre, the shaft of day moves like a spotlight
Leaping across continents in whose bays the entrails of
   ocean-
Liners are rummaged by cranes, and whose angular
   mountains
Are threaded by the steel tape of railways, and whose
   skies are eyed
By the lenses of telescopes, and whose air trembles with
   the echoes
Of radios and the mutter of motors and the nightglare
   of towns.
Here a policevan gongs down empty streets
And here the frenzied fans mob a popstar,
Here are barbed wire and machineguns, and here are
   parliaments
And powerhouses, ballets and bookshops, and mothers
   walking
Their children in sunlit parks. All clocks are striking
Noon together, as three jetplanes slide
Across the air, toward the city of windowed monoliths.

On the right, split clear down the middle, an attempt
To present insoluble enigmas in human terms, the
   future—

All things are possible on this plateau, where at one
   side
A forest blazes, and on the other, glaciers splinter
Into icebergs and between are the terraced hills crowned
With strange towers and crowded with simple but un-
Intelligible machines, for here are earthquake and
   famine,
Plague and buried cities, yet here are men
And women standing in gentle light, absorbed
In unknown activities of mathematics intricate
As dreams and starships of unusual design. From the
   clouds
Two hands offer lightning or music, but not both.

from Leah

2 Jacob

Laban, I curse you for this trick you played!
What have I done that you should use me so?
Your herded cattle fatten in the shade;
Their harvest in, your wine-vats overflow.

Only my corn is blighted in the ear,
Only my grapes tread vinegar for wine,
Have I not served you well this seven year?
By law and love the guerdon claimed was mine.

From that first hour I saw her at the well
Leaning her pitcher and her beauty down,
Her red mouth laughing as the bright drops fell
Like truant rain from brim to flowing gown

My heart was Rachel's—and the longest day
But brief, could it be ended at her knees,
Her hands enticing weariness away,
Her voice a music in the olive trees.

What shall requite her for this mischief done?
And what undo his infinite despair
Who clasped the moon, believing it the sun,
And crying 'Rachel' drowned in Leah's hair.

Green Hammock, White Magnolia Tree
(F.M.G.)

They cannot speak who have no words to say.
If, in my songs, I have not sung of you
It is because I could not find a way.

How in the grace-note of a phrase convey
Such melody, such cadence as we knew?
They cannot speak who have no words to say.

What metaphor, what image dare obey
Love's first command, the praise that is your due?
And though I seek, I have not found a way.

It is the past, the memories that betray,
The backward look, the introspective view,
They cannot speak who have no words to say.

Green hammock, white magnolia, yesterday,
The haunted bough, the great flowers choked with
   dew—
Love, it is here words lost and lose their way.

Is there no homage that my heart can pay?
You were the sun in whose clear light we grew;
But it is vain; I have not found a way.
They cannot speak who have no words to say.

The Islands Where I was Born

I

Fragrances that like a wind disturb
The child's pacific dry in suburban shell
And send it murmuring through time's bony curb
Have caught me in the glassbright thoroughfare:
Pineapples oranges limes, their island smell
A catspaw rocking heart to hoist and dare
The long remembrance. Heart, if you would mime
Journeys to where a child blinked half the truth
Let points of origin be fixed where time
May be measured for a meaningful azimuth;
Your flowery isles are masked in Medusa's blood
And the sapphiry elements wear a darker hood.

II

There was no Pacific then, reef-broken spray
Flared on extremities of childish vision,
Under the mango tree's dim acre, at play
In sunflower groves I lived my changeless season.

When insular hours with morning steps unfurled
Chickens and coconuts, bronze fisherboy,
And old deaf Ka Ngutu's wagon howled
Past the tree of flying foxes it seemed that joy

Was born like my shadow in the sun's presence
With fuming orange in hand and the everywhere
Odour steaming from copra's oily crescents
Soothed and smoothed the least rebellious air.

Then foster speech of my Friendly Islands tongue
Could wag its music, the Ofa Atu sworn

With a white smile and all sweet change sung
For trade or gift or guile where I was born.

And I didn't believe in that realm of banished fairies
The Graveyard of Disobedient Children and hushed
Sleepers who once ran hatless, ate tapu'd berries
Or cut their feet on coral and never confessed.

For then I thought we lived on the only route,
In the apple of a heavenly eye, the fond
Providence of flowery oils and fruit,
Kingdom of Joy and Enjoy to the farthest frond.

It was out of all reckoning one last Steamer Day
When I saw the Pacific skyward beyond our coral;
Farewells fluttered . . . palm-trees turned away
And cool on my cheeks the wind from a new littoral.

III

The key was your clear maternal voice
In stories drolled like a deepsea shell
Except they smacked of human salt
And fancy that your witty mind
Spun from the long-fetched tale,
But colour was counted less than fault
Since truth was nearest to be found
In the swift light of your humorous eyes.

Friends at our fireside listened and laughed.
I blazed with private wonder.
You spoke of places I knew when small
But Oh how far may living stretch?
How many fathoms does heart fall under?
And mind grows—how many mountains tall?
The world's wild wisdom sang out of reach
Till one had learned its tortuous craft.

IV

They were our legends, we flagged them on our lives;
Though tattered with telling I wouldn't haul them
   down!
Sometimes you remembered the two days' journey
—in a boat rigged with twine, leaking at every seam.
When a tall sea rushed upon us
Thrust the roaring tongue-tip of its swell
Under the boozing timbers, how they groaned,
   staggered down!
One small rusty tin was our bailer
And this I scooped in the settling weight of our death
While the Tongan crew prayed and sang for mercy of
   our lives.
And how we survived, by craft or prayer or bailer
Seems crazy now, and the last thing to be dreamed
That land's relief humped on the reddening west.'
      'Jiali was the girl from Nukualofa
Swam forty miles from where a boat went down.
Through the sun-beaten, shark-schooled waters
Armed with a high heart swam the long day home;
When, her hair snatched on coral, the foaming breakers
Shelved her torn and screaming on the reef,
      She said a spirit wouldn't let her drown.'
'Hunting one brilliant midnight by calm lagoon
And burning copra to range the wild pigs near,
No grunting, no scuffle we heard, no sound
But where our horses pulled on their tethered reins
And the inward step by step of mounting fear.
Then smashing mirrored light with gulching waves
Lunged to the shoregrass out of the lagoon
A huge sea-beast, ball-eyed, long-necked, frill-maned.
Leaping to horse we saw with twisted glance
That image, unforgettable, reared at the moon.'
      'Once on an island voyage
A mating of whales, the thing most rarely seen;
How she, pale belly up, lay still on the moving blue,
And was the centre of the circling bull;
How whorling out to the rim of the sky he turned
And shirring a leaguelong wake flashed for his centre.

And they at the clash stood up like two enormous
    columns,
Fell with splashing thunder, rolled over and under,
Down through the sealight's fathoms, into the ocean's
    night.'
        'Eua Iki! Quite lacking in mementoes
And I never thought to bring back seeds and cuttings.
Rips, foam-fierce, guarded the narrow entry,
Bucking between the reefs you were cannoned ashore.
They were silks of sand one stepped on, warm and
    shining
As the island's phantasy. No one would believe .
Flowers, but I can't name them,
Stemmed perhaps from that oldest and richest of
    gardens.
        We skipped on ropes of orchids
In moist rock-hollows hung with trumpeting vines;
        Roamed little valleys
Where grass like green mice meadowed tiny ponies;
        Bathed in crystal—
Clear sweet fathoms, watching jewels of fish in the
    coral-trees—
(They matched I thought the giant butterflies in the
    sun's gleam.)
        Slept at last to the island's
Soft Ariel untragic sigh of a futureless dream.
Sometimes I wonder was it really so.'
Years later you remembered
'Eua Iki lies on the edge of the Tongan Deep.'

V

The stars that sing for recollective sails
With no iron pulling at the point of pleasure
Are child and dreamer exulting in fabled isles
That Maui fished out of the dolphined azure.

'The goldless age where gold disturbs no dreams',
So Byron burning for a south could sigh
With lovesweet oil of his romantic themes
Drawn from the leaves of Mariner and Bligh.

Perhaps that goldless age is the fruit-full sense
Of the islands where I was born, when servitor
Of earthly wishes the sun spreads an immense
Glitter over the Deep's unfathomable sore.

The Tongan Deep! Like death's gut or time's cleft
One grinding yard for dug-out galleon schooner,
Husking bones and bells to pelagic drift,
Repelling our brightest reason, the quick lunar

Tides of our laughter and grief with a quietest mouth.
Thereover we blue-weather-wise would sail
Leaving the wounded day unturned for truth
But mind hears soundings, haulnets a dragon's scale

And must pursue beyond the serving sun
Its utter depth; as Oh, wild-fire-west hurled
To the cod of the track its vast hurricane
Of gilded dreams across the nescient world.

But old as man the island ghosts that rise
From sacrificial stones, purgations of history,
Rinse with undying rains our turnaway eyes
Till the coiled mountain sombres the sapphire sea.

Fear we to know these things? The changing wind
Itself must halt before the Royal Tombs,
Old Lord Tortoise wanders battered and blind
Who shielded his sleep against a thousand dooms;

So in the metropolis panged by the day's alarms
Sail for that strength of witness you recall
By heart to the Friendly Kingdom, its crooked palms
Shall say what pacific hands environ all.

VI

Who is the dancer
Sways at her anchorage
By the salt grave?
The palmtree our sister
Of Adam's red clay;
Slantset by hurricane

Stripped to bone courage
She claps like a scaredevil
Through the moon's and sun's day.

Who are the singers
With timebeat and palmclap
Shake the green grave?
Brown lass, brown lad,
Of sweet banqueting heart:
Earth's night is long
But laughing they clip
Hibiscus and jasmine
In their hair, in their song.

A Simple Matter

So now I'm brooding moodily upon
a bunch of dry dark stems transplanted
when it was a thyme bush thriving green
and I counting on the use ahead,

having forgotten something: its
harsh integrity that likes a tried-
by-fire soil, even a soil that pits
volcanic years against the sharp spade.

I thought how it would like this richer earth
and stoneless tilth, how it would grow here
happier than in that garden with
rough pocked lava strewn everywhere,

forgetting then what I once
had proved with my own eyes and nose: the
sunswept stony uplands of Provence
were thyme's old and true nativity.

Borage, lavender, marjoram,
make a warm site their chief condition
and here have they flourished; only thyme
suffers for a rock to lean upon.

Pencilled by the Rain

1

All walking leans to the left
as time and heart
beat blindly back
to an early luminous pain
and the mountain
on whose slopes we were born
towers before us in the sunset.
From the plucking of the first flower
the pricking of the first thorn
to the last shiver
of the bare branches
in the night wind
all time is illusion
and the end
a cutover waste
where the pukeko screams defiance
at the harrier
circling her nest.

2

Sunrise discovers Cook
still charting imponderable seas.
The long land lies
like the trunk of a tree
washed up by the tide
or the green thigh-bone
of a fallen mountain.
Here at the world's end
we're not exempt
from the harvest of folly.

At our roots
burn Europe's poisons. You'll find
no primal innocence beneath the fern.

3

blue tides of summer
ebbing down
the mussel beaches
of the sky
the heron fossicking the marsh
stands poised
above his yellow eye
autumn
and mist like mown rushes
lies in fallen swathes
along the roots of the mountain

4

Some day shall I too shrug
off loyalty?
below the wing-tip
watch for the last time
the sombre hills
thin-pencilled by the rain and the muscled gull
stride
the enduring sea?

5

There's not much time for cleverness
but a little maybe for love
for this hour I speak
for no other
although I know the lovers
leaning upon the dark
will not heed my words
nor need
any food but each other.

6

So I wander the ways of a squandered country
  till courage quails, purpose and energy flag
   at an empty crossroads
     where a sign-post sagging to dust and weeds
       confuses direction
            and I lose
              the inaccessible name.

7

Beyond the sill
of peripheral mind
walls fall
to footsteps
clattering down the abyss.
Ah! shut the window
hold up a hand
against the traffic
pull down the stars
to light the hour.

8

For you and your kind
I would have built
a tower of words
on an iron crag
but my blows were wild
and this poor ramshackle
lean-to must suffice
to roof my casual phrases
from the rain.

The Wife Speaks

Being a woman, I am
not more than man nor less
but answer imperatives
of shape and growth. The bone
attests the girl with dolls,
grown up to know the moon
unwind her tides to chafe
the heart. A house designs
my day an artifact
of care to set the hands
of clocks, and hours are round
with asking eyes. Night puts
an ear on silence where
a child may cry. I close
my books and know events
are people, and all roads
everywhere walk home
women and men, to take
history under their roofs.
I see Icarus fall
out of the sky, beside
my door, not beautiful,
envy of angels, but feathered
for a bloody death.

Sestina

The body of my love is a familiar country
read at the fingertip, as all children learn
their first landscape. This is the accepted face

secure of harm, in whose eye I am at home
and put on beauty as the thorn in autumn wears
its bright berry, the sky its haycock summer of cloud.

And here in a miracle season no storms cloud
our halcyon day nor prophet stains a green country
with wry mouth twisted to what vision wears
his own griefs. Music is struck off rocks, we learn
the sun ripening behind walls of flesh, the bird called
    home
pilgrim tracing with sure wing a world's face.

He whom I love is more near than this one face
shaped for me at my beginning, dispersed like cloud
in death's careless weather. At the end we come home
to the same bed, fallen like stones or stars in a country
no one travels. Only the mindless winds learn
our history, yet for us each man his mourning wears.

We are what we have been. The living creature wears
like trees his grain of good and evil years. The face
is schooled by daily argument of pain to learn
disguises for the private wound. None knows what
    country
lies under the shut skull, or dazzling beacon of cloud
beckons the always outcast through stubborn exile
    home.

This dear shell, this curve my hand follows, is home
also to the stranger I may not meet, who wears
deeper than tears his secret need. He walks a country
I cannot touch or reach, where the remembered face
burns under brittle glass of winter, and every cloud
holds in its core of ice the dream I may not learn.

Or is he Orpheus, leaving my daylight kingdom to learn
Eurydice for whom he enters the dark god's home?
Hermes, show him this woman, in her cerecloth cloud
of sleep! She is not prey to the subtle worm which
    wears

already at my cheek. No word unlocks her face
or voice answers him out of that silent country.

Yet always we ride out winter and the face
of famine. We return, and O then morning wears
mountains, our signal joy climbing a cloud.

Put Off Constricting Day

Husband, put down Spinoza, Pericles,
the seventeenth century, even the new
nemesis striding after doll or moll.
Private eye or dick, they'll crack the case
as wide as any yawn I'll give, waiting
for bed and casual goodnight.
                      And now
put off constricting day, let sleep release
the obedient body from necessities
of action and response imposed by wills
other, alien, indifferent or hating.

Am I another such, not wife, nearer
than these, more culpable of harm and pain?
Or less, not noticed but by my default?
Look now, before you sleep, am I not still
the one you sought on winter-walking streets,
adding your breath, lonely, to fog and rain?
Then the incendiary blood burned up to spill
its brilliant meteors, crystals of fire
ardent to strike, in doubly shared assault,
from the expectant flesh an answering heat.

Milking before Dawn

In the drifting rain the cows in the yard are as black
And wet and shiny as rocks in an ebbing tide;
But they smell of the soil, as leaves lying under trees
Smell of the soil, damp and steaming, warm.
The shed is an island of light and warmth, the night
Was water-cold and starless out in the paddock.

Crouched on the stool, hearing only the beat
The monotonous beat and hiss of the smooth machines,
The choking gasp of the cups and rattle of hooves,
How easy to fall asleep again, to think
Of the man in the city asleep; he does not feel
The night encircle him, the grasp of mud.

But now the hills in the east return, are soft
And grey with mist, the night recedes, and the rain.
The earth as it turns towards the sun is young
Again, renewed, its history wiped away
Like the tears of a child. Can the earth be young again
And not the heart? Let the man in the city sleep.

from Letter to a Chinese Poet

4 Clouds on the Sea

I walk among men with tall bones,
With shoes of leather, and pink faces;
I meet no man holding a begging bowl;
All have their dwelling places.

In my country
Every child is taught to read and write,
Every child has shoes and a warm coat,
Every child must eat his dinner,
No one must grow any thinner;
It is considered remarkable and not nice
To meet bed-bugs or lice.
Oh we live like the rich
With music at the touch of a switch,
Light in the middle of the night,
Water in the house as from a spring,
Hot, if you wish, or cold, anything
For the comfort of the flesh,
In my country. Fragment
Of new skin at the edge of the world's ulcer.

For the question
That troubled you as you watched the reapers
And a poor woman following,
Gleaning the ears on the ground,
Why should I have grain and this woman none?
No satisfactory answer has been found.

8 Autumn Wind

Words would not have come to write to you
If I had not seen into your heart
As into water,
In a song you made in pity
When a slave-girl ran away,
Water lying over stones,
Transparent,
As at the temple of Wu-Chên,
Or here, by any mountain-side.
Meditating on the symbol of the clear pool,
How could your heart not become clear?

Well you knew,
As the girl did not,
The world beyond the courtyard wall,

And yet, I think you, too, would have run away,
For you were always straining at the world's leash
And had bitterness in your tongue
For every kind of cage.

The tale has grown old,
The unfinished event; something or someone lost
Unaccountably and never found.
We leave the door open for an answer
And only the autumn wind blows,
Idly heaping the leaves against the step.

In the women's rooms the air grows weary.
Embroidery . . . heavily scented hair.
Where is the peasant's daughter who could forget
Though she grew in rags and pain
The taste of the fields and the sweet wind?
This you understood,
Coming from the hills and keeping
Open to the moods of earth and sky,
Sitting still and quiet as a pond,
Out of tune with the social stir.

In the Giant's Castle

My father remembered what it was to be small,
And to nourish rebellion.
My father in the night concocted
From vinegar, brown paper, pepper,
A hot plaster for my jumping ear,
Which was much the same as waving a wand.
I could show you my tommy-axed finger
Bound together without stitches,

Or tell you how my father became a wall
And relied on me to stand as firm
While a doctor scissored off my crushed nail.
But when I grew, and climbed

The hill Difficulty, and at length
Came face to face with Giant Despair,
My father was not there.
Just his initials marked on a stone.

Photographs of Pioneer Women

You can see from their faces
Life was not funny,
The streets, when there were streets,
Tugging at axles,
The settlement ramshackle as a stack of cards.
And where there were no streets, and no houses,
Save their own roof of calico or thatch,
The cows coming morning and afternoon
From the end-of-world swamp,
Udders cemented with mud.

There is nothing to equal pioneering labour
For wrenching a woman out of shape,
Like an old willow, uprooted, thickening.
See their strong arms, their shoulders broadened
By the rhythmical swing of the axe, or humped
Under loads they donkeyed on their backs.
Some of them found time to be photographed,
With bearded husband, and twelve or thirteen children,
Looking shocked, but relentless,
After first starching the frills in their caps.

Girl with Pitcher

The lion and his shadow the lioness
Stalk the terraces above the river.

I balance my pitcher and must pass them.
Terror sticks from my back like an arrow.

I slip with the move-
                    ment of air through the sedges.

The river is not evaporated, as I feared.
I paddle in its shining verge,
Then dip my pitcher full of clear water.
I listen for the sound of the lion's shadow.

Telemachus with a Transistor

A musical man is walking along the shore,
In rags and old sandals, wrist weighted

With voices packaged in London or New York,
Turning down the waves around him,

Beat of tomtoms linking eardrums
To something he can't quite remember,

Thump of his mother's heart, they say,
In the womb beside his own.

Narrowed to rhythms of the blood
Watch the senses grow selective, eyes

Respond to outlines of a human form
As ducklings learn to follow ducks.

It is no longer important, whether
The sea is rough or calm,

Sailing times ill-omened or propitious,
No voyage is contemplated.

Between the wet water and dry hillside
Without eyes, with specialized ears,

The musical man (make way) is walking,
Is walking, make way for the musical man.

KŌHINE WHAKARUA PŌNIKA
(b. 1920; Tūhoe, Ngāti Porou)

He waiata murimuri-aroha

Ka korikori ake i raro rā i te ata o Tongariro maunga
Ka tū au ka wawata, ko wai rā taku iwi
Ko wai rā taku ihi, taku wana, taku tū
Ka hoki ngā mahara, ki te pane o Pūtauaki
Kei tua ko te papa e arohatia nei e
He tohu i taku tūranga waewae, taku noho mauri-tau e

Ka rite ki te rimu teretere i te moana
Ka pari i te akau, te moana i Taupō
Tākiri ko te ata, mau mai ko ahau e tuohu noa ana e—
Ka aupaki kau ake, ki te ārai uhi mai
Kei tua ko koutou, e kui mā, e koro mā, e hika mā, e
    tā mā e—
Ka huri ka titiro ki te ao whai muri e

He oha nā te whaea
E tipu te whakareanga nei, e tipu e
Nāku rā koe i rauhī, i here ki taku pito
Nāku anō koe i pēhi, rutu ake,
I maunu mai ai tō matihe
Tihe! i mauri ora
I ngāngā ai tō waha areare ki te ao mārama e-ai-a

A song of yearning

Beneath the shadow of Tongariro mountain
I stir to a new surrounding
Thoughts fill with anxiety—where am I, who am I, and
    all that I have left behind

The mind penetrates to the peak of Putauaki
Where it shadows from my view the land that I love
The place where I was born—my home sweet home

I'm classed as a seaweed now that drifts in the ocean to
   be stranded by the waves, on the shores of Lake Taupo
Breaks the dawn, and I am caught, in meditation
A gesture of the hand, to an imaginary curtain that veils
   the old folks, the dear ones, the loved ones, gone on
Then, I turn and cast my eyes on the young world,
   moving in

A mother's last words
Grow, the young generation—grow
It was I who nurtured the seed, that was tied to my
   navel
Again it was I who laboured for its rude awakening,
   exhorting the sneeze of life, and the loud burst of the
      lungs
To herald new entry into this world

Translation by Kōhine Whakarua Pōnika

Karanga! karanga!

Karanga! karanga! karanga! karanga rā!
Karanga rā Aotearoa e
I ngā iwi o te motu e
Haere mai rā, haere mai rā, haere mai rā
Ki aku mahi e
Tukua rā ngā kupenga
Kia haere ana i waho e
Tōia mai, kumea mai, tōia mai
Ā tāua mahi e
Ka huri au, ka titiro
Ka huri au, ka whakarongo
Ka huri au, ka tahuri

Ki te awhi mai
I aku aha?
I aku mahi a aku tīpuna e
Te haka tēnā, te poi tēnā, te mahi-ā-ringaringa e
Te hiki i taku mere, i taku taiaha
Te mana, taku ihi e
Pupuritia!
Takahia! takahia!
Kia whakarongo ai ngā iwi
Pupuritia! pupuritia! pupuritia ā tāua mahi e

Call together

Call and assemble together Aotearoa
All the tribes throughout the land
Come and give your support
To my cultural activities
Let the nets be cast
Cast them far and wide
Then drag them back in
Filled with our cultural pursuits
I turn about and look
I turn about and listen
I turn about and begin to embrace all things
What, for instance?
The cultural heritage of my ancestors!
The haka, the poi and the action song
The use of the mere and the taiaha
My prestige, these awe-inspiring activities
I hang onto firmly!
Now tramp your foot
So that all will hear
Retain, and cling to
Our cultural heritage

*Translation by Sam Karetu and the Advisory Committee
for the Teaching of the Maori Language*

Mid Winter

Some newness of the heart I would discern
Imaged upon the nadir of the year.

Continuous cold, the palely flashing sun,
The chill white powder on the dark-brown earth

Proclaim to man, dispirited against them,
An ebb more total than his human weakness.

So may he dream of a despair
In whose still clime such winter-roses bloom

And know a decline purer than his life,
A course for all the ruin in his blood.

At the Discharge of Cannon Rise
the Drowned

One forfeit more from life the current claimed
While, on the horizon, rose white-sheeted spars;
Bare of their canvas when the morning came
They rode the bay that held its prisoner.

Some days then, by our time, of windless rain
That poured and ebbed to shroud or almost show
The unpeopled decks, the looming guardian
On the phantasmal world where no clock marks
Duration of the cold abandonments
And weird acceptances that lead man hence.

Till from the flickering scene one stark vignette
Glares in ambiguous hues of hope and death—
Out of a port-hole bursts a smear of flame,
A blast of thunder from the flood rebounds.
With gliding leap, impelled by answering fire,
Lazarus rises from his restless couch.

Now his corrupted life is as the charge
Exploded in the cannon's narrow depth.
Native no longer of the earth, he springs,
Breaking the waters he surrendered in
And, as he leaves the limbo of vague dream,
Out of the wash and weed he plucks his death.

Back, then, from harbour to the mounting storm,
Into the gale that blows from their high port,
Back from mortality the vast sails slide.

Barbarossa

Addiction to the exceptional event—
That flaw
In something like *My Childhood Days in X*,
And fault-line—as from the Aleutians
Down the Pacific to where I was when
It opened wide one day when I was ten.

The town-hall whistle blows. It's five
To twelve. Now homewards, slow,
Turning a legend like a stone, sea-worn,
Red-streaked. The bearded Emperor in the German cave
Sits in his armour; when will he wake and go
Clanking into the light to lead his hordes?

The gutters heave.
           Upon the rumbling ground
I balance. I sit down.

A stop to stories of the death of kings.
I watch the telegraph
Poles. A great hand plucks the strings.

Upon the other coast Napier, too, sways
Most irrecoverably: flames. Looters are shot
By landing-parties near the gutted shops.
Half a hill
Spilt on the coast-road; squashed in their ancient Fords
The burghers sit there still.

What is Happening Now?

To get a fix on it
I need to have
Three witnesses
In different houses met.

It is the distillate
Of all their lies
I wait. To give the whole harshness
In one sweet swoop.

Conclusions
The mind cannot escape:
The trying hard
May yield some sort of grace.

The streaked façade
Provides a sense of life,
The circus girl
In mauve on the high rope.

The heart may fail
For the illusions
It cherishes
Though it need not.

KĪNGI M. ĪHAKA
(b. 1921; Te Aupōuri, Ngāti Kahu, Te Rarawa,
Ngāpuhi, Waikato)

Te Atairangikaahu
*(Composed especially in honour of Te Ariki Nui,
Dame Te Atairangikaahu, D.B.E.)*

Kia mau ko te rongo ki te whenua,
Te whakaaro pai ki ngā tāngata;
Rau rangatira mā, ngā reo, ngā mana,
Ko te koha paihere i a tātou
Ko te aroha

te kaea	E—tēnā i whiua!
	E piki mai kake mai e ngā iwi o te motu
	Ki runga i a Tāmaki e tū nei!
te katoa	E—hei aha tērā!
	E—haere mai koe i te pōhiritanga o taku manu
	Haere mai koe i te pōhiritanga o taku manu
te kaea	E—ngā mana!
te katoa	Nekenekehia!
te kaea	E—ngā waka!
te katoa	Kumekumea tōtōia ki runga te marae! Kss auē!

1

Pākia mai au e te marangai
Tū ana au i te pūwaha o Waikato;
Titiro atu au ki runga ki Taupiri
Ko Kīngi Potatau he tupua,
Te mauri o te motu he taniwha rā;
Noho mai te torona tapu o ō tūpuna
Te Atairangikaahu e!

2

E tangi e rere e ngā wai o Waikato
Ki ngā aituā o te motu,
Kua eke ki runga Tūrangawaewae marae
Kia tangi kia mihi ngā iwi,
Ringihia te roimata ka ea ngā mate;
Noho mai te torona tapu o ō tūpuna
Te Atairangikaahu e!

3

Ko Tainui te waka Waikato te iwi nui
Kua rūpeke mai ngā hau e whā
Ki te āwhina te kaupapa o tēnei rā:
Me kore e rite te ōhākī;
Tuituia tātou katoa kia kotahi rā;
Tēnei tā koutou mokopuna e noho nei,
Te Atairangikaahu e!
Te Atairangikaahu e!

Te Atairangikaahu

May peace be established throughout the land
And goodwill permeate mankind;
The chiefs, the orators, the leaders,
The gift which binds us all
Is love.

Haka

leader	Begin with a swing!
	Approach, ascend, the people of the land
	Upon Tamaki which greets you!
chorus	Ah! Let it be!
	For you have come in response to the call of my bird,
	For you have indeed come in response to the call of my bird.

leader	All leaders!
chorus	Draw closer!
leader	All canoes!
chorus	Haul and drag them on to this marae!

1

It was an easterly breeze which struck me
Causing me to land at the source of Waikato;
I gaze up to the summit of Taupiri
And there stands Kingi Potatau, a demigod,
The 'life principle' of the land, a supreme chief.
Long may you hold the sacred sovereign power of your
    ancestors
Te Atairangikaahu!

2

May the waters of Waikato continue to flow and grieve,
For the misfortunes and disasters of the land
Which are commemorated at Turangawaewae marae
And are deplored; and for which tributes are paid by
    the tribes;
Whilst tears flow to alleviate our sorrows.
Long may you hold the sacred sovereign power of your
    ancestors
Te Atairangikaahu!

3

Tainui the canoe, Waikato the major tribe,
Whilst assembled are the representatives of the 'four
    winds'
To support the basic significance of this day:
Perhaps the legacy may be honoured,
Binding us together that we may be one;
Here then is the guardian of our heritage who is in
    your midst
Even Te Atairangikaahu!

Translation by Kīngi M. Īhaka

KEITH SINCLAIR (b. 1922)

Memorial to a Missionary

Thomas Kendall, 1778–1832, first resident missionary in New Zealand,
author of *The New Zealanders' First Book* (1815), grandfather of the
Australian poet, H.C. Kendall.

Instructed to speak of God with emphasis
On sin and its consequence, to cannibals
Of the evil of sin, he came from father's farm,
The virtuous home, the comfortable chapel,
The village school, so inadequately armed,
His mail of morals tested in drawing-rooms,
Not war, to teach his obscure and pitied pupils.

There were cheers in Clapham, prayers in Lincolnshire,
Psalms on the beaches, praise, O hope above.
Angels sang as he built the south's first school,
For Augustine had landed with the love
Of God at the Bay; he would speak for his aims were
   full
Of Cranmer, Calvin; would teach for he brought the
   world
Of wisdom, dreamed of the countless souls to save.

But though he cried with a voice of bells none heard,
For who was to find salvation in the sounds
Of English words? The scurrilous sailors spoke
More clearly with rum and lusting, so he turned
To the native vowels for symbols, sought to make
The Word of God anew, in the tribes' first book
Laying in Christ's advance a path of nouns.

Seeking the Maori name for sin, for hell,
Teacher turned scholar he sat at Hongi's feet
And guns were the coin he paid for revelation.

To the south men died when Hongi spent his fees.
Wrestling with meanings that defied translation,
Christian in seeking truth found sorcery,
Pilgrim encountered sex in philosophy.

A dreaming hour he spent at that mast of a tree,
And apple of his eye his mother withheld was that
    love,
The night of feeling, was pure and mooned for man,
Woman was made of earth and earth for wife.
In following their minds he found the men
And reached for a vision past his mother-land,
Converted by heathen he had come to save.

He drank the waters of the underworld
Lying all day in the unconverted flesh,
Entangled in old time, before Christ's birth,
Beyond redemption, found what a nest of bliss,
A hot and mushroom love lay fair in the fern
To suck from his soul the lineaments of desire,
And leave despair, O damned undreamed of pleasures.

To cure the sick at soul the little doctor
Sought out an ardent tonic far too hot,
Though not forbidden, for his infirmity.
With the south on his tongue and sweet he had
    forgotten
His mission, thirsted for infinities
Of the secret cider and its thick voice in the throat,
Bringing the sun all a-blossom to his blood.

But as sudden and in between such dawns his
    conscience
Sharpened his sins to prick his heart like nails.
The hell the Christian fears to name was heaven
To his fierce remorse and heaven and hell
Were the day and night in his life and wasted him
With their swift circling passions, until he cursed
In prayers but hated the flush of his concupiscence.

Did he fall through pride of spirit, through arrogance
Or through humility, not scorning the prayers
Of savages and their intricate pantheon?
He lacked the confident pity of his brethren.
To understand he had to sympathize,
Then felt, and feeling, fell, one man a breath
In the human gale of a culture's thousand years.

The unfaithful shepherd was sent from the farm of
   souls
To live, a disgraceful name in the Christian's ear,
A breathing sin among the more tolerant chiefs.
An outcaste there, or preaching where he fled
To Valparaiso from devils and reproof,
Or coasting logs round Sydney, still he strove
To find the life in the words his past had said.

Drowning off Jervis Bay, O the pain,
For death is a virgin rich in maidenheads
And memories, trees two hundred feet and tall.
The sea is a savage maiden, in her legs
Sharp pangs no missionary drank before,
And the immortality that Maui sought.
O move to Hawaiki, to the shadow of Io's breath.

No man had died such a death of dreams and storms,
For drowning with memories came that expected devil.
He was racked on the waves and spirit wrecked he
   wept
For his living sins, each tear-drop swimming with evil.
O soul be chang'd into little water drops
And fall into the ocean ne'er be found!
Dying he shrank from that chief who would seize him
   forever.

But there no tohunga met him, angels flew
To draw his frightened soul quivering to heaven,
Bright there, bright in the open life of light.
Trying to speak known words that the unbelievers

Might know what was said and bring their ears to
   Christ,
He had sung with the spirit, prayed with the
   understanding,
Thus saved the soul he had paid to save the heathen.

His was the plough, he turned the sacred soil
Where others reaped, a pioneer in Christ's
New clearing, strove with unswerving will
Amidst the roots, the rotting stumps and compost
Of the mind to make a bed where the gospel
Might lie down in the breeding sun and grow
A crucifix of leaves, O flowers of crosses.

Immortal in our mouths, and known in heaven,
Yet as we praise we wish him greater—left
On our fractured limb of time, not yet possessed,
Where north will not meet south, of the south's lost
   gift.
Taught of the sinful flesh he never sensed
That to reach for truth was to reach for God, nor found
God immanent in the cannibals' beliefs.

Father he left us a legacy of guilt,
Half that time owed us, who came from the north, was
   given:
We know St Paul, but what in that dreaming hour,
In that night when the ends of time were tied—and
   severed
Again and so ever—did he learn from the south?
He could not turn to teach his countrymen,
And lost (our sorrow), lost our birthright forever.

The bomb is made

The bomb is made will drop on Rangitoto.
Be kind to one another, kiss a little
And let love-making imperceptibly
Grow inwards from a kiss. I've done with soldiering,
Though every day my leave-pass may expire.

The bomb is made will drop on Rangitoto.
The cell of death is formed that multiplied
Will occupy the lung, exclude the air
Be kind to one another, kiss a little—
The first goodbye might each day last forever.

The bomb is made will drop on Rangitoto;
The hand is born that gropes to press the button.
The prodigal grey generals conspire
To dissipate the birth-right of the Asians.
Be kind to one another, kiss a little.

The bomb is made will drop on Rangitoto.
The plane that takes off persons in a hurry
Is only metaphorically leaving town,
So if we linger we will be on time.
Be kind to one another, kiss a little.

The bomb is made will drop on Rangitoto.
I do not want to see that sun-burned harbour.
Islandless as moon, red-skied again.
Its tide unblossomed, sifting wastes of ash.
Be kind to one another, kiss a little,
Our only weapon is this gentleness.

Sonnet from Below the Age Gap

The middle-elderly have wrinkled necks
like crocodile skins or war-time armour plating;
their nostrils and ear-holes begin to bristle like boars'.
All night they snout and root in the lily swamp
yet never seem to sleep like hearty eaters.

Though some burnt out by alcoholic amps
litter the plain they mostly go straight on,
their eyes lit up by eager, cruel fires
and chomp at anything that's in the way,

ingesting girls, great juicy steaks or dreams,
ferns, trees—all fuels—and belch away
while all around smoking horizons crumple.
The middling-aged advance like beaters driving game
or a line of Tiger tanks chewing up Europe.

KUMEROA NGOINGOI PĒWHAIRANGI
(1922–85); Te Whānau-ā-Ruataupare, Ngāti Porou)

Kaua rā hei huri noa

Kaua rā hei huri noa
Kaua hei whakahāwea
Mā ō mahi ka kitea koe
E te ao, e tō iwi Māori
Kua puāwai rawa ngā purapura
I ruia mai i ngā wā o tūā-whakarere
E toro nei ngā kāwai taura tangata
Hei hono i te aroha o ō tāua tīpuna
Te mana, te wehi
Awhitia ngā taonga kei memeha, kei ngaro
Kei tūkinotia e te ao
Puritia tō mana kei riro e!

Do not turn away

Do not turn away
Nor despise others
By your deeds will you be known
By society at large and by your own Maori people
The seeds sown since time immemorial
Are now in full bloom
And the human links are spread far and wide
Forging the love, the prestige, the respect of our
  ancestors

Give all your support to our cultural pursuits
Lest they become lifeless and die
Or be debased by the world at large
Retain your prestige, lest it be lost for all time!

*Translation by Sam Karetu and the Advisory Committee
for the Teaching of the Maori Language*

Ka noho au i konei

Ka noho au i konei, ka whakaaro noa
He pēwhea rā te huri a te ao katoa—
Ngā rongo kino e tukituki nei i te takiwā,
Ngā whakawai e hau nei ngā tamariki!
Kua kore noa he ture hei arataki
Te mana, te ihi ka takahia mai!
Kia kaha tātou ki te whakahoki mai
Te mauri ora me te wairua! Auē, ngā iwi ē!

Tāpaea ngā hē katoa ki runga rawa,
Kei a Ia te ora me te marama!
Kapohia te aroha nui o te Ariki
Māna e kaupare rā ngā kino katoa!
Whītiki, maranga mai, horahia rā
Ngā kupu hei oranga-ā-tinana ē,
Kia noho ai i raro i te maru
O Te Rangimārie, Te Rongopai, auē, me te aroha!
Te Rangimārie, Te Rongopai! Auē, ngā iwi ē!

I sit here

I sit here and keep wondering
About what is happening to this world
The bad news that afflicts us

The distractions that tempt our youth!
There are no laws to show the way
To the mana men trample down!
We must be strong, we must bring back
O my people, our living mauri and our soul!

Give all our troubles into the care
Of the One above, with whom is life and light!
Hold fast to the love of our Lord
Who will turn aside all evils!
We must gather our strength, rise up
And speak the words that will sustain us
That we may live in the shelter
Of God's love and peace!
O my people! God's love and peace!

Translation by Kumeroa Ngoingoi Pēwhairangi

HONE TUWHARE
(b. 1922; Ngāpuhi, Ngāti Korokoro, Ngāti Tautahi,
Te Popote, Uri-o-Hau)

Friend

Do you remember
that wild stretch of land
with the lone tree guarding the point
from the sharp-tongued sea?

The fort we built out of branches
wrenched from the tree, is dead wood now.
The air that was thick with the whirr of
toetoe spears succumbs at last to the grey gull's wheel.

Oyster-studded roots
of the mangrove yield no finer feast
of silver-bellied eels, and sea-snails
cooked in a rusty can.

Allow me to mend the broken ends
of shared days:
but I wanted to say
that the tree we climbed
that gave food and drink
to youthful dreams, is no more.
Pursed to the lips her fine-edged
leaves made whistle—now stamp
no silken tracery on the cracked
clay floor.

Friend,
in this drear
dreamless time I clasp

your hand if only for reassurance
that all our jewelled fantasies were
real and wore splendid rags.

Perhaps the tree
will strike fresh roots again:
give soothing shade to a hurt and
troubled world.

No Ordinary Sun

Tree let your arms fall:
raise them not sharply in supplication
to the bright enhaloed cloud.
Let your arms lack toughness and
resilience for this is no mere axe
to blunt, nor fire to smother.

Your sap shall not rise again
to the moon's pull.
No more incline a deferential head
to the wind's talk, or stir
to the tickle of coursing rain.

Your former shagginess shall not be
wreathed with the delightful flight
of birds nor shield
nor cool the ardour of unheeding
lovers from the monstrous sun.

Tree let your naked arms fall
nor extend vain entreaties to the radiant ball.
This is no gallant monsoon's flash,
no dashing trade wind's blast.
The fading green of your magic

emanations shall not make pure again
these polluted skies . . . for this
is no ordinary sun.

O tree
in the shadowless mountains
the white plains and
the drab sea floor
your end at last is written.

Monologue

I like working near a door. I like to have my work-bench
   close by, with a locker handy.

Here, the cold creeps in under the big doors, and in the
   summer hot dust swirls, clogging the nose. When the
   big doors open to admit a lorry-load of steel,
   conditions do not improve. Even so, I put up with it,
   and wouldn't care to shift to another bench, away from
   the big doors.

As one may imagine this is a noisy place with smoke
   rising, machines thumping and thrusting, people
   kneading, shaping, and putting things together.
   Because I am nearest to the big doors I am the farthest
   away from those who have to come down to shout
   instructions in my ear.

I am the first to greet strangers who drift in through the
   open doors looking for work. I give them as much
   information as they require, direct them to the offices,
   and acknowledge the casual recognition that one
   worker signs to another.

I can always tell the look on the faces of the successful
   ones as they hurry away. The look on the faces of the
   unlucky I know also, but cannot easily forget.

I have worked here for fifteen months.
  It's too good to last.
  Orders will fall off
  and there will be a reduction in staff.
  More people than we can cope with
  will be brought in from other lands:
  people who are also looking
  for something more real, more lasting,
  more permanent maybe, than dying. . . .
  I really ought to be looking for another job
  before the axe falls.

These thoughts I push away, I think that I am lucky
  to have a position by the big doors which open out
  to a short alley leading to the main street; console
  myself that if the worst happened I at least would
  have no great distance to carry my gear and tool-box
  off the premises.

I always like working near a door. I always look for a
  work-bench hard by—in case an earthquake
  occurs and fire breaks out, you know?

Heemi

No point now my friend in telling
you my lady's name.
She wished us well: offered wheels
which spun my son and me like
comets through the lonely night.
You would have called her *Aroha*.

And when we picked up three young
people who'd hitched their way
from the Ninety-Mile Beach to be
with you, I thought: yes
your mana holds, Heemi. Your mana

is love. And suddenly the night
didn't seem lonely anymore.

The car never played up at all.
And after we'd given it a second
gargle at the all-night bowser
it just zoomed on on gulping
easily into the gear changes
up or down.

Because you've been over this road
many times before Heemi, you'd
know about the steady climb ahead
of us still. But once in the tricky
light, Tongariro lumbered briefly
out of the clouds to give us the old
'up you' sign. Which was real friendly.

When we levelled off a bit at the top
of the plateau, the engine heat couldn't
keep the cold from coming in: the fog
swamping thick and slushy, and pressing
whitely against tired eye-balls.

Finally, when we'd eased ourselves
over a couple of humps and down down
the winding metalled road to the river
and Jerusalem, I knew things would be
all right. Glad that others from the
Mainland were arrowing toward the dawn
like us.

Joy for the brother sun chesting over
the brim of the land, and for the three
young blokes flaked out in the back seat
who would make it now, knowing that they
were not called to witness
some mysterious phenomenon of birth on
a dung-littered floor of a stable

but come simply to call
on a tired old mate in a tent
laid out in a box
with no money in the pocket
no fancy halo, no thump left in the old
ticker.

A talk with my cousin, alone

And afterwards, after the shedding of mucus, the droll
    speeches and the hongi for my cousin in the box,
    we were called to meal at the long tables.
    But I hadn't come for that.

I could hear the Tasman combers shredding themselves
    nearby, wishing then for a cawing beak of sound
    to help me reassemble myself. Taking my shoes off,
    I trudged a steep dune; sand, a cool silken lisp
    spilling through my toes.

Bottomed on a hill of sand, I wondered wry dry leaves
    whether the pakeha marine authorities would sell
    us back ephemeral Maori land (now exposed to bird,
    bleached crab and shrimp) lying somewhere between
    low water mark and high.

A pounding gavel is the sun today—a brassy
        auctioneer:
    the sea, his first assistant. Of this, no instant
    favour offered me in stint. I cushion my elbows
    deeper in sand. I'm the only bidder.
    For this beautiful piece of land/sea-scape, I will
    start the bidding at twenty Falling Axes per square
    centimetre, said the sun looking hard at me for an
    ear-lobe twitch, or, other sign.
    Get stuffed, I reply, holding my middle finger
    straight up—and turning it. Slowly.

Idly I think, that after the eleven o'clock prayers
    tomorrow (and before lunch) my cousin will have
    gone to ground.
    'They may ban tangihangas in the future,' I say
    to him. 'Right now, you're doing *your* job. This
    moment is forever as the splayed fingers of the hand
    drawn together, like a fist.' I look up at the sun
    and blink. The sun is beside itself, dancing. There
    are two of them.

Ron Mason

Time has pulled up a chair, dashed
a stinging litre from a jug of wine.
My memory is a sluggard,

I reject your death, but can't dismiss it.
For it was never an occasion for woman
sobs and keenings: your stoic-heart

would not permit it. And that calcium-covered
pump had become a sudden road-block bringing
heavy traffic to a tearing halt.

Your granite-words remain.
Austere fare, but nonetheless adequate for the
honest sustenance they give.

And for myself, a challenge.
A preoccupation now more intensely felt, to tilt
a broken taiaha inexpertly

to my old lady, Hine-nui-te-Po, bless the old
bitch: shrewd guardian of that infrequent *duende*
that you and Lorca knew about, playing hard-to-get.

Easy for you now, man. You've joined your literary
ancestors, whilst I have problems still in finding
mine, lost somewhere

in the confusing swirl, now thick now thin,
Victoriana-Missionary fog hiding legalized land-rape
and gentlemen thugs. Never mind, you've taught me

confidence and ease in dredging for my own bedraggled
myths, and you bet: weighing the China experience
yours and mine. They balance.

Your suit has not the right cut for me except around
the gut. I'll keep the jacket though: dry-cleaned
it'll absorb new armpit sweat.

Ad Dorotheum: She and I together found the poem
you'd left for her behind a photograph.

> *Lest you be a dead man's*
> *slave*
> *Place a branch upon the*
> *grave*
> *Nor allow your term of*
> *grief*
> *To pass the fall of its*
> *last leaf*

'Bloody Ron, making up to me,' she said, quickly:
too quickly.

But Time impatient, creaks a chair. And from the
jug I pour sour wine to wash away the only land
I own, and that between the toes.

A red libation to your good memory, friend. There's
work yet, for the living.

A Song in Praise of a Favourite Humming-Top

I polish your skin. It is that of a woman
    mellowed by the oil of the tarata,
    humming-top. What stable secret do you

    keep locked up in movement, humming-top?
    skipping away daintily as you do, sidewise
    lurching, nonchalantly coming erect?

    Your drowsy sighs lull and beguile the people
    the many, who've come to hear your talk,
    your whizz your buzz your angry bee-stung

    murmurs—which are simply about nothing
    at all. Ah, see: they're closing in—
    stopping just short of whip range.

Eyeballs plopping like bird's eggs sucked
    deep into your whirlpool, they're surging
    forward again treading on each others' feet.

Lips stretched tightly over teeth, they grin;
    find throat at last to shout; exclaim.
    O, they will leave finally, when they've

    finished fondling you, cooing over you like
    a kukupa. I don't like it: each one of them
    a thief's heart gladdened—but covetous.

The above is a poem developed from a 'Spell for a
wooden humming-top cut out and fashioned from
a totara; matai. Woods which alone hum and
whine beautifully.' Author unknown. Text in
Edward Shortland's Maori Manuscript Notebook
2(b) (MS2), page 73, Hocken Library, University
of Otago, Dunedin.

KENDRICK SMITHYMAN (b. 1922)

Hint for the Incomplete Angler

Not too far north from where I write set dawn
Before your bow precisely. Out there, cast
The kingfish from his feeding while you prey.

Smug blue worms will peck at your neat craft's side.
Show due respect then while you steal the tide.

There was a fisherman once who did things right.

For more than forty years he pulled fish out.
By line, net or pot God's plenty hauled to pout
And puff on the bottomboards, to smack
Themselves silly and die, or be tossed back
Until they swelled a right size for the pan
He kept on the wall by his sink. That man
Had long outgrown the truth of simple tales
Which said if he stroked his arm he showered scales,
That said for years he nourished an old mermaid
All to himself in his bach. Friend, he was staid,
Ordinary, and (it may be) none too bright,
But who could come godlike home with that high light
Morning on morning, to be sane as we
Would claim we are? Yet he did fittingly
More than we'd dream, and with more dignity.

For when he couldn't heave any more at the net,
When the old man snapper clung too hard, he set
His nose to the sea away out east of the Head
To give what was due from good years to the tide.

Watch for the worms as you go, at your dinghy's side.

Colville 1964

That sort of place where you stop
long enough to fill the tank, buy plums,
    perhaps, and an icecream thing on a stick
while somebody local comes
    in, leans on the counter, takes a good look
        but does not like what he sees of you,

intangible as menace,
a monotone with a name, as place
    it is an aspect of human spirit
(by which shaped), mean, wind-worn. Face
    outwards, over the saltings: with what merit
        the bay, wise as contrition, shallow

as their hold on small repute,
good for dragging nets which men are doing
    through channels, disproportioned in the blaze
of hot afternoon's down-going
    to a far fire-hard tide's rise
        upon the vague where time is distance?

It could be plainly simple
pleasure, but these have another tone
    or quality, something aboriginal,
reductive as soil itself—bone
    must get close here, final
        yet unrefined at all. They endure.

A school, a War Memorial
Hall, the store, neighbourhood of salt
    and hills. The road goes through to somewhere
        else.
Not a geologic fault
    line only scars textures of experience.
        Defined, plotted; which maps do not speak.

Tomarata

Learning teacheth more in one year,
than experience in twentie. . . .
                              Roger Ascham

1

Open as experience, this day, this
high-flying island coast, opened
a mile beyond the top of noon's arc

a mile further east than a gumland pond,
severe quartz-brown puritan face
not figured by duck or swan, not by swamp
hen or bittern
                    an indrawn quiet, stiff
as doctrine revised or contracted to
the essential. Maps call it a lake.

Shoreline, regardless of being defined
by reeds, is uncertain. The same maps will
contest its scope. Only
the name is constant, or perhaps what
ever (you might say) was the heart of it
if talking thus were not plainly
alien, to an event in terrain
which may know about physical reason,
nothing readily about feeling.
Tomarata is the name
for which the lake, reserved to
its own logic, has no word. Needs none.

2

We are not called to value, to judge
or be judged.
                    A life other than ours goes
on neighbouring, near while not of the pond.

Like mating and nesting of magpies,
like a single black shag crossing
south to north. East, larks went up
above lupins crouched over drifted sand,
the warm mazy scent of lupins flowering.

3

In which we waded, after a track of sorts
that intended to get to the fishing grounds
through a domain of rabbits overborne
by a harrier coursing slowly, solitary.

The tallest lupin is shoulder-high.
Little that grows—mingimingi, patotara,
sand daphne—has any age, any stature.
The track becomes merely a trail, then no trail.

4

You strike patches where sand is missing,
scurfy clay flakings. Begin to see
movement of change, marking
that formerly swamp was underfoot.
Look against the dune line seaward:
outcroppings from sand's elegant curves,
counterfeit mesas and buttes
where earlier compressed sandstone rots,
eroding to likeness of russet sponges.
Aerial survey shots show you,
ten years ago here was wholly sandhills.
Since then, they have opened. They may
close again, as the plants take over.

A dune is building. Bared,
by water cutting at the weather side
and by what southwesterly winds accomplish,
is old haggard disorder, signifying
a sometime liveliness, less sombre
in temper than the base—canyon,

basin, inept gully system—
by wind and water exposed.

5

We blunder to it,
entering into contriving,
work of total theatre, inordinately
involving. We left responsibilities behind,
locked up in the car. We bring with us
a camera, a set of lenses, a book on botany
and the manner of our lives which is open
to be judged. Or, at least, tested

by a discrete, particular silence.

6

Try to read the text of it, dithering
from one to another shape in experience
where any shape discovers itself,
accidential, substantial; removed from
pity or terror. Seeing into.
Looking up to, and down from.

The datum line is sea's work,
out of hearing, on which built
sandstone dykes. The tops of these,
latest of them, collapse. There have
been others. You read inconstancy.
Some other time, this was forest.

From the lowest open water-channel
I took pieces of fossilized gum.
The stain of soil, difference of textures, told
what became of the tree, where it lay.

Eight feet or so above, different in texture,
a moulding still recognizably humus,
area of stain, plotted

another forest level. After the fall
sand covered the woods, blending itself to some.
Iron grains oxidized; now they show, sculptings
pointlessly carried out in what seem
beggarly rusty skins of oil-drums.
Followed a phase of bog or swamp.

This is the level of moa crop stones,
pebbles of jasper mostly, foreign
to that terrace. They are of two characters.
Mainly they lie clustered, keeping
themselves to themselves.
They are mute, gleam slightly. Nearby,
oven shales still in place, with old shell
which breaks easily or crumbles
almost plastically.
No bones can be seen, no artefacts.

7

The oven stones, transient cooking sites,
ovens still packed together, and shale spills,
they occur from sandstone base to the tops
of the weathered knolls. One midden,
unusual, *Struthiolaria* dominate.
Otherwise the middens are what you'd expect,
in accord with shell of the beaches.

Stratification is probably all to hell;
too much movement. Anyway, I wouldn't know,
not a professional, frivolously puttering
for whom everything is mystery
and error permissible, Doctor Watson.

The puzzle was why the dog did not bark.
Which, resolutely, the dog did not. The hawk refused
to stoop, offering to explain
why, with so many oven stones, so little
shell remains. I turn that over,
turn it again, fingering absence

to have that silence speak, before
the sand comes back again before
the plants take over. Stabilized,
but not open.

8

No, Doctor. That thought occurred,
that the middens dribbled down and were
washed elsewhere. They would seem,
all these cooking sites, to predicate,
the different levels of them too,
so much waste that there should be
obvious scatter or deposits banked
like dykes. Or causeways.

They elude me. Did that happen
long since: the shells were collected, used,
discarded, congregated, exposed, dispersed,
and weather-worn? They are under the dune, then;
they are part of the dune, its calcium
carbonate fraction? I do not need
you, Watson. The matter is more
for Thomas Norton.

9

Open, to experience that satisfying
feeling of what goes unexplained.
Also, of continuity. True is when
whatever was hidden is revealed.
(Our language will not cope well
with reflexives.) It reveals itself

as in the dales earliest in spring
when the grass began to come away
the land spoke out again,
lynchet lines, Celt field marks,
the older presence. In Langstrothdale Chase,
headwater where the Wharfe, over shallow
terracings, prepares transparently
to take on civil properties,

you read a farmhouse back through building,
rebuilding, to the Norse steading
downstream a little from hut circles.

Downstream a little, culturally, is
Tomarata, its sandhills, its questions
which put themselves obliquely.
Partly, one invokes questions of scale,
in perspective, sensible of the proportions
which one tries to keep,
to temper experience

10

as something, so to speak, true.

Like happiness, which you do not
understand, or need to. Compound
wonder, awe, exaltation even
can be admitted. No protesting
or remedying action is called for.

Simply passive response would
not suit, but the getting of insight
may be self-defining, self-sufficient
and justifying. Reserved to its logic,
you have only to stand open to it.
Conceded, correlates may fail to find
themselves objective; communicate,
before understood.

Even here. Not wholly incongruous, then,
to remember the first time I went into
York Minster, just after the excavators
uncovered Roman brickwork
which had not been suspected. You looked up
where scaffolding went, watching
men at work in the church, building;
down, through medieval, through Saxon,
to the Roman, speculating
what water-goddess' site lay further.

All continuous, at once
present. Less than total insight
defines itself uniquely, briefly.

A long haul downstream, to fervid
afternoon in the gumland sandhills.
A quality of difference, recognized,
is to be respected, before
the plants—toetoe, tauhinu, dune
coprosma—take over, usefully.

Circus at the Barber's Shop

Memory, magnesium flare, you single
out—unearthly, static—the village
barber's shop. I shan't ask
why. Tobacconist, bookseller
(newspaper, magazines, pulp fiction)
was he the local booky as well,
and impressario?

Because, the paddock beside
the barber's shop was where any
circus, tentshow, travelling freaks, set down
their burdens briefly. We were
invited to share them a while.
Elsewhere, out of sight, benighted
the River sighed and kept on running.
Rushes that crawled all the way
up from the Heads whistled
at burnt-out trees. We came
when a drum thumped. Cornet, tambourine,
accordion, called us not to our kind.

Yet, could be proved. Common, I mean,
they were; our mothers said.
And looked it, under smoky flarings

stuck by canvas and cages. A mangy lion made
an awful great reeking water,
a bear that would dance stank fiercely.
The rickety seats got harder,
tie-rods and cymbals whanged.

Gumdigger or cowcocky's hand who rode
the buckjumper might pick up five
quid, or stay three rounds with a sadist
for ten bob. We are tested.

Saturday mornings at the barber's
I fondled *Triumph*,
Magnet, Champion and a nameless thing
with blue covers endlessly
serialized 'The Phantom of
Maltravers Towers'. It scared me
silly. Week by week I bought
terror and bathos. This is emotion
recollected in paralysis.
I do not ask why.

They nursed a fire near their Big Top one night.
Every so often the bandsmen took their drum
to the fire, to warm it. Otherwise,
it wouldn't be beaten right.

WIREMU KĪNGI KEREKERE
(b. 1923; Ngāitai, Te Aitanga-ā-Mahaki)

Karangatia e te iwi, te Manu Kōtuku Rerenga Tahi

Karangatia e te iwi, te Manu Kōtuku Rerenga Tahi,
  haere mai
Kōkiri ake te haeata ka mahuta mai i te pae tawhiti.
Haere mai Kuini Riripeti, me tō Hoa Tāne tautangata, a
  Piripi e
Mauria mai rā ō tamariki rangatahi. Haere mai, kia ora
  rā!

Horahia mai ngā mana nui o tō tipuna, arā, Kuini
  Wikitoria
Nānā nei i hora, i hōmai, he oranga mō te iwi Māori e.
Ū mai rā ki Aotearoa, ki te whenua tapu, Tūranganui-a-
  Kiwa.
Tēnei te marae i ū mai ai a Kuki e. Haere mai, kia ora
  rā!
Kei runga te karanga!
Ko wai tērā? Ko Irihapeti! Ka rongo au i tō reo pōhiri
Haruru nei rā Niu Tīreni, tū ake ana rā i te Tairāwhiti.

Pōhiritia e te iwi, te ope tūārangi, nā te aroha nui e.
Ko te tūmanako me te wawata, kia tau ki a koutou rā.
Mā te Matua i te rangi, koutou mā e manaaki i ō haere i
  te ao.
Tēnei te kupu whakamutu a te iwi Māori e. Haere mai!
Kia kotahi e!

A greeting to Queen Elizabeth, the Rare White Heron of Single Flight

We greet you rarest White Heron of One Flight,
Rising as the rays of dawn from the far horizon.
Welcome Queen Elizabeth, and your consort, Philip.
Bringing with you your son and daughter. Welcome.

Bring with you the prestige of your forebear, Queen
   Victoria
To whom we owe our freedom and security.
Come to the Land of the Long White Cloud, to this
   sacred place Gisborne.
The landing place of Captain Cook. So our call of
   'Haere mai!' rings out.
To whom? To Elizabeth our Queen! We heard the call
Resound throughout the land, and are
Assembled on these eastern shores.

The people welcome the visiting party with great love.
Our hope and prayer are with you all.
May our Father in Heaven bless your journey abroad.
We end this message of the Maori people. Welcome.
We are one people.

Translation by Wiremu Kīngi Kerekere

The Place

The place where the floured hens
sat laying their breakfast eggs,
frying their bacon-coloured combs in the sun
is gone.

You know the place—
in the hawthorn hedge
by the wattle tree
by the railway line.

I do not remember these things
—they remember me,
not as child or woman but as their last excuse
to stay, not wholly to die.

The Clown

His face is streaked with prepared tears.
I, with others, applaud him, knowing it
is fashionable to approve when a clown cries
and to disapprove when a persistent sourface
does whether or not his tears are paint.

It is also fashionable, between wars,
to say that hate is love and love is hate,
to make out everything is more complex than we
  dreamed
and then to say we did not dream it,
we knew it all along and are wise.

Dear crying clown dear childlike old man
dear kind murderer dear innocent guilty
dear simplicity I hate you for making me pretend
there are several worlds to one truth when
I know, I know there are not. Dear people like you and
    me
whose breaths are bad, who sleep in and rumble
their bowels and control it until
they get home into the empty house or among the
    family
dear family, dear lonely man in a torn world of nobody,
is it for this waste that we have hoarded words over so
    many
million years since the first, groan,
and look up at the stars. Oh oh the sky is too wide to
    sleep under!

Yet Another Poem About a Dying Child

Poets and parents say he cannot die
so young, so tied to trees and stars.
Their word across his mouth obscures
and cures his murmuring good-bye.
He babbles, *they say*, of spring flowers,

who for six months has lain
his flesh at a touch bruised violet,
his face pale, his hate clearer
than milky love that would smooth over
the pebbles of diseased bone.

Pain spangles him like the sun,
He cries and cannot say why.
His blood blossoms like a pear tree.
He does not want to eat or keep
its ugly windfall fruit.

He does not want to spend or share
the engraved penny of light
that birth put in his hand
telling him to hold it tight.
Will parents and poets not understand?

He must sleep, rocking the web of pain
till the kind furred spider will come
with the night-lamp eyes and soft tread
to wrap him warm and carry him home
to a dark place, and eat him.

When the Sun Shines More Years Than Fear

When the sun shines more years than fear
when birds fly more miles than anger
when sky holds more bird
sails more cloud
shines more sun
than the palm of love carries hate,
even then shall I in this weary
seventy-year banquet say, Sunwaiter,
Birdwaiter, Skywaiter,
I have no hunger,
remove my plate.

The Flowering Cherry

These cherries are not wine-filled bowls for thirsty birds
nor ornaments of the house where sky's the ceiling.
These are the pawnbroker tree's discreet sign,
the wine, tear and blood drops of bondage,

the tree's relentless advantage
taken of the poverty that came when, warmed
with familiar memory of what had been
and had been and would be but is never known
entirely or believed until it is born,
we saw the cherry tree in flower, and at once spent
a life's rich astonishment.

'Why should I be bound to thee?'
Blake asked of the myrtle tree. Why?
He killed to escape. Blood flowed beneath the tree:
a father's blood, an old man's, who must have known
how to bargain with all possession
that makes a tree, a house, a sky into a prison
and each man see the marks of chains upon his skin.

The cherry tree flowers earlier than most,
falls as snow while snow is still falling
sweeps into us and through us and we taste
the flower as fruit, we eat the first
full-blown light unfolded out of winter darkness.
Then, as if the bloom were gone, the tree will hide
in wine-colored shade and pawn signs to pursue its
    trade.

And we are prisoners then, borrowing wonder
to redeem the pledge; or too poor, too ill,
too far away to make the necessary journey,
we plead in writing for the tree's mercy. Why
should a lifetime of marvelling be spent
on this first view of spring light, this burst of cherry
    snow?
Why should the tree house our treasure in blood?

When next you pass the flowering cherry now, in
    September,
look closely at the cool dark wine house
where the blackbirds sing for their supper
where the human senses sing for their survival.

Christmas and Death

Christmas and Death are hungry times
when only the foolish and the dying
with circumscribed vision of Here
learn complete praise, saying
Bravo Bravo to the Invisible.

Who knows to what in the small yard
sunless, the turkey gives violent praise?
Or the sick man spread
On a white plate in his diminishing world?

Letter

Dear friend, the here-there emphasis is made
to keep you at a distance as I write,
to fix you, no captured human specimen
in a crowded corner of a northern world
reminding only how with spear, nail, pen,
I came your way walking from paddock to field
until at noon I fell asleep in an oak tree's shade
and waking saw not manuka and the Southern Cross
but above, Orion, and at my feet, lady-white.

A skin-thin air letter, a ninepenny stamp:
(rata or manuka or koromiko)
or words on a yellow pink green or white page
are the plan I must make, the obstacles overcome
before the public service and the plane take over my
    rage
to speak to you, speed-shrivel the ten thousand miles to
    your home
in the Midlands—fire and blotting-paper damp,
spring-feverishly mourning always the sky's loss
of sun, hanging out to dry bones stained with snow,

gray snow, last winter's fall. What else have I learned
of your city since I traced the millions
crowded on a sinking full-stop as on a doomed raft
in my first geography book and read its important name
and meaning? Small arms, bicycles, heavy drift
of smoke upward all day; diesel fumes, oil-flame, then,
     cultural flame
from science and music where some, not all, once
     burned,
survived by grafting new tissue to others who, wary at
     first,
soon strutted proud and warm in their smart new skin.

Meat markets, medicine, city dignitaries; an electrified
     line
to London from Central Station or Snow Hill.
Edgbaston. Selly Oak. A Chamberlain in office.
A Bull-Ring. Art Gallery. Dustmen. Council Flats.

Association on Association of men in business.
Undertakers, clerks, brokers; with umbrellas and top or
     bowler hats.
And tarnished incomes and incomes that when
     polished, shine.
A city of reservoirs of resigned fluoridic thirst
suckling the sweet channels flowing from the Welsh
     Hills.

Men silent in trains who'd never dare risk
the five-pound fine by pulling the communication cord.
Men with scientific journals; dark eyes
seeing molecules as fellow passengers
or, seeing women, tricking intelligence to tell where lies
the difference as both wrapped in genetic furs
deceive yet are worth study as a lifetime's task.
You'd think I talk of any city, not only Birmingham—
but where else into the mould are men women and
     bicycles poured

with equal reverence? Wheels within wheels
headlights reflectors handlebars
pumps pedals carriers hand and foot brakes,
oh and not to forget the rifles, the agricultural
   machines,
the bath and the kitchen sink; the articles Birmingham
   makes
would equip you from birth to death and after—here
   the touching scene
could be looked at, not through your eyes, but through
   locally made cinema reels,
as taking in the used label of your life, *Tear Round Here.*
   I Am.
You replace it with *Snip, Cover and Fold. I Was.*

My geography book is out of date. Following the new
recognition of humanity by humanity,
the miles of mountain chains everywhere
(you remember their paralysed snowcapped vertebrae)
have been made free, while rivers too have claimed
   their share
in the new deal, have changed their flow and no longer
   obey
the command of the geography book I once knew.
And now Birmingham, to me, is famous not for bicycles
   but for people.
It is the heart profits when facts are produced in an
   enlightened factory.

But it's no use. You are not there. The essence of your
   being
is you flow, lap at far coasts, enter rooms
invisibly to reassure me when I'm afraid
though it's not to be interpreted that therefore
I worship you, regard you as my private God.
When you're an old man you'll have a face like an
   apple in store,
a corner apple smelling of rain and wood, seeing
through narrow eyes nails taller than any steeple,
dead leaves and spiders set beside white scientific
   glooms

—does this image of you seem strange? You'll allow
it's not the usual glimpse of God; it's worse—
a theft of a separate being to complete a torn memory;
a slave-selection more frightening, tyrannical,
than is made in any past or present book of geography;
a callup of a memory-guard I've no right to call.
Death is the only guard who's willing and free Here
   and Now
to stay at my door, to play the memory game,
to plead too often—A bicycle? Had you not better
   choose a hearse?

Tāmaki-makau-rau

Poua ki te hauāuru, hora ana ko Manukau.
Poua ki te rāwhiti, takoto ana Waitematā.
Maiangi ana i waenga, ko Tāmaki-makau-rau,
Tara pounamu o nehe rā, tau tuku iho ngā tūpuna—
Rangi e tū iho nei, Papanuku rā e tau nei!

Tāmaki e! Panuku e! Makau-rau e! Paneke e!
Tau whakairo a te wā, ngā tai e tangi nei—
'Tematā, te hīnga o te rā, Manukau, te tōnga o te rā—
Takoto rā, te takoto roa, tōia mai nei e te wā
Mai i te heunga o te pō i te ao, ka ao, te ao hōu!

Tau wahangū o 'mata e, huri ake rā, ka tūohu.
Nei ngā whare kōrero: Maungawhau, Maungarei,
Maungakiekie, Rangitoto, he piringa no te tini,
He tohenga na te mano—tū atu ana he pakanga,
Hinga mai ana he parekura! A! Mau ana te wehiwehi!

Tau-iwi, maranga, e tau e—me he kāhui kūaka, auē,
Ki runga te tauranga nei! Ko Tāmaki-makau-rau!
Ka ū ki Waitematā, ka piki ki Maungawhau—
Ki Manukau, kua tau! Ki Maungarei, kua eke!
Hinga ana te wao a Tāne, tū mai ana ngā marae a Hōu!

Tamaki of a hundred lovers

Placed in the west, Manukau spreads out.
Placed in the east, Waitemata stretches out.
Between there rises Tamaki-makau-rau,

Greenstone pendant of the ages, the beloved passed
  down
From Rangi standing above, Papanuku lying here!

Tamaki shifts, Makau-rau changes!
The beloved of time and the sounding tides,
'Temata at the rising sun, Manukau at the setting sun,
Lying there, lying long, hauled up by time
When night was parted from day, day, the new day!

Silent beloved of the ages, turn and see!
Here are the homes of speech: Maungawhau,
  Maungarei,
Maungakiekie, Rangitoto, grasped by many,
Contested by multitudes—battles fought,
And battles lost! Oh what terror!

Strangers, come, settle like godwits
On the landing-place! It is Tamaki-makau-rau!
They land at Waitemata, climb Maungawhau,
They alight at Manukau, mount Maungarei!
The forest of Tane falls, the marae of the new men lie
  here!

Translation by Margaret Orbell

Ngā ture whenua

E tuki, e tuki, e tuki ē,
Ngā ture, ture whenua, te tauiwi ē!
Hei aha, hei aha rā, e Tauiwi ē?
Nāu te kī, te kī mai,
'E nuku, e nuku ki Rohe Tāone ē,
Te utu he moni tekihana ē!
Nuku mai i te rohe kāinga ē,
Whenua tuku iho, kāhore he utu ē!'

Rangirua ana ngā mahara,
E tirotiro kau ana te tāngata ē!
Kāhore he mana, kāhore he marae,
E ngaro ana te wairua Māori!
E tū ngohengohe kau ana,
E tū mokemoke ana te tāngata ē,
I ngā ture aki a Tauiwi e—
Ture tukituki tāngata,
Ture hamapaka, koia anake!
Ūkuia nā!

The land laws

Oh men are beaten, beaten, beaten down
By the laws, the land laws, the strangers!
Oh strangers, why, why?
It was you who said, said to us,
'Move, move to the towns,
Earn money for sections!
Move from your homes,
The land you inherited
And don't have to buy!'
Our thoughts are confused,
Men stare about in vain!
There is no mana, no marae,
The soul of the Maori is lost!
Men are helpless, men are lonely
Because of the harsh laws of the strangers,
The laws that beat men down,
The humbug laws, only humbug!
Wipe the shit away!

Translation by Margaret Orbell

Ohakune Fires

There were bonfires on the hillsides
in those days, high
above the raw-boned town
and trees and men giants against the sky
grappling for mastery—not men but bushmen took
their slashers in to hack
blazes on the beech trunks
smacking up a track of sorts,
forced a way to the ridge and stood
straight up to breast the trees
defeated, famished
in the thinning air.

Back on the farm on milder hills
they clubbed second growth
and lit their necessary fires;
women came—sometimes a child
screaming when the blazing
raced up close.
               Dark, and
the booze began, tall tales
of men and bullocks gulped down
in twenty feet of mud or some
such thing in grandad's roaring time.
Round them the spit and snore
of logs' red bodies,
later the blundering
journey home (one, a neighbour,
drunken-drowned in the freezing stream).
And all the time
the hard stars riding by.

Time, it's a moving stage—
bonfires still blaze
and we hold out our hands
across a widening space
calling, hearing now only
the faint snap of the burning
and the far-off pack-a-pack
of the axes.

All Possession is Theft

There had been rain in the morning and a chaffinch,
before we surprised it, strutted beside a pool
on the lawn; the house was white, polite, had nothing
to say, but the trees—the great, well-heeled, patrician
trees—turned their green shoulders aside;
the pohutukawa has lineage, I would be certain
to make faux pas across its genealogies.
And my foot slipped between clay and concrete,
a magpie jeered and left, noisily.
The land agent drooled his obsequies—the previous
occupant, a psychiatrist . . . I thought I saw him
at the window frowning over his sad case histories,
neglecting his paths but cared for by his trees;
and touched one, tentatively, found instead
its green shawl of long three-fingered leaves,
a pink flower luxurious as an orchid, and in
the shadow a single fruit, narrow, golden,
the poised and secret guardian of an old season's
accumulations. 'Banana passion fruit'
—the agent, natural for a moment, pressed on
'The elevation here . . .' I turned aside
breathless, feeling faintly lecherous, closed
my hand about that small old bag of gold
and, with a quick tug, took it. I live here now.

Ghosts II

And after all a slave sits out the centuries
among her betters—a marble general, rows
of emperors—the little *inconnue* some
French committee bought, noticing perhaps
her pert and unpatrician nose, a ghostly
sparkle in eyes long blinded by their dust.

It is as though, unsuitable as ever, she still
slips out into a bustling Roman dusk to where
her lover waits beside his stolen clay, in
a grimy courtyard by the river; she's to sit,
he says, as long as there's a thread of light . . .
stupid! nights she knows are not for that—

and lifts her head and curses, ignorant
little slut; and he, breathless, fire to
his fingertips, catches her magnificence.

Latter Day Lysistrata

It is late in the day of the world
and the evening paper tells of developed
ways of dying; five years ago we would not
have believed it. Now I sit on the grass
in fading afternoon light crumpling pages
and guessing at limits of shock, the point
of repudiation; my woman's mind, taught
to sustain, to support, staggers at this
vast reversal. I can think only of
the little plump finches that come
trustingly into the garden, moving
to mysterious rhythms of seeds and
seasons; I have no way to conceive
the dark maelstrom where men may spin
in savage currents of power—is it

power?—and turn to stone, to steel,
no longer able to hear such small throats'
hopeful chirping nor see these tiny
domestic posturings, the pert shivering
of feathers. They know only the fire
in the mind that carries them down
and down in a wild and wrathful wind.

I do not know how else
the dream of any man on earth can be
'destroy all life, leaving
buildings whole . . .'

Let us weep for these men, for
ourselves, let us cry out as they bend
over their illustrious equations; let us
tell them the cruel truth of bodies,
skin's velvet bloom, the scarlet of
bleeding. Let us show them the vulnerable
earth, the transparent light that slips
through slender birches falling over
small birds that sense in the miniscule
threads of their veins the pulses of
every creature—let these men breathe
the green fragrance of the leaves, here
in this gentle darkness let them convince me,
here explain their preposterous imaginings.

Magpie and Pines

That dandy black-and-white gentleman doodling notes
on fragrant pinetops over the breakfast morning,
has been known to drop through mists of bacon-fat,
with a gleaming eye, to the road where a child stood,
                                                screaming.

And in the dark park—the secretive trees—have boys
harboured their ghosts, built huts, and buried treasure,
and lovers made from metallic kisses alloys
more precious, and driven the dark from pleasure.

A child was told that bird as his guardian angel
reported daily on actions contrived to displease;
stands petrified in the sound of wings, a strangle
of screams knotting his throat beneath the winter
                                                leaves.

Look back and laugh on the lovers whose white mating
made magpie of dark; whose doodling fingers swore
various fidelities and fates. They found the world
                                                waiting,
and broke the silence. A raven croaks 'Nevermore'

to their progenitive midnight. The guardian is aloof
on his roof of the small world, composing against
                                                morning
a new, ironic ballad. The lover has found small truth
in the broken silence, in faith, or the fate-bird moaning.

Here Together Met

I praise Saint Everyman, his house and home
  In every paint-bright gardened suburb shining
With all the age's verities and welcome
  Medalled upon him in contentment dining;
            And toast with gin and bitters
            The Muse of baby-sitters.

I sing Dame Everyone's whose milky breast
  Suckles the neighbourhood with pins and plans
Adding new rooms to their eternal rest,
  The next night's meat already in the pan:
            And toast with whisky and ice,
            The Goddess who keeps things nice.

I honour Maid Anybody's whose dreams are shaping
  Lusts in her heart down the teasing garden-path
Where she stops in time as she must at the gaping
  Graveyard of Hell and rescues her girlish laugh:
            And toast in rum and cloves
            The course of balanced love.

I drink to Son Mostpeople's whose honourable pride
  In things being what they are will not let him run,
But who keeps things going even after he has died
  In a distant desert clutching an empty gun:
            And toast in brandy and lime
            The defenders of our great good time.

Marrows

These lusty plants, complete with blaring sex
have to be helped in the essential act;
beg bee or stud-groom gardener to fix
the man-sized pollen on the female tract.

Their golden horns rear up at poles apart,
attracted, aching, with no power to move
to interpenetration; they've no art
for more than passive hankerings of love.

And many simply rotted till I found
reason and remedy—to take the male
and shake its sperm-stain out upon the round
realistic genital. They never fail

if the job's properly done: the rot is held;
the genes clock over in their natural task,
and marrow-bellies swell: the male is dead.
The rotund widows in ripe sunlight bask.

Bread and a Pension

It was not our duty to question but to guard,
maintaining order; see that none escaped
who may be required for questioning by the State.
The price was bread and a pension and not a hard
life on the whole. Some even scraped
enough on the side to build up a fairish estate

for the day of retirement. I never could
understand the complaints of the restless ones
who found the hours long, time dragging;
it always does. The old hands knew how good
the guardroom fire could be, the guns
gleaming against the wall and the nagging

wind like a wife—outside. There were cards
for such occasions and good companions
who truly were more than home since they shared
one's working life without difference or hard words,
aimed at much the same thing, and shared opinions
on news they read. If they cared

much it was for the quiet life. You cannot hold
that against them, since it's roundly human
and any decent man would want it the same.
For these were decent: did as they were told,
fed prisoners, buried the dead, and, on occasion
loaded the deathcart with those who were sent to the

flames.

Vision

'Elephants in bed,' my daughter says
Disdainfully when asked if she'll explain
The meaning of the picture she has made.
'But at the tops of trees?' I ask, to raise
The matter of credibility, to train
Vision to be exact. This is mere bread

In a world that is made of cake. 'That's what
The ladders are for,' she says, 'because they're big.'
Of course one sees it all when put like that—
Colossal mammals rise above their weight
If there is only vision, and the prize pig
Is indeed a crowned head in the rat's estate.

And so my daughter speaks of size and of
The free flight of the bird's migrating mind
To one who walks on rails and sets his sights
On daily news, apportionments of love,
In a world where all is ordered, easy to find,
Accident-free; where what is known delights.

And for her, possibility is actual.
For me there is only prose and the paper flower
Which needs no explanation. One needs ladders
Or windows more, or a more sensual
Heart which dares to seize the power
To shinny trees with elephants or waltz with adders.

New Guinea Time

Time is mainly a fiction here. There are
Two seasons—and that is near enough—
One for growing, and one for taking stock.
Between them, things gradually disappear.

No feature of the landscape looms as permanent,
And no man stable. Talking of change, we mean
Stages of dermatitis, rust and heat
Etching the native and his habitat.

Near enough is too close: if things get done
Or merely overgrown, who is to blame?
Whom to congratulate? Out of the warm
And septic seas Death grows its territory

Gradually as an atoll in the mind
Might form itself of bone and alcohol
Or failing medication. What stands, skeletal,
Is rock, or the pulse of water, the tale

Of time so quietly running down it tells
Not what one seeks to know, naming the minute,
Placing the day or the week. Things get done
By the season and life goes finish.

Tahiti

A fit place to observe the transit of Venus—
this island, the very body of love—and warm
to the chilled and Horn-tossed sailor whose hungers
trolled empty oceans seeking just such charm.

Those sugar-loaf peaks that rose like nubile breasts
behind palm-fronded beaches, simpering surf,

spoke truly of the island's eager girls,
caught their mood, reflecting them to the life.

What if the instruments gave different readings
of the facts they were set up to trace? There are
transits that defy analysis, transports so deep
the mutinous heart alone responds to, treasures.

And Cook recorded how a mature man
lay in full public view with a younger girl
unwilling to fuse with his needs, while relatives
sat round advising, telling how she should curl

Herself to the shapes of mutual benefit. This
was the sailor's Paradise, where, so soon,
the ravages of Europe's shame and dirt—
disease that fed on love—made itself known.

So, man the reasoner, came and reshaped a world,
discovering only that, wherever he goes,
he takes himself, and nothing truly changes.
The darkness gathers where his shadow throws.

Death of the Bosun's Mate

I, the bosun's mate, John Reading,
this morning, in rum-reeking bedding,
departed this life while full as a tick:
in a sheet I roll in Endeavour's wake.

I had been at the wine, then was given rum,
which oiled my entry to Kingdom Come;
what better way to meet one's maker
than full of Madeira and black Jamaica?

I lived a full life—kept full as I could,
sustained by foods that came casked in wood;

now I must suck at the mermaid's nipple,
the salt Pacific my only tipple.

None can ask more than to die as he lived,
so with these words I'd be engraved:
Content as the groom on his night of wedding,
lies the bosun's mate, John Reading.

The Seventies

These days you keep on meeting,
stooped and desiccated, those
who laugh sadly, describe themselves
as 'the oldest living hippie', or
'the first bikie': looking back over a shoulder
uncertain how they got here so unprepared
for the ongoing, familiar, habitual world crisis.

They're a little out of tune
with the new music and cannot do
much about the falling birthrate.
Perhaps the world will not become
as young as it seemed to be getting
when they were. And if the roads are better
they are not leading anywhere now so soon.

A little less inclined to believe
what they read on placards, and more
amiable about opposing forces,
they see their strength had to be tested—
that even the new was not to be totally trusted—
and power still corrupts. In high places
they recognise no gods; sense father's many faces.

And the pulse of the big machines
still revvs between odd-jobs and going
to funerals. Change has indeed come,

they console themselves, between one suburb
of the global village and others. The road-houses
serve blander plastic steaks: their sons
commute to bread in the dying days of Ford.

The Return

And again I see the long pouring headland,
And smoking coast with the sea high on the rocks,
The gulls flung from the sea, the dark wooded hills
Swarming with mist, and mist low on the sea.

And on the surf-loud beach the long spent hulks,
The mats and splintered masts, the fires kindled
On the wet sand, and men moving between the fires,
Standing or crouching with backs to the sea.

Their heads finely shrunken to a skull, small
And delicate, with small black rounded beaks;
Their antique bird-like chatter bringing to mind
Wild locusts, bees, and trees filled with wild honey—

And, sweet as incense-clouds, the smoke rising, the fire
Spitting with rain, and mist low with rain—
Their great eyes glowing, their rain-jewelled, leaf-green
Bodies leaning and talking with the sea behind them:

Plant gods, tree gods, gods of the middle world . . .
  Face downward
And in a small creek mouth all unperceived,
The drowned Dionysus, sand in his eyes and mouth,
In the dim tide lolling—beautiful, and with the last
  harsh

Glare of divinity from lip and broad brow ebbing . . .
The long-awaited! And the gulls passing over with shrill
  cries;
And the fires going out on the thundering sand;
And the mist, and the mist moving over the land.

Bitter Harvest

The big farm girl with the dumb prophetic body
And shoulders plump and white as a skinned peach
Goes singing through the propped-up apple boughs.

Behind her steps an ancient Jersey cow
With bones like tent-poles and udder swinging.

And last a hairy boy who with a fishing-pole
Drives youth and age before him, flanked by boulders
More yielding than his love. O bitter harvest

When drought affirms and plenitude denies!
Well, let them pass. Assuredly the boy
Will drop his worm into a dusty hole

And fish up . . . death, and the ancient cow
On which so much depends will clear the moon.

from Sanctuary of Spirits

IX   Against Te Rauparaha

Kei hea koutou kia toa—Be brave that
you may live.—Hongi Hika

The records all agree
you were a violent, a pitiless man,
treacherous as an avalanche
poised above a sleeping village.
Small, hook-nosed as a Roman,
haughty, with an eagle's glance,
Caligula and Commodus
were of your kin.

Kapiti floats before me,
and the shadows round the island
prickle
like the hairs of my scalp.
Shadows of war canoes
splinter the bright sea.
And I hear on the cliff below
the low cry of a chief:
'Ka aue te mamae!
Alas, the pain!'

Ironical to think your island pa,
once drenched with the blood
of men and whales,
has since become a sanctuary for birds.
Would this make sense to you, I wonder.
That life is holy would seem
a dubious proposition to you,
old murderer—
most laughable.
Pathetic ghost!
Sometimes you hoot despairingly
across the valley,
and my small daughter sobs in her sleep,
convinced an engine is pursuing her.
Black as anthracite,
issuing in steam
out of the bowels of the hill,
yours is a passable imitation, I'll allow.
But where is the rage that terrorised the coast?
the towering pride not to be withstood?
Imperial violence . . .!
Imperial poppycock!
I saw you slink away in the moonlight—
a most solitary, attenuated ghost
reduced to scaring little girls.
The worst that you can do is raise a storm
and try to tear my roof off . . .

But why deceive myself?
I know you as the subtlest tormentor,
> *able to assume at will*
the features of the most intimate terrors.

Remember Tama who betrayed his friends,
> guests on his marae
to the murderous vengeance of Hakitara—
Pehi and forty others,
> all great chiefs,
> impiously butchered in their sleep!
How, spider-clever, you again escaped
> to spin a web and snare him.
> And how Te Hiko, Pehi's son,
glared at him for fully half an hour,
> lifted Tama's upper lip
> with a forefinger
and tapped the wolfish teeth,
> crying wildly:
'These teeth ate my father!'

> Tamaiharanui
who strangled in the night
> his beautiful daughter
> that she might not be a slave.
But afterwards
> plump goose for a widow's oven,
> plucked of his honour,
what remained of Tama
> but a victim for a ritual vengeance?

Tama and Hiko too were of your kin,
> and vengeful Hakitara—violent men,
> crazed with the lust for blood!
Who would have guessed that they were also
> dutiful sons, affectionate fathers?
or that, decorous on the marae,
> they entertained their guests
> with courtly ease?

Scarer of children, drinker of small girls,
    your malicious eye stares down
         out of the midday sun,
blasting the seed in the pod,
    choking the well with dust.

These teeth ate my father—
    ate the heart of the bright day!

Insidious enmity!
    I know you by these signs:
the walls crack without cause,
    heads show pointed teeth,
leer and fall away,
    the dog barks at nothing,
whimpers and hides his head,
    and something wild
darts into the night
    from under my window . . .
YOU—Te Rauparaha!

The wind rises,
    lifts the lid off my brain—

Madman, leave me alone!

Why Don't You Talk to Me?

Why do I post my love letters
in a hollow log?
Why put my lips to a knothole in a tree
and whisper your name?

The spiders spread their nets
and catch the sun,
and by my foot in the dry grass
ants rebuild a broken city.

Butterflies pair in the wind,
and the yellow bee,
his holsters packed with bread,
rides the blue air like a drunken cowboy.

More and more I find myself
talking to the sea.
I am alone with my footsteps.
I watch the tide recede
and I am left with miles of shining sand.

Why don't you talk to me?

The Dark Lord of Savaiki

I am the one in your dreams,
master of passion,
favourite child
of Tumu and Papauri.
Te Ara o Tumu

I   Under the Tamanu Tree

Who, who and who?
Who is the dark Lord of Savaiki?
    Crab castings,
            convulsions under the house
where the landcrabs
    tell their grievances
to the roots of the tamanu tree.
Agitation of the leaves,
    the palm trees clash their fronds,
and the wind hurries past
    clutching in its fingers
the leaf-wrapped souls
        of children torn
            from the eyelids
of despairing mothers.

                    Hung
on spiderwebs for safekeeping,
            they will dangle there,
until the spirits come
                and eat them.

II   The Witch of Hanoa

When Kavatai died,
    his son Paroa, as chief mourner,
wrapped his corpse in mats
and hung it from the ceiling
    to decay in decent isolation,
neighbour to the stars
            and the grieving wind
that rode the rooftree
                for three months
and terrified Te Tautua people
    with its groans
            and high-pitched whistling.
All this time,
                his widow Puatama,
feared throughout the kingdom
    for her sorcery,
fed his spirit at her breast
            until it grew so vast
it burst apart the ribcage
    of the house,
                    a monstrous storm
that tore up trees
    and levelled villages,
                rampaging
to the west as far as Manihiki.
Her grief assuaged,
    she called his spirit back,
as she would a dangerous child,
and, chastened,
    he returned
                upon a mango's back
and beached at Hanoa,

where he lies in peace
    with Puatama
        in an unmarked grave.

III Teu

Mother, you were there
    at the passage
        when our ship arrived.
The sea, heavy as oil,
    heaved unbroken
            on the reef,
the stars
    lay in clusters
        on the water,
and you wept
    when you laid
        the Southern Cross
upon our eyes.

IV At Nahe

At Nahe, attended by a sandshark,
    I waded in the shallows
that seemed as white and pure
        as happiness,
    or the shark itself.
I was happy being a child again,
    and, careless as a child
        in a treasure house,
I ripped up chunks of coral
    to take home.
        Horrid amputation!
The living creatures seemed
        to shriek,
and bled a kind of ichor.

V   The Doves of Pauma

The surf breaks on the mouth
    of the passage at Pauma,
where the black doves used to play
    when crickets and grasshoppers
drowned out the murmur of the sea,
    and the wind was drugged
by the scent of tipani
                and tiare maori
that flowered abundantly
    along the roadways
now overgrown and sunk in ruin.

VI   Tapu

The sea gnaws at Paroa's bones
    where he lies at Nahe,
but Paetou,
    beloved of Maringikura,
sleeps secure at Hanoa
under an untidy heap of stones.

VII   Brother Shark

The black mango
            is a priest
in his marae
        of blazing coral
where Ataranga's sunken house
    tilts
            towards Savaiki
and the setting sun.

VIII Omoka

It will be like this one day
    when I sail home to die—
the boat crunching up on to the sand,

then wading through warm water
     to the beach,
the friendly voices
    round me in the darkness,
the sky dying out
    behind the trees of Omoka,
      and reaching out of hands.

IX   Trade Winds

You were just a girl,
    one of two wild sisters,
when he came to Tongareva,
    a gloomy trader,
    his soul eaten away
by five years
    in the trenches.
    You followed him
from island to island,
    bore his children
only to see your dreams
      break up
on the hidden reef
    of Savaiki.
      Mother,
your footsteps falter
    outside my window,
where you have waited
    fifty years
for your children
      to return.
The moon comes out,
      lovely
as a mother's face
    over a sleeping child.
The trade winds
    are your fingers
on my eyelids.

X   Bosini's Tomb

Ancestral shapes
           on the beach,
lying beside their drawn-up boats,
chatting and laughing softly
     as they await the dawn—
so many names to remember,
      so many names to honour!
           Grandfather Bosini,
why do you beckon
    from the deeper shadows
         beyond your tomb?
The children of Marata
                   join hands
with the children of Tumu
and have peaceful dreams.
        They smile to see
Father and Mother
    walking hand in hand
across the swirling waters
        of Taruia Passage,
where the leaping dolphins
    celebrate the dawn.

Augury

There are no signs. The sky is entirely bland
and empty of birds. But even if they were flying,
as soon they will be back to night shelter,
even if it were now the season for migration
and the echelons were assembling for departure,
no-one could find patterns in their flying
and predictions in the patterns and a scrap of assurance
to last at the utter limit till the forecast failed.
There has never been a portent but only
a populated earth and an empty sky.
One bird, if it chances to pass, tells more clearly
of a condition so common it needs no prediction:
two narrow wings lifting the great firmament
and only for a moment a fragment of song.

Counter-revolution

Did it go wrong just about a hundred
years ago? A ramshackle self-appointed
cast-off élite of first comers,
promoters, bent lawyers and sham doctors
set it up for themselves, a gentry of sorts,
saw it collapse and crept away with slim gains.
The cities grew, married men left home,
children were tall and wild, women restless.
Something had to be done. Seddon the burly
village policeman, a pattern for the future,
rose like a cork, admonishing finger aloft,
ponderously sly, licking his stub of a pencil,

selecting and rejecting, always with good humour,
not harsh in the least, but in the end obscene.

Parihaka

The province has set up shrines
to its martyrs and heroes Te
Rangi Hiroa to the north
where his vikings landed von
Tempsky well to the south
at the scene of his last encounter
with the spirit of '48
the Richmond cottage with two
volumes of the *Evangelical
Magazine* (but Harry
Atkinson out with the militia
read Mill *On Liberty*
a year after publication)
colonial gothic St Mary's
with neat rows in the graveyard
soldiers sailors settlers
killed by the rebel natives
regimental hatchments
one for the Friendly Maoris
a 20th century second
thought in bright blond wood
to remember all who died
a patch on a war scarred face
no sign for Parihaka
a broken road a set
of ruinous foundations
charred remains of timber
a '38 Chevrolet
under the cloudy mountain.

The Bay

On the road to the bay was a lake of rushes
Where we bathed at times and changed in the bamboos.
Now it is rather to stand and say:
How many roads we take that lead to Nowhere,
The alley overgrown, no meaning now but loss:
Not that veritable garden where everything comes easy.

And by the bay itself were cliffs with carved names
And a hut on the shore beside the maori ovens.
We raced boats from the banks of the pumice creek
Or swam in those autumnal shallows
Growing cold in amber water, riding the logs
Upstream, and waiting for the taniwha.

So now I remember the bay, and the little spiders
On driftwood, so poisonous and quick.
The carved cliffs and the great out-crying surf
With currents round the rocks and the birds rising.
A thousand times an hour is torn across
And burned for the sake of going on living.
But I remember the bay that never was
And stand like stone, and cannot turn away.

Virginia Lake

The lake lies blind and glinting in the sun.
Among the reeds the red-billed native birds
Step high like dancers. I have found
A tongue to praise them, who was dumb,

And from the deaf morass one word
Breaks with the voices of the numberless drowned.

This was the garden and the talking water
Where once a child walked and wondered
At the leaves' treasure house, the brown ducks riding
Over the water face, the four winds calling
His name aloud, and a green world under
Where fish like stars in a fallen heaven glided.

And for his love the eyeless statues moved
Down the shell paths. The bandstand set
On fire with music blazing at its centre
Was havened in his love.
The lichened elm was rafters overhead,
Old waves unlocked their gates for him to enter.

Who now lies dumb, the black tongue dry
And the eyes weighed with coins.
O out of this rock tomb
Of labyrinthine grief I start and cry
Toward his real day—the undestroyed
Fantastic Eden of a waking dream.

Lament for Barney Flanagan

Licensee of the Hesperus Hotel

Flanagan got up on a Saturday morning,
Pulled on his pants while the coffee was warming;
He didn't remember the doctor's warning,
   'Your heart's too big, Mr Flanagan.'

Barney Flanagan, sprung like a frog
From a wet root in an Irish bog—
May his soul escape from the tooth of the dog!
   God have mercy on Flanagan.

Barney Flanagan R.I.P.
Rode to his grave on Hennessey's
Like a bottle-cork boat in the Irish Sea.
    The bell-boy rings for Flanagan.

Barney Flanagan, ripe for a coffin,
Eighteen stone and brandy-rotten,
Patted the housemaid's velvet bottom—
    'Oh, is it you, Mr Flanagan?'

The sky was bright as a new milk token.
Bill the Bookie and Shellshock Hogan
Waited outside for the pub to open—
    'Good day, Mr Flanagan.'

At noon he was drinking in the lounge bar corner
With a sergeant of police and a racehorse owner
When the Angel of Death looked over his shoulder—
    'Could you spare a moment, Flanagan?'

Oh the deck was cut; the bets were laid;
But the very last card that Barney played
Was the Deadman's Trump, the bullet of Spades—
    'Would you like more air, Mr Flanagan?'

The priest came running but the priest came late
For Barney was banging at the Pearly Gate.
St Peter said, 'Quiet! You'll have to wait
    For a hundred masses, Flanagan.'

The regular boys and the loud accountants
Left their nips and their seven-ounces
As chickens fly when the buzzard pounces—
    'Have you heard about old Flanagan?'

Cold in the parlour Flanagan lay
Like a bride at the end of her marriage day.
The Waterside Workers' Band will play
    A brass goodbye to Flanagan.

While publicans drink their profits still,
While lawyers flock to be in at the kill,
While Aussie barmen milk the till
  We will remember Flanagan.

For Barney had a send-off and no mistake.
He died like a man for his country's sake;
And the Governor-General came to his wake.
  Drink again to Flanagan!

Despise not, O Lord, the work of Thine own hands
And let light perpetual shine upon him.

On the Death of her Body

It is a thought breaking the granite heart
Time has given me, that my one treasure,
Your limbs, those passion-vines, that bamboo body

Should age and slacken, rot
Some day in a ghastly clay-stopped hole.
They led me to the mountains beyond pleasure

Where each is not gross body or blank soul
But a strong harp the wind of genesis
Makes music in, such resonant music

That I was Adam, loosened by your kiss
From time's hard bond, and you,
My love, in the world's first summer stood

Plucking the flowers of the abyss.

East Coast Journey

About twilight we came to the whitewashed pub
On a knuckle of land above the bay

Where a log was riding and the slow
Bird-winged breakers cast up spray.

One of the drinkers round packing cases had
The worn face of a kumara god,

Or so it struck me. Later on
Lying awake in the verandah bedroom

In great dryness of mind I heard the voice of the sea
Reverberating, and thought: As a man

Grows older he does not want beer, bread, or the
    prancing flesh,
But the arms of the eater of life, Hine-nui-te-po,

With teeth of obsidian and hair like kelp
Flashing and glimmering at the edge of the horizon.

from Pig Island Letters

2

From an old house shaded with macrocarpas
Rises my malady.
Love is not valued much in Pig Island
Though we admire its walking parody,

That brisk gaunt woman in the kitchen
Feeding the coal range, sullen
To all strangers, lest one should be
Her antique horn-red Satan.

Her man, much baffled, grousing in the pub,
Discusses sales
Of yearling lambs, the timber in a tree
Thrown down by autumn gales,

Her daughter, reading in her room
A catalogue of dresses,
Can drive a tractor, goes to Training College,
Will vote on the side of the Bosses,

Her son is moodier, has seen
An angel with a sword
Standing above the clump of old man manuka
Just waiting for the word

To overturn the cities and the rivers
And split the house like a rotten totara log.
Quite unconcerned he sets his traps for possums
And whistles to his dog.

The man who talks to the masters of Pig Island
About the love they dread
Plaits ropes of sand, yet I was born among them
And will lie some day with their dead.

8

When I was only semen in a gland
Or less than that, my father hung
From a torture post at Mud Farm
Because he would not kill. The guards
Fried sausages, and as the snow came darkly
I feared a death by cold in the cold groin
And plotted revolution. His black and swollen thumbs
Explained the brotherhood of man,

But he is old now in his apple garden
And we have seen our strong Antaeus die
In the glass castle of the bureaucracies
Robbing our bread of salt. Shall Marx and Christ

Share beds'this side of Jordan? I set now
Unwillingly these words down:

Political action in its source is pure,
Human, direct, but in its civil function
Becomes the jail it laboured to destroy.

Ballad of the Stonegut Sugar Works

Oh in the Stonegut Sugar Works
The floors are black with grime
As I found out when I worked there
Among the dirt and slime;
I think they must have built it
In Queen Victoria's time.

I had the job of hosing down
The hoick and sludge and grit
For the sweet grains of sugar dust
That had been lost in it
For the Company to boil again
And put it on your plate;

For all the sugar in the land
Goes through that dismal dump
And all the drains run through the works
Into a filthy sump
And then they boil it up again
For the money in each lump.

The bricks are held together by dirt
And the machines by rust
But I will work in any place
To earn myself a crust,
But work and never bow the head
As any grown man must.

And though along those slippery floors
A man might break a leg
And the foul stink of Diesel fumes
Flows through the packing shed
And men in clouds of char dust move
Like the animated dead,

To work beside your fellow men
Is good in the worst place,
To call a man your brother
And look him in the face,
And sweat and wash the sweat away
And joke at the world's disgrace.

And sweet on Auckland harbour
The waves ride in to land
Where you can sit at smoko
With the coal heaps close at hand
And watch the free white gulls a while
That on the jetty stand.

But the Clerk and the Slavedriver
Are birds of another kind,
For the clerk sits in his high glass cage
With money on his mind,
And the slavedriver down below
Can't call a slave a friend.

Instead they have (or nearly all)
The Company for a wife,
A strange kind of bedmate
That sucks away their life
On a little mad dirt track
Of chiselling and strife.

But work is work, and any man
Must learn to sweat a bit
And say politely, 'OK, mate,'
To a foreman's heavy wit,
And stir himself and only take
Five minutes for a shit.

But the sweat of work and the sweat of fear
Are different things to have;
The first is the sweat of a working man
And the second of a slave,
And the sweat of fear turns any place
Into a living grave.

When the head chemist came to me
Dressed in his white coat
I thought he might give me a medal
For I had a swollen foot
Got by shovelling rock-hard sugar
Down a dirty chute.

But no: 'I hear your work's all right,'
The chemist said to me,
'But you took seven minutes
To go to the lavatory;
I timed it with my little watch
My mother gave to me.'

'Oh thank you, thank you,' I replied
'I hope your day goes well.'
I watched the cold shark in his eye
Circling for the kill;
I did not bow the head to him
And so he wished me ill.

The foreman took another tack,
He'd grin and joke with us,
But every day he had a tale
Of sorrow for the Boss;
I did not bow the head to him
And this became his cross.

And once as he climbed the ladder
I said (perhaps unkindly)—
'I'm here to work, not drop my tweeds
At the sight of a Boss; you see,
The thing is, I'm not married
To the Sugar Company.'

As for the Company Union,
It was a tired thing;
The Secretary and Manager
Each wore a wedding ring;
They would often walk together
Picking crocuses in spring.

You will guess I got the bullet,
And it was no surprise,
For the chemists from their cages
Looked down with vulture eyes
To see if they could spot a man
Buttoning up his flies.

It's hard to take your pay and go
Up the winding road
Because you speak to your brother man
And keep your head unbowed,
In a place where the dismal stink of fear
Hangs heavy as a cloud.

The men who sweep the floors are men
(My story here must end);
But the clerk and the slavedriver
Will never have a friend;
To shovel shit and eat it
Are different in the end.

from Jerusalem Sonnets
Poems for Colin Durning

1

The small grey cloudy louse that nests in my beard
Is not, as some have called it, 'a pearl of God'—

No, it is a fiery tormentor
Waking me at two a.m.

Or thereabouts, when the lights are still on
In the houses in the pa, to go across thick grass

Wet with rain, feet cold, to kneel
For an hour or two in front of the red flickering

Tabernacle light—what He sees inside
My meandering mind I can only guess—

A madman, a nobody, a raconteur
Whom He can joke with—'Lord,' I ask Him,

'Do You or don't You expect me to put up with lice?'
His silent laugh still shakes the hills at dawn.

2

The bees that have been hiving above the church porch
Are some of them killed by the rain—

I see their dark bodies on the step
As I go in—but later on I hear

Plenty of them singing with what seems a virile joy
In the apple tree whose reddish blossoms fall

At the centre of the paddock—there's an old springcart,
Or at least two wheels and the shafts, upended

Below the tree—Elijah's chariot it could be, Colin,
Because my mind takes fire a little there

Thinking of the woman who is like a tree
Whom I need not name—clumsily gripping my beads,

While the bees drum overhead and the bouncing calves
    look at
A leather-jacketed madman set on fire by the wind.

18

Yesterday I planted garlic,
Today, sunflowers—'the non-essentials first'

Is a good motto—but these I planted in honour of
The Archangel Michael and my earthly friend,

Illingworth, Michael also, who gave me the seeds—
And they will turn their wild pure golden discs

Outside my bedroom, following Te Ra
Who carries fire for us in His terrible wings

(Heresy, man!)—and if He wanted only
For me to live and die in this old cottage,

It would be enough, for the angels who keep
The very stars in place resemble most

These green brides of the sun, hopelessly in love
With their Master and Maker, drunkards of the sky.

37

Colin, you can tell my words are crippled now;
The bright coat of art He has taken away from me

And like the snail I crushed at the church door
My song is my stupidity;

The words of a homely man I cannot speak,
Home and bed He has taken away from me;

Like an old horse turned to grass I lift my head
Biting at the blossoms of the thorn tree;

Prayer of priest or nun I cannot use,
The songs of His house He has taken away from me;

As blind men meet and touch each other's faces
So He is kind to my infirmity;

As the cross is lifted and the day goes dark
Rule over myself He has taken away from me.

Haere Ra

Farewell to Hiruharama—
The green hills and the river fog
Cradling the convent and the Maori houses—

The peach tree at my door is broken, sister,
It carried too much fruit,
It hangs now by a bent strip of bark—

But better that way than the grey moss
Cloaking the branch like an old man's beard;
We are broken by the Love of the Many

And then we are at peace
Like the fog, like the river, like a roofless house
That lets the sun stream in because it cannot help it.

from Autumn Testament

12

The wish to climb a ladder to the loft
Of God dies hard in us. The angels Jacob saw

Were not himself. Bramble is what grows best
Out of this man-scarred earth, and I don't chop it back

Till the fruit have ripened. Yesterday I picked one
And it was bitter in my mouth,

And all the ladder-climbing game is rubbish
Like semen tugged away for no good purpose

Between the blanket and the bed. I heard once
A priest rehearse the cause of his vocation,

'To love God, to serve man.' The ladder-rungs did not
   lessen
An ounce of his damnation by loneliness,

And Satan whistles to me, 'You! You again,
Old dog! Have you come to drop more dung at
   Jerusalem?'

42

The rata blooms explode, the bow-legged tomcat
Follows me up the track, nipping at my ankle,

The clematis spreads her trumpet, the grassheads rattle
Ripely, drily, and all this

In fidelity to death. Today when father Te Awhitu
Put on the black gown with the silver cross,

It was the same story. The hard rind of the ego
Won't ever crack except to the teeth of Te Whiro,

That thin man who'll eat the stars. I can't say
It pleases me. In the corner I can hear now

The high whining of a mason fly
Who carries the spiders home to his house

As refrigerated meat. 'You bugger off,' he tells me,
'Your Christianity won't put an end to death.'

48

The spider crouching on the ledge above the sink
Resembles the tantric goddess,

At least as the Stone Age people saw her
and carved her on their dolmens. Therefore I don't kill
   her,

Though indeed there is a simpler reason,
Because she is small. Kehua, vampire, eight-eyed
  watcher

At the gate of the dead, little Arachne, I love you,
Though you hang your cobwebs up like dirty silk in the
  hall

And scuttle under the mattress. Remember I spared
  your children
In their cage of white cloth you made as an aerial castle,

And you yourself, today, on the window ledge.
Fear is the only enemy. Therefore when I die,

And you wait for my soul, you hefty as a king crab
At the door of the underworld, let me pass in peace.

from Five Sestinas

3 The Dark Welcome

In the rains of winter the pa children
Go in gumboots on the wet grass. Two fantails clamber
On stems of bramble and flutter their wings
In front of me, indicating a visit
Or else a death. Below the wet marae
They wait in a transport shelter for the truck to come,

Bringing tobacco, pumpkins, salt. The kai will be
  welcome
To my hungry wandering children
Who drink at the springs of the marae
And find a Maori ladder to clamber
Up to the light. The cops rarely visit,
Only the fantails flutter their wings

Telling us about the dark angel's wings
Over a house to the north where a man has come
Back from Wellington, to make a quiet visit,
Brother to one of the local children,
Because the boss's scaffolding was too weak to clamber
Up and down, or else he dreamt of the marae

When the car was hitting a bend. Back to the marae
He comes, and the fantails flutter their wings,
And the children at the tangi will shout and clamber
Over trestles, with a noise of welcome,
And tears around the coffin for one of the grown-up
    children
Who comes to his mother's house on a visit,

Their town cousin, making a longer visit,
To join the old ones on the edge of the marae
Whose arms are bent to cradle their children
Even in death, as the pukeko's wings
Cover her young. The dark song of welcome
Will rise in the meeting house, like a tree where birds
    clamber,

Or the Jacob's-ladder where angels clamber
Up and down. Thus the dead can visit
The dreams and words of the living, and easily come
Back to shape the deeds of the marae,
Though rain falls to wet the fantails' wings
As if the earth were weeping for her children.

Into the same canoe my children clamber
From the wings of the iron hawk and the Vice Squad's
    visit,
On the knees of the marae to wait for what may come.

TE AOMUHURANGI TE MAAKA
(b. 1927; Te Whānau-ā-Apanui, Kāi Tahu,
Te-Aitanga-ā-Mahaki, Ngāti Porou)

Haka: Hinemotu

Kōpare ō whatu
Whakaara mai ana ngā wai
O ngā moana ki runga o Hinemotu
Aha! ha!
Whakatau ake e hika mā
Ki ngā wai e whakarehurehu mai rā
Aha! ha!

Riu atu riu mai
Whati atu whati mai
Mau tonu
Aha! ha!
Whakaranga ngā kupenga

Tūpou ka ea
Tūpou ka ea
Whakaranga

E kuia e ia
Whāngaia mai ō kūhā!
Kūhā! Kūhā!
He kai ma ō mokopuna
Aha! ha!
Koe koe kōeaea ea ea
Hoki atu he tai
Ara mai he tai
Aha! ha!
Kī atu he kete
Ara mai kupenga
Tēnā i karawhiu!

Haka: Hinemotu

Open your eyes and stare
The waters of the sea rise up over Hinemotu
Aha! ha!
Give thanks people
To the waters misting before us
Misting with fry
Aha! ha!

The waves cut this way and that
They flee here and there
Held by the river
Cast out the nets

Dip in and dip out
Dip in and dip out
Cast out again

Oh ancestress dear
Open up your thighs
Yes your thighs, yes your thighs
Give up food for your grandchildren
Aha! ha!
You! You! Koea the wriggling guest, ea, ea, ea
The tide goes out
The tide will come back to us
Aha! ha!
The kete basket stands full
The net comes out full
Let's make for home!

Translation by Te Aomuhurangi Te Maaka

E tō e te rā i waho o Mōtū

E tō e te rā i waho o Mōtū i te pae raro o Whakaari
Pūmau ana tō heke i tō heke raro e hika ee
Kore rawa koe te tatari noa ki te huringa muri e
Engari mārō ana tō tū ki te poroporoaki mai e
Ki te ao mārama ki te ao tangata, ki te ao hurihuri
Tīahoaho ana te murara mai o tōu kanohi
Whakakoi ana ko' i āu hoari hei aha ee

Tērā pea kei tua o te pae raro o Whakaari tāu e hiahia
nei. Ahakoa a Ranginui i whakapekapeka i tō huarahi ki
ngā taura kapua kore rawa koe mō te tōmuri e.
   Pōhēhē ana koe ka whai atu au e, i āu mahi
maminga! Aha! ha! Taotū ana i a koe te pae raro o
Whakaari. Kākari mai ana kōrua—riro atu ana koe i te
pae raro. Tōtohe ana koe ki te haere i tāu haere ā,
toromi ana koe. Nanati ana te wheke a Tangaroa i tō
kakī—whakatahataha ana tō haere, whakatakataka
ana moata i muri tonu mai i tō whakaāhuatanga i a koe
i runga i te kare o te wai o te Moana-nui-a-Kiwa. Pīata
ana te moana i a koe, engari kua tīmata kē a Hine-
ahiahi ki te toha i tana huru. Kia hiwa rā! Kia hiwa rā!
   Mokemoke ana te tū a Whakaari i waho o te moana.
Ānō he whenua mahue. Ko te kare anake o te ia o te
moana e papaki kau ana i te akau e rongona atu ana.
   Rere pōpoto noa, te rere a te kawau i runga i ngā wai
pōpokorua—he kai rā mā taku noho puku e. E tō e te
rā, e moe e te rā i tekau-ma-rua e. Hei tō hokinga mai
ka ao, ka ao, ka awatea!

Go down, o sun, out from the Motu River

Go down, o sun, out from the Motu River
And over the horizon at Whakaari Island
Your going down, down to the underworld

Is a journey we all make, my friend
You cannot pause or turn from your path
But move unflinching in sorrow and farewell
To the world of light and men turning cold
As the lights glint on your face
The sword-lights you sharpen—for what?

Your desires are beyond Whakaari, out of reach, and
though Ranginui tries to turn you with his hanging
ropes of cloud, not even he can hold you back in your
wild haste.

Don't think to lure me with your tricks—aha! ha!
You stab the watery body of Whakaari, both of you
struggling together—until you're sucked down. You
jumped wildly, not caring, and now you drown.
Tangaroa's octopus tightens around your throat, makes
you slide down deep into the water, makes the empty
shells of light flicker out in your ghost lying on Kiwa's
great sea. Now you make the ocean red with light—but
briefly, for the evening maid pulls her cloak around the
world. Guard yourselves now, guard yourselves!

Whakaari Island stands out at sea a lover abandoned.
For now only the slap of the sea on the shore can be
heard.

The lone shag skips from one pool to the next, and so
do my silent thoughts. What food for thought you are,
o sun, sinking, dying at the twelfth hour. Only when
you come alive again will I see the light of another new
day.

Translation by Te Aomuhurangi Te Maaka

Overture for Bubble-Gum and Flute

When the bones are no longer curious
                and the shells
           are no more than shells
the whale's way
the wine-dark waters
have been pricked out
                 for tourists
when the terrible children
                Brunton
                Marx and
    the man who fixes television sets
have written all their books
finished their intricate fiddling
            have exhausted themselves
are
               no longer brilliant
               nor even very clever
Hephaestus
puts down his tools
             in bewilderment
             limps from his cellar
what will there be left to do
               on Lemnos?

A woman walks by the water
        talks to the wind and the sand
            she has combed back
the hair of her daughters
given her sons
              to the land:
on the rim of her horizon
rise

         office blocks and dormitories
the enclosures and the cages
               of the municipal zoo.
Her sister's in the nut-house
her brother died in gaol:
                    though
       the sun still rises in the morning
the stars ascend at night
         the moon is what she married
         the moon provides her light.
What's to be done on Lemnos
when the merry-go
                won't
             go round?

At Chelsea
feeding
         the Sugar Company ducks
woman dwarf and child
         entice cajole and plead
play out their separate phantasies
           in secret
         as they must.
What the woman does
         you know
the child
attends mechanical toys
         in theatrical full-dress
the dwarf
     that's me
         of course
Narcissus-like examines
the woman in the child
and sees reflections of himself.
This hand holds out the bread-crumbs
          this eye
       concedes the womb
in a mirror wrought on Lemnos
a gargoyle-mask

                half-covers
the waters of the moon.

Down on the lake
where algae
            leap blushing into bloom
the mayors of all the cities
              stir Lemnos with their spoons.
                    We wake
                      and
take the bus to Bristol
explore the public gardens
              examine Lenin's tomb
              admire
whatever's pretty
return to rented rooms:
            while Kitty gets the cholera
              Jack takes up the pill
we face with Agamemnon
the host of human ills
              the Great Pacific Ocean
                slides slowly
        down the eroded throats of shells.
What's to be done on Lemnos
when the merry-go

                    won't
                go round?

from The Toledo Room

I, ix

They do it with knives—
a kind of juggling act designed to lift
eyebrows, raise eyeballs
excite admiration, astonish, delight.

And when the bone is pierced
the brain falls out, the blood runs down

there's this sudden quiet—
a nervous laughter, a clapping of hands

as if at first, no one believed
it real, imagined it done with mirrors;
mock bones, mock brain, ketchup—
like on TV or at the drive-in movie house.

But it's the reality
of the thing that excites the laughter
the knowledge that the knives
are REALLY knives, have fine-honed edges

that they can be used
for opening arteries, removing intestines—
cut, pierce, hurt, do exactly
those things for which they're designed.

It's done with knives
and the best of it's when the victim himself
is no longer in doubt
the skin opens up & the gut tumbles out.

from Incantations for Warriors

5 Incantation

The warrior is going a journey:
    he travels like everyone else
      across a great rift
   a wide valley filled with stones
which block his way
  which he falls over in the darkness—

And he discerns that the rocks
    serve the same purpose
   as the water he wades through
    the dust by the roadside

mornings & evenings he has never seen
             mountains falling into night.

He is enclosed within a circle
          encompassing everything he feels
              everything he thinks:
        'chestnut blossoms in the mind'
children by a river at nightfall—
        his ignorance & his own stupidity.

And he carries with him
             across that wide valley
          a vision of the sun rising
          light falling over the land
of the sad sounds earth makes—
          hills, clouds, & the sky.

22 Complaint

I look for an explanation
of the way things are
      for everything miraculous in women
               (their mockery & disguise
prevarication, particular preference)
& most of all for that terrible giving ...
          & can't understand what it is
          (beyond the power of words)
that mothers give their daughters:
a suspension of the reasonable & actual—
          the language of surprise.

Lady, I remember your body
& the body of the spiritual world
          locked in that double helix
            of the first begetting:
the worst & best of wild surmise ...

It runs beyond reason
   beyond the sense of spring or summer
           the seasons that make good
whatever falls apart, dies, decays:
clouds breaking, leaves falling
         silence & the world's last day.

Lamentation on Ninety-Mile Beach

Hills afloat across the water are
immediate and remote as you
are now, Hohepa Kanara
this is Maringinoa
you said, and here
the Maori dead
look back
and weep
these
are waka au
braided leaves
left to guide those
that follow, whirlwinds
I said, look, see how that wind
goes chasing its tail, round and round
up the hill. And you replied calmly
'that may just as easily be a soul
as it passes, braiding the grass
exactly as I said', and you
were not joking, not even
offended that I did
not accept your
explanation
now I feel oddly
guilty that I did not
and I'm wondering, did you pass
like cloud shadow across the grass
did you braid waka au all the way up
the hill, leaving such vacancy no wind
can fill, let it whirl all it will
'and this', you said, 'is the road
taken by the many dead
te ara wairua, the way

the departing spirit
journeyed to join
its ancestors on
Hawaiki
a misty day
like this, you can
hear their voices, a high
singing on the edge of sound
or a sudden bright burst of words
out of nowhere, it is not frightening
it even makes you feel good about dying
that is te reo irirangi, sky voice.' But I
hear only your voice, Hohepa Kanara
in the crackling surf, the roar of
each wave as it rises and topples
against the shore, telling and
retelling its tales of
loneliness and loss
my courage is
not that of
a man
on his own
but of the many
how does that saying go
'e hara taku toa i te toa tahi
he toa takitini taku toa', ae, pono
as your people say, even to this day
we are the people of the long
memory, the flesh may die
but the spirit remains
yes, not only in surf
and dry grass along
a sacred beach
where once we
walked and
where
we may
remember
but today it is
only the surfcaster with

his supple rod, fibre or plexiglass
come to try his luck, take home a tale
of snapper and shark boasting, as well he might
having gone further than most, but not as far
as he will one day go, up this same toppling
shore where old friends pass, froth falls
like petals on black, reflecting pools
silent places at the edge of the surf
where you see yourself distorted
like clouds briefly reflected
as they pass, in endless
progression across
sea, land and sky
remember them
their name
is on the wind
Hohepa Kanara, Tangi Te Paa
Rarawa Kerehoma, each one a friend
haere, haere, haere atu, haere ki o tipuna–
te hono i wairua, i Hawaiki nui, Hawaki roa
Hawaiki pamaomao, the far distant gathering place
of your ancestors, to remain there, in peace, lie there
leave this small town, unable even to reconcile
the living, let alone the reproachful dead
poor Ahipara, our sad psalms falter
the thousand mile lamentation
of the beach beyond makes
mockery of our small
service for
the dead
we cluster
about the open doorway
to the night, the small neat plot
the bowed head, the droning word, the sound
of the sea overwhelming all, 'on low misty days
such as this', you said, 'and yes I am a heathen
if it is heathen to believe heaven and hell exist
they are on this earth and we make them
each for the other', but even that
matters less than the sullen

roar of wave upon wave
absolute universal
reiterated unique
death
of a shape
against a shore
shaped of their shape
no escape except
in the shape
of a wave
go
ka haere
ki o tipuna
haere, haere ki
te hono i wairua
haere, haere atu, haere atu
haere atu
aue.

ARAPERA HINEIRA BLANK

(b. 1932; Ngāti Porou, Ngāti Kahungunu, Rongowhakaata, Te Aitanga-ā-Mahaki)

He kōingo

I reira ahau
Tūtaki tāua
Haurangi ana
Ka kite ahau
I a koe
Me te mea nei
He taniwha
Ka minamina
Kia piri.

Hei konei rā
Ka huri
Te marama
He maramara
Marama rākau
Huri noa
Marama nui
Ahakoa rā
Mau tonu.

Kakai ana
Kongakonga a
Kikokiko
Kore he
Timatanga
Kore he
Mutunga
'Ka mate ka mate
Ka ora, ka ora'!

Ināianei kua
Kite ahau
Ki te minamina
Koe
Ki te pīrangi
Koe
Ahakoa wawata noa
Me kai kia kī
Engari kia tika te
Haere!

A yearning

I was there
We met
Drunk
And I saw
You
As if
A magic bringer
Then I wanted
To be close.

That was all
The moon
Turned to
Bits and pieces
Became lean
Was
Swollen
No matter what
It was there.

Eating
Bits and pieces
Then flesh
As if there

Were no beginning
And
No end
'From darkness
Into light'!

Now I
Have seen
If you desire
Or want
Whether only
A dream
Satisfy
Your hunger
But be
True in spirit!

Translation by
Arapera Hineira Blank

The Iceman

What happened to the iceman after all?
Amazing how we waited for his call
and ran across to pick up chips of light
as the iceman's hook would beak-like bite
deep into ice, which he shouldered on a sack
and carried to our verandah at the back,
invisible the winter halo round his head.

We have other means of freezing now instead
of ice; it only lasted half a day
unwinding summer's waterclock away,
filling the tank, falling on zinc
under the icebox.

      Nowadays I think
the nameless birds outside have hauled
some massive block of silence called
the morning to my door; with beaks well-ground
have started chipping splinters made of sound,
have sung me almost unaware how sick
I felt one childhood day, the embryonic
pain of seeing yolk and shell all splashed
together yellow where a bird's egg smashed;
yet pain evolves, perception grows more keen
as fits the many-coloured bird that might have been.

What happened to the iceman after all?
Amazing, how we waited for his call.

The Sirens

We sirens, since we rigged up stereophonic sound,
can take life easy. The tunes we use are played
from timed magnetic tapes and speakers placed around
at all the sixteen compass points. Dumb divers wade
through wrecks in leaden-heavy sleepwalk yet have
    found

no evidence soever of the hidden cause
which keeps insurance brokers busy, leaves the kin
of crew and captain searching for the laws
laid down, or dropped, by heaven. The divers spin
out hopefully that coil of dream the captain was

uncoiling so that they might walk where he had tried.
But somewhere along the line they find a severed
end which points in no direction save the tide's.
From storm-stacked files one diver has discovered
the ship's log lying, its pages blank both sides.

Our solvent sea is darker for those entries' ink
and makes the divers' task more difficult; but, as I say,
our work is easy these days—certainly we sink
more ships than did the old-time sirens trained to play
so many roles and voices, making captains think

their loved ones called. The former sirens had to learn
to pitch their voices high so only old sea-dogs
could hear the note whilst helmsman mate and crew
    would turn
blank faces to their captain yet be deaf as logs
or men with wax-sealed ears. You really had to earn

your immortality in classic times. We see
no great advantage to be gained from underhand
devices; one tune from sixteen places seems to be
harder for all to follow to the promised land,
or, if heard as danger, harder still to flee.

Waiata mo te whare tipuna

Kekē kekē pakitara
Me te hamumu pī
Ngā ihi o te rā
E wero mai nei
I ngā matiti kōpapa
Whiti pahū ana
Ki te whatu kōtahi o te tekoteko
E takoto whārōrō mai rā i te whare

Runga arawhata ahau
Me taku ringa e toro nei
Ki te whai haere
Ngā tuhinga kōwhaiwhai o neherā
Uku pāpango uku tea uku kōkōwai
Ngā rākeitanga rara
O te whare tipuna

Hoki wairua mai ra e hika!
Mai i ngā tangatanga tukutuku
Ārahina te ringa kūare e!

Nukunuku marumaru
Kikī rawa te whare
Pukepuke kiwikiwi
Whakapukupuku ana i te whāriki moe
Ngote kai horohoro ra te piripoho
Te waiū o te whaea
Kōhumuhumu whaiāipo i te kokonga
Me ngā koroua e ngongoro ra

Engari he pūngāwerewere noa iho ēnei
Me ngā tāhae pī

Ko rātou ngā kaitito pakiwaitara
Me ngā korokoro waiata
Mo te roanga o te pō
Kāhore he tamaiti
Kāhore he whaiāipo
Me ngā koroua e whākana nei
Whakaāhua horetea
Hauarea roto tīrewa kōrapa
Tū haurangi ra i te pātū

Me au hoki
Runga arawhata tūretireti
Me te tae mōhinuhinu
Me te rongoā mo te tuarā manumanuā
O te tekoteko e!

Restoring the ancestral house

Old walls creak
amid mason-bee hum
through cracked timbers
sun splinters ricochet from
the one good eye
of the tekoteko
supine upon the floor

And I . . .
ladder perched
hand poised tentatively
to trace aged scrolls
of clays blue-black and white and kokowai
adornments on the ribs of
the ancestral house
let the master craftsman return
from the loosened tukutuku panel
to guide the untutored hand

The shadows move
and the house is full
grey mounds humped upon the whariki
sleeping
a child slurps upon his mother's nipple
in the corner
muffled lover shufflings
and the old men snoring

But only spiders
people the house
they
and the marauding mason-bee
are the spinners of tales
and the long night singing
no child
no lovers
and the old men stare
faded photographs
morose in their warped frames
drunk against the wall

And I . . .
ladder shaking
and shiny acrylic
and cement for the dry rot
in the tekoteko's back.

English interpretation by
Katerina Te Hei Koko Mataira

C.K. STEAD (b. 1932)

April Notebook

1

April, and a fool's good day.
My salary escalates.
In the brisk morning
Anticipating fires
I think of insurance.
Preserve me from Justice.

2

Girl
You'd have me moon
In littered corners.
The dead are yours
Muse.
Keep them!
It's the living who die.
Listen.
Hear their rage and fret?
Set it to music.

3

She
After a night of serenades and skirmishing
Drags in her seasoned wake
This taut, bow-legged
Big-shouldered tom.

Catching his mean eye
A boot's throw from our door
I call him Purpose.

4

A padlocked trunk keeps
My days accounted
In draft and revision.

Iron grave
It's womb too.
I sentence myself.

An oak-headed catechist
A Swedish captain and
His daughter whose exact blood
This world affronted
Meet there the black Celt
Uttering
History, music.

5

Paulina, I was your first
Petitioner. It still galls me
In this month to remember
How hard I hammered
On the gate to your garden.
True patrician
You kept your legs crossed.
You married a maker
Of plastic gnomes and bird-baths
And bore him (they say)
A succession of grudges.
I took my seed elsewhere.
Paulina, I'm still your poet
Celebrating today
Baldly your locked gate
And the cobwebs in your tomb.

6

April 21. Far north
The sun enters the Bull.

I buttress this garden corner
With chimney bricks and plant
One palm, one pink hibiscus
One bronze flax.
All roads lead to it
A neighbourhood where
The dogs of war have never gone unfed.
Cracked brick in hand
Ears full of children
I stand between the columns
The unerected statuary of this garden
Caesar, and Henry Ford.

The wing of fire is clipped.
I look towards the dark,
Into the sullenness of its coming on.
Beneficence of the Eagle
Corrupts our days.

7

Happy birthday Shakespeare
the comedy of errors escalates
there aren't enough nettles to go round
among the grasping statesmen
Babel's headphones burn
Bermudas are long shorts
happy are you receiving me
their kitchens make ice
sleep tight Shakespeare
we can tell you now
it won't hurt
none of your blood survives

8

The last grape resolves beneath the vine.
Fruit-fly and wasp defect.
I watch
Pampas captains mount in the azure field.
Autumn. Auckland.

Spotless enamel
Scuffed by dusters.

9

Climbing on that same gun
Below the bloody flags, above the harbour,
I learned as you do my son
While April swept the vault and seemed to show
The place they'd sailed to
How boots and trumpets of good men shook down
Walls, and whole towns.
Medals aren't worn on sack-cloth.
The dead are ashes. Orations won't bring them back.
That jaw-bone of an ass was God's wrath.
We call it Anzac.

10

April decays in the grape.
It taints the air. Which of us two
Lives to see the other die
Not waiting on the proof
Will give what's borrowed back.
While one lives
So do we both, fortunate so far
Beyond deserving
It is a kind of faith
Refuses to see
In this bland sky
In every blade and branch
That grows to please us,
Injustice, ruling the world.

11

Each day He dies to do me good.
I sign a protest, join a march.
What Wolf began, Eagle accomplishes.

Minerva had a mouse in mind.
It was a weasel, tore her beak.
What Owl began, Eagle accomplishes.

Eagle bears the Snake to die.
Up there it twists about his throat.
Out of the sun they fall like brass.

I signed a protest, joined a march.
Today he dies to do me good.
What Eagle began, Serpent accomplishes.

from Quesada

Je pense . . .

   aux vaincus!

1

All over the plain of the world lovers are being hurt.
The spring wind takes up their cries and scatters them
   to the clouds.
Juan Quesada hears them. By the world at large they go
   unheard.
Only those in pain can hear the chorus of pain.
High in the air over winds that shake the leaves
High over traffic, beyond bird call, out of the reach of
   silence
These lovers are crying out because the spring has hurt
   them.
No one dies of that pain, some swear by it, a few will
   live with it always,
No one mistakes it for the lamentations of hell
Because there is a kind of exaltation in it
More eloquent than the tongues of wind and water
More truthful than the sibylline language of the leaves
The cry of the injured whose wounds are dear to them
The howl of the vanquished who cherish their defeat.

10

Odysseus under wet snapping sheets
Quesada in the saddle—all men are travellers
Astride, under sheets, travellers and lovers, they go
To prize the world apart, to learn the spaces
In Circe's cave, on couches of blue satin
In brown grass under summer olives.
As long as seasons change don't look for stillness
Dulcinea, don't ask for kindness or rest—
Only the long reach of the mind always in love.

17

That the balls of the lover are not larger than the balls
    of the priest
That the heart of the miser is not smaller than the heart
    of Quesada
That the same sun warms the knight and the squire
That the long lance and the short sword open equally
    the passages to death
That the barber may wear a beard and the hangman
    have long life
These are the opaque equities of our world.

That the breast of Dulcinea is whiter than the driven
    snow
That the strength of her knight is as the strength of ten
    because his heart is pure
That the empire of true love is boundless and its
    battalions unconquerable
These are the translucent hyperboles of art.

Where was Quesada whose grapes fattened uneaten at
    his door
Whose fields were ripe, whose mill-wheels were always
    turning?
He was beyond the horizon, riding against the
    sunspears
Remembering the foot of his lady tentative as a white
    penant in the cold mountain stream.

Pictures in a gallery in his brain
Were turned facing the wall, his limbs jolted
Coming down into a valley, night coming down
Sun catching flax and pampas along a stream
A church white in the foot-hills, the dead on his mind
The empty world full of their singing ghosts.

Owls in the poplar candles, a pheasant dead on the
    road
Thunder over the treeless mountain burned brown by
    summer
Thunder over the flooded fields, thunder over the
    dunes
Thunder over the darkened ocean shafted with light
Thunder in the long line of the surf breaking against an
    offshore wind
Thunder in the long line
Exaltation in the defeated heart of Quesada.

Who but a Christian would sing the broken body of
    love?
Who but a lover would sigh to be a plaything of the
    gods?

from Twenty-One Sonnets

2

Rain, and a flurry of wind shaking the pear's white
    blossom
Outside our kitchen window and tossing the lassiandra

As it did that morning four-year-old Michele Fox
Sat at our table painting shapes she said were flowers

While we listened to the news: a coaster missing up
    North,
A flare sighted in the night over Pandora Bank,

Radio contact lost—the ship's name, *Kaitawa*.
That was eight years ago. On the bus north

To Reinga and Spirits' Bay the driver remembers it—
Not a man saved, not even a body recovered,

Only smashed timber scattered down miles of coast
To tell how quickly it can come. I kept that painting—

It was the world she saw believing she had a father—
He was third engineer, a Scotsman, a good neighbour
   lost.

from Walking Westward

Walking westward
you have it all before you
the great out-reach
pale blue with a clean white edge
the downing sun bright orange
rabbits among lupins
       a dog in the distance
no human shape.

Out there is the world
is nothing but the sun bleeding
         cloud cerements
ocean
     darkness enfolding.

The fish of Maui is under your feet
the hook of Maui is in your guts
here is all the beauty of Lackland
the surf is blind as Homer and forgetful
in Paradise are no legends

the drowned angels are silent
        as the millenial stars.

         *   *   *

Mediterranean
a room with southern light
that strikes off sea through vine leaves
light reflected
                caught with
a brush in its hand
or playing on the ceiling
the only movie ever made in heaven.

Picasso's horned figure   brows in leaf
broods over her nakedness
why did they call it modern?

and at the Auckland Art Gallery
we stood breathless before it
knowing that room though we had never been there
where the sun lay on its back and with delicate strokes
painted light over light on the ceiling
above the brooding lovers.

Mougins, Notre Dame de Vie, Antibes
statues on ramparts against the sea
terraces, orange stone, deep windows, tiled parterre
and the lover with wreath of oak about his brows
taking in her nakedness
as a man takes in a painting.

'Holding that energy is near to benevolence'
and add to that
                l'occasion
the times that release it
so that the blessings of the heavens
holy influence

                    the rain and breath of stars
these are intelligible
as to say that she the lover looked on
was Proserpine
          responsible for the weather
for the way light struck light from water
          green from branches.

Or any morning like this one
that is a world of webs.

When the lovers die their stars are not withdrawn.

from Clodian Songbook

7

     Air New Zealand
                    old friend of Catullus
you offer a quick hike
                    to Disneyland
                    the South Pole
Hong Kong's hotspots
to ease a jealous ache.

     Thanks brother
                    but I'd rather
you flew downcountry a message to Clodia.

Tell her she's known to her 300 loveless lovers
as the scrum machine.
                    Tell her
          Catullus loves her
as the lone lawn daisy
                    loves
                    the Masport mower.

13

Fucking, I feel at one with the world
Clodia
it's like rowing into heaven.

                    Through glass
       the moonlit ferns and pongas
sculpted in the grove of Priapus
                       approve.

           On this coast are white
wine
and oysters.

A Popular Romance

will you have me?
groaned the frog
my squashy love
is all agog

do you care?
complained the crab
a true heart serves
this horny scab

the prince exclaimed
if you agree
your love could change
the brute in me

they're all the same
the princess said
it's like a bestiary
in my bed

My First Forty Years

all I wanted was to brew him rhubarb wine
to roast meat and onions for some good man
to lumber him in bed

to take his babbling children to the zoo
call nothing mine
scan his pores through a lens of candlelight

stare into his redness his hooked his twisted mouth
own his hidden breath
look down from a cushioned chair

and watch him jot his plans out like a child
with coloured pens with pads
and books and papers tipped across the floor

how differently it all turned out:
a man's grizzling bileful ambitions
his gay crabbed carnivals performed in meanness

behind his squinting foul-mouthed doors
so many pitiful unhot unkind bodies
stacked up like dummies in his head

I was brought up to a horror
of such domestic debt: the shame
of lover's prison: that blind and shabby hole

where relatives and friends would have to bring
pastries full of knives and files
and words knotted like climbing-nets:

after all there was that crisis just beyond recall
to anyone my age—that time when payments and
    instalments
chilled like a wet patch in the bedclothes

when our fathers' dabbling certainties
and our mothers' baffled hearts seemed to foreclose
and we had first knowledge of guilt in the last glance

of the windows of the huge houses as they were
    boarded up
in the silence of the mill in chains
in the way pride lay on its back and stared:

all I wanted was a microscope skis a pony
I wanted to stay
not to be taken from home like a pound of flesh

now the boys I grew up with have won their way
into success—in their offices they dream of wondrous
heroic uncomplicated transcendental debaucheries

my short-sightedness both appals and amuses them—
it makes them think me eccentric—they still shout
drinks then try to borrow their luck from the dark

the world faces ruin: this century costs too much:
and here am I desired at forty by many but loveless
what should a good woman do

there is no dawning of truth as white as my breast
no poem that smiles of my need
to be loved

all I want seems so reasonable: he should brew
rhubarb wine do his share of the chores
never snarl but sit there as part of all that I am

watching me unfold my plans like a child
curling up in his cushions and gloating
in his gnarled his dazzling his stubborn heart

Note on Propertius

Among the Roman love-poets, possession
Is a rare theme. The locked and flower-hung door,
The shivering lover, are allowed. To more
Buoyant moods, the canons of expression
Gave grudging sanction. Do we, then, assume,
Finding Propertius tear-sodden and jealous,
That Cynthia was inexorably callous?
Plenty of moonlight entered that high room
Whose doors had met his Alexandrine battles;
And she, so gay a lutanist, was known
To stitch and doze a night away, alone,
Until the poet tumbled in with apples
For penitence and for her head his wreath,
Brought from a party, of wine-scented roses—
(The garland's aptness lying, one supposes,
Less in the flowers than in the thorns beneath:
Her waking could, he knew, provide his verses
With less idyllic themes.) On to her bed
He rolled the round fruit, and adorned her head;
Then gently roused her sleeping mouth to curses.
Here the conventions reassert their power:
The apples fall and bruise, the roses wither,
Touched by a sallowed moon. But there were other
Luminous nights—(even the cactus flower
Glows briefly golden, fed by spiny flesh)—
And once, as he acknowledged, all was singing:
The moonlight musical, the darkness clinging,
And she compliant to his every wish.

Wife to Husband

From anger into the pit of sleep
You go with a sudden skid. On me
Stillness falls gradually, a soft
Snowfall, a light cover to keep
Numb for a time the twitching nerves.

Your head on the pillow is turned away;
My face is hidden. But under snow
Shoots uncurl, the green thread curves
Instinctively upwards. Do not doubt
That sense of purpose in mindless flesh:
Between our bodies a warmth grows;
Under the blankets hands move out,
Your back touches my breast, our thighs
Turn to find their accustomed place.

Your mouth is moving over my face:
Do we dare, now, to open our eyes?

from Night-Piece

2 Before Sleep

Lying close to your heart-beat, my lips
Touching the pulse in your neck, my head on your arm,
I listen to your hidden blood as it slips
With a small furry sound along the warm
Veins; and my slowly-flowering dream
Of Chinese landscapes, river-banks and flying
Splits into sudden shapes—children who scream
By a roadside, blinded men, a woman lying
In a bed filled with blood: the broken ones.
We are so vulnerable. I curl towards
That intricate machine of nerves and bones

With its built-in life: your body. And to your words
I whisper 'Yes' and 'Always', as I lie
Waiting for thunder from a stony sky.

Advice to a Discarded Lover

Think, now: if you have found a dead bird,
Not only dead, not only fallen,
But full of maggots: what do you feel—
More pity or more revulsion?

Pity is for the moment of death,
And the moments after. It changes
When decay comes, with the creeping stench
And the wriggling, munching scavengers.

Returning later, though, you will see
A shape of clean bone, a few feathers,
An inoffensive symbol of what
Once lived. Nothing to make you shudder.

It is clear, then. But perhaps you find
The analogy I have chosen
For our dead affair rather gruesome—
Too unpleasant a comparison.

It is not accidental. In you
I see maggots close to the surface.
You are eaten up by self-pity,
Crawling with unlovable pathos.

If I were to touch you I should feel
Against my fingers fat, moist worm-skin.
Do not ask me for charity now:
Go away until your bones are clean.

Over the Edge

All my dead people
seeping through the river-bank where they are buried
colouring the stream pale brown
are why I swim in the river,
feeling now rather closer to them
than when the water was clear,
when I could walk barefoot on the gravel
seeing only the flicker of minnows
possessing nothing but balance.

The Net

She keeps the memory-game
as a charm against falling in love
and each night she climbs out of the same window
into the same garden with the arch for roses—
no roses, though; and the white snake dead too;
nothing but evergreen shrubs, and grass, and water,
and the wire trellis that will trap her in the end.

Poem Ended by a Death

They will wash all my kisses and fingerprints off you
and my tearstains—I was more inclined to weep
in those wild-garlicky days—and our happier stains,
thin scales of papery silk . . . Fuck that for a cheap
opener; and false too—any such traces
you pumiced away yourself, those years ago
when you sent my letters back, in the week I married
that anecdotal ape. So start again. So:

They will remove the tubes and drips and dressings
which I censor from my dreams. They will, it is true,
wash you; and they will put you into a box.
After which whatever else they may do
won't matter. This is my laconic style.
You praised it, as I praised your intricate pearled
embroideries; these links laced us together,
plain and purl across the ribs of the world . . .

Visited

This truth-telling is well enough
looking into the slaty eyes of the visitants
acknowledging the messages they bring

but they plod past so familiarly
mouldy faces droning about acceptance
that one almost looks for a real monster

spiny and gaping as the fine mad fish
in the corner of that old shipwreck painting
rearing its red gullet out of the foam.

Below Loughrigg

The power speaks only out of sleep and blackness
no use looking for the sun
what is not present cannot be illumined

Katherine's lungs, remember, eaten by disease
but Mary's fingers too
devoured and she goes on writing

The water speaks from the rocks, the cavern speaks
where water halloos through it
this happens also in darkness

A steep bit here, up from the valley
to the terraces, the path eroded by water
Now listen for the voice

These things wane with the vital forces
he said, little having waned in him
except faith, and anger had replaced it

One force can be as good as another
we may not think so; but channelled
in ways it has eaten out; issuing

into neither a pool nor the sea
but a shapely lake afloat with wooded islands
a real water and multiplied on maps

which can be read in the sunlight; for the sun
will not be stopped from visiting
and the lake exists and the winds sing over it.

Rowley Habib (Ngā Pitiroirangi)
(b. 1935; Ngāti Tūwharetoa)

Moment Of Truth
(Maori Land Protest Sit-in)

They said a while ago that the fuzz were coming to take
    us away.
Someone said they were massing outside the Town Hall
and that there were a lot of them. Someone cracked a
    joke
and a nervous giggle rippled through the crowd.

Your mind, not wanting to believe, searches around for
    an explanation.
It might be a brawl in a hotel or a gang of bikies.
But you have to face the truth. It's you they're after all
    right.
Shit, what do I do? (It's not just a saying then that your
    feet turn cold.)

I've never been to prison before and the only
    confrontation
I've had with the fuzz was when one handed me a
    summons
for a driving offence, years ago. And I'm forty now.
And what about my wife? And what about my kids?

How will they get on? And will I be branded criminal
for the rest of my life? There is little comfort
in someone saying that we will be political prisoners.
And even less when he assures us that thousands will
    side with us.

I think to myself, 'Brother, there might just be you.'
And someone else, trying to persuade us to leave

tells us we could get up to thirty years for what we're
    doing.
We would have laughed at him before. But there is only
    silence now.

When will they be arriving, the fuzz? I'm a layman to
    this sort of thing.
What will I do? Do I stretch out stiff and make myself
as awkward as possible to carry? Or make myself all
    floppy—
or is that just what the girls do? Or worst of all, will I
    chicken-out and run?

And will they bash my head with batons in the dark
because one of the others called them pigs the other
    day?
And how long will this go on? Will this be just another
    false alarm?
Like the one the other night? I mean, I want to get on
    with other things.

I wish they'd hurry up and come, the fuzz and get it
    over with.
This waiting is getting me down. My nerves are packing
    up.

Ancestors

Where once my ancestors grubbed for the fern's root
They build their hygienic houses now.
And where the wild pig roamed and rooted
They've measured the land into precise sections
Worth 3000 dollars (or to sound better
For the prospective buyer, 1500 pounds).

And here where once on an excursion up the back
Jacky pissed on a scrub

And thought no more of it
A house stands worth 10 000 (quid that is).
And where Tamati did something worse
There stands yet another house
Even more expensive than the first.

MURU WALTERS (b. 1935; Te Aupōuri, Te Rarawa)

Haka: he huruhuru toroa

He huruhuru toroa te rere o te kapua
    ka pae ki runga o te tihi o Pukekura e
Auē! I ahu mai koe i Hawaiki nui
    Hawaiki roa, Hawaiki pāmamao e
Auē! Nō te ao pani, nō te ao mahue
    kua hoki mai koe ki te awhi
    i tō whenua
E! I roto i ngā whenua raupatu
Noho i te whakamā! Noho i te momori!
Noho i te whakamā! Noho i te momori!
Hore kau he oranga kei roto i
    tōku ngākau
Hōmai he whakahauora!
Toroa nui! Toroa roa!
Toroa rere mai! Toroa pāmamao e!
Auē! He tau pōuriuri
    He tau pōtangotango
    He tau pō tiwhatiwha e!
Hena! Te marama o runga o
    Aramoana tiaho ki te kāinga e
Auē! Pōuri nui! Pōuri roa!
Kia kite i a tauiwi nui!
Tauiwi roa! Tauiwi pāmamao e!
Auē! Whakaparu ana i tō
    tātou whenua
Hena! Mātakitaki! Mātakitaki!
    Mātakitaki! Mātakitaki!
Ki ngā kaipuke o tauiwi
    E rere mai nei!
    E rere mai nei!
Kei hea ngā waka Māori?
Kua tangohia e!
Kua tangohia e!

Ki te kōpū o te tai
I a Kōpūtai e!
I a Kōpūtai e!
Maringi ana ngā roimata ki raro
Ka kake anō ki runga
Tīheia ngā tini mahara
Ka awhi i roto i te pōuri
Te poupou whakairo ko Āraiteuru
Hei kāmaka!
Mō te kāinga e! Hi!

Haka: the feathered albatross

Like a cloud the feathered albatross
        alights on the summit of Pukekura
Aue! You came from the great Hawaiki
        the lofty Hawaiki, the distant Hawaiki
Aue! From a world of orphans, from a world deserted
        you have returned to embrace
        your homeland
To your confiscated homeland
Remaining in shame! Remaining bare!
My heart is sick within me
Inspire me!
Great albatross! Lofty albatross!
Flying albatross! Distant albatross!
Aue! A time of dark night
        A time of intense darkness
        A time of intense sadness!
Look! The moon over Aramoana
        illuminates the ancestral home
Aue! Great darkness! Deep darkness!
Witnessing great foreigners!
Lofty foreigners! Distant foreigners!
Aue! Polluting
        our land
Look! Look! Look!

Look! Look!
At the foreign ships
    flying here
    flying here
But where are the Maori canoes?
Taken!
They have been taken
In to the stomach of the tide
By Koputai!
By Koputai!
Tears fall underground
And rise again
With a great burden of memories
Embraced in the darkness
Is the carved post Araiteuru
The foundation
Of the ancestral home!

Translation by Muru Walters

VINCENT O'SULLIVAN (b. 1937)

Elegy for a Schoolmate

On the other side of the world I heard
That she died in a Newton kitchen,
Her head in someone else's oven.

I'd never thumped her nor called her names
With the others, and so I had nothing
To sorrow or anger about.

                        Her big
Wet-nosed face just the same for me
As if she was sitting in the desk beside me.

Her clothes were always dirty
And she said stupid things.
The stupidest when she was trying hardest.

And I wish now that I'd thrown
A rock at her, had her caned for smoking . . .
Then I could feel pent-up for a day
            And forget her.

But she takes her place among immortal things.
With the potter's wheel at the bottom of a dry pit,
With the hands of Egyptian ladies held like thin, brown
    leaves,
Their collars of beaten gold, and a basalt dog.

Home

When they came to that blue harbour,
saw the narrow gap,
and the waterfront seemed to stand
in its own reflection,
they heard in either ear the voice of poets,
one saying
            now you know what Ithaca was,
the other
            you have sailed past remembering,
are you any better than tout, or grocer?

            Rather than listen to either's talking,
rather than have the nets of both at once
cross their shrunken backs,
cutting against their ears
as against soft figs,
they shouted 'No! This is not our harbour!
We did not defy the sun and the earth's camber
for a town like squares of sugar
along the edge of a plate.'

Several cracked what was left of their hearts
against oars that fought them.
One broke his image in the glassy water.
Others moved and sang and thrashed
their feet on the deck,
expecting perhaps some god to be impressed.

And those young men who had run
from the high white houses
to the crusted wharves,
threw down their plaited branches.
They said 'Who shall tell their children?
Who shall call them father?
We have waited how many years
to be handed shit?'

Dogknotting in Quezaltenango

In a town with a name as beautiful
as you'll come by, which hand-outs tell you
is known for its hardworking, peaceable
natives, its fragmented cathedral
with provincial baroque façade,
a view of a volcano smooth as an ice-cream,
I witness, for the first time, dogs knotted
as in a dozen jokes—a large, grey
disconsolate mongrel dragging up the street
another, a third its size, which will not screw off.
Appropriate and natural as the weather
in a country which carries parable like a machete,
where the divine system of co-ordinates
splays out from each act like pins from their cushion,
where dogs knotted between cinema and church,
observed by mothers, children, an officer
whose pearl butt cheeks the declining sun—
those dogs as much as the vaunted quetzal
yelp of eternal order, the stellar path.
One watches, hears this sad bitch of a country
ridden by the iron hound whom one day will find
taking his turn on the vet's table,
another muzzle to greet you as you cross the border,
the same emblem waiting, one town or another.

from The Butcher Papers

Still Shines When You Think of It

Stood on the top of a spur once
the grunt before Sheila sharp beside him
a river shining like wire ten miles off
the sky clean as a dentist's mouth
jesus *Was* it lovely!

and the hills folded and folded
again and the white sky in the west
still part of the earth
            there's not many days like that eh
when your own hand feels a kind of godsweat
fresh on things like they're just uncovered.

And not fifty feet from the spur
a hawk lifted
            and for two turns turned like one wing
was tacked to the air
            and then she's away
beak a glint as she's turning
so the grunt sighs like in church
and even Butcher
                        yes Butcher too
thinks *hawkarc curries the eye all right*
gives your blood that push
while the mind corrupts as usual
with 'proportion' 'accuracy' etcetera
those stones we lift with our tongues trying to say
            ah! feathered guts!
And she's closing sweet on something,
death, that perfect hinge.

It still shines when you think of it,
                        like that river.

Look Sheila Seeing You've Asked Me

Life is *not* a horse with a winner's garland
on its sweaty neck, across its chugging veins;
not a rosette hung to a pair of agreeable norks
the world pants at like a scrum;
nor *quite* a flushy sunset and its pouring ribbons
from God's theoretic bosom either, lady—
Yet *I don't know what it is* says Butcher
                        hardly know what it is
if it isn't this as well—
                        which is light walking

the dreamy edge of steel
which is pulse where his wrist lies on complacent death
which is water pure as silence before speech is thought of
from the tap in the back room
                    splashed on face, on boots,
so he stands with chin tingling,
                        with feet like jewels.

from Brother Jonathan, Brother Kafka

13

To be in a place for spring and not have lived its winter
is to get things on the cheap—it is asking from sky
as much as taking from earth, what has not been
    earned,
it is food without its growing, pay without labour,

love and not its unpredictable effort
at kindness, tact—in fact, it is how we live.
I sit in a room where each day the heaters
burn for an hour less; I see trees

which I saw neither in leaf nor when their leaves
were called for, prepare for spring,
                            I am like a man
arriving too late for Friday's riddled flesh
or Saturday's dreadful inertia, and then on Sunday
    hearing

a corpse walks on the hillside, shining and placid,
asks 'What's so special?'
                        A man in spring
without winter or the fear which is properly winter's
is Thomas's gullible brother,
                    so much sillier than doubt.

27

A figure who stands on the beach and beckons,
invites to the green room behind the fangs of surf,
walks again in my dreams—a little too far off
to catch his features.

                                He is patient, sure.
He looks back, pauses, moves further on.
He could be a parent walking with a child,
waiting while shells are pocketed, while driftwood
the shape of a bird or of a figure is brushed and carried
to prove how the child had come to the sea's edge.

He walks on a bit, once more he is waiting.
His shirt is open at the throat, the sun
razors his stubble,
                    his step is pretty much my own—
then that slow encouraging sweep of his signalling arm.
Through his hands the sea glitters, the hands which are
    glass.

40

Last things:
            the turning leaves slip in the wind
as turning fish; the wind stills and the long branch
outside the window rubs at the late sky,
behind it the library tower, the power poles,

the dead paraphernalia of an ordered world.
The leaves if you like are now spread hands
or clipped identical banners or metaphor
fading against the stalled comparative sky.

The slight ephemeral leaf is the size of night.
The single word swamped in the gob of silence.
There is sky at the window, dark where even dark was.

    The veering fish slip on, there is breeze again
outside . . .

an undersea of leaves is schooling,
a branch berths at the wall.

One remembers light
as a quaint hook let down
through day's wrack,

home.

Don't Knock the Rawleigh's Man

Don't knock the Rawleigh's Man
when he opens his case and offers you
mixed spices, curry powder, chilblain
ointment, Ready Relief, brilliantine,
don't say *Not now*, don't think
Piss off, but remember:
think of a hill called Tibi Dabo
behind Barcelona and the legend
that up there Satan
showed J.C. just what he was missing.
What he offered was not simply
the vulgar things—the girls
with buttocks like mounded cream
or enough money in brewery shares
to take a Rotarian's mind off mowing lawns
for octogenarian widows, .
or the sort of drink we all know
Vice-Chancellors drink when they drink
with other Vice-Chancellors—
not that but more deftly
the luciferic fingers fondled
buttons nostalgic with little anchors
as in the Mansfield story
and bits of coloured glass from old houses
and variously, these: good punctuation,
unattainable notes, throaty grunts
at bedtime, the nap of the neck
of lovely ladies caught in lamplight

like the perfect compliance of the pitch
in the last over when the last ball
takes the intransigent wicket—
yes, he did. Satan offered those things,
those were the things turned down,
that's how serious it was.
And what was round the corner as we know
was a tree already chopped
waiting to be a cross and a woman
at home rinsing a cloth white as she could
and Joseph of Arimethea still thinking the rock
he had hollowed at phenomenal expense
was going to be his, forever,
not Some Body Else's, for a spell . . .
So when the bag snaps on *your* doorstep,
flies open like leather wings
and you see instead of feathers
the tucked-in jars, the notched tubes,
the salves the spices
the lovely stuff of the flesh,
ask him in, go on, in for a moment.
There's no telling what else he might show you—
what mountain he has in mind
you may cast yourself from,
what price that your hair shimmer
like a diving hawk.

Waikato-Taniwha-Rau

We have a fiction that we live by: it is the river
that steps down, always down, from the pale lake
to the open jaws of land where the sea receives it,
where the great body of the sea sucks the river on,
absorbs it, where river ceases as river,
joins the past of rivers:
              and we say as it
slips beneath the fingers of willows,

as it jerks from the narrow guts of white rock,
taniwha rau—good name, eh?
        We see the logs pinned at the bend
the child on the sandbank with a lasso or a chain
the drowned sheep puffed to a blurred balloon
the old men along the bridge spitting into the current
the pumice's small skulls on the black drift.
We join the men on the bridge, look into the river,
we hear them say *ah* when they say
'Even twenty years back the trout came this far',
or 'See that brown froth there? That's what gets the
    fish.'
They talk of 'upstream' as though of a time
when the girls rose as the fish did
and they fall silent for a bit and look down
at the mottled backs of their hands on the rail.
They say 'See you then' when we nod, walk on over
    the river . . .
We have a fiction and the fiction itself is a river,
it has upstream, lake, sea, current, much as this.
We say *taniwha rau*—'a spirit at every bend'.
We open and close our fists on the edge of the bridge,
raise and lower our eyes to the black water,
its sandbar and sacred mountain, reflected cliffs, the
    narrows.
We have a fiction to live by, talking of rivers.

Maui

I have snapped off my burning
fingers, and given them to you
one by one, but you have thrown them
in the stream to amuse yourself.
I am fed up with you!
When next you come to me begging
for fire, I shall be ashes.
I hear that you intend to cheat
Death—a serious matter—
but, when I see you crushed
between her thighs, I shall laugh
until my fires rekindle,
and my tears steam, and spit.

Journeys

At the end of the journey we built
another pyramid, intending
to rendezvous with the gods.
Each contributed a massive brick
and it was placed according
to his rank. At the top,
with a foot-hold in the heavens,
was our priest-king
with his mathematicians
and war-lords who planned it all.
As our energies ripened we were
driven on, remembering certain
promises that we carried in a chest.

Once, at sea, we gathered by the mast
to see an angry child, curled
head to tail, unfurl himself
as the ship rocked. Morals
spilt from his throat and sank
unfathomed, and, tongued
by faint light, he searched the sky.
It was a one-way mirror by day
he said—a gold and pink lie.

We left the chest behind—all
that we cared for was in the sky,
because of a small and swarthy
man-god we had learned to love.

We loved him for the curved
rib of his nose, and, because,
where he had walked, God sprang
from the soil like mushrooms
at a witch's heel. But now
he is staked out in the sky
with stars for nails, while we watch
stiff-necked and giddy,
and full of inarticulate belief . . .

Mushroom clouds like fairy rings
surround the earth. Forgive me—
I write hastily, in the shadow of my hand.

Vlaminck's tie, the persistent imaginal

Vlaminck's tie survives.
It is made of wood & painted yellow;
it has purple polka-dot moons
that once were sighted floating around
the town, walking Vlaminck in every
direction.
      When I tell my son
it is resting now in a glass case,
it looks like, say, the beginning
of the world, he says, measuring
the space between his outstretched
hands, oh—like a crusader's sword
you mean.
        Yes, perhaps that's it
I reply, looking out over the yellow
fields, the tall sword-grass battling
the air. I see, now I see Vlaminck
in his wooden tie sailing right by
the day-moon, milky & far.

Poem then, for love

1 The anima has a predilection

Always you are there—standing
outside the door when someone
shakes the house down, packs
the children away. You appear
at the bedsides of friends who
are leaving town, and finally.

Shadows grow out of your hands;
you bring hills into a room.
There is no question of regret,
you are busy with the secret
joy of one who is inconsolable.
Tomorrow, we may swing on the
bell of the sun, hang by a song;
we may sing. Oh, there is some
small promise when you say *I do
not believe, I know*. When I
touch your body there is light
buried in my hands; there is the
distinct possibility of romance.

2 And just now

The way light swarms over
your shoulders.
The day is remarkable that lifts
the town to walk on stilts.
The sun wheels down,
windows shine.

In the crowns of flowers
small fires leap; seeds spill
in the bright air.
Like planets spinning
into sight, passatempo our bodies
turn the hours.

For love your hair sings,
and earth's curve.
For love I pour light
into your body like this—
oh, there is music to be heard,
and just now.

3 The arrangement

Your letters arrive
almost daily, and on time;
there may be songs filled
with light, there may be none.
'When you appear on the balcony
like spring undressing, I will fly
through the points of your eyes.'
And what about that fine calligraphy
of sky?, I add as if to meet you
in the middle of a story that's
half gone: oh, we are happy, love
to make use of words even
if it is a trial.

Of course there is an
arrangement. When you say
it's time to move on; that your body
is a heave of old desires you are
ready to shake down—I can see
we are on the way to a fine future,
even if I refuse to know what comes
next (a cause de ma folie). Oh well,
somewhere there is a sentence
chasing time; there is a story
we may need to sleep on,
and always.

4 The right touch

You undress
by moonlight; your body is an adventure.
The mirror goes on
forever. I begin to suspect
you are leaving the story
I have been holding in my arms
all these years, or almost.

If I walk
from this room, return with a
small song for company
and the right touch to write in
the ending, will I find
the mirror may be taking you
away; the moon
a perfect accomplice?

Will I hear that cry
in the dark space
behind you?

5 My love in bed I will not lie

My love in bed I will not lie,
You take flight in the middle of it all;
Of course the moon is right on time.

I would wrap my legs around your waist
On point in air pin you against
The light, but too much is happening
Elsewhere, and already.

When you fall, if you have that
In mind, I will not be here despite
The pleasures of an old regard; there is
A boisterous affection in how we hate, and lately.

It is a comfort to know this speech
You make on leaving is also
About love, and clearly.

6 Leave it

leave it :
on the table
with these small
islands of stones,

and that fine Bakubu king
in ebony, his plum-coloured belly
a wishing-ring.

On the way out
you may be looking for words
to sing the perfect pitch
of morning; unriddle why last night
certain stars light years
from here were discovered
leaving town. Let be
what is, love, you know
every/thing that is
in the world changes
what is real.

Leave it :
but keep in mind
no doubt you will,
these chevrons of lavender
shedding their points,
that there is of course
no 'commercial outlet'
even if it is
invisible.

The Tall Wind

He said to them, Look at this: you see
where the tall wind leans against your window-pane?
And they said Yes; the cold has come again.
Which being true, he dared not disagree.

Instead he said, If that wind once more blows
like that, your house will fly away like straw.
But they, of course, had thought of that before.
And also, though he did not dare suppose

they might have done, they'd seen a dead man lain
for laundering on half a fallen tree.
He thought, How strangely that man looks like me;
and said aloud, With luck there'll be no rain . . .

and just as he spoke, it started in to pour.
One of them laughed, and one said, Thar she blows:
we'll find out now what this young charlie knows.
There's a tall wind out there, leaning on our door.

Fish and Chips on the
Merry-Go-Round

In caves with a single purpose
fish were drawn deliberately
from room to room.
Pallid Romans employed them
in a kind of masonry.
They even had their own day of the week.

Before that, though,
presumably,
before the nails from Calvary went back
like bullets into the dove on Ararat,
there must have been a fish or two
sharked many a household bare,
great bloated sunfish, ogling octopi,
between the bedstead and the hearth with relish
tearing apart all shining, arkless men,
competing for the viscous eyeballs loose
like opals on the suffocated floor.

A seasonable peripety assures
contemporary hygiene,
symbol and ancestor alike
hosed out, or splintered off.
Little, or large as eels, fish
fodder us; best of all
on the six days in between.
They build us up.

Still,
on a slow wheel, sharpening fins
give glints.

from The Four Last Songs of Richard Strauss at Takahe Creek above the Kaipara

2   September
(Hesse)

I am assembled here, at ease
in foreboding. I have measured the shadow
dying, and the brilliant wind
is alive with new things, lambs and petals and light,
asserting permanence. And yet,
this little thrush, that madly

flew through the scents of newness, now
grows cold within my hand. Strange noon,
to smite so casually, to freeze so small a thing
and drop it on warm grass!
I watched this little bird. It sped like a thistle
recklessly, bucketing on the air,
and very loud: implying, I think,
mortality, because I watched it all the way
from the long soft grass through that abandonment
to the tree so landmark-large, to the last and sudden
blindness, staggering ecstasy, light
singing
      death.
           I am assembled here, at ease
in foreboding. And my desire?
My love should bury this with love.

My love would not. My love would
toss it in the air.

Te Kaha

oh well tonight or some other night
you or someone else will put
the usual proposition and I
will warm and waver and decline

there are nappies snapping
at the soggy breeze
white is the baby's
Invercargill flesh
he bites Makwini's brown breast

the conger eel has been undressed
and the shark is a white knife
wanting a woman this time

you will or will not know my want
blunt as a boulder
sleek as a butterfish

but I am a boat afloat
and I see many a fin

I could rock you in the sun
I could be babied and reborn
but I age, I rage at other men
laughing and lying at their wives
and trying the tips of their knives

bird-woman

this is awkward I apologise
if it hurts as I hook in

we are tail-heavy I was planned
for lighter loads

I'm taking you north Rimutakas Tararuas
it's been a hard snowy season but
you'll love it

see my cosy sticks and stones see
my clever library For Sale Rest Area
Beware of Wind

I peck off your squeal do not shake like that
you need some titbits of possum

at this level I need a superman
with your leathery head and your gristly legs
you looked almost worthy

but close up you are the same
pale pulpy mixture as the rest
well you will have to do

you are cold come under my wing
I am an angel
I am a ladybird

stop whingeing please
yet I desire your voice

the snow is blind the wind bores me
and I am the only one of my kind

let me work your tongue with my claws
this is the way it is done
I need to hear my name

OK if that's your game
forget it we shall mate instead

excuse my claws it is a tricky business
must I spell this out? lie still

after all I've done I feel
wounded

my views my home my food refused
my words even my singular body

at least there are a few red
meals on your bones
you may think this is fun but for me

it's a nightmare
you've got everything
but I am lonely

first your eyes I hate
to be watched while I eat

next my beak on your tonsils
down there down there
are the words I need

how you love me or how you don't
how you miss the Olden Days
how wonderful/lousy I am as a lover

the soft bits while they are warm
and your limbs for later
safe from scavengers

you grow hard and cold
I told you you were hard and cold

now let us look at the sights
now let us fly in the sunset
light in the head
with love

from House Poems

xiii

the house flatters her ankles
with purple pink and green
the house prefers me to mention
spring in a soft voice often

polyanthus and peppermint
parsley and periwinkle
violet, viola, Virginia stock

rock tulip, jasmine
oreganum, angelica
forget-me-not, iris, crocus and chives

I plaited a litany of flowers
so we would have some syllables to sing
something feathery and savage
to celebrate come September

these are all the names we need
for our September song
this has always been the song
of a square yard garden in the city

my lai/remuera/ponsonby

she
holds th mirror to her eye

whole villages burn.

2 million years have proved nothing
she

did not already know.

th lines on hr hand
speak out clear   &

serene

also those beneath her eyes
& in between . . .

she
sits in th kitchen
'boiling an egg'

she
inverts th tiny
'hourglass'   &

30 seconds pass   &

she
contemplates th sand
                    &

she
holds a hand over each dark eye
in turn
     &

children burn.

at pakiri beach

(for adrienne)

here
I sing th green branch
th lost hymn
to earth's green blood
& sap
& slime
to hold back time . . .

let me here give praise & tongue
to your bright flesh & hair & bone
to mouth & nostril/ salt & lime
to breast & belly & that cool line
from throat to thigh; to all yr mouths
& voices/ winedeep/ lovestung
to silken down beneath th sun/ about
th nipple
& all along th length of supple spine . . .

so hold/ time! & let us stand
since we are naked &
th blood is up
stay your bitter hand!

& let me here give praise & tongue
to teeth & earlobe; sigh & chime
of deepest wells of love; to breasts

like bells; to distant cries within
th drifting head/ awash with swan pain
to these soft, inland eyes, gone out
this day on tides of goat pleasure
under
          sensual capricorn . . .
&
flesh i sing; th heavy vine; th green
voice branching up through throat
& down through spine; as thick as starmilk
or that yolk of springtide lust caught high
within the ancient ring of sea
& bone & sky
like dawn's blood in th midnight eye . . .

so hold/ time! & let us stand
since we are naked &
th blood is up
stay your bitter hand!

& let me here give praise & tongue
to your bright flesh
within whose silent web this moment past
have sprung; pale seeds as clear & warm
as tears; to this white rainbow; come
with dawn
to where th song fades bird like
on th feathered stave & broken
spoke of light . . .
to where th song fades O but does not die
lark ringing down
a waste of sky
                    to where we lie.

Silences

who seeks wisdom in words
honours (justly) th head
but/ O
        as the eye opens; so
closes th heart . . .

from th first breath
i drew in silence & i
discerned
            that all had gone
& had t'be relearned . . .

who seeks wisdom in words
seeks best between th lines
& below their bland faces—
who
faces silence in fear; fears
also
        th silence in faces/ at best
then
may try t'sing & shout
all night long!
& year after year
or come apart at last on looking in
to self
like harlequin aghast
against th thin
& painted cloth of life/
of 'art'
its feast or fast . . .

ah! words. words! WORDS!

        words
are pretty, petty
        icons

    yet man
has set them
        up

since this fell time began/ this
time round/ this spare & dying
        sun . . .
            &

who is there, here, with heart
who does not fear at last or least
in some fool part or wise/ th dark
blue frieze of
    silences
            to

    come?

i work towards words to realise
th silences that speak through 'art'
to live th dream & dream no death
            as he who
'would some kind'
            of wisdom seek
at that just folding of the eye
& closing of th breath
            opens
                / also
                        th heart.

Van Gogh

the iron bells toll
th train pulls in

the evening carries
birdsong
gracefully

against th pines
& cypresses

& on th distant scroll of th sea . . .

madame comes from th gloom

she bears a little flag

she cuts th twilight with her arm

her flag

she is doing her duty

it is pleasing for to see

her uniform is blue against th varnished sleepers . . .

along th narrow platform

th pullman passengers are making haste

vincent appears

carrying a cardboard suitcase

he looks a little ill
at ease

he doesn't look like he's got much time
to waste

over th mediterranean angle of his left shoulder
th stars/ the stars

are falling & climbing/ & going to gaseous waste

as is their wont . . .

some are blazing it seems/ far too brazenly
some waver & dip at th rim at th rim
of th sea

some tumble & roll, it seems, aimlessly
                                aimlessly . . .

like an unwritten law
like a yacht that will not come about

th train pulls out
th footsteps fade
the white waves roll
th dark bells toll.

Guy Fawkes '58

The stars all fell out of the sky
in a single night,
and boom, they sounded cannons too.
I'd thought, till then, he'd father kids for me,
for that was our inheritance
        those 'fifties years
to plan the wedding day
        and decorate the cot,
between the rugby and the beer,
the dreamy aftermath of the game won,
which carried us through the whole weekend,
Saturday night and Memories are Made of This
        on the car radio,
till Sunday tea
of piecart pigs' trotters,
        and love on a blanket by the lake,
fortifying us for the long week of work,
broken only by the current ball season—
clouded in 20 yards of chiffon,
Howard Morrison just a kid,
the potted ferns
and will Don Clarke do it again?
All this and no regrets.
(The single misplacement of innocence
is simply a technical aberration.
See how it begs to be taken back
every time it goes away.)
But at season's end, always the same.
As winter turned
        so did love,
put away with the football boots and hockey sticks,
waiting for another year.
A cold wind off the lake,

that fiery night he said,
                'Well see ya round sometime.'
He married, wisely and Catholicly,
                the chain store lolly counter girl.
Last count I heard,
sweet, sweet, the family numbered six.
Someone tacked the stars back in the sky;
I saw them there one night and wondered
if he saw them too, or whether it was just
                the last thing he'd done for me.

Train Song

It is hard to remember parents at their loving
Shoo-sh-shoo-sh-shoo.

In the austerity of wartime, the bravest front was at
    home
Shoo-sh-shoo-sh-shoo.

And after, in the bleary dawns of milking morns
Shoo-sh-shoo-sh-shoo.

Farm hands were made for sickles and lips for whistling
    dogs
Shoo-sh-shoo-sh-shoo.

Still, in '43, when I was three, in a night train full of
    Yanks
Shoo-sh-shoo-sh-shoo.

He in blue, she in best, my heavy lids spied hands
    locked fast
Shoo-sh-shoo-sh-shoo, shoo, shoo.

Return from Luluabourg

My report is not of schools
we built out there, or market gardens
planted to help the poor
but of an evening after work
when through a ruined iron gate I saw
a garden overgrown with weeds
and entered it.

Before me rusted boats, swings
dislodged like giants on a dungeon rack,
seesaws split, unpainted, thrown aside,
a wall from which I could not turn my back,
my own hands tied.

That concrete prison drop was set
with broken glass along the top,
bottles once put to European lips
at evening on a patio.
I climbed a metal staircase,
looked across a land scarred red,
huts roofed with grass on which
bone-like manoic roots were dried
to rid them of their arsenic.

But poisons which had touched that place
still kept it out of bounds;
pleasures were gone; children's voices
were not heard
except beyond that wall, in villages
or in the dusk, the garden, one night bird.

The Red Flag

A night of iron wheels and rain,
the judder and crash of wagons
coupling each valley to a metal road
and the nasal shriek of the train's
severing echo half way from home
to nowhere, I listen to you play
The Red Flag on your harmonica,
railroaded into cinder yards
on the abrupt last day of childhood.

1931. Your father just come back
from three months jail; you stand
among his comrades in a smoke-filled
railway waiting room; the train
blacks out the lamps; they take him
away. A child then, four years
old, accomplice to events
you do not understand, and your mother
won't or can't explain.

For the need of heroes in a hard time
the orphaning of those who wake
to the night train whistle in the hills,
play *Tannenbaum*, pine tree, wind, cones
and branches on an iron roof. In
Marion Street you wait for your girl
while west of Himatangi the barrow
of an old embankment covered with lupins
covers your father's tracks.

The Moths

Our house had filled with moths,
a slow silting of lintel and architrave
a cupboard dust,

until I looked much closer
and found the wood-grain one,
the white quill paperbark, the blotched
shadow of a patch of bush,
an elbowing riverbank that had gone deep blue.

The soft perimeter of forests
had entered our house
fluttering around the moon.

Then for five days they drowned
in sinks and pools or seemed to wane
into sanded wood or ash on windowsills
until they became
what they were when I first noticed them:
fragments of a dull interior.

Macrocarpas

Those most assailed trees
that go with rack and torn barbed wire
for don't we stack
such dog season stuff
always under a macrocarpa.

Always the roughest corner of
the farm, someone has worked his anger off
hacking at trees
so that like crabs
their pincers cut

They claw the northwest gales.
In macrocarpas there is no delight,
only the blown fleece
on a broken fence
magpies scatter

Across the plough; scarfed
and splintered when words were not enough
the revving saw
and the axe
do for them now.

Socrates' Death

That he was ugly we have no doubt,
but little survives of what he said;
remembered for his paunch, barefeet, indifference to death,
an ill-dressed master of argument.

I think of his accusers:
Anytus, a politician,
Lycon, a public orator,
Meletus, a tragic poet with lank hair,
scanty beard, whom Plato called
'a hook-nosed unknown man'.

Did death come any easier to them?

I see no change.
The thirty rule our city.
What we do not know we still condemn.
Sages wait without audience
and the trials go on.

Mask-Maker

For years we endured his insolence
as he worked on, carving

in the avoided wood
faces we could not see.

At festival or market
set by the stars, a grim display;
how he became us and mocked our chief,
found out bad parentage, illicit
love, confronted our intent
with consequence.

To me he gave this mask
smudged with charcoal and red clay,
to my neighbour this
abandoned hearth,
and to another madness, smoke and ash,
and to us all the curse of secrecy.

Clotho, Lachesis, Atropos

1 Clotho

I learn you were hurt my sweet and hurt again
      from loving too much
and of this wound and loss regretted nothing—

a slave in subject to voluptuous pain
      which caused you such
an ecstasy of bewildered weeping.

I the animal whose quick teeth nipped your vein
      now seize a bolder clutch—
lie down my whore you are not finished bleeding.

2 Lachesis

look at me sleeping I am somewhat disfigured
      like a statue from malice
with strong wrists and proud lips broken.

you the vandal in my private park who fled
      from mutilating this
creep back to gape at love so quaintly stricken.

oh then I grope blind arms across my empty bed
      and sadly wait your kiss—
and smile to think it is my hate you'll waken.

3 Atropos

I whom you touched am other things beside
        your only mourner trailing
an infamous coffin through each sullen rank,

friend you are dead your flesh is putrified
        and no clean-smelling thing
nor memory obliterates the stink.

As for convention I have wept dry-eyed
        from numbness having
greatly loved you for a time, I think.

Observations

Observations i

arranged on the opposite porch is a male
waist-coated and posing to catch my eye
you are far too unsubtle for such as I
dear sir, who prefer whipped cream and spice with
  pudding

besides you've a paunch and I've done with loving.

I've too sick a humour to take the veil
salvation oh lord's not in praying but work
till a board-hard bed in a prickling dark
of half-heard taxi wheels and footsteps hesitating

and a clock not kisses to wake me in the morning.

that girl with the cat-yellow ponytail
sixteen and slim and (thank you) quite ready
swaying my street like a sailor's lady
plucks and shreds he-loves-me leaves in passing

so what. I did that once myself when walking. . . .

Observations ii

daily the neighbour's dog is withdrawn to the park
ignores his mistress and courts her
the mongrel in a canine pas-de-deux
I have a dog most like to this which bites the heels of
    men

I must subdue it then.

my old dog blindly whimpers in the dark
hunts for its bounding hare in dreams
through my thorned channels and deep streams
and twitches bloodwet at my feet till I am rudely woken

so I shall whip it then.

I have a hound too weak and too afraid to bark
which cringes for the flesh that I withhold
and aching nuzzles me when nights are cold
till I allow my animal to feed and thrive again

it will devour me then.

Observations iii

turn again, maiden, twice slain and rotten—
no leaves and roses heat a coward's grave
and I'm no miracle to save
your citadel from civil war

cry armistice and resurrect once more.

cure me, physician, bloated with poison—
a wound I got in strife last year's not dead
but leaks and festers where ran red
in sweet and murky agony

and stained the cunning blade that gave it me.

fortify, proud one, survey the field again—
so foreign warriors flushed with victory
assault your trade-worn territory
thus sickening from my strange advice

and plunder you, commodious drab, as prize!

PITA SHARPLES
(b. 1941; Ngāi te Kikiri-o-te-Rangi, Ngāti Whatuiāpiti,
Ngāti Kahungunu)

Te mihini ātea

I motu koe e Hōri
Tuakana ē
Ki te Mangukaha ē
Tangi ana Mama
Ka riri Papa
Kua ngaro koe tuakana ē

Ka haere atu au
ki te mihini ātea
taku hoa pūmau
taku hoa mau tonu
e rua tekau heneti te whiu

Papā ana ngā ngutu wahine ē
Pahore ana te tuarā
I te hapū a Mereraina ē
Mataku ana
Ngā tamatāne ē

Ka haere atu au
ki te mihini ātea
taku hoa pūmau
taku hoa mau tonu
e rua tekau heneti te whiu

Horo ra te haere
O te moni e
Na te hōiho na te pia
Tangi ana Mama
Ka riri Papa
Kua ngaro koe tuakana e

Ka haere atu au
ki te mihini ātea
taku hoa pūmau
taku hoa mau tonu
e rua tekau heneti te whiu

The space invaders machine

You were separated from me Hori
My big brother
You joined Black Power
Mum cried
Dad was angry
Now you're lost to me my brother

So I'm off
to the space invaders
Spacies is my best friend
my true friend
and only costs twenty cents to play

The gossips are hard at it
The 'back' has been eaten away
Because Mereraina is pregnant
And all the local boys
Are worried

So I'm off
to the space invaders
Spacies is my best friend
my true friend
and only costs twenty cents to play

The money at home is still being
Frittered away
On the horses and beer
Mum cried

Dad was angry
And you're lost from me my brother

So I'm off
to the space invaders
Spacies is my best friend
my true friend
and only costs twenty cents to play

                    Translation by Pita Sharples

Haka: te puāwaitanga

Tēnā i tukua
          Hei auē hei!
Nāku te haka taparahi
Tōku mata kia whakarewa
          I ahaha
          kia whakarewa
          ki te wai ngārahu
          ko te pāwaha
          te uhi a te tohunga
          whakatara koroaha
          me te whānakenake!

Auē, moe hurihuri ai
taku moe ki te whare,
          He tangata pūtohe
          o te riri,
          he tama a Tū-kai-taua,
          he tama a Tūmatauenga!

Mā te hau rokuroku
e whiu i ahau
          Kss kss
Ki te pakanga
o tēnei rā!

Auē ko te kairākau
te taua kai-tangata
I ahaha!
Tū ki te whakarewarewa,
tū ki te tūtū ngārahu
pērā ngā tai
pakū ki waho
ki te toka tapu a Kupe!

Kia māia, kia niwha,
Kia para, kia toa!
    A, kia para,
    kia para, kia para!
    A, kia toa,
    kia toa, kia toa!
    I ahaha!

Ka kohekohe
taku korokoro
    te roro reka
    o te hoariri!
Kohekohe
taku korokoro
    Te Reo Rangatira
    kia puta atu
    ki ngā tamariki!

Ko te au mārō,
    ko te au mārō!
    Nene aku niho
    ki te tuna kaha—
    ngau, ngau, ngau!

Ko te tuna kaha
    Te Tū Āhua Rangatira
    o te rangatahi,
    te puāwaitanga,
    te puāwaitanga!

Pakanga parekura,
  Tīhorea te rae,
  tapahia te taringa—
  ka patu ki te ihu
  ka patu ki te tā!
  Ngā hoa ngārara,
  whakangaua ki te riri!
  Auē auē auē,
  Hei auē hei!

Haka: the blossoming

Put down your weapons
  Hei aue hei!
Mine is the haka taparahi
Let my face be adorned
  I ahaha
  Adorned
  with the tattoo pigment,
  marks of rank
  from the expert's chisel
  on the mouth,
  nose, cheek,
  and the forehead markings!

How I toss and turn
in my sleep at night
  For I am a warrior
  born to fight,
  a son of Tu the devourer of war parties,
  a son of Tumatauenga!

Let the gusty wind
carry me forth
  Kss kss
To where the battle is
being fought this day!

These are the tried warriors,
the war party that will destroy the enemy
I ahaha!
Dance the war dance,
perform the weapon dance
like the tide
that claps beyond on
Kupe's sacred rock!

Be bold, be courageous
Be brave, be strong!
Yes be brave,
brave, brave!
Yes be strong,
strong, strong!
I ahaha!

How my throat
tickles
for the sweet brains
of the enemy!
Yes my throat
tickles
for our proud language
to be imparted
to the young!

Be strong in battle,
be strong in battle!
My teeth clatter
for the big eel—
bite it, bite, bite!

What is this big eel?
It is dignity
for our youth,
it is the blossoming,
the blossoming of our people!

It is like a battle to be fought
  Where foreheads are gashed
  and ears are severed,
  noses are clubbed,
  necks are the target,
  enemies are made
  to eat the dirt of battle!
  Aue aue aue,
  Hei aue hei!

   Translation by Pita Sharples

The best cowboy movie

The best cowboy movie I ever saw
Began with a notice sticking on a cactus
I mean the beginning was the best
Ever begotten by the torn word. WANTED
Or GOLD RUSH and half a hat.
In excitement I recall they turned the coach
About and before nightfall the classic
Town showed its boardwalk arse
To the red sky. The bar door swung loose
As a hooker's thighs. The cards
Spread out, well-thumbed, the honkytonk
Gulped to fan the silence. Three guns
Split the mirror above the coward barman.
The standard pattern, classic cultures—
The virgin schoolmarm on the outer
Inside the charmed picket fence of sharks' teeth
Was overthrown later in the piece
By the hero with eyes like guns.
In the end string tie and waistcoat
Triumphed and the domestic stage
Flew fast as airmail between the towns;
They all were wanted in that place
That stayed or lived twelve hours and
Twelve and raised a golden glass of lead.

The terrapin

Gabrielle, the terrapin, whose tiny eyes
Blink sideways like the flaps

Of the digital clock telling time
Is crouched on the floor of the
Gardening shed. A few hydrangea leaves
Left over from hibernation stain
Into her shell. It's spring.
We lift her out into a world of blossoms
And watch her neck come out
Sniffing the whole two feet to
Her submerged pool. Quarter of an hour.
Will the scents of spring still hold
Through sleep's dead leaves? It seems
They may. We turn our heads, talk
Softly. Then with a sudden plunge
A passion like rage drives the shell
Over the top angry as Patton:
The angry grass of spring blazes
Against crabbed grey winter claws.

City girl in the country

The rooster crows like someone being sick.
How Nature stinks! The fecund pots
Of time-embalming herbs visibly
Eat what sun there is embalming us.
The proper oils, the proper bread
Seem offerings to a beetling god
Whose hair sprouts under the flagstones
Whose orisons arise in fleas.
The busy ant, pernicious wasp
Devour their mutual hemispheres.
The girl in the garden calls out 'Shit!'
Aimlessly pulling out the weeds.

Temptations of St Antony
by his housekeeper

Once or twice he eyed me oddly. Once
He said Thank God you're a normal woman
As though he meant a wardrobe and went off
Humming to tell his beads. He keeps
A notebook, full of squiggles I thought, some
Symbolism for something, I think I've seen
It on lavatory walls, objects like chickens' necks
Wrung but not dead, the squawking
Still in the design, the murderer running.
He's harmless, God knows. I could tell him
If he asked, he terrifies himself.
I think it makes him pray better, or at least
He spends longer and longer on his knees.

from Casanova's Ankle

Casanova's ankle

Casanova was turned by an ankle
Over and over. His glance ascended
To towers of conquest, snares set
In the shade of trees. Too bad
He had to toil as well in the trap
To free the booty used
And stained by capture. Distasteful
Somehow what he possessed
When the time for possession came.
It was better in the stalking light
With the moon half-hid
Following the scented glove, the ankle.

Close-up

A woman inside an enormous sunhat
scrapes at a hillside. Below her a string road
winds round the corner and out of sight. Above
her, a storm mass creeps across the sky.
　　She tussles, she tugs at the earth.
White hairy roots lie crumpled at her feet.
Overhanging tussock cuts her hands.
　　She is clearing a space to paint on.

Have you heard of Artemisia?

Have you heard of Artemisia of Halicarnassus,
　　or Cartismandua? or Camilla?

Have you heard of Hiera of Mysia? Or Julia
　　Mammaea who ruled Rome? Or Tomyris the Celtic
　　queen who killed great Cyrus of the invading
　　Medes and Persians?

Have you heard of Boadicea who fought
　　an attacking empire—who would not be a Roman
　　Triumph and died by her own hand?

Have you heard of Martia Proba, Martia the Just?
　　Her Martian Statute, after a thousand years,
　　was the source of Alfred's code . . .

And what of Hypatia of Alexandria? head of
　　the School of Philosophy—logician, astronomer,

mathematician—torn to pieces by a Christian
bishop's flock . . .

Have you heard of Thecla the Apostle, or Aspasia,
or Nausicaa? and if you know passionate Sappho
what of Corinna, St Bridget, or the Lady Uallach?
and since you know Joan of Arc, should I
mention the Papess Joan or good Queen Maud,
or Philippa the beloved queen whose merchants
bought her pawned crown back . . .

I did not learn them at school, these queens
and scholars . . . but scan names such as Mary,
Elizabeth, Shulamith, for their story—vivid
women who lived as the Celts did, with audacia,
and loved their sisters . . .

In a wheel's radiation all spokes fit the motion . . .
old Europe's strain has crossed the Pacific Ocean
and I have heard it, who am a descendant
in a train, going back to a flat with a goddess
wall, whose connections travel countrywide
in quiet woman's guise . . .

dedicated to Elizabeth Gould Davis and Max Jacob

Theology and a Patchwork Absolute

Time and again,
time and again I tried to write a goddess song.
Now that I have fleshed the lyric tongue a poem
stirs. It breaks from its inhabitants. Red shapes
blaze in the patchwork quilt. Here are two women
naked on a bed.
  Such proximity is heretical and a sin
to theologians and borough councillors. Their voices

shake the boardrooms. Bearded ones look stonily
from blazoned coats of arms. Thick carpet corridors
choke between the walls.

And we strip absolution. We have become
our own theologians and counsellors. Our skins are
moon washed. Our laughter escalates. If sometimes
we hear Unclean Unclean we ascribe it to the mythical
leper, mournful behind his bell. From driftwood
fire to loft we heal the biblical landscape.

We have unpicked the spiral staircase.
We have pieced out a goddess ancestry from digs
and neglected pottery to risk her gifts.

One is the faculty of clearing a Selective
Hard of Hearing. Libraries and presses yield
their fast. Shelves inch out to accommodate new
limbs. A poem holds the shell of an inner
chamber.

Voices between the breasts. Satin
and seersucker edged with feather stitch. Arms
that slide down forearms. Yellow plums.
Serenities.

Proximity of old lyric tongues and this.

Responses to Montale

1

It wasn't in my time, or so I suppose
and we left off loving long ago.
It is tragic only if we allow it
where the loser is lost and the lost defeated.
Leavings of rumour and want
and a smidgen of truth time will concede.

Look, see how the sun topples
to its known rest on the far side of everything:
and the breeze, begrudging nothing,
carries summer in its arms
wandering across fields that are youth's.

2

You rang to say goodbye
and I could hardly speak.
'That's all right,' I said, lying.
Look how I manage!
Do I survive in your memory
not quite a legend? Hardly.
You will survive in mine
as a cactus extremes of weather.
Because you are not here.
Because you knew better,
supremely, and it grows later.

3

Recognition cannot be taken away from us
as time consumes. It is not

the flower's fragrance that survives
but the flower,
or nothing at all.

4

To speak of larger truths
pre-supposes a knowledge of truth,
and we don't have that, Montale,
or if we do we cannot share it.
We cannot buy it, we cannot
sell it, yet the possibility lingers
in all its haunting ambivalence
and that is enough.

5

If your feet touch the earth
you are lucky. If your tongue speaks
of wealth
accruing in the spirit
then the sun glows in you
and your memory
is charged with remembering.

Coming Home

Coming home late through the smoky
fuzz of late autumn, winter rackety
on the elbows of birch trees,
a storm of finches pecking an apple,

I feel some things are never
lost in the conspiracy of evening,
the garnered and gathered
puddling silences of chill air.

I find you, wet hair glistering,
lying in a bath of foam, so I soap
your back, my hands revived
by your smooth skin, its perfect slither,

and then I go in my dubious mind
to stand in the damp and addling
dark beside the beetle-browed barn
and wait for tribulation to pass, music to begin.

Nichita Stanescu

You say you 'live inside a full-stop'
even though you hate them
and much prefer to 'whistle up the moon'.
'A single great life' seethes
in your tired, wrought
Romanian's face.
                    The hurt we inflict
upon animals and trees haunts you,
is raw as wind accompanying rain.
Nothing is pure enough
to cleanse centuries of infection.

A moon rises white
and floats like a full-stop.
The light is as clear
as the tears that flood your eyes,
wet your stubbled cheeks.

Each life is a 'great life',
but some are greater than others.

Psycho

At your silver wedding in '64 we gave
you the name Psycho—partly out of ignorance,
partly out of mixed-up pride.
Roared along Ponsonby road drunk on rum
celebrating the sixteen piston transplants
you underwent in 3 rodbending years;
took you to an empty suburban beach
at midnight, where you watched
with hot wisdom the voodoo fires jump
between our jeans as we drank
to your honour.
   Psycho, the word the darkdressed beachraiders
wrote in their notebooks as they gathered
the underaged from the underground hangouts;
smooth-dressed underground raiders
too busy under the beds counting stolen goods
to notice the smokey getaway—
eight bodies crammed into a single seated
4 wheeled psychopath;
gearlever between the legs of a knocked-out
catholic girl screaming for the next party.
   In '39 they respectably named you Ford.
By '64 your owners had turned to suicide,
& the underaged runaways had entered the womb
of your trunk to kiss the ejaculating
petroltank at each rubberburning curve . . .
   But now, after 3 years & 8 hundred
gallons of illegal gas has been shoved down
your chronic alcoholic throat,
we watch you die under the shaking hands
of the carwrecker;
his hammer smashing into your stretchmarks,

while the people you educated, dragged
thru fast narrow streets
stand by, dreaming of the next party.

My Mother Spinning

Sit too close
& the spinning bobbin cools you.
Leave the room
& the foot pedal beats
on a raw nerve.
Leave the house

& a thread of wool follows.

Thoughts of Jack Kerouac—
& Other Things

I work nights at the University Bookshop:
Junior, Intermediate, Headman, Honorary Caretaker,
Master Cleaner. I work in every conceivable position
from toilets, Foreign Language to Herbal Cookery,

sometimes singing 'Oh What a Beautiful Evening' and
sometimes not. Mostly, I just race about like
Neal Cassady with an overstuffed vacuum
cleaner snarling on my tail, cornering fast on one

sneaker past SUPERWOMAN and gassing like a madman up the BIOGRAPHY Oneway Section—chewing-
   gum,
cigarette-butts, paper-clips and brains dissolving before
my foaming fury . . . Zap, out the back, empty a tin,

grab a bucket one mop one broom, flash back
past LAW, Modern PSYCHOLOGICAL Medicine,
  Heavy
Granite Colour-filled Graffito ART, Sex Cornered
PAMPHLETS, miles of wrapping paper and up the
  stairs

to the staff room for a coffee break at 8. Ten
minutes only. Into the toilets, scrub shine wipe
on hands and knees, sometimes thinking 'The Closest
I Come To God and Other Things' and sometimes not.

Mostly, I just thank the Lord for the Detention
Centre Experience many Rocky Youthful Years back
and get the hell out of there down the stairs (4 at
a time), jump over a hot PAN Paperback, switch off

the lights (5 second silence by the NZ POETRY
Section), scratch my backside, straighten the doormat,
lock up, slam the outside door tight, run to the pub
(9 PM), sweat, feel proud, get half drunk,

crawl home, sit down, try to write a love poem
to a girl who works in the Bookshop Office . . .
Her typewriter and hairpin, her mystery yoghurt con-
tainers, her tiny footscuffed secrets and solitary chair.

fox glove song

it was last year
    same time
same time as this
the sweet peas were black
  by the side of the road
i did not know the fox gloves then

    last year
    same time
  same time as this
i was hidden hidden by the walls
    dark red

a long road
  lay between us
the hills were burnt black
  black the manuka trees
black black the sweet peas
  by the side of the road
i did not know the fox gloves then

the throats of the fox gloves
      are spotted spotted inside
      the black storm has passed
    leaving the river yellow swollen
        at the foot of the house

      the leaves of the fox gloves
      are pale fur
      between the hills

i shall never know the river
      yet i bathe my head

in its waters
walk on its smooth stones

i shall never know the trees
that stand on the other side
i know only the fox gloves
the foxgloves

waiheke 1972—rocky bay

i came
heavy with child in the fierce sun
the house was a dull yellow
lying
below the road
the front door was shaking
in the heavy house
the gate was wire
the fallen stars on the path
were hidden
by dry mud
lying in heaps
on the bank grew endless daisies the colour of the
house
near the clothes line
where the clothes hung
dry & empty
was a swaying wooden cross
the chimney rose up
in the painted sky

all summer the cicadas screamed
glued to concrete walls
their bodies heavy and painted
i did not know the way outside
rats with shining eyes
skimmed up trees

the heavy pods
of the nikaus
crashed
in the heat
my baby clung to me
his eyes seeing beyond
later
when he died
i walked
through the wire gate
down a long dusty road
at the end
was a shop
a telephone box
and a little crushed beach
where the sea ran
in and out

1974—the sounds

After much driving
on broken roads
we came to a place
where the hills rose on each side of the water
the house sat beside a magnolia tree
it had no leaves
only grey twisted branches
the wind ran over the grass
there was a dog on a chain
black and ginger
his eyes demented
a lamb running beside its mother
in a bloody coat

We walked until we came to a deep pool
below the road

that night i slept with my child
under a picture
of fish
gasping on a beach
lilies
in a broken vase

from Black and White Anthology

8

I say hello to the sunshine
     how nice to have you here
ignore my bile, oldtimer
                      since the stars
                      split us
                      oh
                      north &
                      south
tell you one thing however
this one here (gestures)
is gonna be
(PAUSE)
       my last duchess
(coughs) (reaches for the horehound)
for I declare (declares)

:we are no longer strangers!

10

her voice is like some angel picking at the door
her voice is like some angel (spits)
in some whores' caravan park saying
'it's $20 for a blow job, Mac'
oh she
(laughs like a cracked mosque)
oh she burns
        really
        she rides the trade winds
like the early winter rains . . . (it never rains)

18

oh me

is that the ambulance chasing out of town?
is that the rain dying away in the hills?
there is a shadow against the sun
a door opens
                & the dry season begins
our last supper
oh me
I do what everyone else through here has done

What Happens in Shakzpeare
(for Chrissie)

it's a rheumatic world if you ever stop to listen:
some country doctor down some country ways
nodding to the sun
oh lord, he say
you got cancer shacking in your lungs
(something about it that I can't get quite right
turning around now)
ah streets drowning in junk
(beat me brother beat me)
there's people on Aro St with guns & knives
just to see how the law stands
and the armed offenders' squad
is ripping down hungry tenements
on the black side of town.
the proud young princes of this generation
are greasing pipes in the engineroom
oh yes
they need to travel on the other side of the world
a diet of Hangchow eggs
(here they come now
coming home with the sunshine in their eyes)

alas
oh
alas
(sometimes I can't even feel the pain)
everything gets a little easier
clearly green
is the colour of fear
green
is the colour of the wild man coming over the hill
green is the hair of the child on the corner
trying to get her medicine
with her left leg stuck out too
ah
too terrified to run for the other side.
meanwhile
bankers and commercial attachés cruise the allnight
    revues
in cars built like hotel rooms,
direct telephone connection with their dealers
(bring me a miracle,
I need to cry tonight)
& with their forgers
& with their hired hands in the universities
who send them bones
(any man's bones)
that have deformations
as a result of genocide,
for example—
welcome to drink friend,
        welcome
            yes
life is reduced to a tired biology
played
oh
by a rock 'n' roll band
called maybe the Four Gone Conclusions.

meanwhile
downtown in bourgeois city streets

the magicians and Pharoah's men and the Great
   Copt
are making a line hand in hand
and kneeling down before they stand
& honest citizens out in the housing projects
turn on the television
to hear the town crier from his closet
give the stock exchange report—
it's a rheumatic world surely
when the people come to town
to ask the banks back for their money
(ha)
what strange three wise kings are these
slouching towards Bethlehem?
it's never been this cold before
the night porter has been to see the Chinese
and has done some acupuncture
the American Embassy is full of plumbers
who want to recommence the opium wars
out on the border
where professional soldiers kick each others' shins
through the barbed wire
green
green
green are the exquisite fascists of Europe,
hhhmmmmmmmmmmmm mm m
like Renoir of old
all feeling has gone from my wrists
now to paint down trying one last time
the dainty peach of a schoolgirl's trembling buttock
and dreaming of huge black mesmerists fucking Paris
about
oh
(about the year 1914)
oh
that shake in the wrist
when all the manufacturers say
that all your labour
will
have to come cheaper than this

(oh Jerusalem!)
(oh Calcutta!)
and the wide world groans
my fingers get tired of hanging on,
there is no feeling in my bones
welcome to the drink,
friend
a foreign city is beautiful seen from the hills
but seen from the ghetto it's a pile of shit

(somewhere precursory to this:
war is a cow
with an udder of thorns)

despite all the promises
there is no fast way home
and where
oh
where
is the laughing saviour with the easy answers
and why
the dealers are packing their bags
and standing hand in hand
in line
at the station
where a red light is shining
hey hey
who will point a golden finger and say
that's the way
yes
way to go

so it goes

so it does

so let it be

(here they come now
called maybe the Four Gone Conclusions)

At Castor Bay

I found the colour of your
flesh again this morning:
a tidal bank exposed
at dead low water, shells
the colour of your flesh.

This coast again . . . sun rising
over islands this blue May
morning reefed inside the bay
where sunlight floods:
wading to my knees, fat
black seagulls on the smooth hard sand
and water clapping, the rock-pools
drained . . . familiar
but no less bright,
your silken crevices.

Sunday Evening

This morning gathering wood
at the old mill up Moonshine
Valley Road: all a little
pointless, these fires, with no one
here but myself a little
drunk and out of booze.

                And all
the afternoon, combed the edge
of the estuary, kindling
for a month.

With an almost
sickening smell of gum, night
settles in the macrocarpas.

The first sharp drops of cold rain
fall. I think of her, five foot,
no more, maybe dead: a black
raven crouching in her thighs.

Porirua Friday Night

Acne blossoms scarlet on their cheeks,
These kids up Porirua East . . .
Pinned across this young girl's breast
A name-tag on the supermarket badge;
A city-sky-blue smock.
Her face unclenches like a fist.

Fourteen when I met her first
A year ago, she's now left school,
Going with the boy
She hopes will marry her next year.
I asked if she found it hard
Working in the store these Friday nights
When friends are on the town.

She never heard:
But went on, rather, talking of
The house her man had put
A first deposit on
And what it's like to be in love.

Bottle Creek Blues

The wind can't blow any harder,
the air's as heavy as Hell . . .

I watched blue diesel smoke like mist
hanging on a high suburban hill:
wind I thought would blow it away
but the wind itself is diesel.

And yet the smoke disappeared
absorbed by that suburban hill:
the problem of disposal was
solved by the lungs of the people.

Two years ago we used to row
to an island here called Cockleshell:
gather cockles in a sack,
warm them up and gorge ourselves.

A friend I used to do this with
near died from typhoid fever:
they had the cockles analysed—
shit from down the coastline further.

Barefeet on the beach is madness,
this beach that was once made of sand:
the sun shines bright on broken glass,
cockles from Cockleshell Island are banned.

Sad protest songs are sung and heard
like this one here. And afterwards
the audience goes home convinced
the shit's cleared clean away with words . . .

The wind can't blow any harder,
the air's too heavy for the birds.

My Father Scything

My father was sixty when I was born,
twice my mother's age. But he's never been
around very much, neither at the mast
round the world; nor when I wanted him most.
He was somewhere else, like in his upstairs
Dickens-like law office counting the stars;
or sometimes out with his scythe on Sunday
working the path through lupin toward the sea.

And the photograph album I bought myself
on leaving home lies open on the shelf
at the one photograph I have of him,
my father scything. In the same album
beside him, one of my mother.
I stuck them there on the page together.

Maintrunk Country Roadsong

Driving south and travelling
not much over fifty,
I hit a possum ... 'Little
man,' I muttered chopping
down to second gear,
'I never meant you any harm.'

My friend with me, he himself
a man who loves such nights,
bright headlight nights, said
'Possums? just a bloody pest,
they're better dead!'
He's right of course.

So settling back, foot down hard,
Ohakune, Tangiwai—

as often blinded by
the single headlight of
a passing goods train as by
any passing car—

Let the Midnight Special shine
its ever-loving light on me:
they run a prison farm
somewhere round these parts;
men always on the run.
These men know such searchlight nights:

those wide shining
eyes of that young possum
full-beam back on mine,
watching me run over him . . .
'Little man,
I never meant you any harm.'

My Father Today

They buried him today
up Schnapper Rock Road,
my father in cold clay.

A heavy south wind towed
the drape of light away.
Friends, men met on the road,

stood round in that dumb way
men stand when lost for words.
There was nothing to say.

I heard the bitchy chords
of magpies in an old-man
pine . . . '*My* old man, he's worlds

away—call it Heaven—
no men so elegantly
dressed. His last afternoon,

staring out to sea,
he nods off in his chair.
He wonders what the

yelling's all about up there.
They just about explode!
And now, these magpies here

up Schnapper Rock Road ...'
They buried him in clay.
He was a heavy load,

my dead father today.

Birth of a Son

My father died nine months before
My first son, Tom, was born:
Those nine months when my woman bore
Our child in her womb, my dad
Kept me awake until the dawn.
He did not like it dead.

Those dreams of him, his crying
'Please let me out love, let me go!'
And then again, of his dying ...

I am a man who lives each breath
Until the next; not much I know
Of life or death; life-after-death:

Except to say, that when this son
Was born into my arms, his weight
Was my old man's, a bloody ton:

A moment there—it could not stay—
I held them both. Then, worth the wait,
Content long last, my father moved away.

Requiem

They say 'the lighthouse keeper's world is round'—
The only lighthouse keeper that I know
Inhabits space, his feet well clear of ground.
I say he is of light, of midnight snow.

That other lighthouse keeper—he they say
Whose world is round—is held responsible
For manning his one light by night; by day,
For polishing his lenses, bulb and bell.

My man, my friend who lately leaves, is quite
Another type. He climbs no spiral stairs:
But go he does, for good, to man the night;
To reappear, among his polished stars.

The Prayer

I

What do you take
away with you?

Here is the rain,
a second-hand miracle,
collapsing out of Heaven.

It is the language of
earth, lacking an audience,
but blessing the air.

What light it brings
with it, how far
it is.

*

I stayed a minute
& the garden
was full of voices.

II

I am tired again
while you are crossing

the river, on a bridge
six inches under water.

Small trees grow out of
the planks & shade the water.

Likewise, you are full of
good intentions
& shade the trees with your body.

III

Lord, Lord
in my favourite religion
You would have to be
a succession of dreams.

In each of them
I'd fall asleep,

scarred like a
rainbow, no doubt,
kissing the visible bone.

On originality

Poets, I want to follow them all,
out of the forest into the city
or out of the city into the forest.

The first one I throttle.
I remove his dagger
and tape it to my ankle in a shop doorway.
Then I step into the street
picking my nails.

I have a drink with a man
who loves young women.
Each line is a fresh corpse.

There is a girl with whom we make friends.
As he bends over her body
to remove the clothing
I slip the blade between his ribs.

Humming a melody, I take his gun.
I knot his scarf carelessly at my neck, and

I trail the next one into the country.
On the bank of a river I drill
a clean hole in his forehead.

Moved by poetry
I put his wallet in a plain envelope
and mail it to the widow.

I pocket his gun.
This is progress.
For instance, it is nearly dawn.

Now I slide a gun into the gun
and go out looking.

It is a difficult world.
Each word is another bruise.

This is my nest of weapons.
This is my lyrical foliage.

The trees

Barques we ride on over the sea:
we like to come in on the tide
alone and when it's morning, first
light shattering the bodies.
We want to go under completely,
a well-heeled relic of devotion.

Shapes in the dusk, the faithful
breathing, happens under leaves;
though what does it matter, let's suppose—
'under the circumstances' is where *we* are.
The truth is a requisite urge,
nobody's lover. Sweet sweetheart,

I have a good intention to be better.
I mean to be a silence,
a hair on the floor of the forest.
Why, I sometimes hope to be your pleasure,
the raft you swim out to in lake-water,
shaking a little when your body touches.

Contemplation of the heavens
After Camille Flammarion

Innumerable worlds! We dream of them
Like the young girl dreaming
Who separates with regret from her cradle.
What cannot this adorable star
Announce to the tender & loving heart?

Is it the shy messenger
Of the happiness so long desired?
What secrets has it not surprised!
And who bears malice against it?

And yet, what is the earth?
Is not the great book of the heavens
Open for all to see?
Seek, talk, find out in your conversation.

The Selenologist

Is gazing at the moon again.
He stares as usual through his optic lens,
The length of tube with glass at either end.
There, as it happens, is the outside cat;
And there are the fox & the flower & the star.
Among all these his life takes place.

There also is the river of light
Which moves past stars with golden rays
Too bright to contemplate or gaze upon.
The river itself begins in snow,
Far out in space. It travels under cloud,
And those who travel in the boat upon the river

Are pleased to hold beneath the cloud
Because there they are always safe.
(Of course, they will never again traverse
The space they have just left
And which they have just deserted forever,
They will never again embrace brothers or sisters:

They are looking for life on another planet.)
Imagine, before the selenologist was born
They were on their way. They dipped their oars
In cloud and thought of water. Even now
They hardly know if they are touching water
Through the cloud—for they are going with

The current anyway. They are unknown life
But not to each other. They know each other
By their voices and the songs they sing; yet
They can only assume the content of these songs,
The golden stars past which they journey,
They can only assume the water.

This is not strictly true
For they can almost guess at death.
They can imagine the faces, growing older;
Also, they know that if one should fall
From the boat, then it is one voice less;
And yet that such a splashing will confirm the water.

It is then they sing with purest pleasure.
The selenologist can hear across all space
The sound that water makes when violently displaced
And fancies he can hear them singing.
He knows that before he was conceived
This noise was on its way; and smiles

And sighs and gives the cat its supper.
He tells the story of the fox & the flower
& the star, he writes how happy all these are.
He sighs and writes: 'Life is motionless
In consequence of all the time it takes.'
He sighs and writes: 'Distance sets limits

Where our vision fails in space.'
He tries to imagine the boat upon the water
But can see only grass in a small field
By the river at the edge of cloud.
It is immense vegetation, fixed in place:
Green as emerald, soft like a lake.

The Late Victorian Girl

A friend thinks he knows best
and says only because you love him.
And because you make a point of entry
he is grateful and knows where he is
and will do without the usual summary
of facts. Oh he is lost
in the complicated forest of your heart,

he is lost in the forest of your heart
and soon will be obliged to climb a tree and scan
the wide horizon. But it is darker up among
the branches than it is down here, and here
he already knows there is nothing: not the light
of the moon or the light of the stars disappearing,
none of the things he still believes

are needed, not even you.

Children

The likelihood is
the children will die
without you to help them do it.
It will be spring,
the light on the water,
or not.

And though at present
they live together
they will not die together.
They will die one by one
and not think to call you:
they will be old

and you will be gone.
It will be spring,
or not. They may be crossing
the road,
not looking left,
not looking right,

or may simply be afloat at evening
like clouds unable
to make repairs. That
one talks too much, that one
hardly at all: and they both enjoy
the light on the water

much as we enjoy
the sense
of indefinite postponement. Yes
it's a tall story but don't you think
full of promise, and he's just a kid
but watch him grow.

Zoetropes

A starting. Words which begin
with Z alarm the heart:
the eye cuts down at once

then drifts across the page
to other disappointments.

*

Zenana: the women's apartments
in Indian or Persian houses.
Zero is nought, nothing,

nil—the quiet starting point
for any scale of measurement.

*

The land itself is only
smoke at anchor, drifting above
Antarctica's white flower,

tied by a thin red line
(5000 miles) to Valparaiso.

London 29.4.81

King Solomon Vistas

1

Gazelle-girl/gazelle
your small breasts leap to your dancing
at the crest of the mountain.

Your feet play upon the brink
knocking the quartz pebbles together.

Your flank draws taut along lithe sinew.
Your narrow breasts leap to your dancing.

The rattle of pebbles down the mountainside,
ankle cymbals at the rim of space . . .

2

You are borne up
by the love of others.
You put words in their mouths.
You the king enter the bodies of women

& speak through them
in the flat
clonic syllables of trances.
Their dark eyes roll up.

They dance before you
groaning your impersonal strophes
clashing their ankle-cymbals.
Their fine joints turn back impossibly.

3

At the rim of space
                    mind's
archimedian point

on which it tosses
itself up & over
                    like the long
flung back hair of a dancer whose

spine cracks like a whip or
a quartz boulder striking half
way down the mountainside
& sailing outward.

from Earthly: Sonnets for Carlos

9

'If thy wife is small bend down to her &
whisper in her ear' (Talmud)

                              —what shall I
whisper?   that I dream it's no use any
more trying to hide my follies. If trees &

suchlike don't tell on me I understand
my son will & soon, too. His new blue eyes
see everything. Soon he'll learn to see
less. O the whole great foundation is sand.

But the drought has broken today, this rain!
pecks neat holes in the world's salty fabu-
lous diamond-backed carapace & doubt comes
out, a swampy stink of old terrapin.

What shall I say? 'I hid nothing from you,
but from myself. That I dream, little one,

10

by day & also by night & you are
always in the dream . . .' Oh you can get no
peace, will get none from me. The flower smells so
sweet who needs the beans? We should move house
   there
into the middle of the bean-patch: a
green & fragrant mansion, why not! Let's do
it all this summer & eat next year. O

let's tear off a piece. It's too hard & far
to any other dreamt-of paradise
& paradise is earthly anyway,
earthly & difficult & full of doubt.

I'm not good I'm not peaceful I'm not wise
but I love you. What more is there to say.
My fumbling voices clap their hands & shout.

26 *power transformer*

Dozens of wrangling sparrows have built their
shitty serviceable nests high up Three
Mile Hill in a power transformer. I see
them every day unscorched & lusty where
they're getting on with it in that airy
crass penthouse with its fine view of the sea,
shouting & breeding among the deadly
grey buzzing conduits . . . oh you were born there

first of all little Carlos, in the mind,
& there you live now in faith & in hope
before a horizon that could skate right
up to you! (closer than *this*, than these lines,
& closer than the thought of love, the 'shape
of things to come')
                    —let them see/
                              who have sight.

31

Diesel trucks past the Scrovegni chapel
Catherine Deneuve farting onion fritters
The world's greedy anarchy, I love it!
Hearts that break, garlic fervent in hot oil
Jittery exultation of the soul
Minds that are tough & have good appetites
Everything in love with its opposite
I love it! O how I love it! (It's all

I've got
              plus Carlos: a wide dreaming eye
above her breast,
                    a hand tangling her hair,
breath filling the room as blood does the heart.

We must amend our lives murmured Rilke
gagging on his legacy of air.
Hang on to yours Carlos it's all you've got.

Those Others

1

The sea does not
                  meet the sky. They kiss only
in our minds. They are priceless
                              in that space
which recedes forever
                      where we make them lovers
forever
        O my dear friends I reach out
as though across the sea
                        to embrace you
between sea & sky
                 or between earth & sky, that space
where the imagination feels your warm
                              breath upon its cheek.

2

Teraweka, Sleeping Indian, Signal,
                              Flagstaff, Cargill, Saddle,
& those other
                nameless hills
just beyond the public ridges

                                        which frame
the world we can admit: we come upon
                                those others
as we come upon certain ideas,
                        a hinterland, that we know
but pass through always
                        going *to* somewhere,
a friend's place or a place
                        where friends were once—
'those others': ideas
                        like the idea of an endless space
where sea
        & sky kiss,
ideas without names,
                        beyond the frame of the world.

3

This is a letter
                which must travel through that hinterland
without knowing its destination.
                                Or perhaps it is returning
by way of the same
                anonymous familiar hills,
a sign
        that friends have gone, that the house
(on the cliff, by the small lake, in the paddock,
                                in any case
there, *there, stop!*)
                has been drawn into that hinterland
where we cannot stop, because the space
                                goes on forever,
the embrace goes on
                forever, as the horizon,

which eye & mind
                    unroll   a highway
leading
        forever to where *you* are.

4

How can I speak of the
                        sadness in this? The infinite
regression of love? The weariness
                            of that distance?
In that same space, in the
                        imagination, you are embraced!
By way of those highways,
                    of the heart, you are always closer.
Day by day, more of the hinterland
                                is named:
Communion, Love, Imagination—
                            these hills are dark,
wooded, sometimes alight
                        with yellow flowers,
a dogged clasping
of gorse, barberry, kowhai, broom, lupin, ragwort.
The road follows their perfumes.
                        From the summits of the hills
we look out at the sea
                    turning forever to the sky.

from Angel

& this is where
you get
off, Angel,
that tender miracle your child's
foot   treads the glass
shard doesn't feel a thing
till it hits bone

it goes in so clean.
& this is where you get off, Angel.
Hey, & across there
where the ozone blows down from the north
& then blows
back again from the south
'in one ear &
out the other'
your own sentences coming back at you
backwards off the
windy Straits off the snowy shoulders
of Tapuaenuku: a shrug, who
cares? clouds as heavy
as a drink of water—hey, across there's
Mt Crawford. The millionaire embezzler
plays 500
for cigarettes
there. That's
where you get off
Angel. That's where your
sentence comes back
at you. You
cheap bastard. This is where
you never listen. This is where the cloud
you drink's
so heavy it
rams you into the dirt
you never had on your hands
Angel. This is where you get off
oh Angel child here's
where your miraculous glass foot
slashes the beach. Down to
the bone
where it hurts.
This is your beach-head
right here
         right here
Angel. One step back
& you're off & there's nothing
behind you

but what you came from
the bitter waters you
rode in on   ah they
filled your nostrils then Angel like an offshore breeze
in spring yes
gorse-flower & jasmine, something
rare like that.

from Tales of Gotham City

The Beggar at the Gate
(for Tony Fomison)

The first
tale of Gotham City, the Beggar
at the Gate. Gunshots
across Evans Bay, believe that,

a breeze from paradise, smoky
cloud cover, commuter cars
on the coast road by the yacht marina, tax
free collateral, leisure scam.

But while you set the scene, shooting
your language
out like carat cufflinks
from under good cloth, your

mohair & wool mix, or
Donnegal so plain like
real taste, don't forget
the beggar at the gate.

Mount Crawford Prison is keeping a
cool elevation, below it
the Shelly Bay Defence Base tricked out
for a picnic spot, & evening lights the bony sea

as it might 'strike' the
brow bone &
nose bone of the
beggar at the gate. Looking up

at your bright window.
There's no war on but they're practising
for one. They've got him
dead in their sights, the enemy
within. Look out! When he

starts to howl & howl they'll turn
the hounds loose all over town.
The Minister of Defense will toss
a red hot coin down
to the beggar at the gate.

As the manikins fall back with broken hearts
behind the bunker at the
practice range, as your money
burns through your pocket,

as the blue ribbons fray
on the trailer-sailers, as the flood
lights come on at Mount Crawford
& the Bridge St dogs bark the sun

down, light reveals
the watching still face of
the beggar at the gate.

from Georgicon

hardon ('get one today'

It's a south wind that drives you back
     inside   your dream is her dream

you imagine the world as a giant flitch
curing in the cold smokehouse, of
time, were you going to say? stop while you're ahead.
                                   As you
            climb the steps
there's a smell of toast
& the sound of Elgar on the breakfast programme
comes out your neighbour's open door
the young woman stands there   her clouds of sleep
burn off   morning breezes into her dark house
she has her baby under one arm

                              you want
              sunshine on her breasts. Instead
you go up the steps to your room to write
you have this funny idea that the world is bacon

                                 you have to
see what you can make of it. Title: *Full Moon in Gemini:*
Killing the Pig. where frost & moonlight were . . .
Remember Auntie May at Tuamarina years ago?
how the old lady ran into the sty
            to catch the blood in a milking bucket?
black puddings   white puddings   guts hung & stripped
in the barn
               sage in the sausages   brawns
you'd find pig toenails in.
                          Opposing eye to opposing
ear   where those lines cross on the forehead your
bullet scrambles the pig's cupful
of perceptions.   Imagine! if your beautiful neighbour
   was a
farmer's daughter you could unbutton her warm work-
   shirt
                           in the barn you
            could be happy to just go on missing out
   on all the fun
'out there'

KERI HULME

(b. 1947; Kāi Tahu: hapu Ngāterāngiamoa, Ngāiteruahikihiki)

He Hōhā

Bones tuned, the body sings—

See me,
I am wide with swimmer's muscle, and a bulk and
    luggage I carry curdled on hips;
I am as fat-rich as a titi-chick, ready for the far ocean
    flight.

See me,
I have skilled fingers with minimal scars, broad feet that
    caress beaches,
ears that catch the music of ghosts, eyes that see the
    landlight, a pristine womb
untouched, except by years of bleeding, a tame unsteady
    heart.

See me,
I am a swamp, a boozy drain with stinking breath, a
    sour sweetened flesh;
I am riddled with kidneyrot, brainburn, torn gut,
    liverfat, scaled with wrinkles,
day by day I am leached, even between smiles, of that
    strange water, electricity.

See me,
I am my earth's child,

        and she, humming
        considers her cuts and scars, and debates our
        death.

Mean the land's breast, hard her spine when
    turned against you;
  jade her heart.

Picture me a long way from here—
back bush, a rainbird calling,
the sea knocking shore.

It is cliché that once a month, the moon stalks through
    my body,
rendering me frail and still more susceptible to brain
    spin;
it is truth that cramp and clot and tender breast beset—
    but then
it is the tide of potency, another chance to walk through
    the crack between worlds.

What shall I do when I dry, when there is no more
    turning with the circling moon?
Ah suck tears from the wind, close the world's eye;
Papatuanuku still hums.

But picture me a long way from here.

Waves tuned, the mind-deep sings

  She forgot self in the city, in the flats full of dust
      and spiderkibbled flies;
  she forgot the sweetness of silence in the rush and
      roar of metal nights;
  no song fitted her until she discovered her kin, all
      swimmers in the heavy air of sea;

  she had lost the supple molten words, the rolling
      thunder,
  the night hush of her mother's tongue;
  she had lost the way home, the bright road, the
      trodden beach, the mewling gulls,
  the lean grey toe of land.

In the lottery of dreams, she gained prize of a
nightmare, a singular dark.

But picture her a long way from there,
growing quiet until she heard herself whispered
by the sea on the blackest night,
and echoed in the birds of morning.

Keening, crooning, the untuned spirit—
I am a map of Orion scattered in moles across this
firmament of body;
I am the black hole, the den where katipo are busy
spinning deadhavens,
and he won't go, the cuckoo child.
Jolted by the sudden thud and shatter, I have gone
outside to find
the bird too ruffled, too quiet, the barred breast broken,
an end of the far travelling.

Tutara-kauika, you father of whales, you servant
of Tangaroa,
your little rolling eye espies the far traveller—
quick!
whistle to him, distract, send him back to the
other island;
I don't mind ever-winter if summer's harbinger is
so damaged, damaging.

He turned full to face me, with a cry to come home—
do you know the language of silence, can you read
eyes?

When I think of my other bones, I bleed inside,
and he won't go, the cuckoo-child.

It is not born; it is not live; it is not dead;
it haunts all my singing, lingers greyly, hates and hurts
and hopes impossible things.
And Papatuanuku is beginning her ngeri, her anger is
growing, thrumming in quakes and tsunami,

and he won't go, the cuckoo's child.

> O, picture me a long way from here;
> tune the bones, the body sings;
> quiet the mind, the spirit hums,
> and Papatuanuku trembles, sighs;
> till then among the blood and dark
> the shining cuckoo spreads his wings
> and flies this hōhā, this buzz and fright,
> this wave and sweat and flood,
> this life.

Island Waters

separating one by one
this knot of serpents
dadakulaci
          or banded coral
snakes the colour of ambivalence

for fifteen years they have nested
under the jetty in my memory
easing themselves at dusk
out into hard blue water

and we fine combers of the reef
thick river silt had fouled
ran dove and swam there
days before we noticed

toads too were numerous
live heaps of muck at night
that blurted and flopped
across the yacht club lawn

or tossed on a sleeping
mate's face wept slime
that like *yaqona*
numbed the lips and nose

between tides the serious play
of our transect went on
where we scraped chipped and measured
tilling the reef's immobile garden

observing the work light does
or depth and salinity

and the pitted vehemence of species
born at one kind of edge we know

to raise the head was to
acknowledge once again the stale
ingredients of fancy's jigsaw
scurrying into view

the tall palms mopping the wind
and always as if on a loop
some svelte schooner
white moustached offshore

asides of the paradise business
like the smiles and flowers
our limp excuse of science
turned briefly solemn at the airport

and going back now without it
would embrace the slick deal whole
sun surf and sand
and the tourists' glittering tits

no better and no worse
an eden simplified
than that of the boys we weren't
who knew without the aid

of quadrat wires and trowels and formalin
the shape of a habitat
where nothing innocent lasts long
and clean fangs weave and glint

HIRINI MELBOURNE (b. 1949; Tūhoe)

He aha te hau mai nei

Ka kūtere ngā tarawai
I ngā haehaenga
O te whenua tipua
E takoto nei

Ka mumura ake
Ngā tūākiri o mua rā
Me he waiari koropupū
E kore nei e nawe

Ko ngā roimata
O te whatumanawa
E whakamoremore
Iho nei i te ngākau

Mimiti kau ko ngā
Wai o ōku kamo
Tetē ake ngā rei
O Te Ngaki ki te ngau

He hau taua
E hau mai nei
Hai whai i te tika
Mōu e te ūkaipō.

Why the wind comes

The sap weeps
From the lacerations

Of the ancestral land
That lies here

The old wounds
Fester up
Geysers
Never healing

The constant tears
Of the heart
Wearing away
The soul

The waters from my eyes
Cease
Snarling teeth
The bite of revenge

An avenging war party
Comes the wind
To seek justice
For you, my mother.

Translation by
Hirini Melbourne

Tāmaki-makau-rau

Pōteretere
Ana ahau
I runga i te hau
O waku poi hurihuri

Ka rewa nei au
Ki ngā kapua teretere
Ki tawhiti nui
Ki tawhiti roa
Ki pāmamao e

Me he āniwaniwa
Piri ki te rangi,
Ka titiro iho au
Ki Tāmaki-makau-rau

Pīratarata ana mai
Ngā wai o Waitematā
E tauhuna nei i te
Riri kai runga o Takaparawha e

Kia tangi iho ahau
Ki ngā wai o Manukau
E takoto pōuri nei
I roto i te rikoriko

Kei raro ko Ākarana
Te urunga te taka
Ki te pokorua
O te pōpokoriki

Kātahi au ka kite
I te hē, i te mate
E taupokitia nei
E te pōuriuri.

Tāhurihuri kau ana
Te hunga kia puta
Ki te whai i ahau
Ki te ao mārama.

Tamaki of a hundred lovers

I float
On the wind
From my twirling pois

Soaring high
In the drifting clouds
I travel
Far away

A rainbow
Suspended in the sky,
I look down
On Tamaki-makau-rau

The sparkling calm
Waters of Waitemata
Veil the rage on
Bastion Point

I lament for Manukau
Lying there
Darkened
Polluted

Below is the town of Auckland
A trap door into
A nest
Of ants

Now I see
The abuse and destruction
Done under the
Cover of the night.

The masses
Clambering to
Escape into the
World of light.

                    Translation by
                    Hirini Melbourne

Poem

A puriri moth's wing
lies light in my hand—

my breath can lift it

light as this torn wing
we lie on love's breath.

'When the wild goose finds food
he calls his comrades'—*I Ching*

It is not enough to drink
this cup alone,
but you there, Olavi,
on that rattan chair
and you there, Gwendolyn,
on that checked cushion,
your toes on the cool parquet,
drink with me tonight
this last honey-coloured light,
that so slowly folds itself
under the eyelid of the dark.

Letter to the Immigration Officer

We did kowtow to a blazing sun,
tease the towkay

into bargain price for chicken rice,
pick our way through shit on coast sands,
throngs of brown bright children
gaze at green eyes, blue eyes of
oh so strange orang putih:
    'hello peace hello, you got twenty cents?'
watching ancient hands
silently gut tiny silver fish,
mother, cross-legged in saronged ease,
the beach crashing her men, their boats,
another catch to shore.

So many weddings,
the bride shy as a limpet,
the groom stoned on ceremony,
all the relatives bearing on cushions
new underwear, a handbag and high-heeled shoes,
singing in the fashion of a river
winding its slow peopled tail
at sunset, through coconut groves
to the bride's house.

Malaysia Exotica,
a new breed of orchid,
a cheongsam slit from breast to thigh,
she is the mistress of the Tunku,
she, the fifth wife of the Sultan,
and she, oh how she lies
hung from the neck of Siam,
an emerald pendant between two seas,
provocative as a fruit
with jambu, rambutan rolling from her hips.

    'You fall in love here'
said the rubber-soled expatriate
sweating from squash
disappearing into rubber trees,
    'so many shades of green.'

So many shades,
enough to write a book
by candlelight when the generator fails,
by the light of Mercedes Benz star
standing over Ipoh
taller than a minaret,
louder than a horn-blast.

'Auntie has no gold?' asked the Indian amah
sympathetic as she hand-washed Auntie's cotton
    clothing:
'Auntie has an uncle and a car and a house,
where is Auntie's gold?'

Ah, Sarasa,
the gold's in the teeth of the Sultan,
hung from ear-lobes of girls in the harem,
the gold's in the goblet
raised to the lips of seekers after ringgits,
not in the hands of beggars
rattling on the pavements,
not in your hands or mine—
                    the gold's in opulent palaces
extravagant as elephants, the gold's in poppy seed,
in piculs of tin, but not scanners' hands,
girls bonneted like nuns
cycling past rubber trees to work the mines.

Our gold's in the sweat of the arc of a scythe,
in the succulent mango you planted,
in the wrist of the wok-man,
in the silken wind on yellow-green padi,
in the shoulders of bullocks
pulling rickety carts over stones,
in the night guard's sleeping on his rope bed
with no bars to fence him.

from The Grafton Notebook

Von Tempsky's Dance

In No. 64 Von Tempsky has his picture up
I am uncertain where he lived
I am uncertain where he lives
& he is out of breath
& out for blood
in a dance that yearns to know
how old, how far, & when & where to go.

We are not antipodean mediterranean
but perhaps Big Sur breathes a yearning
into the dust that wakes & rises
out along the West Coast road/
manuka forces its indigenous reminding
white flower up, & out westward to the sun
going down/& out along that road
to the headlands where the distance
blooms upwards & the flat sea is foreshortened.

East, the Gulf, Gt Barrier,
a coast of wrecks & Maori ghosts
& from there where the feet of the mind
dance, quitting to Valparaiso, Santiago,
NE Easter Island/Easter on that latitude!
The reckless twirl & swell of anachronisms
the uncertain pulse of breath & blood
that cant be exiled from this body
too hulked & mutant to subsist.
& on that island, in South Chile too,
the gold sophora grows. The voice too
is indigenous as it walks about
where it is.

Von Tempsky has his picture up, swordslung,
& the gully-clay lies flat, fat,
in my guts, a grave still indigestible
want where some sword questioned me
with its desiring finger into living/
and there *was* a stream!

Where shall I go now/take the road
south, back into the inland dust & heat
of desire & illusion, back always back
transporting the electric yellow peat-haze
in my head where-ever I go.
Time & its heats are here coital
in my voice & head, in my gully,
its clay & people.

My dance is a yearning east where
'the light gains'/another white flower
opens, luminous, desireless, the feet of light
themselves, *om mane padme hum*/
where my voice sends itself & yearns
dangling on Von Tempsky's hilt.

What is it they are digging up
with such bravado in the gully?
Yellow metal scoops & scrapes a surface,
steps out a road, artery of desire,
stream of illusion, a certain sword
thrust through the gully's broken crutch.

A Sprig of Karo

A sprig of karo—
starlings gabbling and whistling—
she lifts her arms
above her heavy belly
to the washing line

and brings the football jerseys down,
one by one.
A glance over her shoulder
tells her I am watching her
from the window
as I put these tight, velvet-red, karo flowers
in a small vase.
But really, she needn't worry,
I am only half watching her
as I go on to water
the parsley, the sage, the geranium—
if there was some song like
      'I know a lady
      who sleeps by day,
      I know a lady
      who wakes with the moon'
something like that
to sing,
I would,
but there's only the starlings
squawking at the end of the day,
stumping on the power lines
and jumping on the chimney stacks.
Vaudeville! Sunshine! Springtime!

The karo flower is dark,
so dark, the moths cannot see it
at night, so it gives off a scent,
a sweet scent, a guiding scent,
a scent to bring all alert moths
homing in—a centering scent!

(And in summer the burnt, black,
sticky, piecrust seeds bursting open—
but that is another song—
      'And the birds began to sing.')

Ah, she has gone inside
and all the washing's gone as well
except for one, heavy woollen jersey.

I hear her feet, upstairs,
in the flat above—
back and forward they go
as now she cooks the dinner.

And you are asleep on the bed—
up and down your breathing goes
loud and strong as her footsteps.
I can still hear the starlings
distant now, as night approaches,
and the dark red flowers
prepare to pour out that scent
which leads on the unwary,
beckons the reckless,
calls to the eager,
summons the urgent—

Ah, I hear the soft wings beating closer.

from Poems of the End Wall

House

Last night as I lay beside you all the desire had gone
   out of me
and I was cast up like a heap of sand, porous,
   shapeless, shifting,
a thing of shape, an entity, only by virtue of its million
   parts.

Here I live on a cliff in a tiny house at the end of the
   island
and in the face of the wind from the north and the
   wind from the south
I surround myself with this thin wall of wood, this
   shape in space

and you are there asleep in the bed, curled to the end
  wall of the house,
your breathing blowing shapes in the cold air, your
  dreams dreaming,
your dreaming holding up the whole fabric of paint and
  wood and tin.

If you stop wanting to dream it will collapse. Your
  desire to dream holds it up,
all the bare longing of the imagination holds it up, the
  desire of the nail
to enter the wood, the desire of the wood to embrace
  the nail,

the desire of the paint to hide the wood and reflect the
  light,
the desire of the roof to contain a secret shape of
  darkness,
the desire of the glass to shine like the sun in the face
  of the sun.

And the earth desires to lie asleep under the house and
  dream,
it dreams the very shape of the house as though it was
  something organic,
whole as a body, breathing and seeing and standing
  cold in the wind.

The house is the container and you are the thing
  contained.
Its membrane protects you and your life gives it energy
and stops the walls from collapse. And the moment of
  seeing this

and the moment of saying this are two separate
  moments:
the first, the moment of seeing is a moment without
  desire,
at night, by the bed watching you sleep, alone, still,
  chill,

but not cold, watching, as the silence of space watches
   the grinding earth,
when all the desire has gone out of me and I get up,
get up out of the bed, go out the door, out through the
   end wall,

and grasp hold of the string on the balloon and rise
   slowly, steadily,
shimmering like a giant eye over the house, the whole
   town, the capital city,
rising over the island and the ocean, the earth opening
   like a flower.

But the second, the moment of saying, involves me in
   the grammar of desire.
I have to touch you with my speech to be heard.
And grammar itself is a thing of desire, announcing its
   capacity

to evolve infinitely more complex systems out of bits of
   nothing,
to put together the grains of sand to make rock and the
   rock to build
a cliff and the cliff to hold a house, many houses, a city

to stand at the end wall of the island, the end wall of
   the land
turned like smooth wood in the yielding shape of the
   bay
to embrace the random desiring waves of the sea.

Somewhere a child is sacrificed and buried at the foot of
   the posthole
which comes to hold up the whole house. Building
   walls for the compost heap
I smash a post in half and in its rotted core a weta lies,
   soft and sleepy,

hiding until its new exoskeleton hardens enough to let
   it safely live,

to let it grow vulnerable, as earth to light, as sand to
 sea.
Tonight I embrace you and trust the roof will hold up
 till morning.

Here

Dream behind the
unknown door.

A small woman, an empty
house with flat weatherboards,
a garden that had always
been there, the cherries
the lemons & the apricots.
A broken gate & a road
we knew only how to take . . . her face

her face . . . the road to the sea,
the season's fever of apples
& other dreams that bank
up like clouds against
a distant rim of hills.
Hills that resist the idea
of thought. Hills that are
themselves as thought. Take me

into them.

Parable

She came walking
along the street
by the building site
in her white shirt &
tight jeans . . . the woman
in the beautiful sandals.

She was in the sun
stepping lightly
she was stepping on lightly.
& the men of course stopped
working. Then they whistled
hard at her—they yelled at
her that she had a good arse
they told themselves she'd be
a good fuck. The woman
in the white shirt & tight jeans
the woman in the beautiful sandals.
She walked in from
                    the street
she walked past concrete pillars
she walked past scaffolding
she walked against the noise
of hammers & saws & drills
she walked into their words
that still hung in the air
like chisels. She walked &
they wished that she would
keep right on walking.
                    She did.
Walked through them as if they were
dreams. Walked through them. Left them.
Puzzled & unhappy she left them
& left them free. The woman
in the white shirt & tight jeans
the woman in the beautiful sandals.
None could remember what she wore.
A man in a crane gently moved
a cloud
          across the sky.

Studio Poem

On the mantelpiece
there are green lemons
sent by a man who
has lost his wife.

I spend a lot
of time tearing pictures
out of old magazines.
Today I found

a fallen idol a volcano
and a man with birds
on his head. Yesterday
there was a home-made

aeroplane, and I looked
for a long time at soldiers
doing target practice
on a Chinese Laundry.

Living under a green
verandah among trees
water and normal sounds
I look up from a

U.S. helicopter manhunting
across paddyfields out
at fog gobbling the
peninsula and back to the

life of the honeybee,
finding it hard to keep

up. I would like to say
that I admire closeness,

poets who say what they
mean with words that
have nothing to do
with it. One of my

favourite photos is the
white madonna half buried
in ashes, victim of
another of those volcanoes.

To Ben, at the Lake

See, Ben, the water
has a strong soft skin,
and all the insects dance
and jump about on it—
for them it's safe as
springy turf. You see,
it is a matter of ensuring
that you are lighter
than the medium you
walk on: in other words,
first check your meniscus
And also, to hell with the
trout—you can't afford
to look down, anyway.
You and I have lots of
golden sticky clay on our
gumboots—the world
is holding us up
very well, today.

DAVID EGGLETON (b. 1953)

Painting Mount Taranaki

Mainly I was led to them, the casinos of aluminium,
by the gift of eyebright whose hollow core contained
a vision of the coast and on it the cone shape,
like a pile of drenched wheat, of Mount Taranaki.
In a world covered in silica and
chucked up alkáthene, fibrolite, aluminium
it is just a peak surrounded on three sides by water.
For the Soviets, holding down a floor
of the Los Angeles Hilton is a forbidden
progression of the open society.
So, to the French, whose own symbol is an ageing
                                        Brigitte Bardot,
the mountain, just the same,
could be a logo for the butter they've no-noed,
dismissing a country's living tannery with a sniff:
the hides of rainslicked cows only acceptable
in the corner of a page by Frank Sargeson.
Corrupt innocence, a young brain, prodded Techtones,
featureless Features, a shot Texan burgerbar,
the list is endless but not one story seems complete
on its own, even tying up the numbered dots proves
less efficient than you might at first think
and, anyway, this absurd reductionist format is one
which can only begin to hint at the complex,
underlying reality.
Gossamer threads in air, truck belting down the drive,
irresistible wind urging on the silver mist threads
over the split, cheap graves and into green Norfolk
                                        pines.
During the Vietnam War Against Imperialist Aggression
I was schooled in classrooms near Mangere International
                                        Airport

as venerable millenium temples blew into
millions of fragments in lovely orange and black
negatives—in a variation on a theme
a close study of the status of stainless, chrome, plastic
superheroes revealed wild discrepancies.
Over the various eye witness accounts
whirred the blades of gunships trailing and corpses
surfed by on an extravaganza of black Coke.
Later, as I put down another batch of jungle juice,
I began to learn that Man cannot live
on homebaked bread and granola alone.
So much up, I moved closer under the mountain
until I stood inside a convention of car dealers
in an Inglewood hotel.
Young and hopelessly flippant I felt
I should be in an environment where it was easier
to make a buck and people were more understanding
about 'in' references to tribal totems.
I swan-dived through the sex-shops of Wellington,
reaching towards vibrators in a glass case only
to catch onto a picnic papercup then an electrified fence
as it threw the other way
on an elliptical approach towards the majestic
funereal mountain that figures at the violet centre
of the windscreen first dotted before being laced
by the rain caught in the drum machine motion of
                                        Jupiter,
spearing the side of a punga with a flaming asteroid,
the cosmos being full of hauhau vistas.
In the snowstorm black-visored Samurai rode on
hornet-yellow Yamahas past a chipped, white,
enamel basin on a window ledge,
a plant trained to crawl up that same window,
the richly decayed caskets of autowreckers' yards,
the tea kiosks of tourist stops
and up the winter volcano to the extinct lip.
From ash to dove to puce to brandy
the undersea turbines smashed the tints
of the glassy waves into sloppy froth and stiff whites.

A litany of rejects from dye vats,
the unwanted energy of their beauty decorated the feet
of the giant for whom the many Victorian explorers
also left souvenirs.
A string tie, cedarwood fan, lace-edged cambric,
saddlestrap, sherryglass, wristwatch, nightgown, velvet
ribbon.
In the centre of ferns they were given back
the ghost images of sedated depressives in the foetal
position.
As I scrubcut my way around a backblock wilderness
as unknown as Europe it was I who began to crack not
it.
The mountain 'Egmont' rained down its ciphers as I
slept
until I entered the psychologically tropic world
of heat and fever, lava village of the last upthrust.
Dealing with the giggling mountain, walking it,
you felt you had seen one of the quadrants,
fundament and crotch scored
between the arched legs of the world.
This province began to experience happenings.
A two-headed calf was born at Stratford,
at Bell Block at evening an old age pensioner
hung himself by his shoelaces in a Corporation bus,
Dow Chemical Plant mutated into a radioactive centre,
firing out supernovae.
Sacred sites became fictions and sensitised scraps
of computer card in plastic envelopes were irrevocably
drawn into the throbbing whirlpool of events.
A drudge in a hotel kitchen cornered the market
in replicas of credit cards by fabricating a deception
which played on the public's mounting fears of
eruption.
His prolific operation soon saw him zooming
to the top of the money tree.
Bizarre mission for a steamy morning, hunting
through the underbelly's growth canopy
for signs of the tribe as showers sweep down

and a rackety V8 is driven from under
a dilapidated carport overhang with the rain seeping in,
the tribe collapsed like a rusty barbed wire fence
in front of a wedding cake house with soft pink icing
spelling out blushes and little tears of joy
in the happy hour.
Scrawny wetas skipping across cushions of green moss
on fallen old totaras. Neat, eh, to see
ragwort, cocksfoot, fennel, catmint growing
round a shagged dinghy on a rusted cradle trailer
as wraiths ascend supplejack and the beekeeper
is rooted to the spot with a curse.
And now with the art that goes through daily life
the fundamentalist preacher, like a page of old history,
speckled, damp with mildew spots,
his brylcreemed waffle of hair catching the morning
                                                    sun,
walks in the foreground of cones of gravel,
central and terminal.
Stained stacks of 'Truth' newspaper in the skew-whiff
                                                    shed
adjacent to the off-balance dunny.
In the wool shearers' abandoned quarters
a few stained, bloody mattresses, stuffed with kapok,
have burst.
Cherubim perch on the shingle, ice-cream
types of gentlemen swing their partners
like candyfloss in a spin.
A bruised young mother
with her mother in a trouser suit
and upswept wings of punished hair
recalling knitting needles of the circle clicking
like train wheels
in the pink wafer light that reminiscing imposes.
Quattrocento fanatics didn't have it like this.
From them we borrowed cardinal red and pageboy
                                                    hairstyles,
our larders and pantries stuffed with wholemeal loaves
on the rise, in ferment.
Beans swelling, sprouting out of their jars.

Nuts pouring from plastic sacks.
The stillness leads on into a chapel hush.
Grated carrot bristles. The dinner guests shrunk
back from the gurgling wine like tarnished coins
thrown into a pocket
the questing forefinger seeks.
A model T Ford carhulk planted
in front of the mind like a zombie chariot before the cult
of skis.
A battery of children
winding in a crocodile, candles aloft,
their seed teeth bared at the effort of the pilgrimage.
Those ropey arms and flayed legs are not
starved of sensation nor the sharp black/white
as the light snaps on.
Don't knock yourself out,
Taranaki will be there in the morning,
the snow a gunky white blob of brilliantine,
an ornament, a gargoyle for Bat-Stud.
The town hall, pub, gymnasium and squash court
cluster
below, everything we have learnt reduces to a search
for the pyramid they burned down.

These Rumours of Hexagonal Rooms in
Gone Bee City

These rumours of hexagonal rooms in gone Bee City
over the Strait, just north of Leper's Footprint Island
are like being in a hexagonal room, spectacular lattice,
stalking the sweet elixirs of the rewarewa.
Homages, tears and smiles,
all alone with a spluttering kerosene lamp of shadows,
sodden bruised blossoms,
fragile stems of herbs, embattled comfrey roots,
pale throats of mushroom,
and in the lounge the closed basilisk eye

of television, dense grey amid the shrieking orchard
swirling in the carpet.
It's Autumn, that gymnasium of harlequins;
snow's dirty coat's ready to appear in mid-year.
Velvet purple-cherry blood
on a saint's statue and the carved benches in a
cheapjack church early settlers slaved to establish,
bequeath the momentum of heritage.
They were so distracted by all this space on their hands.

APIRANA TAYLOR
(b. 1955; Te Whānau-ā-Apanui, Ngāti Porou, Taranaki)

Taiaha haka poem

I am Te-ngau-reka-a-tu
I once danced with killers
who followed the War God
beyond the gates of hell
to kill in the gardens of pleasure

I am the taiaha left among people
who dance and twirl poi
in gaudy halls
of plastic Maoridom

Father give me guts
Evil one why
have you forsaken me

Sad joke on a marae

Tihei Mauriora I called
Kupe Paikea Te Kooti
Rewi and Te Rauparaha
I saw them
grim death and wooden ghosts
carved on the meeting house wall

In the only Maori I knew
I called
Tihei Mauriora
Above me the tekoteko raged
He ripped his tongue from his mouth
and threw it at my feet

Then I spoke
My name is Tu the freezing worker
Ngati D.B. is my tribe
The pub is my marae
My fist is my taiaha
Jail is my home

Tihei Mauriora I cried
They understood
the tekoteko and the ghosts
though I said nothing but
Tihei Mauriora
for that's all I knew

The womb

Your fires burnt my forests
leaving only the charred bones
of totara rimu and kahikatea

Your ploughs like the fingernails
of a woman scarred my face
It seems I became a domestic giant

But in death
you settlers and farmers
return to me
and I suck on your bodies
as if they are lollipops

I am the land
the womb of life and death
Ruamoko the unborn God
rumbles within me
and the fires of Ruapehu still live

Portrait of a Lady

Some people are incurably gentle.
I am thinking of one. She
is thin as a bird
as if she might
be rescued by the wrists or ankles, if she is light.
She is the lady of the house
though her face moves like
the face of a thief
at the window of her house.
When she breathes, she breathes in
the air of aftermath.
Imagine her
alongside a wall
where the roof is bombed out and
the choir missing.

She may provide
food and bedding.
We find everything she gives is ash.
Why wait. Already you could say
turning away, Yes. It was a growth, internally.

Queen of the River

Here the boat set me down, and I wait. The oarsman
    swung on the pole
and we came to the bank, lifted my belongings, and I
    got out.
Four days and five nights, the canoe does not return.

I waited at the river bank. Oh, the river. How I wept,
   and now
how dry I am.
                   This is only a tributary, and a thousand
   miles to the sea,
a lifetime to the other side. The river bends, or is it that
   my eye
bends what I see with distance and time.
                                        The military
   walk in the town.
The old giantess behind her stand in the market refuses
   to bargain
selling fallen fruit smelling of diarrhoea, golden and
   black,
and she looks down. The tiny captured monkeys
tethered to her, they also look down.

In the evening I walk to the river, at the end of town
and I watch the sun set in equatorial calm.
I see the circles on the slow-swift stream
and I hear the monkeys scream. It is all one.
I walk back to my hammock and lie down.

Opposite in the street is the tailor's shop, a carbox with
   an open side
where the tailor works through the night. In the
   evening
his family come and sit with him, a laugh breaks, and
   one sings out.

Outside my room the night has turned to flowers. The
   tailor's daughter
lines up her back with the side of the shop, looks down
   the street.
The military drift, looking in at bars
                                 I am the Queen of
   the River
and I go as I please. The river is as wide as this arm of
   mine,

I reach out and measure the river with my arm and
  touch on the far side.
I will leave now. Why should I not go down?
A mosquito steps on to my arm and clings.
My arms are bitten by the dark bougainvillea
  and ignored by the spines.
                        I am the Queen of the River,
I know all the songs to this hour in time, and I drive
  the oarsman mad.

The tailor's little daughter kicks a foot at midnight.
It is cool now, and I who have flown in my dreams and
  died
stop sweating, pull the sheet up on to a shoulder, and
  sleep.

Notes

Ko tumi euwha, page 63

The Chatham Islands were settled from New Zealand
by the early Maori, within a few centuries of their
colonisation of the main islands. In the late eighteenth
century there were some 2000 people there, who
spoke of themselves as Moriori and lived fairly well on
seals, sea-birds, fish, eels and fern-root. After the arrival
of Europeans these peaceable people suffered from
introduced diseases and were conquered by Maoris who
arrived on a European ship. There are now no people of
full Moriori descent.

According to Moriori mythology Rangi-tokona made
the world by separating the sky and earth, then formed
the body of the first man by heaping up earth and
chanting this spell. The man is seen as growing like a
tree; and it was in fact customary among the Moriori to
plant a tree when a child was born, and to identify its
growth with that of the child.

Moriori traditions were recorded by Alexander Shand.
This spell appears in the second of a series of articles
which he published in the *Journal of the Polynesian Society*
in 1894 (vol. 3, p. 129).

He hari no mua, page 65

John Savage, visiting New Zealand in 1805, noted that the
people sang both at sunrise and sunset: 'On the rising of
the sun, the air is cheerful, the arms are spread out as a
token of welcome, and the whole action denotes a great
deal of unmixed joy; while on the contrary, his setting
is regretted in tones of a most mournful nature.'

This hari (recited song of rejoicing) was one that
greeted the sun. It was titled by the unknown Maori
writer who recorded it. The text is from John McGregor,
Popular Maori Songs, supplement 1, Auckland, 1898,
p. 21.

Ngā taura, kumea kia ita, page 66

This work song comes from the wide reaches of the
Kaipara Harbour, where it was sung by fishermen as
they hauled in their nets. The mythical Tangaroa was
associated with the sea, and his children were fish.
Kahukura was said in Northland to have been the first
man to make nets, having tricked the fairies into
showing him how to do it.

The text is recorded in a manuscript article by George
Graham, 'Legendary origins of Maori arts and crafts',
which is in the library of the Auckland Institute and
Museum. The translator is indebted to the Librarian and
to Marguerite Scale for permission to publish it.

He oriori mo Te Hauapu, page 67

Noho-mai-te-Rangi was a chief who lived at Heretaunga
(Hawke's Bay) in the middle of the eighteenth
century. During his lifetime there was bitter fighting.
This oriori for his son dedicates him to war and sends
him on a spiritual journey to his ancestors in the sky,
who will give him strength.

The last lines assert that the poet has saved his
people from destruction. 'The albatross plume of the
land' was a poetic expression for the red feathers of the
kaka, which were bound around the heads of taiaha.
The stormy waters are the enemy, and 'the albatross
plume of the sea' represents the poet's tribe and their
lands.

The text is from Apirana T. Ngata, *Nga Moteatea*, part I,
The Polynesian Society, Wellington, 1959, pp. 104–107.

Na Murupaenga ra, page 68

In about 1810 the northern tribe of Ngati Whatua, under
the leadership of Murupaenga, made a raid on the
Taranaki tribes. Among the prisoners they brought back
with them was a young woman of good birth who came
from Tarakihi, near Warea. When she was told she was

to become the wife of one of her captors, she composed
this waiata addressed to her former lover at Tarakihi.

The text is from S. Percy Smith, *Maori Wars of the
Nineteenth Century*, 2nd ed., Christchurch, 1910, pp.
62–63.

Mātai rore au, page 69

Hill tops were traditionally associated with melancholy.
(This may be a pao rather than a waiata.)

The text is from a manuscript collection of poetry
made by Robert Maunsell, now among Sir George
Grey's papers in the Auckland Public Library
(GNZMMS 32: 69). The translator is indebted to the
Librarian for permission to publish it.

He waiata aroha, page 70

The image of the man as paddler and the woman as
canoe is a traditional one. The text is recorded in a
manuscript written in 1876 and entitled 'Maori material
contributed by Mohi Ruatapu and Henare Potae' (vol. II,
Henare Potae, p. 61) which is among the Elsdon Best
papers in the Alexander Turnbull Library. The translator
is indebted to the Chief Librarian for permission to
publish it. Since the writers of the manuscript belonged to
Ngati Porou, the waiata is probably an East Coast one.

E kui mā, e koro mā, page 73

This waiata tangi by an unknown composer is still sung
today. Musically it is unusual, being similar in some
respects to an oriori and in others to a patere.

Hirini (Sid) Waititi and others of Te Whanau-a-Apanui
and Ngati Porou tribes recorded this song in 1964 for
Mervyn McLean. It was published in Mervyn McLean
and Margaret Orbell, *Traditional Songs of the Maori*,
Wellington, 1975, pp. 264–267.

He tangi mo Te Heuheu Herea, page 75

Te Heuheu Herea, a high chief of Ngati Tuwharetoa in the Taupo district, died in about 1820 and was mourned by his son with this waiata tangi. The translation of the last line is conjectural. Probably the meaning is that Te Heuheu died because he had inadvertently broken the ritual restrictions which his great tapu, or sacredness, required him to observe, and that as a consequence he had offended his family's ancestral spirits. 'Natural' deaths were often ascribed to this cause.

The text is from Apirana T. Ngata, *Nga Moteatea*, part I, The Polynesian Society, Wellington, 1959, pp. 196–201.

He tangi mo Te Iwi-ika, page 78

This waiata tangi was recorded in about 1894 at Waikouaiti, north of Dunedin, by Moses Wood, who wrote it at the dictation of his aunt Pinana. The manuscript is among the papers of F.R. Chapman which are in the Hocken Library, Dunedin (MS 416A, song no. 3). For permission to publish the song, the translator is indebted to the Librarian.

It was almost certainly composed by a South Island poet, for its allusions to the myth of Tane correspond exactly to a version of this myth which was known in the south.

The story of Tane explains the origin of death and also that of life. Tane created the first woman, married her, then later married their daughter, who was called Hine-titama. But Hine-titama discovered that her husband was also her father, and in great distress she rushed down to the underworld. Though Tane tried to persuade her to return she would not do so, but said, 'Go back to the world, Tane, to rear up our progeny, and let me go to the underworld to drag down our progeny'. So now she drags men down to death, along with her daughters Tahu-kumea and Tahu-whakairo (or, as they are in this song, Tahi-kumea and Tahu-whaera).

But in the world above, new generations replace the
old: after going back, Tane made his way up to the
highest of the skies, found there 'the living waters of
Tane' from which come the souls of new-born babies,
then returned and set about his task of making the
earth fruitful.

The anonymous poet laments her husband's death by
speaking of the journey his soul must make to Hine-
titama in the underworld, but she then ends her song
by telling of Tane's ascent to the skies and his creation
of new life. In this way she affirms that life will
continue and that 'the world of light' will be
triumphant.

The second line is of uncertain meaning, and may
have been inaccurately recorded, and the translation of
the first line is conjectural; possibly the multitudes are
'seeking the reason' for Te Iwi-ika's death. Where the
letter *k* is italicised in the Maori text, it is equivalent to
ng in North Island Maori.

He pōkeka, page 80

Pokeka are recited laments for the dead which are
composed only in the Arawa and Matatua tribal areas.
They are generally performed at tangi ceremonies on
the last night to 'cheer up' those present, and are often
performed with impromptu actions.

The titi kura or titi kawe kura spell was recited to
heal the sick, and apparently also to restore life to the
dead. The 'greenstone tiki' is the dead person. The
mythical, paradisial land of Hawaiki is the place from
whence men come and to which they return after death.
The mythical Tiki made the first man, thereby
introducing death into the world; the mythical
Ruaumoko lives under the earth, so is associated with
death; the defeat of the mythical Manaia and his
warriors occurs in poetry as an archetypal image of
defeat. The meaning of some of the last words is
uncertain. An affirmation of harmony and wellbeing,
they occur at the end of many recited songs.

Turau and Marata Te Tomo of Ngati Tuwharetoa
recorded this song for Mervyn McLean in 1963. It was
published in Mervyn McLean and Margaret Orbell,
Traditional Songs of the Maori, Wellington, 1975,
pp. 200–201.

E Hōhepa e tangi, page 82

This must have been one of the first songs to celebrate
the coming of Christianity. The Turner who is
mentioned is Nathaniel Turner, one of two Wesleyan
missionaries who in 1823 established a mission station
at Whangaroa in the far north. Four years later, tribal
warfare forced them to leave the district.

The text is from Ernst Dieffenbach, *Travels in New
Zealand*, London, 1843, vol. 2, pp. 312–313.

Kia nui ō pākiki maunga, page 84

Kie Tapu probably lived on the West Coast of the North
Island and composed her song during the period from
about 1820 to 1850. When it was published in 1905, it
was accompanied by an explanatory note. In translation,
the note is as follows:

> Kie Tapu, who lived here, married a man, Tukaiora. Now
> after they had been living together for many years, her
> husband became jealous, thinking his wife had been
> unfaithful to him—this was an idea he had. Now the
> woman was shamed, and she composed a waiata for
> herself. This is her waiata.

So the song is a face-saving device. Accused of having
taken a lover, Kie Tapu seeks to redeem the situation
not by refuting the charge but by defiantly singing of all
those who have—she claims—been her lovers in the
past, and by sending herself on an imaginary journey to
visit them. It does sound as though at least two of these
men, Tangi-noa and Uta, have in fact been her lovers,
probably before her marriage. In speaking of them she

refers to their wives also, as a matter of politeness. Her song is addressed to her husband, Tukaiora.

In the first lines, Ship is a personification of a word used of European vessels, and Kawa is probably a Pakeha; often in such songs the poet speaks of a neighbouring chief who she claims will allow her to travel under his protection, and sometimes in the nineteenth century an early Pakeha trader occurs in this role. The fourth line is a complaint about gossip. In the ninth, the word 'mine' refers to her genitals; Tangi-noa eventually tired of Kie Tapu, and she blames this on the destructive god Maru, saying he has made her unattractive to him. In the last line the poet employs a traditional image equating a woman with a canoe, and a man with a paddler: Uta, having lost Kie Tapu, is now only a steering paddle without its canoe.

The text is from John McGregor, *Popular Maori Songs*, supplement 3, Auckland, 1905, p. 70.

He tangi na te tūroro, page 86

The poet composed this waiata tangi in her old age, when she was suffering from asthma and tuberculosis. Mihi-marino is a hill on the coast south of Tokomaru Bay. The seventh line is addressed to the morning star.

The text is from Apirana T. Ngata, *Nga Moteatea*, part I, The Polynesian Society, Wellington, 1959, p. 72.

Tangi a taku ihu, page 88

After the wars of the 1860s the prophet Te Whiti-o-Rongomai founded a religious movement at Parihaka in Taranaki, teaching the doctrine of passive resistance. Many of his followers were people who had been driven from their land. Te Whiti and his fellow prophet Tohu gave new hope and meaning to their lives, and for some thirty years Parihaka was a flourishing community.

This well-known song sung by Te Whiti's followers was composed by his close kinsman, Te Whetu. It is still performed today; it is accompanied by the double

poi, and differs from earlier poi songs in being sung
rather than recited. The poet complains of the
antagonism and slander of the hostile Pakehas, and
celebrates the leadership of Te Whiti and Tohu. In the
first line, a sneeze was thought to be an omen that a
person was the subject of talk: the poet and his people
are being 'raised up' on the lips of their opponents. In
the second line, the tongue (which protrudes vigorously
in grimaces in the haka) symbolises enemy aggression.
The queen is Queen Victoria, and Titoko is Titokowaru,
a famous guerrilla leader in Taranaki. Te Whiti's
'plumes' were the white feathers worn as an emblem by
his followers.

The text is from Mervyn McLean and Margaret
Orbell, *Traditional Songs of the Maori*, Wellington, 1975,
pp. 234–235.

Ē, i te tekau mā whā, page 90

An old story has it that the missionaries told the Maori
to look up towards God in the sky, and they did so, but
when they looked down again, Pakehas had taken their
land. The first missionary was Samuel Marsden, who in
1814 preached for the first time at Oihi, in the Bay of
Islands. In this song, which probably dates from the
late nineteenth century, he is held responsible for early
land sales in which the Maori were persuaded to part
with broad acres in return for implements of iron and
articles such as blankets and jew's harps. The poet also
blames the Governor, who represents the New Zealand
Government.

Aotearoa is a Maori name for the North Island, or
sometimes for New Zealand. The image in the last line is
traditional: land which was lost to a tribe was sometimes
said to have gone out to sea.

The text is from an article by Apirana T. Ngata in *The
Maori People Today*, edited by I.L.S. Sutherland,
Whitcombe and Tombs, 1940, p. 346.

He waiata tohutohu, page 91

From 1868 until 1871, Te Kooti Rikirangi, the prophet and guerrilla leader, was sheltered by the Tuhoe tribe in the mountainous Ureweras from the government expeditions that pursued him. He then lived in the King Country under the protection of King Tawhiao until 1883, when for political reasons he was pardoned by the Government.

Meanwhile the Pakehas had been trying in vain to 'open up' the Ureweras, for the Tuhoe would not allow any surveying or road-making in their territory. Te Kooti, who was now free to travel, visited the Tuhoe to strengthen them in their stand against the Government, and composed and sang this song urging them not to permit their land to be surveyed and not to sell it.

In the first lines Te Kooti names three things possessed of mana, or power and prestige. The first two are seen as instruments devised by the Pakehas for the purpose of wresting control of the land from the Maori, and thereby destroying their mana. Te Kooti opposes to these 'te Mana Motuhake', the followers and allies of King Tawhiao who were maintaining their independence and holding out against the Pakehas. The expression 'Rohe Pōtae' usually refers to the King Country, where Tawhiao lived, but here refers to the territory of the Tuhoe tribe.

This waiata tohutohu (song of instruction) was recorded for Mervyn McLean in 1958 by Puke Tari of Tuhoe and others of Tuhoe, Whakatohea and Whanau-a-Apanui tribes. It was published in Mervyn McLean and Margaret Orbell, *Traditional Songs of the Maori*, Wellington, 1975, pp. 37–43.

Ko te tangi mo Tāwhiao, page 95

When King Tawhiao died in 1894, this haka was performed by hundreds of mourners at the tangi ceremony at Taupiri. Mokau and Tamaki marked the boundaries of the traditional territory of the Waikato tribes. Tupu was Tupu Taingakawa Te Waharoa, who held the high position of Kingmaker in the King Movement, and Whiti was Whitiora Te Kumete, another leading figure. The Kauhanganui was an assembly of elders who met in a Parliament modelled on that of the New Zealand Government; the Ministers were the king's leading councillors, the Manukura were chiefs, and the Matariki commoners.

The text is from John McGregor, *Popular Maori Songs*, supplement 1, Auckland, 1898, p. 31. Some of the words were called by the leader and the rest were shouted in response by the assembled men, but it is not known how this division was made.

He pao, page 99

Each of these couplets, or pao, is a separate song. In the fourth one the English expression 'good ladies' occurs in transliteration, its unexpected use being witty and, of course, ironical.

Para Iwikau of Ngati Tuwharetoa recorded these songs for Mervyn McLean in 1962. She said that they were composed before her time. They were published in Mervyn McLean and Margaret Orbell, *Traditional Songs of the Maori*, Wellington, 1975, pp. 66–69.

Pōkarekare ana, page 105

Paraire Henare Tomoana was one of the best composers of waiata-a-ringa in the early decades of this century. 'Pōkarekare ana' is not an 'action song' however, but has been called a waiata whaiaipo, or love song, a term usually applied to older songs.

Published with the permission of the Tomoana family.

E pari rā, page 106

This song, adopted by the RNZN as their official slow march, was composed in memory of the son of Hemi

Rapaea from Kairakau. The latter was a contemporary of other famous Te Aute College graduates, such as Sir Apirana Ngata, Sir Peter Buck (Te Rangi Hiroa), Hemi Huata, Raniera Ellison and Paraire Tomoana.

The text is from Sam Karetu and the Advisory Committee for the Teaching of the Maori Language, and is published with the permission of the Tomoana family.

E rere rā te kirīmi, page 119

This famous waiata-a-ringa was composed early this century by Apirana Ngata, the Maori leader and statesman, at a time when he was encouraging his tribe of Ngati Porou, on the East Coast, to take up dairy farming. His song helped his cause and also, it seems, served to welcome the Prime Minister when he attended the opening of the dairy factory at Ruatoria.

The name Nati is a slang expression for Ngati Porou. Maui Pomare was the well-known Taranaki politician.

The text is from *Waitara, 1859–1936: Souvenir of Pomare Memorial Meeting*, edited, anonymously, by Apirana Ngata, p. 72, and is published with the permission of H.K. Ngata.

E noho, e Rata, page 133

This popular song celebrating the Kingitanga, the Maori King Movement, was composed in 1917 by Te Puea Herangi, one of the leading figures of the movement. In her song the King, Rata, is sent on an imaginary journey around the tribal territory of his people, visiting places on the West Coast which are rich in associations for them. Te Akau, literally 'The Coast', is the stretch of shore between the mouth of the Waikato River and Whaingaroa (Raglan Harbour). Just south from Whaingaroa is Mt Karioi, then come Aotea and Kawhia harbours; the saying about Kawhia refers to the abundance of its sea food and the great numbers of its people. The Tainui, the ancestral canoe of the

Waikato people, lies turned to stone at Kawhia; Karewa
is Gannet Island; the Twelve are the men who make up
the Cabinet of the Kauhanganui, the Maori Parliament
established near Cambridge by Tawhiao, Rata's great
predecessor. Tawhiao moved to Cambridge after living
at Alexandra, which is now the town of Pirongia; Te
Paki o Matariki is a name given to his followers.
However Tawhiao, whose other name was Matutaera,
prophesied that the centre of the Kingitanga would one
day be at Ngaruawahia. Te Puea recalls this prophecy in
her song. She was soon to make it come true.

The text was provided by the late Arapeta Awatere,
and is published with the permission of Te Ariki Nui,
Dame Te Atairangikaahu, and the kahui ariki of the
Kingitanga.

Arohaina mai, page 188

Tuini Ngawai was one of the most talented and
best known of waiata-a-ringa composers. This song
was composed in the early years of the Second World
War and was first performed at a Final Leave farewell
held at Tokomaru Bay for the men of Ngati Porou who
were going overseas with the Maori Battalion.

In the traditional Maori religion, Tu is the name of
the god of war. The ancient pronouncement *tihe mauri
ora* is an affirmation that all will be well.

Published with the permission of Kumeroa Ngoingoi
Pewhairangi, the poet's niece, and the Secretary of the
Tuini Ngawai Printing Fund, Hokowhitu a Tu, Tokomaru
Bay.

Ngā rongo, page 189

Text and translation from Kumeroa Ngoingoi
Pewhairangi; published with her permission.

He tangi mo Kēpa Anaha Ēhau, page 194

Arapeta Awatere had a deep knowledge of Maoritanga, and wrote many songs. Kepa Anaha Ehau (1885–1970) was a rangatira of Ngati Tarawhai and Ngati Whakaue subtribes of Te Arawa. Muruika and Te Papa-i-ouru are the names of Arawa marae. The path of Tane is the light of the setting sun upon the western ocean, and Tatau-o-te-po literally is 'The door of the underworld'.

Text and translation from the late Arapeta Awatere. It was first published in *The New Quarterly Cave*, and is published here with the permission of Donna Awatere.

I ngā rā, page 223

This is the best-known of Hera Katene-Horvath's songs and was composed between 1970 and 1971. Its simplicity in translation is deceptive, as is often the case with such material. The familiar cry of *Auē! Auē! Auē!* is an expression simultaneously of distress and urgency. The plea to 'raise up' coming generations in the Maori language is expressed with great force, using a term (hāpai) which refers to the commencement of a song, and as a noun to an advance guard, and to the dawn. The kahu kiwi is an object of great value: the kiwi-feather cloak worn by rangatira, and endowed with exceptional significance.

Text and Author's translation from Sam Karetu and the Advisory Committee for the Teaching of the Maori Language; published with the permission of Hera Katene-Horvath QSO.

Kaua rā hei huri noa, page 273

As in other regions throughout the country, annual competitions in haka, waiata, poi and waiata-a-ringa are held in Gisborne for the area known as Te Tairawhiti. This waiata-a-ringa was composed for the competitions held on 15 October 1977.

Text and translation from Sam Karetu and the

Advisory Committee for the Teaching of the Maori Language; published with the Author's permission.

Ka noho au i konei, page 274

Text and translation from Kumeroa Ngoingoi Pewhairangi; published with her permission.

Karangatia e te iwi, te Manu Kōtuku Rerenga Tahi, page 295

This waiata-a-ringa has twice been used to welcome Queen Elizabeth to New Zealand. Text and translation from Wiremu Kingi Kerekere; published with his permission.

Tāmaki-makau-rau, page 305

Tamaki-makau-rau, Tamaki of a hundred lovers (see also Hirini Melbourne's poem p. 498), is a traditional name for the Auckland isthmus, and Manukau and Waitemata are its two harbours. Rangi the sky father and Papanuku the earth mother were the first, ancestral parents. Maungawhau is the ancient name for Mt Eden, Maungarei is Mt Wellington and Maungakiekie is One Tree Hill.

Text from Merimeri Penfold; published with her permission.

Ngā ture whenua, page 306

First published in *Into the World of Light*, edited by Witi Ihimaera and Don S. Long, Heinemann, 1982. Text from Merimeri Penfold; published with her permission.

Haka: Hinemotu, page 349

Hinemotu is the name of a landmark at the mouth of the Motu River. In legend it is a rock in the form of a woman who can only flirt with her lovers, two rocks further out to sea. She is the guardian of the river and the food it provides, including the whitebait (kōeaea), the subject of this haka.

Text and translation from Te Aomuhurangi Te Maaka; published with her permission.

E tō e te rā i waho o Mōtū, page 351

Text and translation from *Te Kaea*; published with the Author's permission.

Haka: he huruhuru toroa, page 394

Pukekura is the name of the albatross colony at Otago Heads. Aramoana is the name of an area adjacent to Pukekura, proposed site of an aluminium smelter. 'Kōpū o te tai' translates as 'stomach of the tide'; 'Kōpūtai' as one word is the Maori name for Port Chalmers, but was originally the name of the beach off Aramoana. Araiteuru is the name of the Maori culture club which won the 1982 South Island competitions with this haka.

Text and translation from Muru Walters; published with his permission.

Te mihini ātea, page 438

In the manner of the old waiata-kori, this waiata-a-ringa depicts events of common life. It was composed for the group Te Roopu Manutaki and, having been performed at the Polynesian Festival in Hastings in 1983, was given to the Ngati Kahungunu people of that area.

Text and translation from Pita Sharples; published with his permission.

Haka: te puāwaitanga, page 440

This haka, composed for Te Roopu Manutaki and subsequently given to the Ngati Kahungunu people of Hawke's Bay, identifies the challenges which face the young Maori today with the battles of the past. It incites the taua to warfare: the 'enemy' is the task of keeping the Maori language alive.

Text and translation from Pita Sharples; published with his permission.

Select Bibliography

Major poetry publications only; contributions to other literary forms, minor pamphlets, and editorships are not included. New Zealand is the place of publication unless otherwise indicated. In some cases bibliographical entries postdate selections for this anthology.

FLEUR ADCOCK

The Eye of the Hurricane, A.H. & A.W. Reed, 1964
Tigers, Oxford University Press, London, 1967
High Tide in the Garden, Oxford University Press, London, 1971
The Scenic Route, Oxford University Press, London, 1974
The Inner Harbour, Oxford University Press, London, 1979
Below Loughrigg, Bloodaxe Books, Newcastle upon Tyne, 1979
Selected Poems, Oxford University Press, London, 1983

K.O. ARVIDSON

Riding the Pendulum, Oxford University Press, 1973

BLANCHE BAUGHAN

Verses, Constable, London, 1898
Reuben and Other Poems, Constable, London, 1903
Shingle-short and Other Verses, Whitcombe and Tombs, 1908
Poems from the Port Hills, Whitcombe and Tombs, 1923

JAMES K. BAXTER

Beyond the Palisade, Caxton Press, 1944
Blow Wind of Fruitfulness, Caxton Press, 1948
The Fallen House, Caxton Press, 1953
In Fires of No Return, Oxford University Press, London, 1958
Howrah Bridge and Other Poems, Oxford University Press, London, 1961
Pig Island Letters, Oxford University Press, London, 1966
The Lion Skin, The Bibliography Room, University of Otago, 1967
The Rock Woman: Selected Poems, Oxford University Press, London, 1969
Jerusalem Sonnets, The Bibliography Room, University of Otago, 1970
Autumn Testament, Price Milburn, 1972

Runes, Oxford University Press, London, 1973
The Labyrinth, Oxford University Press, 1974
The Treehouse and Other Poems for Children, Price Milburn, 1974
The Bone Chanter: Unpublished Poems 1945–1972, edited by J.E. Weir, Oxford University Press, 1976
The Holy Life and Death of Concrete Grady, edited by J.E. Weir, Oxford University Press, 1976
Collected Poems, edited by J.E. Weir, Oxford University Press, 1979
Selected Poems, edited by J. E. Weir, Oxford University Press, 1982

CHRISTINA BEER

This Fig Tree Has Thorns, Alister Taylor, 1974

MARY URSULA BETHELL

From a Garden in the Antipodes, pseud. 'Evelyn Hayes', Sidgwick and Jackson, London, 1929
Time and Place, Caxton Press, 1936
Day and Night, Poems 1924–1935, Caxton Press, 1939
Collected Poems, Caxton Press, 1950

TONY BEYER

Jesus Hobo, Caveman Press, 1971
The Meat, Caveman Press, 1974
Dancing Bear, Melaleuca Press, Canberra, 1981

CHARLES BRASCH

The Land and the People and Other Poems, Caxton Press, 1939
Disputed Ground, Poems 1939–1945, Caxton Press, 1948
The Estate and Other Poems, Caxton Press, 1957
Ambulando, Caxton Press, 1964
Not Far Off, Caxton Press, 1969
Home Ground, edited by Alan Roddick, Caxton Press, 1974
Collected Poems, edited by Alan Roddick, Oxford University Press, 1984

ALAN BRUNTON

Messengers in Blackface, Amphedesma Press, London, 1973
Black and White Anthology, Hawk Press, 1976
O Ravachol, Red Mole Publications, 1979
And She Said, Alexandra Fisher for Red Mole Enterprises, New York, 1984

ALISTAIR CAMPBELL

Mine Eyes Dazzle, Poems 1947–1949, Pegasus Press, 1950;
   revised editions 1951 and 1956
Wild Honey, Oxford University Press, London, 1964
Kapiti: Selected Poems 1947–1971, Pegasus Press, 1972
Dreams, Yellow Lions, Alister Taylor, 1975
The Dark Lord of Savaiki, Te Kotare Press, 1981
Collected Poems, Alister Taylor, 1982

MEG CAMPBELL

The Way Back, Te Kotare Press, 1981
A Durable Fire, Te Kotare Press, 1982

GORDON CHALLIS

Building, Caxton Press, 1963

ALLEN CURNOW

Valley of Decision, Phoenix Miscellany 1, Auckland University
   College Students' Association Press, 1933
Enemies, Poems 1934–1936, Caxton Press, 1937
Not in Narrow Seas, Caxton Press, 1939
Island and Time, Caxton Press, 1941
Sailing or Drowning, Progressive Publishing Society, 1943
Jack Without Magic, Caxton Press, 1946
At Dead Low Water, and Sonnets, Caxton Press, 1949
Poems 1949–1957, Mermaid Press, 1957
A Small Room With Large Windows, Oxford University Press,
   London, 1962
Trees, Effigies, Moving Objects, Catspaw Press, 1972
An Abominable Temper, Catspaw Press, 1973
Collected Poems 1933–1973, A.H. & A.W. Reed, 1974
An Incorrigible Music, AUP/OUP, 1979
You Will Know When You Get There, Poems 1979–1981,
   AUP/OUP, 1982
Selected Poems, Penguin Books, 1982

RUTH DALLAS

Country Road and Other Poems, 1947–1952, Caxton Press, 1953
The Turning Wheel, Caxton Press, 1961
Day Book, Caxton Press, 1966
Shadow Show, Caxton Press, 1968
Walking on the Snow, Caxton Press, 1976

Song for a Guitar and Other Songs, edited by Charles Brasch,
   University of Otago Press, 1976
Steps of the Sun, Poems, Caxton Press, 1979

EILEEN DUGGAN

Poems, The New Zealand Tablet, 1922
New Zealand Bird Songs, H.H. Tombs, 1929
Poems, Allen and Unwin, London, 1937
New Zealand Poems, Allen and Unwin, London, 1940
More Poems, Allen and Unwin, London, 1951

LAURIS EDMOND

In Middle Air, Pegasus Press, 1975
The Pear Tree, Pegasus Press, 1977
Wellington Letter: A Sequence of Poems, Mallinson Rendel, 1980
Seven: Poems, Wayzgoose Press, 1980
Salt from the North, Oxford University Press, 1980
Catching It, Oxford University Press, 1983
Selected Poems, Oxford University Press, 1984

MURRAY EDMOND

Entering the Eye, Caveman Press, 1973
Patchwork, Hawk Press, 1978
End Wall, Oxford University Press, 1981

A.R.D. FAIRBURN

He Shall Not Rise, Columbia Press, London, 1930
Dominion, Caxton Press, 1938
Poems 1929–1941, Caxton Press, 1943
The Rakehelly Man, Caxton Press, 1946
Three Poems: Dominion, The Voyage, To a Friend in the Wilderness,
   New Zealand University Press, 1952
Strange Rendezvous, Poems 1929–1941, with additions, Caxton
   Press, 1952
The Disadvantages of Being Dead, Mermaid Press, 1958
Collected Poems, edited by Denis Glover, Pegasus Press, 1966

JANET FRAME

The Pocket Mirror, Braziller, New York, and W.H. Allen,
   London, 1967; Pegasus Press, 1968

Ruth France ('Paul Henderson')

Unwilling Pilgrim, Caxton Press, 1955
The Halting Place, Caxton Press, 1961

Ruth Gilbert

Lazarus and Other Poems, A.H. & A.W. Reed, 1949
The Sunlit Hour, Allen and Unwin, London, 1955
The Luthier, A.H. & A.W. Reed, 1966
Collected Poems, Black Robin, 1984

Herman Gladwin

In Praise of Stalin, Alister Taylor, 1977

Denis Glover

Thistledown, Caxton Club Press, 1935
Six Easy Ways of Dodging Debt Collectors, Caxton Press, 1936
Thirteen Poems, Caxton Press, 1939
Cold Tongue, Caxton Press, 1940
The Wind and the Sand, Poems 1934–1944, Caxton Press, 1945
Summer Flowers, Caxton Press, 1946
Sings Harry and Other Poems, Caxton Press, 1951
Arawata Bill: A Sequence of Poems, Pegasus Press, 1953
Since Then, Mermaid Press, 1957
Enter Without Knocking: Selected Poems, Pegasus Press, 1964;
    enlarged edition, 1972
Sharp Edge Up, Verses and Satires, Blackwood and Janet Paul,
    1968
To a Particular Woman, Nag's Head Press, 1970
Diary to a Woman, Catspaw Press, 1971
Dancing to my Tune, edited by Lauris Edmond, Catspaw Press,
    1974
Wellington Harbour, Catspaw Press, 1974
Come High Water, Dunmore Press, 1977
Or Hawk or Basilisk, Catspaw Press, 1978
To Friends in Russia, Nag's Head Press, 1979
Towards Banks Peninsula, Pegasus Press, 1979
Selected Poems, Penguin Books, 1981

Michael Harlow

Edges, Lycabettus Press, Athens, 1974
Nothing but Switzerland and Lemonade, Hawk Press, 1980
Today is the Piano's Birthday, AUP/OUP, 1981
Vlaminck's Tie, AUP/OUP, 1985

'PAUL HENDERSON'

see Ruth France

PETER HOOPER

A Map of Morning and Other Poems, Pegasus Press, 1964
Journey Towards an Elegy and Other Poems, Nag's Head Press, 1969
The Mind of Bones, Hazard Press, 1971
Earth Marriage, published as *Fragments 3*, D. Young and D. Waddington, 1972
Selected Poems, John McIndoe, 1977

KERI HULME

The Silences Between (Moeraki Conversations), AUP/OUP, 1982

SAM HUNT

Bracken Country, Glenbervie Press, 1971
From Bottle Creek, Alister Taylor, 1972
South Into Winter, Alister Taylor, 1973
Time to Ride, Alister Taylor, 1975
Drunkard's Garden, Hampson Hunt, 1977
Collected Poems 1963–1980, Penguin Books, 1980
Running Scared, Whitcoulls, 1982

ROBIN HYDE

The Desolate Star, Whitcombe and Tombs, 1929
The Conquerors, Macmillan, London, 1935
Persephone in Winter, Hurst & Blackett, London, 1937
Houses by the Sea and the Later Poems of Robin Hyde, edited by Gloria Rawlinson, Caxton Press, 1952
Selected Poems, edited by Lydia Wevers, Oxford University Press, 1984

KEVIN IRELAND

Face to Face, Pegasus Press, 1963
Educating the Body, Caxton Press, 1967
A Letter from Amsterdam, Amphedesma Press, London, 1972
Orchids, Hummingbirds, and Other Poems, AUP/OUP, 1974
A Grammar of Dreams, Wai-te-ata Press, 1975
Literary Cartoons, Islands/Hurricane, 1977
The Dangers of Art, Poems 1975–1980, Cicada Press, 1980
Practice Night in the Drill Hall, Oxford University Press, 1984

MICHAEL JACKSON

Latitudes of Exile, John McIndoe, 1976
Wall, John McIndoe, 1980

LOUIS JOHNSON

Stanza and Scene, Handcraft Press, 1945
The Sun Among the Ruins, Pegasus Press, 1951
Roughshod Among the Lilies, Pegasus Press, 1951
New Worlds for Old, Capricorn Press, 1957
Bread and a Pension, Pegasus Press, 1964
Land Like a Lizard, Jacaranda Press, Brisbane, 1970
Selected Poems, Mitchell College of Advanced Education,
   Bathurst, NSW, 1972
Fires and Patterns, Jacaranda Press, Brisbane, 1975
Coming and Going, Mallinson Rendel, 1982
Winter Apples, Mallinson Rendel, 1984

M.K. JOSEPH

Imaginary Islands, the Author, 1950
The Living Countries, Paul's Book Arcade, 1959
Inscription on a Paper Dart, Selected Poems 1945–1972, AUP/OUP,
   1974

JAN KEMP

Against the Softness of Woman, Caveman Press, 1976
Diamonds and Gravel, Hampson Hunt, 1979
Ice-breaker Poems, Coal-Black Press, 1980

FIONA KIDMAN

Honey and Bitters, Pegasus Press, 1975
On the Tightrope, Pegasus Press, 1978

HENRY KIRK ('THE MIXER')

The Transport Workers' Songbook, New Zealand Worker, 1926

HILAIRE KIRKLAND

Blood Clear and Apple Red, Wai-te-ata Press, 1981

ANTE KOSOVIĆ

Dalmatinać iz Tudjine, U. Vajarin and I. Rujna, 1907; Splitska
   Drustvena Tiskara, Split, 1908

Uzkrsnuće Jugoslaviji, The Excel Printing Co., 1920
Uzkrsnuće Slavena!, Johnson Press, 1947

RACHEL McALPINE

Lament for Ariadne, Caveman Press, 1975
Stay at the Dinner Party, Caveman Press, 1977
Fancy Dress, Cicada Press, 1979
House Poems, Nutshell Books, 1980
Recording Angel, Mallinson Rendel, 1983

HEATHER McPHERSON

A Figurehead: A Face, Spiral Publications, 1982

CILLA McQUEEN

Homing In, John McIndoe, 1982
Anti Gravity, John McIndoe, 1984

BILL MANHIRE

The Elaboration, Square & Circle, 1972
How to Take Off Your Clothes at the Picnic, Wai-te-ata Press, 1977
Good Looks, AUP/OUP, 1982
Zoetropes, Allen & Unwin/Port Nicholson Press, 1984

R.A.K. MASON

The Beggar, the Author, 1924
No New Thing—Poems 1924–1929, Spearhead, 1934
End of Day, Caxton Press, 1936
This Dark Will Lighten, Selected Poems 1923–1941, Caxton Press, 1941
Collected Poems, edited by Allen Curnow, Pegasus Press, 1962

BARRY MITCALFE

Thirty Poems, Hurricane House, 1960
Migrant, Caveman Press, 1975
Harvestman: Poems, Coromandel Press, 1979
Uncle and Others, Coromandel Press/Caveman Press, 1979
Country Road, Coromandel Press, 1980
Beach, Coromandel Press, 1982

DAVID MITCHELL

Pipe Dreams in Ponsonby, Stephen Chan, 1972; reprinted, Caveman Press, 1975

'THE MIXER'

see Henry Kirk

PETER OLDS

Lady Moss Revived, Caveman Press, 1972
Freeway, Caveman Press, 1974
Doctor's Rock, Caveman Press, 1976
Beethoven's Guitar, Caveman Press, 1980

W.H. OLIVER

Fire Without Phoenix, Poems 1946–1954, Caxton Press, 1957
Out of Season, Oxford University Press, 1980
Poor Richard, Port Nicholson Press, 1982

BOB ORR

Blue Footpaths, Amphedesma Press, London, 1972
Poems for Moira, Hawk Press, 1979
Cargo, Voice Press, 1983

VINCENT O'SULLIVAN

Our Burning Time, Prometheus Books, 1965
Revenants, Prometheus Books, 1969
Bearings, Oxford University Press, 1973
Butcher & Co., Oxford University Press, 1976
From the Indian Funeral, John McIndoe, 1976
Brother Jonathan, Brother Kafka, Oxford University Press, 1980
The Rose Ballroom and Other Poems, John McIndoe, 1982
The Butcher Papers, Oxford University Press, 1982

ALISTAIR PATERSON

Caves in the Hills, Pegasus Press, 1965
Birds Flying, Pegasus Press, 1973
Cities and Strangers, Caveman Press, 1976
The Toledo Room, Pilgrims South Press, 1978
Qu'appelle, Pilgrims South Press, 1982
Incantations for Warriors, Earle of Seacliff Press, 1984

GLORIA RAWLINSON

Gloria's Book, Whitcombe and Tombs, 1933
The Perfume Vendor, Hutchinson, London, 1936

The Islands Where I Was Born, Handcraft Press, 1955
Of Clouds and Pebbles, Paul's Book Arcade, 1963

WILLIAM PEMBER REEVES

New Zealand and Other Poems, Grant Richards, London, 1898
The Passing of the Forest and Other Verse, the Author, London,
   1925

KEITH SINCLAIR

Songs for a Summer, Pegasus Press, 1952
Strangers or Beasts, Caxton Press, 1954
A Time to Embrace, Paul's Book Arcade, 1963
The Firewheel Tree, AUP/OUP, 1974

ELIZABETH SMITHER

Here Come the Clouds, Alister Taylor, 1975
You're Very Seductive William Carlos Williams, John McIndoe,
   1978
The Sarah Train, Hawk Press, 1980
The Legend of Marcello Mastroianni's Wife, AUP/OUP, 1981
Casanova's Ankle, Oxford University Press, 1981
Shakespeare Virgins, AUP/OUP, 1983

KENDRICK SMITHYMAN

Seven Sonnets, Pelorus Press, 1946
The Blind Mountain, Caxton Press, 1950
The Gay Trapeze, Handcraft Press, 1955
Inheritance, Paul's Book Arcade, 1962
Flying to Palmerston, Oxford University Press for Auckland
   University Press, 1968
Earthquake Weather, AUP/OUP, 1972
The Seal in the Dolphin Pool, AUP/OUP, 1974
Dwarf With A Billiard Cue, AUP/OUP, 1979

CHARLES SPEAR

Twopence Coloured, Caxton Press, 1951

MARY STANLEY

Starveling Year, Pegasus Press, 1953

C.K. STEAD

Whether the Will is Free, Poems 1954–1962, Paul's Book Arcade, 1964
Crossing the Bar, AUP/OUP, 1972
Quesada, The Shed, 1975
Walking Westward, The Shed, 1979
Geographies, AUP/OUP, 1982
Poems of a Decade, Pilgrims South Press, 1984
Paris, AUP/OUP, 1984

APIRANA TAYLOR

Eyes of the Ruru, Voice Press, 1979

EDWARD TREGEAR

'Shadows' and Other Verses, Whitcombe and Tombs, 1919

BRIAN TURNER

Ladders of Rain, John McIndoe, 1978
Ancestors, John McIndoe, 1981
Listening to the River, John McIndoe, 1983

HONE TUWHARE

No Ordinary Sun, Blackwood and Janet Paul, 1964; reprinted, John McIndoe, 1977
Come Rain Hail, The Bibliography Room, University of Otago, 1970
Sapwood & Milk, Caveman Press, 1972
Something Nothing, Caveman Press, 1974
Making a Fist of It, Jackstraw Press, 1978
Selected Poems, John McIndoe, 1980
Year of the Dog, John McIndoe, 1982

IAN WEDDE

Made Over, Stephen Chan, 1974
Earthly: Sonnets for Carlos, Amphedesma Press, 1975
Spells for Coming Out, AUP/OUP, 1977
Castaly, Poems 1973–1977, AUP/OUP, 1980
Tales of Gotham City, AUP/OUP, 1984
Georgicon, Victoria University Press, 1984

HUBERT WITHEFORD

Shadow of the Flame, Poems 1942–1947, Pelorus Press, 1950
The Falcon Mask, Pegasus Press, 1951
The Lightning Makes a Difference, Brookside Press, London, 1962
A Native, Perhaps Beautiful, Caxton Press, 1967
A Possible Order, Ravine Press, Harrow, 1980

DAVID McKEE WRIGHT

Aorangi and Other Verses, Mills Dick, 1896
Station Ballads and Other Verses, J.G. Sawell, 1897
New Zealand Chimes, W.J. Lankshear, 1900
Wisps of Tussock, A. Fraser, 1900
An Irish Heart, Angus and Robertson, Sydney, 1918

Index of Poets and Translators

Index of Titles and First Lines

Titles are set in *italic* type.